SKY DANCE

A Novel

Richard M

This is a work of fiction. Names, characters, businesses, events, and incidents are either the product of the author's imagination or are used fictitiously, and any resemblance to actual persons, living or dead, business establishments, events, or locales is entirely coincidental.

ISBN: 1500472476
ISBN 13: 978-1500472474
Library of Congress Control Number: 2014912530
CreateSpace Independent Publishing Platform
North Charleston, South Carolina

To Carol,
Always my inspiration.

Table of Contents

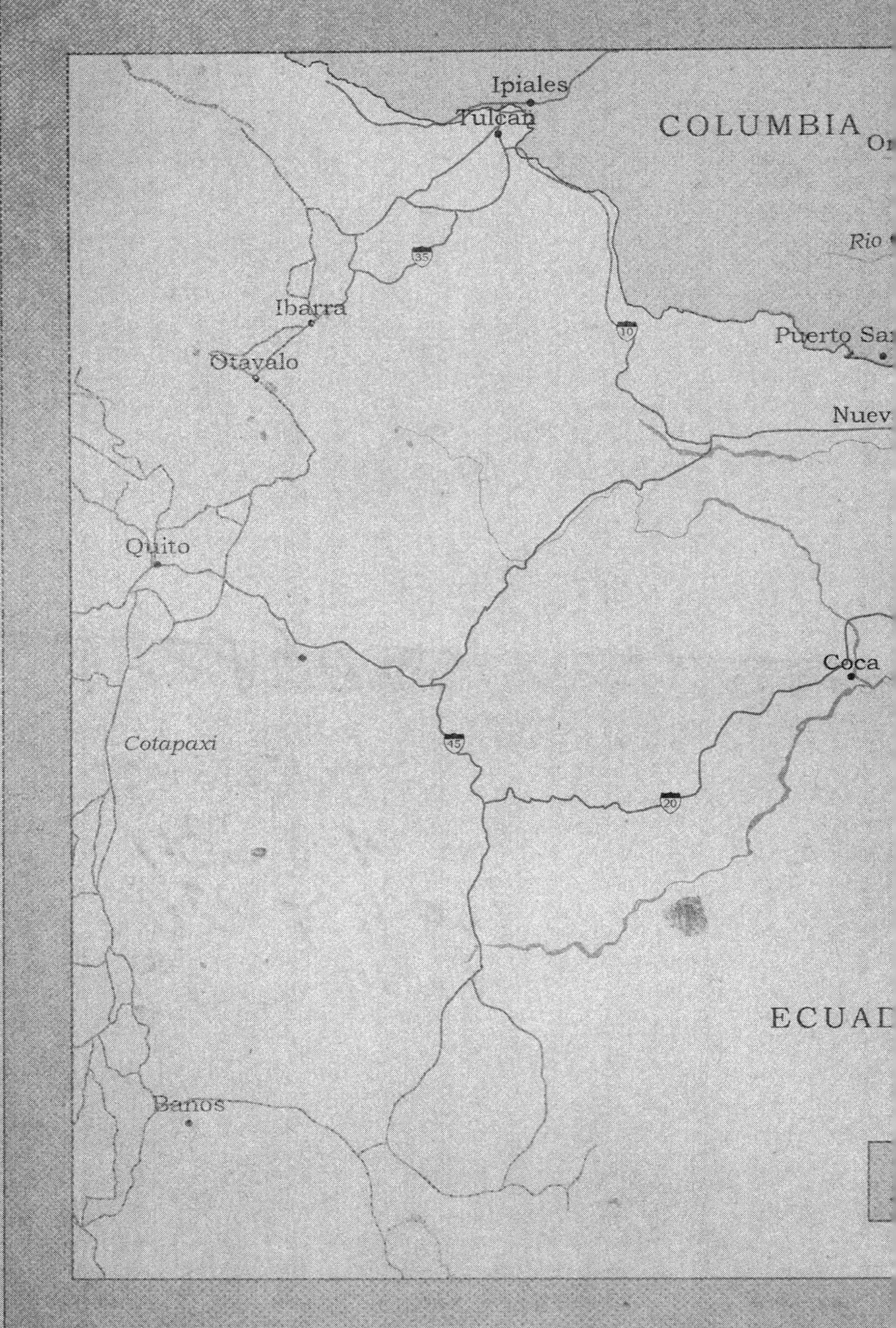

Ipiales
Tulcan
COLUMBIA
Rio
35
Ibarra
10
Otavalo
Quito
Coca
45
Cotapaxi
20
Banos

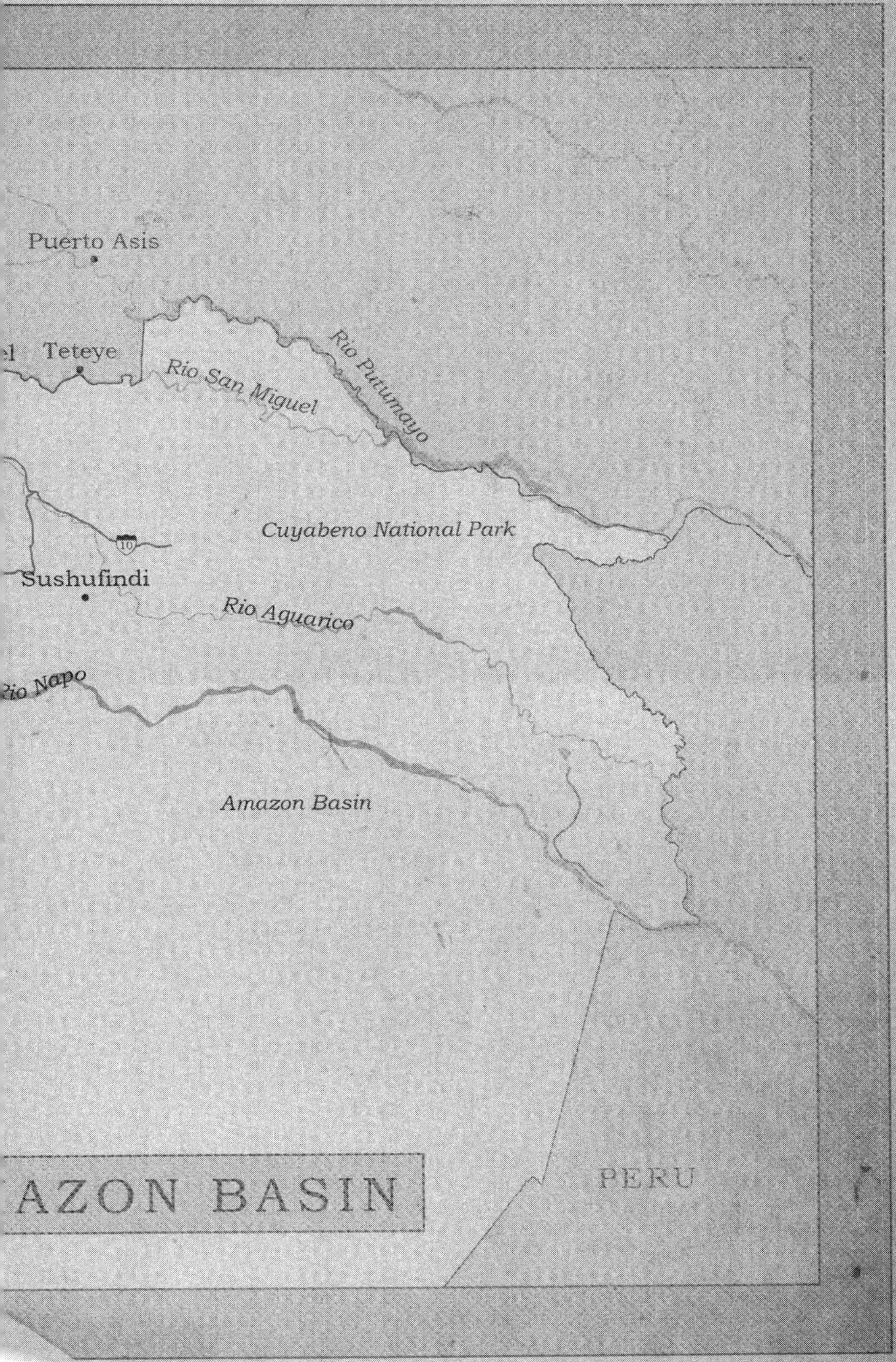

Puerto Asis

el Teteye

Rio San Miguel

Rio Putumayo

Cuyabeno National Park

10

Sushufindi

Rio Aguarico

Rio Napo

Amazon Basin

AZON BASIN

PERU

<Prologue

Near Puerto Asís, Colombia

Carlos arrived just before dawn, knowing the comandante would be leaving early to tend to his obligations and before Señor Martinez returned from yet another "business" trip to the city of Cali.

He had climbed the tree to avoid the stone wall with its embedded glass shards and the alarm sensors that surrounded the hacienda. He brought only the minimum of equipment—a long hollowed tube from the branch of an *Iryanthera* tree, a small quiver formed from a gourd, and a half dozen ten-inch darts, each whittled to a sharp point. The darts had been dipped into a concentrated, highly toxic exudate from the skin glands of the golden dart frog.

As he had for so many hunts, he waited. Silent. Invisible.

Just after seven, he saw the comandante open the front door, kiss Señora Martinez good-bye, and walk toward his Land Rover.

Carlos pulled a dart from the quiver, wrapped the blunt end with fiber from the bark of the kapok tree, and inserted it into the breech of the blowgun. He took careful aim, and with one swift blow, the dart sailed invisibly through the heavy morning air until it struck the comandante in the middle of his back.

The comandante felt a gentle pinch as the dart penetrated his skin to the blood-rich dermis tissue below. He turned to look behind him but saw nothing. He reached back, but the dart was beyond his fingertips. Believing he'd been stung by a bee, he continued to his vehicle. Meanwhile, warm blood was quickly dissolving the dried resin on the dart, and the fluid was surging through the comandante's circulatory system—a poison so potent that one microgram, the equivalent of a grain of table salt, is deadly.

After a few steps, the comandante felt another pinch. This time, he felt the thin lance in his back. He pulled it out and examined it. He looked around again but saw no one. Realizing what was in his hand, he made a desperate retreat to the house. Too late. Already the batrachotoxin was short-circuiting his nerve cells, freezing his muscles. In sheer panic, he called for help, but only a silent scream echoed in his ears. Before the comandante could reach the door, his heart went into ventricular fibrillation, and he no longer could stand, as his legs buckled in paralysis, which was quickly followed by cardiac arrest and then darkness.

It was several hours before the returning Señor Martinez saw the dead man at his doorstep. The Colombian police were jubilant—some of them at least—when they notified Bogotá. The señora mourned in secrecy. And Carlos returned to Ecuador with his friend Gustavo's blowgun. Justice was sometimes ugly, but the debt had been repaid.

Week One

CHAPTER ONE

Approximately One Year Earlier; Monday; Lago Agrio, Ecuador

Jorge looked skyward. The slim silhouette was all he saw as the osprey strained mightily to clear the tall trees at the river's edge. As it turned, Jorge caught a glimpse of the large piranha clasped tightly in the bird's talons. The fish writhed furiously in its last moments as the osprey struggled to reach its roost in the bare branches of a long-dead kapok tree. There, safe from predators, the bird would consume its last meal of the day before drifting to sleep. It had been a frenzied life the past months and six thousand miles north. The bird had repaired the winter damage to its nest, fed its mate, reared three chicks, and then returned south. Now, on its wintering grounds, it was enjoying a well-deserved rest and storing reserves for the next migration north to the jack pine forest in Northern Michigan.

The momentary distraction over, Jorge returned to his work. He had been digging for almost the entire day and, as dusk approached, had little to show for his effort—just four fifty-five-gallon drums partially filled with a rich black soil, along with sweat-drenched clothes and the familiar aches of a man accustomed to hard work.

Dirt? Why does he need so much dirt? And why here? I can get dirt anywhere, he thought, as he leaned against the side of the last of the three holes he'd dug in the grassy field.

But Muniz had been very insistent; the man knew what he wanted. When they had arrived just after dawn off an overgrown road east of Nueva Loja, in an area locally known as Lago Agrio in the Amazonia region of northeastern

Ecuador, Muniz had taken out a map of the old oil-well pad and carefully determined the three places where he wanted Jorge to dig.

"You need to dig at least five feet down. You'll know the layer when you see it. It'll be dark, almost black, and I need at least two drums," Muniz had told him, pointing to the plastic drums they'd offloaded from Raul's pickup truck. "We'll be back to get you after dark."

Jorge didn't question the jefe and busily went to work with just a pickax and a couple of shovels. Fortunately, the soils in the rain forest were soft and loose, and the digging was easy, but the blazing midday heat made the work difficult. Only in the last few minutes had conditions eased as the sun sank behind the forest canopy.

Muniz was right; the soil color changed very abruptly. The surface layer was light, almost a tan color, for about a foot, then ocher red for a few more feet, and then it was black. And the bottom layer was different—it didn't have the musty smell of the other soil. The black stuff smelled like chemicals, sort of like rotten eggs, and it felt slippery.

I'd better get this last one filled, or there will be hell to pay when Muniz gets back, Jorge thought, as he hefted another shovelful from the hole. *But I could get him much better dirt than this stuff.*

CHAPTER TWO

Monday, Outside of Sacha, Ecuador

Palumbo Muniz sat in his sparse front room in an old farmhouse on the outskirts of Joya de los Sachas (Sacha). Unlike Lago Agrio, which had been a direct result of the oil boom, Sacha, thirty miles to the south, was once a small Quichuan Indian village. The wave of oil workers and, more important, the *colonos*—land-seeking peasants from the cities of the Andean Plateau—had transformed it into a major jungle town of twenty thousand people.

The population boom in Sacha had been an indirect consequence of the oil industry. Oil production required roads to transport equipment and personnel from the cities. Once access was provided, and with the prodding of the national government to relieve dense urban populations, peasants flooded the area to homestead land along the new roadways. While the footprint of the oil industry was extremely small, it induced major land clearing for farms and timber. Much of the oil industry eventually left, but the settlers remained.

Muniz glanced at his watch. It was only 5:30 p.m.—he had a couple of more hours to wait. He had told Raul to pick him up at 7:00 p.m. when the roads would be dark and abandoned. No one needed to see what he was doing.

At night, few ventured on jungle roads. There were great distances between villages and no lighting, and the conditions were treacherous. These roads, and the rivers, remained critical links between Peru and Colombia for cocaine smugglers, and the jungle held few benefits for the night traveler.

Muniz never thought he'd be involved in anything that would require such secrecy.

He had intended for his organization to help the poor Indians and farmers of the area. Like many of them, he had been raised in the tumult of the oil fields, but at least the industry had provided work for some of his family—not the high-level technical work valued on the rigs, but the more menial tasks, like clearing forests, milling wood, and building roads.

At the company-sponsored schools, his teachers found that he had great curiosity, and he easily outperformed students two and three years older. It wasn't long before he caught the attention of a local priest, who encouraged him and found sponsors for his continuing education.

He had studied sociology at the Catholic University in Quito, which became a hotbed of protest against the oil industry and its impact on the indigenous peoples and the rain forest. Because of his knowledge of the industry and experience in the region, he became the natural leader of the Native Peoples Forest Project (NPFP) after his graduation ten years earlier.

Through a series of completely inexplicable and random events, Muniz was now working with a group of lawyers trying to help the Indians and *colonos* harmed by oil pollution. The lawyers had told him that they could sue Steator Energies in the United States for the loss of their lands in Sacha contaminated by the oil and for the poor health they suffered because of the pollutants in the water, air, and soil.

As the lawyer's local representative, Muniz had the task of interviewing as many people as he could and determining whether their lands had become less productive in recent years and whether they or anyone they knew suffered health problems.

Muniz attended to his task diligently, and by the end of three months, he had interviewed and prepared dossiers on more than one hundred people.

Señor Luis Curruca flew in from Quito to collect the reports, had them translated into English, and sent them to the United States. Curruca complimented Muniz on the fine job he had done but said more work would be required in the coming months to provide further documentation for the courts.

True to his word, Curruca came up with other tasks. However, tonight's work was unexpected and concerned Muniz. But it was something he was told was necessary.

He looked out the window as daylight was beginning to fade and saw the first raindrops on the glass pane.

***

"Slow down!" Muniz shouted at Raul, bracing both his hands against the dashboard as the small truck slid and skidded for the third time in the rain-soaked muck. "You're going to get us killed."

It had rained steadily and hard for the past two hours, and if he didn't have Jorge sitting alone at the old drilling pad, he never would have left the farmhouse, especially with Raul behind the wheel. But events had conspired against him. He needed Jorge, and he needed Raul's unlicensed truck.

The roads were always a menace, particularly at night and especially when wet. They were pocked with ruts, and most of the gravel had eroded with the rains and floods. What had once been a substantial two-lane road used for long convoys of semitrailer rigs hauling oil-drilling equipment was now barely one lane wide because of the encroaching forest. And ever since the oil companies had left, there was no maintenance; the government was supposed to do it, but like other things in the jungle, it was low-priority work.

"You worry like my old grandmother. Just hold on!" Raul laughed through the slapping and squeaking of the windshield wipers, trying but failing to keep up with the torrent. "How did you know of this place anyway?"

"I saw it when I was a teenager. There was an oil well there."

"What happened to it?"

"Once they drilled to the oil, they left," Muniz said. "A small crew came by later and leveled the drill pad and filled all the pits. They planted some trees and grasses and walked away."

***

Jorge awoke with a start underneath the plastic tarp that protected him from the downpour. The rain had masked the sound of Raul's truck, and it had come within two hundred feet before Jorge's brain sounded an alarm.

"Sleeping on the job, Jorge?" Muniz shouted from the driver's seat.

"Just a little after shoveling all day. I have four half-filled drums," he responded. "If I filled them any more than that, we wouldn't be able to lift them."

Muniz exited the cab and helped Jorge and Raul roll the drums toward the truck. With considerable effort, they muscled the three-hundred-pound containers into the truck bed and secured them with cargo straps.

With only the truck's headlights, Muniz scanned the area. *It didn't seem possible,* he thought, as he looked around the small one-acre field wrested from the dense forest.

Just fifteen years earlier, an eighteen-story oil derrick nearly reached the canopy of the towering kapok and *Guarea* trees. The rotary drill and attending army of roughnecks, drillers, and roustabouts were in constant motion, searching for oil ten thousand feet beneath the jungle floor. New roads were slashed through the forest to deliver more drilling pipe, workers, and heavy equipment to clear even more land to drill more wells. And then, as quickly as it had started, it was over. Once the oil was found and taken, the derrick was dismantled and all the equipment and workers were moved to another well pad to start all over again.

The industrial clamor and miasma were gone, and except for an occasional farmer in search of a wayward cow grazing on the lush tropical grasses that had overtaken the field, the drilling pad was deserted. The only evidence of its past life was the small rusty valve that still connected the underground well to the pipeline that once delivered the oil over the Andes to the Pacific Coast port of Esmeraldas, where it was shipped to California in huge oceangoing tankers to sate the starving refineries.

Lago Agrio was now a ghost town.

"Are the drums tied down?" Muniz asked.

"They're tight," Raul replied.

"Let's get these back to the farm," Muniz said. "We'll need them in a few days."

As the three drove out, Muniz was pleased with Jorge's work. He had what he needed, and Jorge had left no evidence—all the holes had been refilled and leveled. In a few days, nature would do the rest, and grasses would cover everything, he thought, as Raul accelerated to the main road.

Crunched uncomfortably into the back of the cab, Jorge thought, *All this just for some dirt.*

CHAPTER THREE

Thursday, Near Lago Agrio

The minivan pulled into a small clearing shrouded by second-growth forest. With trees reaching more than a hundred feet high and a thick, latticed understory arching over the slow-moving waters of the Río Aguarico, this was a prime location to spot the Cocha antshrike, a very rare bird that sometimes nested in the area. With the precision of a military drill team, the van's occupants exited simultaneously through three doors, jostling daypacks and scopes, while two-thousand-dollar binoculars swung precariously. The scene could have been mistaken for an L. L. Bean photo shoot with all the Gore-Tex boots, quick-dry convertible trousers, and ripstop nylon, sun-blocking shirts.

"A pair was spotted here three days ago, just above ground level in that thicket over the stream," explained Tom Steps, the Australian field leader for the trip, as the group hurriedly but quietly extended tripod legs, uncapped scopes, and methodically scanned the foliage for a hint of cinnamon-red and black contrasted against the thousand shades of green.

"It may fly through the canopy first before heading into the clearing. But because of the heat and lateness of day, it may also just hunker down and say, 'Sorry, not today, maybe *mañana*,'" added Carlos Serrano, the local guide and driver, his face furrowed in gloom.

This wasn't what the group wanted to hear. They had each spent six thousand dollars for the ten-day birding excursion, not including the airfares from California, Michigan, and England, and just as the group was about to give up hope, Carlos's expression changed instantly into a beaming smile.

"Got ya!" He laughed.

The group, only together for the past four days, had yet to fully appreciate their mischievous guide. His youthful face, slight five-foot-six-inch frame, and high energy level had everyone believing this thirty-two-year-old was a teenager.

The relief showed on the group's faces. These were serious birders who had planned years for the chance of a ten- to fifteen-minute encounter with this unique, elusive species. Sure, they would collectively see more than three hundred species of birds as they descended the Andes from Quito into the Amazon Basin, which was only a fraction of one of the most diverse and rich bird populations in the world, but this was the one they'd most regret missing. The Cocha antshrike was a species that had been presumed extinct only to be "rediscovered" twenty years earlier. Its resighting was no wonder, though, because until the discovery of oil, very few from the outside could venture in. There were no roads, no airstrips, and no places to stay—only canoes and Indian villages. Now, with luxurious ecolodges and easy access from Quito, many more eyes were searching the trees. It wasn't just the intrepid graduate student hoping to gain immortality by discovering and naming a new species; now grandparents from Topeka could trek through a once inaccessible rain forest.

"It's a hard bird to find," Tom said. "Its main defense is its skulking habit. It hunkers down in the vegetation to hide from predators. It takes patience, skill, and a heavy dose of luck to find it."

"I saw my first one when I found a horde of army ants raiding the jungle. The bird doesn't actually eat the ants; the ants are loaded with formic acid to ward off predators. Instead, the ant-shrike, like its relatives—the antpitta, ant-birds, antwrens—feed on the insects and other critters escaping the marauding ants," Carlos explained.

"Geez, here we go again. Every time he tells this story there are more birds, more ants, and he had to run for his life to escape," Tom laughed.

"My memory is just getting better with age," Carlos countered.

"Or with more beers."

"This humidity is something else. It's fogging up my bins. It's like looking through cotton," lamented Jack Sinclair, as he fumbled to wipe the lenses of his binoculars. The California native was used to the ninety-degree heat, but the humidity and lack of a breeze was maddening. "I'll bet if I squeeze my hands together, I can make a cloud."

"Please. No more clouds! Every time one floats over, it's more rain!" exclaimed Ben Cales, looking skyward as a billowy cumulus cloud, snow-white against a bright blue sky, slowly passed over. "And I don't think Marsha or I have one dry shirt between us."

"R-a-i-n forest, honey. Deal with it," teased Marsha. "At least the rain keeps the bugs off me."

She and Ben, both recently retired, always tried to schedule trips to the tropics at the height of the winter. They maintained that now that they were over sixty, Detroit was a three-season city for them. While they eschewed being anchored to a winter home in Florida or the Caribbean, they sought warm respites during their snowbird migrations. Being serious birders provided more than sufficient justification for these exotic tours.

"Jack, this weather should be easy for someone your age—and condition," Ben said.

At forty-six, Jack was still in pretty good shape, with a lean body on a five-foot-eight-inch frame. He did his share of path pounding while chasing birds, but he also conditioned for an occasional half marathon or triathlon. His face retained a youthful appearance. Only his short-cropped hair and trimmed beard gave him away, as a bit more salt than pepper was beginning to show.

Jack was the quiet one in almost any crowd—not really an introvert but possessed of a certain natural shyness, which was probably why he pursued individual sports. He was competitive, but mostly, he challenged himself. He didn't avoid groups—he was always there for meals and always ready to share a beer. But he would slip into himself, and after an hour or so, you'd forget he was there.

"I agree," added Vincent Murray, the fourth and final member of the tour group, as he mopped the back of his neck with a handkerchief. "You should be carrying all our gear and maybe ferrying me over the streams and mountains." Vincent was approaching eighty, and while his trousers were now belted at midchest and his pate mostly bald, he too was in pretty good condition, which he attributed to his daily search for birds, butterflies, and all other manner of wildlife. Since the death of his wife, Betty, ten years earlier, it gave his life a purpose other than his part-time medical career with England's National Health Service.

"Listen for a low and repetitive *co-co-co*," Tom said, attempting to refocus the group. "It's not very loud, but it's distinctive. It's sometimes difficult to hear it over the insects and other birds," he continued, wiping a strand of his long, prematurely white hair from his eyes. His hair had started to turn gray in his first year of college, and the full conversion hadn't taken long. He actually liked it, setting off his surfer tan as it did—probably his only vanity. The length hadn't changed since he was a kid either, when he had adopted the look of the other surfers at Bondi Beach in Sydney. Back then, when he wasn't at the beach, he was venturing with his uncle into the forest, looking for birds. By the time he was twelve, he was very accomplished at both.

"How can you hear a call with all the noise?" Marsha asked.

"Your first trip to the rain forest, right? I remember my first experience," Tom said with a knowing smile. "I thought... rain forest...wilderness, a little solitude, huh? Boy, was I wrong. It was real cacophony. It reminded me of a severe case of tinnitus or maybe even a Stones concert! And every frequency is hit—from the booming roar of the howler monkeys to the high-pitched shrill of the cicadas."

"Yeah, and you rarely see them," Carlos added. "They are either high in the canopy, hidden in the tangle of brush, or on the dark forest floor."

"I guess that's why we shell out so much cash for the binoculars and spotting scopes. They level the playing field for us presbyopian," Ben added.

"Well, you better make use of them while we have a chance. We've probably got about an hour or so of good light," Tom advised, without even looking at his watch. "So let's keep all eyes on that area to the west." As he had explained to the group on the first day, it would be ten hours of light, ten hours of dark, and four intervening hours of dusk and dawn, all week, all month, all year. That was the predictability of the equator.

"I've got something here but can't really make it out," Jack said as he slowly backed away, making space for Tom to step up to the spotting scope. All conversation ceased.

"Maybe. The body color looks right." He hesitated and then exclaimed, "Yes, I see the black hood!"

The others quickly lined up behind Tom for their turns. After a few minutes, the antshrike, having performed its duty, tired of the situation and flew from sight. For the birders, the desire for a rare bird was sated, at least temporarily.

The group searched for another twenty minutes, and just as the dappled light in the forest dimmed, Tom announced, "Start packing up. We've got an hour's ride back."

"No complaints here. My neck and back are aching. I'm in need of a double dose of vitamin I," Vincent replied, referring to the use of ibuprofen by the group before, during, and after long days in the field.

"Washed down with a cool cerveza?" Ben asked.

Almost as quickly as they had exited the van earlier, the group was repacked in their familiar seats and ready for the bone-jarring drive to the lodge.

Just before they turned onto the main road, headlights from a small pickup truck parked off the road illuminated the river enough so that they saw a man standing near the top of the steep bank.

"Local fisherman?" asked Marsha.

"Maybe," responded Carlos. "Probably collecting his nets and putting the catch in those drums. But it's getting awfully late to be working in the river."

As the van turned onto the main road, three snoring tourists in the back—the true sign of a successful day, overtook the drone of the engine.

But the eyes from the riverbank fixed ominously on the van. "Natura Sucumbios," they read.

***

After the minivan passed, Muniz walked back to the riverbank. Jorge and Raul were sliding the drums of soil they had collected three days earlier down the bank and out of sight of the road.

Muniz recalled how weeks earlier he had carefully surveilled the field station for several days. It was from there that the field technicians left in the morning and returned with the water samples in the afternoon.

The station was an inconspicuous concrete-block building topped with a rusted corrugated-metal roof. Situated near the outskirts of Sacha, it was similar to many of the one-story warehouses dotting the area. It was also a convenient quarter-mile walk from the Sacha Inn, which provided the accommodations for visiting crews.

Muniz learned that the two-person field teams consisted of a technician employed by Xebec Environmental and an assistant who was hired locally based on his knowledge of both the geography and residents. He recognized several of the assistants but knew none personally. One day, however, while relaxing under the porch of the bodega across the road from the field station, he noticed a young woman enter the building. She was more than familiar; she was family.

It was his cousin Clarita who provided him with the information that a Xebec team would be collecting water samples at a small tributary to the Río Aguarico near the Teteye Bridge in a few days. He telephoned the information to Curruca, who e-mailed the dates to his contact in the States. They decided the Teteye location would be their best chance.

Muniz had calculated that with the sluggish flow of two feet per second, it would take only three hours for the contents of the drums to arrive at the bridge four miles downstream. He couldn't release it farther upstream for fear of greater dilution, or any closer for fear of detection by villagers. He would just hope he was releasing enough at the right time and that the water sample would be collected at the correct location.

So, on the night before the sampling, Muniz and his men were at the bank, waiting for the call from Clarita the next morning to inform them that the sampling team had left the station. Clarita's warning would give them about ten minutes to get ready and another thirty to empty the contents of the drums into the river. Muniz hoped to create a mile-long plume, just in case the samplers arrived late.

In the meantime, he had a call to make to Quito about the van full of tourists.

Jorge shook his head. *First I have to dig it up, and now he throws it in the river?*

CHAPTER FOUR

Thursday Evening, Philadelphia, Pennsylvania

The phone rang at the offices of Reynolds Environmental Consultants, LLC, on Sansome Street in Philadelphia's Center City. It wasn't really an office—actually an apartment building, just a three-room flat. But you couldn't tell this from his business card and website. It appeared to be a prestigious and established company, which was the point of the illusion. Not many offices would be answering the phone at nine thirty in the evening.

"You can't be serious. What happened to your foolproof plan? Did they see anything?" shouted Douglas Reynolds, the agitated sole proprietor of the firm.

"Muniz says they saw the truck near the river, but his men were out of sight down the riverbank. They may not have seen the drums," replied Luis Curruca, his lawyer in Quito.

"How the hell could that happen? I thought you said they found the perfect location and that there wasn't anybody around."

"It was some tour group. Muniz wasn't sure why they were there, but I did some checking and the van is owned by a company that leads nature tours to different parts of the jungle."

"This could ruin everything. If they saw anything, they could blow our whole case. We have billions at stake with the settlement talks. Those tourists can't tell anyone what they saw until the testing is completed. Do you understand?"

Reynolds shouted more loudly with each successive thought. *I should have known this would happen. No one ever gets it right,* he thought. *I need to do everything myself. But, I can't be everywhere at once.*

He leaned back in his chair and tried to concentrate, but his head was pounding and his guts were wrenched.

Just as quickly, he calmed and, in a slow and controlled voice, said to Curruca, "You must try to locate the van and identify who was in it before they can alert anyone."

Now accustomed to Reynolds's mercurial moods, Curruca said, "They don't know what they saw, and even if they happened to report it, the authorities don't know anything. What would they report? A man by the river? The police wouldn't investigate because there was no crime."

"You don't get it. It's a loose end. We can't afford to take any chances. You don't think Steator won't have teams of investigators combing the entire area and interviewing everyone they can find just to discredit us? Wise up. You're the one who's supposed to know everything going on down there. It's about time you take control, or do I have to fly there and do it myself?"

"How do I keep them quiet? Bribe them?"

"Make them disappear."

"Kill them?" Curruca asked. "That would bring in the national police and probably US officials, and then we'd have even more people investigating."

"Not kill them, maybe just detain them for a short while until we get the green light from the judge."

Curruca thought for a few moments. Sucumbios Province could be a very dangerous place. There were always plenty of thieves, drug runners, smugglers, and hostile Indian tribes and, most important, the Columbian terrorist group Revolutionary Armed Forces of Colombia, also known as Fuerzas Armadas Revolucionarias de Colombia (FARC). Curruca's law practice relied on that slice of society.

"Well—maybe they could have an encounter with drug runners," Curruca suggested. "There's a reason that area is called the 'ski run' with all the snow passing through."

In fact, FARC financed their paramilitary and terrorist operations through kidnapping and extortion but mostly by providing protection to the drug cartels. Of late, Ecuador, and other friendly leftist governments bordering Colombia, turned a blind eye to those activities, as long as FARC fostered no hostilities in their countries.

"What are you suggesting?" Reynolds asked.

"If a group of tourists came upon some smugglers, they could be a lucrative target, and who would suspect anything except kidnapping?"

"But wouldn't that bring in the authorities like you said?"

"The kidnappers would tell the families not to alert anyone or the hostages would be killed."

"I don't care how you get rid of them. Just do it before they can talk to anyone, and there can be no links to us. Is that clear?"

"Yes," Curruca said.

"Remember, no e-mails, no texting, and only calls from the secure phones," Reynolds finished and hung up. He drew a deep breath and threw his head back hard against the leather chair. As he stared at the emptiness of the yellowing white plaster ceiling, he thought back on the strange path that had led him to this day.

He had been an average college student at an average state university studying environmental science with great expectations of solving the pollution problems vexing humankind. It would be him, he believed, who'd be called in to solve the thorniest of issues. Unfortunately, his professors had lacked the vision to recognize his potential. In a field that required much cooperation and collaboration, he, instead, resented his fellow students—he didn't like working with them. He knew he could do so much better alone; they were competitors and looking to take away the recognition he felt should be his.

Reynolds was a small man, barely five and a half feet tall and maybe 150 pounds. Many attributed his sense of superiority to his diminutive stature—a Napoleonic complex of some sort. But it wasn't that; he would have felt superior if he were seven feet tall. His compulsion for success was just hardwired into his soul.

He tried to appear indifferent to the trends surrounding him and took to wearing nothing but black jeans topped with a black T-shirt with his unruly skein of long, curly blond hair twisted into a tight braid and tucked under his shirt as an antifashionista statement. But it had the opposite effect—people though he was trying too hard. At least he was being noticed.

He tired of school after he had got his master's degree and needed something different. He thought about pursuing a doctorate but wasn't sure what interested him, and he wasn't looking forward to all the years of research it would require. He wanted something with a little action. So, he began looking for work. Jobs in his field were difficult to find unless he wanted to work for the government, which he saw as little better than college with all the paper shuffling involved. He wanted to be in the field and not tied down to a desk.

He landed a job as a field technician for a large environmental consulting firm and was promptly assigned to monitoring the cleanup of leaky tanks at gas stations. The work was steady, maybe a little routine and repetitive, but he was making money and thought he could work his way up the chain.

He did, and within a couple of years, he was managing a team of technicians. All the time he was learning as much as he could about the petroleum industry and compiling a sizable list of contacts.

Over the course of five years, he changed companies two more times. He'd been advised that the only way to move up was to move on, and he did, each time taking a slightly higher position with additional responsibilities, but it was really the same old thing dressed up in a new package. He found that while the money was good, he still toiled in relative obscurity and was only making incremental advances. Few even knew he existed, and his fantasies of great success and being the envy of others went unrealized. He needed another ticket to get into the club.

He finally realized that every company he had worked for had obtained their work from the different oil companies, and if he was going to really advance, he should be handing out contracts not chasing after them. He wanted to make big money, run a large department, and get to travel worldwide. He wanted to be one of the big guys, but that hadn't worked out so well.

Reynolds remembered the call years ago that triggered his present situation.

"This is Doug Reynolds," he answered.

"Hi, Doug. This is Bill Haller at Steator Energies. We met after your interview here in Houston last month."

Immediately, Doug felt a flush of excitement; his heart was pounding, his palms sweeting. He had been waiting for this call. He had thought his interview had gone very well, and this was his big chance.

"Oh yes, Mr. Haller. How are you? It isn't often that you get to meet a vice president when you come in for an interview. It was great meeting with you and the selection committee. You were very gracious hosts."

"Well, the position of chief of regulatory compliance is in my division, and I felt I should meet each candidate and not rely only on the committee. I am a business guy, not a scientist, but I know how important the position is—keeps the regulators off our backs and our asses out of jail, hopefully," Haller said with a slight laugh. "Let me first thank you for your time and particularly the note you sent. But I am afraid I have bad news. This is the very worst part of my job, but it is only fair that you hear it directly from me. I only apologize for having to do this over the phone. The committee deliberated for more than two weeks. We had three very well-qualified candidates, and after much soul searching, we selected another candidate, Dr. Rebecca Rainey from Tolle and Worth of Chicago."

After a longer than comfortable pause, Reynolds said, "Well, I am disappointed, but I had an inkling when it took so long." He tried to be upbeat, but the rejection deeply angered him.

"Doug, if it's any consolation, the committee was split almost down the middle. Just two votes made the difference in the final vote."

"Can I ask what was the deciding factor? Where did I come up short? I want to be ready next time, if you know what I mean. It's not all negative if I can learn from the experience."

"Doug, it was a couple of things," Haller said. "You lacked any real corporate-level experience in the industry. Your history and practical knowledge of the field management and regulatory matters are superior, but Dr. Rainey has the academic credentials. She had a PhD and several publications in the field. These are factors that weigh heavily in legal negotiations and congressional hearings."

"It's a void in my experience."

"I don't want to close the door on future opportunities with you. You are very talented, and the entire selection committee recognizes that. You do know that we rely very heavily on outside experts, and I'd like to keep that door open for you. Let me know if you are planning a trip to Houston. Maybe we could do dinner."

"Thanks, Mr. Haller. I appreciate that. And next time you're in Philadelphia, dinner is on me."

"Deal. I've always wanted to try those cheesesteaks I've heard so much about."

"Hey, we can do better than that."

Haller chuckled lightly. "Again, Doug, sorry to be the bearer of bad news. Hope to talk soon."

"Looking forward to it. Good-bye."

Reynolds wanted to slam the phone but composed himself. He knew his chances had been slim, and he had little experience in the oil industry, but he didn't like to lose—not at anything. He was now thirty-five, ten years out of college, and he saw his options lessening each year. He had to make a move

He thought that if he didn't get the position, than it would certainly go to the in-house guy, but he bristled at the thought that a PhD mattered. *I've never even heard of Rebecca fucking Rainey. Harvard, I'll bet. They all hang together, maybe a consort with a committee member. This ain't over,* he assured himself.

Reynolds couldn't admit it to himself, but Steator became an obsession. It was confirmation that the system was stacked against him. It didn't matter how much he had accomplished—the system only choose from within, and he hadn't attended the right college or worked for the right firms. It wasn't so much a glass ceiling as an invisible door—one he never would be able to find, let alone enter. Steator, and Rebecca Rainey in particular, became the target of his wrath.

If I can't join them, maybe I'll own them. And with a little seed money he'd set aside, the enterprise began.

***

He needed something big; he needed to make a name for himself but didn't have a clue where to begin. What he did have, in spades, was perseverance. He was tireless, and he kept looking for the opportunity.

Any other day, he would have breezed right by it, but something caught his attention. It was a short and obscure article from the *New York Times* about a group of activists in the Amazonia region of Ecuador who had unsuccessfully sued the national oil company Andean Power for its failure to clean up oil spills that were harming indigenous Indian groups. It wasn't until the fifth and final paragraph that he read, "The oil fields had been developed by the US-based firm Steator Energies, which turned the facilities over to the national company when its lease expired."

It was just a germ of an idea, but it kept growing. Could the tribes sue in American courts? He didn't have a clue, but he began researching endlessly, taking advantage of dozens of lawyers offering "free initial consultations" just to run it by a professional.

"First, you can't sue Steator in US courts—you have no standing. You need to find somebody who has been harmed from the pollution, either physically or economically," the first lawyer said. "You then have to show that it was a direct cause of Steator's action. That could be very difficult because they allegedly cleaned up the pollution. But if you could show that they were somehow negligent and some pollution remains, then you might stand a chance of getting a court to hear it."

Intimidated at the prospects of suing one of the largest corporations in the world and standing toe-to-toe with the top legal minds in the country, many of the attorneys Reynolds consulted declined to take such a case on contingency—it was just too speculative and would take years and financing they did not have.

But Reynolds persisted. He continued his research. The time had come to make a move, and Reynolds Environmental Consultants was born.

His first encounter with Ecuador, however, left him wanting. He hadn't come to tour; he just wanted a quick in and out. He needed to know if it was fertile ground for his scheme.

He had contacted a man named Palumbo Muniz who had been interviewed in the *Times* article and asked if they could meet. Muniz had obliged but told Reynolds he couldn't afford the trip to Quito. Reynolds agreed to meet him at his home in Sacha, not realizing the effort that entailed on the rough, poorly marked roads in the jungle, but needing to see the area firsthand.

As he drove to Muniz's farm, he was too focused on his idea to pay much attention or appreciate the effort it must have taken to rip the small plot from the clutches of the surrounding jungle. He had no idea of the thousands of trees felled to clear the precious few acres of cropland. Nor could he know the care it took to preserve the thin, fragile soil or the constant battle to keep the jungle from reclaiming the land. All he saw was a primitive house, a few sheds, and small fields.

"Hello, Mr. Reynolds," Muniz spoke in his best English as he greeted Reynolds outside the house. "Please come in."

"Hello to you, Mr. Muniz. Thank you for taking the time to meet with me," Reynolds said, looking around the room. He noticed that the computer and printer on the desk against the far wall looked strangely out of place—a twenty-first-century convenience in a structure that would not have been unfamiliar two hundred years earlier. The floors were unfinished wood planks covered with handwoven wool rugs, all prizes from the enterprising llama ranchers in the highlands. The walls were also rough timbers with a thin and ageing veneer of blotchy paint.

Muniz signaled Reynolds to sit in one of the two upholstered chairs while he sat opposite him on a long wooden bench against the front wall.

"May I get you some tea or water?" Muniz asked. "I am sorry that I do not have anything cold. I try not to run the generator during the hot part of the day."

"Tea would be great, thanks," Reynolds responded. As he sat, his eyes were drawn to a small banner pinned over the two small windows on the front wall. It read, "Native Peoples Forest Party." Next to it, Reynolds saw photographs of Muniz and others at what appeared to be either a protest march or political demonstration. Next to the photographs, Muniz had proudly hung his college diploma.

Returning from the kitchen with two cups of tea, Muniz asked, "How can I help you?"

"I am interested in learning as much as I can about your troubles regarding the oil pollution in this area. There were some newspaper articles in the US, but they only provided sketchy details. Could you explain what happened?"

"There has been much oil spilled in the jungle, and it sometimes gets into the water," Muniz replied, handing Reynolds a small cup of steaming tea. "Many areas have so much oil from leaking pipelines that the farmers cannot use parts of their land. Many of us worry about the health of our children."

"Why wouldn't the government force Andean Power to clean it up?"

"The government *is* Andean Power. It does not want to spend money cleaning up the oil. They just want to pump as much as possible for the money. That is why we tried to sue them. But no court would hear our case," Muniz explained. "The presidente and his party have promised so much to the people, and they need the oil money to pay for everything. They claim they don't have enough money for both the social programs and the pollution problem, so we just have to wait."

Reynolds knew that the current president and his party had been swept into office on the promise of extensive social reforms. They delivered, but doing so was very expensive. They could ill afford to have anything jeopardize the country's oil production—the economy's lifeblood. As a consequence, oil production had been ramped up to the extreme, particularly when the price rose to historic highs. Money slated for equipment upgrades, pollution cleanup, and even pipeline maintenance was diverted to find new fields and to drill new wells.

"Who were your lawyers working on the case?" Reynolds asked.

"We had a couple of young attorneys paid for by the Amazon Tomorrow organization. But they were from the US and didn't know much about our legal system," Muniz explained. "They were very good at public relations and got many reporters here from all over the world. But in the end, that didn't help. They probably should have hired one really good Ecuadorean lawyer who understood how things get done here, but it would have been difficult to find such a lawyer. None of them would be eager to fight the government over oil."

"Do you know such an attorney?"

"I did suggest an attorney from Quito who often works here in the Oriente region, but he wanted nothing to do with the case."

"Who was it?" Reynolds asked.

"His name is Curruca, Luis Curruca."

***

Two days later, after Muniz gave him a brief tour of the oil fields, Reynolds was back in Quito, this time at the office of Luis Curruca, *abogado.*

"Welcome to Quito, Mr. Reynolds," Curruca said, motioning Reynolds from the waiting area to his inner office.

"It is a pleasure to meet you," Reynolds said, thinking this wasn't the man he had envisioned. He stared into Curruca's dark-brown eyes as they shook hands. He guessed the man to be in his early forties. He was about his height, maybe a tad shorter. He appeared trim and fit, even slimmer in his European-cut pale-gray suit. He was reasonably handsome but not overly so. His face and hands were sun-bronzed from days on the golf course or hours by the pool. And his black hair with a slight tinge of gray was slicked back in a stylish cut. He had that refined, cosmopolitan Euro-chic quality that was prevalent in the capitals of South America.

Reynolds took a seat in a stiff leather chair opposite Curruca's dark-stained and highly polished mahogany desk. Curruca closed the office door and sat behind his desk.

"How may I assist you, Mr. Reynolds?" Curruca asked.

"As I indicated in our phone call from Mr. Muniz's farm, I have been following the oil pollution situation in the Oriente," Reynolds explained.

"It is an issue that I know very little about," Curruca said.

"Mr. Muniz explained that many are reticent to involve themselves against the government's oil interests. It would be bad for future business opportunities."

Curruca nodded. "That would be a fair assessment."

"I understand there would be little chance of winning against the government in its own courts, but what if a suit were brought in US courts?" Reynolds asked.

"How is that possible? The US courts have no jurisdiction over Andean Power."

"I'm not concerned about Andean Power; I'm interested in Steator Energies," Reynolds explained. "And it is a US corporation."

"Yes, but they left the country years ago."

"Is it not possible that some of the pollution in the Oriente may be leftover from Steator's operations?"

Curruca shrugged, "I wouldn't know. And if this were the case, how would you prove it resulted from their work? What evidence do you have?"

"I don't have any evidence…at least not yet."

"So, why are you here? What does this have to do with me?"

"Let me ask you this," Reynolds said. "If I could sue Steator, would you be interested in assisting me? I haven't researched everything yet, but what if this could be worth a hundred million dollars in damages?"

At the mention of such a large number, Curruca stared back in disbelief. He tried hard not to show the excitement he felt.

"What would you need me to do?"

CHAPTER FIVE

Thursday; Quito, Ecuador

Reynolds had chosen wisely. Curruca knew Ecuador's legal system inside out. He knew when to play, when to pay, and when to walk away. But, most important, he knew, well, everybody. More fixer than lawyer, he possessed connections both above and below the radar that ensured his success.

Curruca had developed a wide network of contacts within and outside of the government, which was necessary since leadership could change rather abruptly. Most important, he knew their price and how to get their money into accounts in the Caymans and other refuges, safe from the grasp of the Servicio de Rentas Internas auditors.

Immediately after his call to Reynolds about the tourist van, Curruca picked up his phone and dialed the number of one of his contacts, a client he'd worked with a few years earlier. Once the appropriate "bail" had been paid, his client's arrest records hadn't so much been expunged as permanently misfiled. Better still, the fifteen kilos of coke had found its way back into his client's trunk.

"Señor Rodriguez, *por favor*," Curruca said after the phone was answered on the third ring.

CHAPTER SIX

Friday, Verde Vista Ecolodge

It was still pitch-black on the veranda when Tom devoured his breakfast of scrambled eggs; ham; a platter of guava, papaya, and melon; and fresh-baked bread from the lodge's kitchen. The black lagoon was below him but barely visible through the dim glow of the solar-powered lights that dotted the shoreline.

As Tom jotted notes on the day's itinerary, Carlos pulled out the chair across from him and placed two plates heaping with food on the table.

"*Buenos días*, jefe. How was your sleep?"

"Very good, Carlos. Long days make for deep sleep. You plan on eating all that yourself, or are you sharing with the army?" Tom said, amused, as always, how the short, rail-thin man could eat so much yet not ever gain weight. *He's got the metabolism of a teenager*, he thought.

Carlos grinned. "Long days make me hungry. Any signs of the group?"

"Not yet. Let's give them another fifteen minutes. They're going to need it, and so will you." Tom laughed, staring at Carlos's plates.

Within thirty minutes, the group had ambled to the veranda, devoured breakfast, and praised the accommodations of Verde Vista Ecolodge.

"We're in for another long, productive day," Tom announced. "We won't be back until after dark. I've arranged for the lodge to have dinner trays ready for us, but don't forget your box lunches for whenever we have a chance to eat. Carlos loaded a case of bottled water into the van, but if you want anything else, you'd better grab it now."

"We're going back to those old oil roads because they provide the only access near the várzea," Carlos said, referring to the seasonally flooded forests that transition between the upland (terra firma) forest along the eastern slope of the Andean foothills and the permanently flooded swamps of the Amazon Basin.

"Once we reach the edge of the rain forest, there are no more roads—only canoes and boats—from here to Brazil," Tom explained. The topography of Ecuador was always a curiosity to him, particularly since he'd been raised on the flattest continent, where mountains were rare.

"This is a small country, but its rivers flow across the continent and empty into the Atlantic Ocean," Tom explained. "Just imagine a raindrop that falls along the spine of the Andes. It has an equal chance of flowing west for two hundred miles to the Pacific Ocean, or east three thousand miles down the Amazon to the Atlantic!"

"Great speech, jefe, but I've heard it a thousand times before." Carlos laughed.

"But I have a new audience now," Tom said, "and you're going to hear it another few thousand times before I retire."

"No bickering, boys." Ben said, looking around the table. "I think our guides deserve a toast." He raised his glass of guava juice. "To another great day of birding."

"To great birding," Vincent responded.

Tom remembered when it was called "bird watching." The term was popular with the media and projected the image of little old ladies with binoculars, tennis shoes, and floppy hats. But it was a misnomer. Watching does occur, but Tom detected most birds by their vocalizations—songs and calls. *I see…what…maybe eighty percent,* he thought. *The rest I just hear. Yeah, "birding" works better.*

"Look," Jack shouted. "Hate to break up the celebration, but we've got our first bird of the day." As they peered out over the lagoon in the palest of light, an osprey was soaring low in pursuit of a meal.

"Let's hope that's a sign that we'll see many more birds today," Marsha said.

"I don't know about that," said Vincent. "To the Micmac people of Canada, the osprey is a sign of danger to come."

"Thankfully, we're in Ecuador," Tom said, laughing. "Let's hope the bad mojo isn't intercontinental."

The group left the dining area and assembled at the van with their gear, all of which they had carefully inspected, dried, and cleaned the night before.

"*Vámonos*!" Carlos shouted as he steered the van from the lodge.

CHAPTER SEVEN

Friday, Outside Verde Vista Ecolodge

Arturo Rodriguez knew what he had to do. Although he and his men were outnumbered, he didn't expect much resistance. But he had to do it fast and away from any prying eyes.

They sat in the white Isuzu Trooper outside the gates of the lodge. Tracking the group hadn't been difficult. Muniz had spotted the name of the tour group on the side of the van the previous night, and there were only a few high-end places in the area where tourists stayed.

After Curruca's call, Rodriguez and his men had quickly assembled in the bustling river-port city of Puerto Francisco de Orellana, "Coca" for short, located at the confluence of the Napo and Coca Rivers.

They weren't able to locate the van within the fenced compound of the lodge until about three in the morning because of their long drive north on Highway E55. There was always the chance that more than one van from the tour company could be in use, but they found only one.

Not expecting any activity until dawn, the three slept uncomfortably and intermittently for the next few hours, out of sight of the security guard who manned the front gate.

"Look," announced Tepe. "The van is pulling out."

"Don't start the engine yet," warned Rodriguez. "How many are in there?"

"Five, maybe six," Tepe responded, "but I can't see very well through the tinted windows."

Unbeknownst to the birding group, for the rest of the day, stop after stop, they, like the birds, were being stalked.

***

In the late afternoon, Carlos turned into an abandoned well pad. The road was barely visible because of the six-foot-tall grasses overtaking the gravel surface.

"We'll park here and walk along an old trail to the Río Aguarico for about a half mile," Tom informed the group. "Tuck your pant legs into your socks—this place is teeming with chiggers. Spread out along the trail for better coverage."

"Keep your radios on, and alert us if you see or hear anything," Carlos added.

They checked their Family Radio Service (FRS) radios, made sure they were tuned to 11-22—the frequency used by most birders—lowered the volume to avoid startling the birds, and set off.

During the next few hours, they dashed between cinchona, Guarea, and otaba trees as they alerted one another of a new bird or a large flock.

Exhausted by their day in the field, the group was walking slowly toward the van when Ben and Jack spied a troop of spider monkeys brachiating high in the trees.

"Set up a scope," Marsha said excitedly to Ben. "I want to get a look."

They all stopped momentarily to enjoy the commotion in the canopy.

"We'll be right along," Ben said as he extended the tripod legs. "Give us ten minutes, and we'll catch up."

"I'll stay with them," Carlos informed Tom. "They may not hear the approach of *el tigre*," he joked.

As the rest of the group headed into the clearing from the trail, Jack was the first to notice. "Where'd that SUV come from?" he asked no one in particular. "I don't see anyone, do you?"

Two men emerged from behind a large tree that stood between the group and the van parked one hundred feet in front of them. The shorter of the two men held a pump shotgun.

"Are they friendlies?" Jack asked.

"Don't know. Maybe they're oil-field security," Tom replied.

A third man appeared from behind them, blocking any retreat to the trail. After grabbing Vincent from behind, he pulled a revolver from his waistband.

Vincent, not seeing the man's approach, was startled and fell toward the gunman. Reflexively, the gunman swung away from the tottering man as Vincent grabbed for his arm. As they stumbled, the revolver discharged, thundering through the jungle. In an instant, flocks of squawking parrots exploded from the trees in a frightened frenzy.

Deeper in the forest, Ben heard the shot and turned to Carlos. "What was that?" he asked.

"I don't know, but it came from the direction of the van." He picked up his radio. "Tom, what was that?" Silence. After a few seconds, he tried again. "Tom, are you OK?"

Hearing the call, Rodriguez sprinted toward Tom and grabbed the radio hanging from Tom's vest.

"Tom, Tom, are you reading me? Over," Carlos repeated.

At the third hailing, Rodriguez depressed the transmitter and said, "We have your men, and you'd better get here in a hurry. The old man looks like he's badly hurt."

"I'm perfectly fine," Vincent protested, getting to his feet. "I just tripped."

Back on the path, Ben warned Marsha and Carlos, "This doesn't sound good. We'd better get back to the van fast."

"Hold on," Marsha insisted.

"Yes," replied Carlos. "Let me check it out while you two stay here. I'll call you when it's clear," he added, pointing to Ben's FRS.

"I don't know," Ben said apprehensively. "I think we should stay together."

"Let him check it out, Ben," Marsha told him. Warily, Ben nodded.

Carlos moved slowly and cautiously. As he neared the clearing from the cover of the forest rather than the open trail, he saw his three friends surrounded by armed men.

Carlos radioed Ben. "Three men have guns on Jack, Tom, and Vincent." He immediately regretted making the call, realizing the armed men had Tom's radio.

Ben jumped into action. "Marsha, we don't have much time before they find us. There's no way out of here except the trail to the van. Without a canoe, we have no chance down the river."

He emptied their daypack. Two water bottles, a field guide, a small first-aid kit, a tube of sunscreen, a notepad, a pen, a pocket knife, three energy bars, and Marsha's FRS radio fell onto the path.

Whoever they are, Ben thought, *they'll never let us keep the radio or knife.* He directed Marsha to turn on her radio and set the dial to the international distress frequency of 9-9-9.

"Start calling for help," he told her, trying to allay the rising fear he saw on her face. But he knew full well that the range of these units was measured in miles, and there was little chance that anyone would hear them.

Ben grabbed the Swiss Army knife and unfolded the main blade. *Too long,* he thought, *and they'll suspect something if it's missing.* Opting for the smaller blade, he drove it between the rubber sole and the leather welt of his right hiking boot, inserting it to the hilt. Then he jerked his wrist, snapping the blade. Using the large blade, he pushed the exposed portion of the broken blade completely into the sole. He repeated the process with the file blade in his left boot, folded the knife shut, and placed it back into the daypack.

He then had Marsha gather up the water bottles, sunscreen, and energy bars while he ripped pages from the field guide.

"Marsha, as we head down the trail, I want you to place these items in the bushes along the path," he instructed. He grabbed a sheet of paper from the notebook, scribbled his and Marsha's names, the date, and the following message: "Three armed men." He grabbed the first-aid kit, took out the roll of adhesive tape, and secured the transmit button in the "send" position. He then taped the note and the FRS radio onto a vine overhanging the trail.

"I don't know how long the batteries will last, but maybe someone can pick up the signal," he said. "I'll keep my radio with us."

That done, they started back down the trail, carefully littering the landscape with the jetsam of their existence.

CHAPTER EIGHT

Friday, Río Aguarico

As he had at three previous sites earlier in the day, John Lacker donned his neoprene waders and slowly and carefully slid down the four feet of bank to enter the stream. He walked cautiously to avoid disturbing the bottom sediments.

He pulled a plastic bag from the chest pocket of his waders and removed one of the three sample bottles. He removed the cap and filled the first of the plastic one-hundred-milliliter bottles to the top, displacing any air, and secured the cap. He then filled the other two bottles and placed them back into the bag and into his wader pocket.

As the water gently eddied around his calves, Lacker shoved a stainless-steel sampling tube into the river's soft mud bed. He quickly removed the tube and emptied the stream's sediments into a clear polyethylene bag. He squeezed the bag to expel as much air as possible and then sealed it. After carefully wading back to the bank, he removed a felt-tip permanent marker from his vest and wrote his name and the date, time, sample-site location, and sample number on the bag and bottles. He handed the collections to his assistant at the top of the bank, who placed them with other samples in the fifteen-gallon red cooler chilled with chemical cold packs.

The assistant then handed him what looked like a portable radio trailing a long cord. In fact, it was a sophisticated portable analyzer designed to record the dissolved oxygen, pH, turbidity, temperature, and other physical and chemical properties of the stream. His assistant had calibrated the probe on the bank with deionized water. Lacker depressed the "on" button, selected the automatic function, and placed the probe into the stream.

As the analyzer cycled through its preprogrammed menu, Lacker, reading the digital output, announced, "Temp twenty-five Celsius, dissolved oxygen seven parts per million, pH seven point four, turbidity fifteen units." Even though each parameter was automatically recorded in the SD flash memory of the analyzer along with the date, time, and latitude/longitude coordinates from the internal GPS chip, the assistant duly recorded each one by hand on the sampling log.

After exiting the stream and removing his waders, Lacker and his assistant signed and printed their names to the chain-of-custody sheet for all the samples.

Walking back to the Nissan pickup, Lacker glanced at his clipboard. "The next station is three miles downstream, next to the old Colibrí-6 well pad and near the confluence with the Río Aguarico," he said. He knew roughly where the site was, since this was his second assignment to the area. During the first series of samplings conducted over a period of two weeks the previous year, he had sampled approximately fifty locations and had ridden or driven over most of the roads in the old petroleum production block.

As the field technician, Lacker was only vaguely aware of the painstaking process involved in developing the sampling protocol in which he was now engaged.

His company, Xebec Environmental, had been selected to conduct the sampling based on an agreement between a federal judge in Houston, Steator Energies, and the representatives of the plaintiffs, Victims of Sucumbios Contamination.

The federal court in Houston had sent a request for proposals to a number of qualified firms in the United States, Canada, and Ecuador. Each responding company supplied a comprehensive work plan, an estimate of costs, and statements of qualification to conduct the water-quality study. A three-member evaluation committee, consisting of the special master selected by the court and technical representatives of the defendant and plaintiff, evaluated the proposals and ultimately selected Xebec.

The selection was based principally on cost, since all firms were equivalent in experience and skills. But as Xebec was located in Miami, logistics also proved a major advantage for it. With flights between Miami and Quito and major analytical labs located near the Miami airport, time-sensitive sample testing was assured.

When Xebec was selected, its first task had been to prepare the sampling and testing protocol. This involved determining the most appropriate sites to sample, including potentially contaminated sites near abandoned oil facilities and uncontaminated control sites outside the influence of the facilities. In painstaking detail, the company spelled out the type and number of samples to collect, how to preserve and transfer the samples to the analytical labs, and chain-of-custody procedures to prevent tampering.

The sampling protocol was reviewed only by the court to ensure operational security. The dates and locations of sampling were known only to the in-field coordinator, who assigned the six two-person field teams on a daily basis. Only on the morning of collection did each field team know where they were heading. Only two people in the entire hierarchy knew in advance: the field coordinator, who selected the sites, and a secretary, who typed the assignments two or three days before the sampling. The protocol was almost foolproof.

CHAPTER NINE

Friday, Late Afternoon, Abandoned Drilling Pad near the Río Aguarico

As a young seaman just out of high school in 1968, Ben had attended the US Navy's Survival, Evasion, Resistance, and Escape (SERE) training on Whidbey Island, Washington, before shipping out to Vietnam as a gunner in the brown-water fleet. Lesson one, painfully learned and never forgotten, was "Don't get caught." Suppressing the urge to turn and run to the security of the river, Ben, fearing for the safety of the others, now entered the clearing, hand in hand with Marsha, toward an unknown fate.

Off to the side, Carlos, crouched low and out of sight of the intruders, waved to catch the attention of the couple.

"Don't look, Ben, but Carlos is signaling us," Marsha whispered.

"I saw him. We'll approach as if we're the last ones on the trail. Hopefully, they'll buy it." Ben slapped his leg as if shooing an insect to acknowledge to Carlos that he saw him and to alert him that the strangers were fast approaching.

The couple was immediately seized by the pistol-wielding man who had been sent down the trail to see who had made the radio call.

Javier led them toward the rest of the group, who stood next to the Trooper. Out of the corner of his eye, Ben saw Carlos duck deeper into the brush.

"Empty your pockets and packs," Rodriguez demanded.

Ben and Marsha placed their wallets, passports, keys, knives, cell phones, watches, binoculars, notebooks, and field guides on the hood of the SUV.

Realizing these men were hardly a security force for the oil fields, Tom pleaded, "Please take the money and leave us alone. We're here on vacation and don't want any trouble."

Rodriguez examined the passports, trying, with some difficulty, to interpret the English. "Who was speaking on the radio?" he asked, staring at Ben.

"Me," Ben responded, pointing to his radio on the hood.

Rodriguez eyed him suspiciously, unable to identify the voice veiled by the static. All the while, Tepe scrutinized the cell phones, ejecting batteries and SIM cards.

"Who's your driver?" Rodriguez asked.

"Me," said Tom. "I'm a guide with Natura Sucumbios. I've been leading trips to Ecuador for fifteen years. We're staying at Verde Vista Ecolodge, and they're expecting us back for dinner."

Rodriguez caught himself before he blurted out that he knew exactly who they were and where they were staying. *The less they know, the better*, he thought.

Tepe finished counting the money. "There's about three hundred dollars US and another hundred fifty thousand sucres. Eight credit cards, two phone cards, and four ATM cards. Maybe they have more money in their luggage. Add these cameras and binoculars," he said while pocketing the cash.

"Maybe so," Rodriguez acknowledged, but he really wondered how much they were worth to their families.

"If it's money you want, I can get it for you," Tom said. "Let the others go, and I'll have my company drive the money from Quito. Once it arrives, you can let me go."

Rodriguez said nothing but nodded to Tepe, who began to bind Tom's hands behind his back.

Jack saw this and knew that once his hands were bound, they had no alternatives, and if anyone had the strength to overcome the men, it was him. *It's now or never*, he thought.

As Tepe was focused on Tom's hands, Jack swung violently to his right and grabbed Tepe around the neck. He torqued Tepe's right arm into a half nelson. He hoped the others in the group would follow his lead, but instead they froze, as surprised as Tepe.

Rodriguez, just two steps away, leaped toward Jack as he reversed his hold on the Remington 870 shotgun. The butt of the shotgun caught Jack squarely on his forehead, grazing Tepe with the follow-through. Stunned and disoriented, Jack released his grip on Tepe and fell to the ground on one knee. Blood gushed from a three-inch gash over the bridge of his nose.

"He's bleeding." Marsha gasped at the sight of Jack as he collapsed to the ground.

Rodriguez pivoted again, this time facing the group with the shotgun aimed directly at them. "Don't anyone move or try something like that again," he said menacingly. "Tepe, get him tied tight," he added, lowering the barrel toward Jack's twisted body on the ground.

Still unbound, Vincent stepped forward with his arms up in a sign of surrender. "I'm a doctor. Please let me look at him," he pleaded.

Considering the old man's age, Rodriguez nodded in approval. "Javier, keep an eye on the others," he said, pointing to Ben and Marsha.

Vincent bent down alongside Jack. "Hand me that first-aid kit on the hood," he told Rodriguez, who, in turn, motioned for Marsha to get it. Marsha unzipped the nylon bag as she knelt and placed the kit on the ground next to Vincent.

Vincent grabbed a large gauze pad, unwrapped it, and held it with pressure against Jack's wound. "Can you hand me another pad and peel off some tape?" he asked Marsha, who looked to Rodriguez for approval.

"It'll probably require sutures, but this should stem the bleeding," Vincent said as he taped the pads tightly to Jack's forehead. He cradled Jack's head in his hands. With the bleeding slowed, he was able to see Jack's pupils were equal in size and reactive to light. A good sign, he noted.

"Jack, can you hear me?" he asked. Jack responded with a low, unintelligible murmur. "He's responsive but concussed. We'll have to be careful with him. We don't want any brain injury. Can we lay him down in the van?"

Rodriguez motioned to Tepe, who had finished tying Tom's hands, to help Vincent get Jack into the van. "Make sure you tie his hands and feet to the seat frame," he cautioned Tepe.

Once they were all bound and in the van, Rodriguez said, "Tepe, you drive the van. I'll sit in back. Javier, you follow in the Trooper."

Resigned to the situation, each member of the group was alone in his or her thoughts, not wanting to repeat what had happened to Jack. They weren't silent but spoke little so as not to draw attention to themselves.

Ben, sitting beside Marsha, nudged her with his shoulder and, with a nod and smile, tried to reassure her. Marsha understood. After so many years, their body language—a squeeze of the hand, a gentle stroke of the cheek—was all that was needed. She slowly turned to Ben and, with just the hint of a smile, mouthed, "I love you."

Tepe drove the van on Highway E45 northward to the village of Jivino Verde, where he turned right and headed toward the small jungle town of Shushufindi. Then he followed E10 through Tarapoa, finally terminating outside the village of Tigre Playa on the Río San Miguel. The route directly to Lago Agrio was faster but also more traveled. Their route was through nearly deserted forest with neglected roads, which minimized unwanted encounters with isolated villagers.

After what seemed hours, though it was just a little more than forty-five minutes, the vehicles pulled off the main road onto a two-rut trail that led to a small landing along the river. Moored to a makeshift piling was a twenty-five-foot wooden canoe with a square stern on which a fifty-horsepower outboard motor was mounted.

Canoes like this were the principal transportation for 90 percent of the Amazon. Trade was wholly dependent on an armada constantly cruising the river channels, flooded rain-forest swamps, and ancient oxbow lakes. Usually, the canoes were laden with manioc, coffee, cacao, and plantain. But sometimes, as on this evening, cargos were more nefarious. This was the night fleet, *flotilla de noche*, slowly and quietly navigating the blackness of the jungle night.

Javier and Tepe carefully eased the group into the canoe and onto wood planks strapped between the gunwales that served as seats. Tom was seated first, followed by Ben and Marsha and then Vincent. Jack was still dazed when Javier helped him into the boat.

"Thank you, Carlos," he said.

Javier looked over to Rodriguez. "Who's Carlos?"

Rodriguez looked at Tom. "Who *is* Carlos?"

"One of the cooks at the lodge," Tom replied. "Looks a lot like your man there."

"No, Tom. He was our driver, remember?" Jack blurted.

Rodriguez glared at Tom, but Tom stared right back, unblinking.

"Tepe, hand me that bag," Rodriguez said.

Rodriguez rummaged through the gear collected from the hostages. When he found a digital camera, he turned it on and scrolled through the photos. They were mostly snapshots of birds and other wildlife, an occasional landscape, and the group in various combinations. Then he saw a photograph of a handsome Ecuadorean man with piercing green eyes and bright white teeth grinning widely through the open window of the minivan they had just purloined, then another of the same man with his arms around Ben and Marsha, and another of him peering through a spotting scope mounted to a tall tripod.

"What's your cook doing in the jungle? Shouldn't he be back at the lodge preparing dinner?" Rodriguez asked Tom in a threatening tone. He grabbed Tom by the throat with both hands and choked him violently. "If someone doesn't tell me the truth, your leader will be a meal for the piranhas in a few seconds."

"Carlos is our driver," Ben yelled. "Let him go."

"Where is he?" Rodriguez demanded.

"Back at the clearing. He was hiding when we left," Ben said.

Rodriguez released his death grip on Tom, who coughed and gasped for air.

"You've made our trip a little more complicated," Rodriguez said as he regained his composure. He thought for a moment and signaled Tepe to his side. Together, they walked from the landing out of earshot of the captives. "We can't let him get away. He'll go straight to the police."

"But they could never catch us—we have too much of a lead, and we'll be out of the country soon."

"He saw our truck. He saw *us*. We can't take any chances."

"What should we do?" Tepe asked.

"Go back and find him. He can't get far on foot, and there was no one around to help him. I can't wait around with the hostages. I need to get them out of here. Once you find this Carlos, bring him back here tomorrow evening. I'll have Javier come back in the canoe to pick him up. After that, you can get rid of the van and wait until Javier and I return in a few days."

Tepe didn't like the idea of returning for the man alone, without any backup; he'd be more vulnerable. It was possible the police were looking for them already.

"Wouldn't it be easier if I just got rid of him? Lose him in the jungle?"

"No. The jefe said, 'No harm.' They are too valuable," Rodriguez insisted. He then tossed Tepe a cell phone from the bag.

"Here, take this and call me when you find him."

The two men returned to the boat. Rodriguez taped the hostages' mouths shut; then he moved to the bow seat, and Javier, the motorman, sat at the stern. From the bank, Tepe tossed the daypacks into the rear of the canoe and pushed them off into the invisible stream.

***

It was dark when Tepe sped from the landing. He had many miles to cover, but fortunately, the man he was after was on foot and couldn't have traveled more than a few miles. Tepe would have more than enough time to intercept him before he reached the nearest village.

He parked on the roadside about twelve miles from the oil-pad site and waited. He stayed in the truck; he didn't like the jungle. He was raised in the city, and the only reason he had found himself there was because of Rodriguez. And just like Rodriguez, he made his money in petty crime in Quito. It was Rodriguez's Indian friend, Javier, who was the jungle man; he worked the roads and rivers smuggling contraband for the cartels.

Tepe could see nothing through the windshield, so he occasionally turned on the headlights to illuminate the road ahead. He had parked the Trooper just before a bend so a person walking the road couldn't see it until he was mere yards away.

There he waited and didn't leave the vehicle unless he absolutely had to, which was twice because of all the water he'd been drinking.

***

Javier motored the canoe downriver, close to the bank and under the shroud of the overhanging trees with lianas and vines streaming from their branches. It wasn't likely that anyone would see them, and if they did, no questions would be asked. Just the same, it was prudent to avoid detection.

Ben shifted slightly to ease his discomfort from the wooden seat; all was quiet, except for a few moans from Jack. He made out an occasional passing boat working its way upstream from the east. A few had small lights tethered to a jury-rigged mast to signal their approach. But not this boat.

Along the way, Ben also spotted widely separated villages. Even at this distance, he heard the rumble of diesel generators, which provided power for the occasional light. At one point, he thought he saw the ghostly blue cast of a television screen in the distance. He tried to remember landmarks and directions, but it was impossible. In the blackness, he could only count the number of villages they passed.

Javier knew the river well. When they neared a village, he steered the boat to the opposite bank. Long, slender sandbars constantly changed the river's channel, but he avoided them all.

What other cargo has he transported so that he knows the river so well at night? Ben wondered. *Maybe I don't want to know.*

As his eyes adjusted gradually to the conditions, he was reminded of night patrols on his PBR (patrol boat, river) in the Mekong Delta. Only about seven feet longer and wider than the canoe, it possessed twin diesel engines and jet drives that were considerably louder, even in stealth mode, than the little outboard propelling the canoe.

What I wouldn't give for that M60 machine gun right now, he thought.

Marsha was leaning against Ben for support as she tried to sleep. Ben felt her drifting off, her breathing slow and rhythmic. He was grateful that she could sleep, as he knew she could be free of fear for least a few minutes. Ben, unfortunately, was wide-awake, his brain on overdrive. He couldn't remember a rush of adrenaline like this since he'd taken fire from sniper teams. But he knew he had to pace himself. He was in a no-win situation, and the rest of his group would pay the cost of any bad decision he made. Now was the time to reconnoiter. Pay attention. Observe. Remember. Plan.

With that, he finally relaxed as the canoe continued its meandering course.

***

Carlos had watched silently as Ben and Marsha had surrendered to the gunmen.

I will not desert you, he vowed.

When Rodriguez had butted Jack with the rifle, Carlos was tempted to run to his assistance, but he didn't. It wasn't out of fear, not completely; rather, he sensed he would be more valuable if he stayed concealed. He could get help. But his gut wrenched when he saw Jack motionless on the ground. Not since the death of his father five years ago had he felt such helplessness. There was nothing he could do to help the group, just as he could do nothing to free his father of cancer.

Sitting motionlessly, he had carefully surveyed his surroundings, looking for an escape route if the gunmen discovered he was missing. He had enough of a lead that he could outrun them to the river, but he would be better off hiding in the forest. The men didn't dress like locals, so they probably didn't know the area as well as he did.

The tension in his body eased as he watched the two vehicles drive off. He rose and brought the binoculars to his eyes. He looked for a license plate on the Trooper, but it apparently had been removed. In the last second before the Trooper and minivan turned onto the road and out of sight, Carlos stared hard, trying to remember everything he could.

He made his way back to the clearing and began to head for the road but decided to hide for a little longer. He knew his best chance to elude them was to travel at night.

He racked his brain trying to figure out who those men could be. He hadn't heard of a kidnapping in the area for many years, not since the oil company had left.

Maybe smugglers? But they would work at night. Surely they would know the police would launch a search for the tourists, which would bring many unwanted eyes to the area. That wasn't what smugglers would want.

Carlos was baffled but knew he had to get out of the area as soon as it got dark. He was within ten miles of a couple of villages, but that would be where the men would look for him after searching the old drill pad. It was sixty miles to Lago Agrio, where he could go home and contact the police, but only thirty miles to the lodge. He could do that distance in half a day under normal circumstances, but traveling at night would slow him. He would need to proceed carefully because the gunmen weren't the only danger he could encounter; in the jungle—Carlos knew that man was not always the top predator.

He checked his pack and saw the two full water bottles. They would have to do; giardia was rampant in the jungle rivers.

He saw a large kapok tree near the road. It had several large buttress trunks that flared like rocket fins from the main bole. He found a crevice between two six-foot-high buttresses; another animal obviously had used it for the same purpose, because the vegetation was worn away, exposing reddish jungle soil laden with animal tracks. Fortunately, none were large enough to have been left by *el tigre*, which he had jokingly warned the group about a few hours ago. The tree offered good cover. He thought about sleep, knowing he wouldn't get much in the next twenty-four hours, but he was too wired. Instead, he bided his time.

An hour later, Carlos squeezed out from his makeshift den and slowly stretched to relax his knotted muscles. He pulled a headlamp from his pack and turned it on. Then he slowly scanned the terrain until he saw the road. By then, it was pitch-black; the moon was only a sliver and still low in the eastern sky. A few stars were visible, but they weren't much help. He would have to use the light sparingly to preserve the batteries and, just as important, not to advertise his presence.

He began his walk down the road. He listened hard for sounds of civilization but heard only the din of the nocturnal jungle. He thought how much he'd rather be home right now with Cecilia and the kids. The whole family—which now included his mother, his younger sister, and her daughter—would have finished dinner and would be readying themselves for the next day. He had to think for a minute. *What day is it? Are they going to school and work tomorrow, or do they have the day off?* For Carlos, one day merged with the next, and none was much different. He was always on the road or in the field.

Staying at home in Lago had become more and more of a luxury. But the more work he got guiding these trips, the more money he made.

He had become a sought-after guide by the tour companies and also by scientific expeditions to the Oriente. If he wanted, he could be working fifty weeks a year. Fortunately, he worked for Natura Sucumbios, which allowed a fairly flexible schedule. Also, their clients were the best. They wanted to see the rarest birds, which made it a particular challenge for Carlos. Before a weeklong tour, he would be out scouting bird-sighting locations; that way, the birders got to the perfect spots. Because of the specialized clientele, tips were very generous and more than doubled his salary.

After about two hours, he stopped. He searched the primitive road and found a dry spot to sit and rest for a few minutes. He grabbed a water bottle from his pack, along with a plastic bag with a few *galletas* that Maria from the lodge had slipped him the day before. The sweet, buttery treats were just what he needed. He only wished she had packed more. He still had a can of tuna, which he would save for breakfast. After that, he'd have to forage in the forest.

As he walked, he occasionally swept the forest with his flashlight in search of eyeshine from an unsuspecting animal. Seeing nothing was reassuring, but he still heard the grunts, moans, cackles, snorts, hoots, and other sounds as the rain forest went about its business. Carlos was attuned to the forest and relished his solitary moments immersed in its bounty.

Just past dawn, as darkness began to lift, Carlos contemplated finding a place to settle for the day. Although he had seen and heard no one in the past hours, there was no telling what would happen when civilization awoke.

As he rounded a slight curve alongside the road, he looked up and there, not thirty feet away, was the Isuzu Trooper he'd seen yesterday. He instantly recognized the man leaning against the hood, and the man seemed to recognize Carlos too, but Carlos didn't know how.

The man ran toward Carlos, who instinctively dove into the forest to escape. Carlos leaped over fallen trees, dodged between limbs, and ducked under vines. He thought he was making headway when a bullet exploded into a tree trunk less than three feet to his right.

"*Alto*!" the man shouted.

Carlos stopped and turned toward the voice; the man had him in the sights of his pistol. Slowly raising his hands over his head, Carlos looked to the ground in submission.

The man was a few years older than Carlos, maybe in his early forties and not in the best of condition. He wore jeans, running shoes, and a short-sleeve T-shirt, not the best clothes for the humid jungle. Carlos surmised he was from the city.

"Your friends are waiting for you, señor," Tepe said.

"What friends are you talking about?"

"I know who you are. You are Carlos. You are the driver with Natura Sucumbios."

"You are mistaken. I am Juan, and my village is just down the road."

"Juan, you should know your friends had very expensive digital cameras. And they must like you very much because they had many photographs of you with them in the forest."

Carlos had no response; he just knew he had to escape. He was the last chance the group would have. He remembered his silent pledge to Marsha, but he was smaller than the stranger and unarmed. He knew the jungle better, however, which was his only advantage right then.

As Tepe ushered him toward the Trooper, Carlos noticed a thicket of about twenty peach palms off to his left. This species of tree had been carefully cultivated for at least three millennia for its sweet fruit and rich oil. The Incas were responsible for its wide distribution as a food crop, but the tree now propagated on its own throughout the Amazon. These trees were tall, reaching seventy-five feet, but they were also very thin, not much more than a foot in diameter. Because of this, they were very fragile and vulnerable to damage by climbing animals. So they had developed a very effective defense mechanism: at about one-foot intervals above the ground, they had as many as one hundred spines encircling the trunk, some up to seven inches long and a quarter-inch in diameter. The spines were so effective at repelling invaders that the local Indians called them "monkey no climb" trees.

Carlos knew he had to make a move before they reached the Trooper, and this place was made to order. He faked a stumble and fell hard to the ground. "My ankle! I broke my ankle!" he screamed. He drew his left knee to his chest with both hands, lifting his damaged ankle off the ground, and rolled back and forth in a display of agony.

Tepe ordered him to stand up.

"It is too painful," Carlos replied. "Help me to the car. Then I will be all right."

Sensing the vulnerability of the younger, smaller man, Tepe went over and lifted him by his left arm and steadied him.

"I can't stand on it," Carlos said, eyeing the .22 pistol now in the man's left hand.

Carlos made a couple of feeble hops with Tepe supporting his left side. Then he pretended to try to bear weight on his left foot but cried in pain again.

"Let me put my arm around you," he said to Tepe.

They walked a few more steps until Carlos was in the position he wanted.

"I need to rest. Please stop for a moment."

Tepe stopped.

When Carlos felt Tepe relax slightly, he braced himself firmly on his miraculously healed left foot and pivoted until he was face-to-face with him. In an instant, he drove his shoulder into Tepe's chest and sent him reeling into the peach-palm thicket. Tepe screamed in pain as hundreds of spines penetrated him from his calves to his neck. Carlos grabbed for the pistol in Tepe's immobilized right hand, but Tepe was strong and wouldn't release his grip. Impaled, Tepe tried to struggle, but each movement drove the spines deeper and intensified the pain.

"Don't move," Carlos said. "You could puncture a lung or maybe open an artery."

But with a force of will that Carlos hadn't expected, Tepe pulled himself forward and free from the tree. He fell face-first to the ground, still in agonizing pain. Before Tepe could regain his senses or his aim, Carlos knew this was his only chance to run.

Jesus Cristo, how did he do that? Carlos wondered.

Running through the jungle wasn't possible. Even a fast walk would be difficult. Trees, shrubs, vines, and downed logs were everywhere; it looked like an impenetrable green maze. But this was Carlos's country—he knew the landscape. He slithered his way through the tangle. He stopped for a moment and heard the man in pursuit. Unlike Carlos, who was smooth and graceful, Tepe was stumbling and bulldozing his way through the mass of vegetation. Carlos heard him grunting, wheezing, and cursing in the distance.

***

Carlos kept moving, but Tepe quit after a few minutes; it was too much for him. He couldn't keep up, and he was afraid he would get lost if he followed Carlos farther into the forest. So Tepe returned to his truck. He would check each village along the road until he found Carlos.

***

Carlos had stopped a few times to listen. When he was sure he no longer could hear the man barreling through the understory, he thought about circling back but decided it was better to get farther away. He knew that if he continued east, he eventually would arrive at the river near the kidnapping site, which he could try to follow. But that would be treacherous. Instead, he would stay close to the road, just far enough in the forest to hide at the approach of any vehicles. But first he had to find a place to bed down for the day.

***

"I couldn't find him. He must be hiding in the jungle or maybe got a ride out of the area," Tepe explained to Rodriguez over one of the stolen cell phones.

"Keep searching. I won't send Javier back, but when you find him, make sure you hide him. We will deal with him after we turn over the others."

Rodriguez was sorry he'd had to send Tepe—Javier would have been a better choice because he knew the jungle. But Javier was also the only one who knew the river, and, right then, that was most important. Although he'd been in the jungle many times, for Tepe, it was still foreign and foreboding without Javier.

Rodriguez understood Tepe's trepidation. Both were mountain people born in the slums of Quito and had turned to crime early to survive. Rodriguez had specialized in smuggling and knew of the many hidden mountain trails and passes leading into the jungle. Some, he had been told, actually had been used by the Incas to hide from the conquistadors. Now they were used to hide from rival gangs and the police.

In his many years as a criminal, Rodriguez was proud that he had only been caught twice—the first time landing him in jail for two years. However, for a professional criminal, prison was time well spent. He developed a web of contacts and learned new skills, which he quickly put to use. It was in jail that he met Tepe, who taught him the skills he needed in the urban environment—breaking and entering heavily protected homes, neutralizing car alarms and ignition switches, and finding the fence offering the highest returns. But he tired of the high-risk, low-reward crimes—he wanted something bigger, and he convinced Tepe to come along.

It was on his second bust—this time working for a cartel—that he met Curruca. Rodriguez was amazed what a good lawyer and bad judge could achieve with enough cartel money. He had spent less than a day in jail and, even better, met a local Quichuan Indian, Javier, who knew the jungle like he knew the mountains.

Rodriguez never understood why he became the leader—he wasn't the oldest, the smartest, or the most experienced—but the others never challenged him, and so far, it had worked well for them.

CHAPTER TEN

Saturday, the Landing

They approached the landing near dawn while the sky was still and black. With his hands bound behind him, Ben discreetly struggled to twist his arms into a position to read the illuminated dial on his watch and then realized it was part of the booty confiscated by Tepe. He had no way of judging time, distance, or even direction. All he knew was they first had motored downstream but then turned and now were running against the current. With all the meanders and side channels, they could be heading in any direction. And the darkness offered no frame of reference to judge speed. But something in Ben's mind—maybe an internal compass, maybe his experience in the muddy delta forty years ago—told him they'd been traveling for five hours, more or less. He wished he knew celestial navigation, for the stars on this clear night had provided a road map.

After Javier eased the bow onto the shore, Rodriguez leaped to the bank and tied off the canoe on the stilt root of a *Cecropia* tree.

Unknown to the captives, they had traveled easterly on the Río San Miguel to its confluence with the Río Putumayo, then northward, arriving just south of Puerto Asís, Colombia. However, this was no passport-control entry port. In fact, in Bogotá, 450 miles away, this was considered no man's land—FARC country.

Rodriguez scrambled up the bank and searched the wooded area with a flashlight. Satisfied they were alone, he returned to assist Javier in offloading the group.

Fatigue, coupled with age, was beginning to affect Vincent. He barely had the energy to stand, and it required the assistance of both men to get him up the steep bank—likewise with Jack in his somnambulant state.

On the bank, Ben stretched and tried to arouse all the muscles numbed from the confined seating arrangement. Glad to be on land, he rubbed his bound arm against Marsha, who also was gathering her strength.

Certain they were out of earshot of anyone, Rodriguez removed the tape from his captives' mouths. Immediately, Marsha exclaimed, "I really have to pee!" a sentiment also expressed by the others.

One at a time, Javier untied their hands and walked them behind the large trunk of a river palm while Rodriguez, his rifle in hand, oversaw the rest of them. Upon returning to the group, Javier bound each of them again, this time with their hands in front. Then he gave each of them a bottle of water and an energy bar from one of the daypacks Tepe had tossed into the canoe.

"Let me check on Jack," Vincent requested.

Rodriguez nodded and motioned to Javier to untie Vincent's hands.

Vincent kneeled next to Jack, who was sitting on the ground. He checked Jack's eyes and lifted a corner of the tape holding the bandage on his forehead.

"Looks like the bleeding has stopped. How are you feeling?" Vincent asked Jack.

"I'm a little dizzy, and my head's still throbbing," he replied.

"Here, drink my water. You don't need to be dehydrated, too," Vincent said. "I'll walk behind you. Let me know if anything gets worse."

"Thanks, Doc," Jack said, realizing he had been saying that a lot lately.

Within minutes, the group was walking. This time, Javier led. As Ben had surmised, Javier knew this area well.

CHAPTER ELEVEN

Saturday Morning, Verde Vista Ecolodge

Maria was managing the reception desk at the lodge all evening. She had expected the birding group to return sometime around dinner. But knowing Tom, she wasn't surprised they were late.

Probably chasing some bat or owl, she thought, laughing.

But now it was really late—one o'clock in the morning—and she was beginning to worry. Before needlessly waking anyone, she tried Tom's cell-phone number. Nothing. She tried the contact numbers from the guest-registration forms. After the fourth nonresponse, Maria became even more anxious. She dialed again.

"*Sí,*" answered Oscar Malin in a sleepy, barely conscious voice.

"I am so sorry to wake you, Señor Malin, but I am worried about the Natura Sucumbios group. They have not arrived, and it is very late. I tried to call Tom but received no answer or voice mail. I also tried the guests' cell phones. I didn't know what else I should do."

"No, Maria, you were correct in calling me," replied Malin, the lodge manager. "I will be at the desk in fifteen minutes. Could you call the Natura Sucumbios office? Maybe the group contacted them."

"Yes, Señor Malin. I will call right away."

Malin reached the desk from his small cabin on the grounds in less than ten minutes.

"No one is answering in Quito at this time. I just get an answering machine," Maria informed him. "I will keep trying, but they probably won't open until the morning."

Malin pondered his options. There wasn't much chance of finding them by himself at this time of night. He didn't even know which direction to start. He could call the police, but they probably wouldn't do anything until daylight.

"Try the cell phones again, Maria. I see no reason why they shouldn't work," he said. Because of the need for cheap, efficient, and reliable worldwide communications, the oil companies had subsidized the cellular telephone network in the country, particularly in the oil production areas in the jungle. While some locations had marginal coverage, he thought that Tom's group could not be that far away.

After several failed attempts, Maria turned, looked at Malin, and shrugged in exasperation.

"OK," he said, feigning confidence. "Here's what we will do. Please awaken Colonel Hernandez in room seven and explain the situation. Tell him I will drive north on Sacha Road for twenty-five miles and try to contact the group with my cell phone in case they're just out of range. I will call you if I proceed farther north. If I am unsuccessful, I will return here and head south. Give the colonel my cell-phone number, and I will keep him updated also."

Malin reached under the reception desk and grabbed a set of car keys that dangled from an eye hook.

"*Sí*," Maria responded, as Malin headed through the door into the night.

***

Colonel Xavier Hernandez of the Ecuadorian Army was in the lobby when two of his officers arrived at 5:30 a.m., just as the first glimmer of sun backlit the eastern rain forest. A study in contrasts, the colonel was dressed uncharacteristically in a flowered tropical shirt, khakis, and sandals—appropriate attire for his long-overdue family vacation—while his men wore starched green-camouflage uniforms with service belts and highly polished boots.

Fifteen minutes earlier, Malin had returned tired and frustrated. Four hours of driving and calling had yielded nothing.

"Colonel, please, you and your men join me for breakfast, and I will fill you in. I hesitated to call the police since you were here at the lodge, and our police force is so small."

The colonel, Malin, and two soldiers walked to the buffet line, which was beginning to attract the early risers heading out on tours. After they sat down at a table a discreet distance from other guests, Malin related everything he knew, the areas he had searched, and his failure to contact the group by phone or radio.

Colonel Hernandez shifted uncomfortably in his chair. "There is no plausible explanation for no service to five cell phones. It is not likely that all were out of batteries or turned off for this duration," he said. *Maybe for a few minutes to preserve power…but simultaneously? No*, he thought. "I am reluctant to begin a search before we contact Natura Sucumbios," he stated. "Maybe there was a change of plans, and the group left the Oriente for the mountains, or maybe they are at another lodge. Do we have phone numbers for anyone else with the tour company?"

After excusing himself, Malin rose and headed to the reception desk. A few minutes later, he returned and informed the colonel that Maria would try the number of the driver's family in Lago to see whether they had heard from him. She also would call another local guide who worked for the company.

Satisfied that additional contacts were being made, Colonel Hernandez said he would put the army post on alert in case a search was necessary. He then returned to his room to let his wife and children know that Papa would not be joining them today on their hike to the lagoon to see the *cocodrilos*.

CHAPTER TWELVE

Saturday Morning; Near San Miguel, Colombia

The trail from the river was well traveled. The dirt was compacted and the understory cleared two to three feet on either side. Nipped, leafless branches on the shrubs, along with hoofprints in the dirt, indicated that teams of mules were regular visitors. Ten feet from the river, the trail wasn't visible; the dense vegetation masked any view from water or sky. Sunlight was barely able to penetrate, which further obscured the group's presence.

Tom's ears were tuned into the sounds from the canopy. His encyclopedic knowledge of birdcalls was almost as good as a map. From his extensive travels throughout the Amazon, he was able to discern which habitat, which province, and in this case, which watershed he was in by the sounds of the assemblage of birds. He'd had no chance to exercise his skills in the boat because of the motor noise and the darkness. And what he had heard was typical of all the major rivers in the area. But now he was able to fine-tune. The groaning of the tiger-heron and squawks of the oropendola told him he was in a várzea lowland, and the "whet" and "chree" calls of the black-capped donacobius pretty much confirmed he was in south-central Colombia. Like Ben, he was mentally cataloging everything, not knowing which scrap of information he may need.

Tom felt a leaden responsibility for the group. They had placed their trust in his company. It was his planning, route, and timing that had led to the encounter with the kidnappers. *If only we had left fifteen minutes earlier,* he tortured himself, unaware of the futility of his angst.

This sense of responsibility for others had developed early in Tom. Birding had begun as an escape, a way to distance himself from his father, who had taken to the bottle heavily after Tom's mother's death. His guilt about leaving his brother and sister alone with their father—even for a few hours—had eaten at him. As a teenager, he often had confided in his uncle Billy on their treks and prayed his father wouldn't turn his wrath on the younger kids. Tom could take it; he was tough. But the kids—well, they were just kids and were much more vulnerable. Billy often confronted his brother-in-law, which always ended in a shout fest with no resolution. Billy wanted to call the police and have Tom's father arrested, but Tom always pleaded against it, afraid the authorities would break up the family.

Finally, when he was only sixteen, he'd had all he could take—his father had slapped his younger sister. Tom raced across the living room, lowered his head, and slammed his left shoulder into his father's rib cage. He heard and felt the cracking of bone—some his, some his father's. Though Tom's father was considerably larger than his son, the combination of surprise, his drunken condition, and the force of a 150-pound object hurtling through the air sent him tumbling backward four feet, and he landed flat on his back. Tom's father gasped for breath but was able to get to one knee to gather his strength. He saw his son twisting in pain on the floor due to a fractured clavicle.

Tom's father exploded in rage, jumping on his son and pummeling him with both fists. Shocked and fearing for her brother's life, Tom's sister grabbed a butcher-block cutting board from the kitchen counter and, with a well-placed blow to the back of the skull, knocked her father out. His limp body collapsed on top of Tom.

The police arrived in minutes, and Tom's father was taken in cuffs from the house. The family's situation had been a poorly kept secret among the neighbors, who erupted in a collective cheer as Tom's father was placed in the police car. Tom left by ambulance, but not before Uncle Billy came and took the kids home with him; it was an arrangement later approved by the courts.

At least now Tom didn't feel he had abandoned anyone, but he did feel guilty for having put the group in such a dangerous situation. He tried to analyze their prospects. *Harming us will do them no good if they want a ransom,* he thought. *They're too practiced not to know that proof of life will be required. This was well planned; they've done this before. Amateurs wouldn't have ready access to a boat and know this trail so well.*

Their only mistake so far was Carlos. *But why us?* he wondered. *Did they prowl the roads looking for victims? And what are the chances of finding us on that deserted road? If they have a history of targeting tour groups, I would have heard about it. It seems too coincidental.*

He thought about Carlos. He was sorry Ben had told the captors about him, but he probably would have done the same under the circumstances. He just hoped Carlos would reach the authorities quickly.

Tom turned slowly to look over his right shoulder. Behind him was Jack, followed by Vincent, Marsha, Ben, and Rodriguez. Javier was leading in a slow, measured pace so as not overtax to Vincent or Jack.

They had walked for about an hour and a half, and the jungle slowly was waking to the new day. The air was warming and the humidity rising. The songs and calls throughout the forest were increasing. Not a single sign of human habitation was apparent, which came as no surprise to Tom. This trail had been established for a purpose, and it wasn't to access villages. In fact, it seemed to encourage the opposite—no logging, no clearing, no crop plots, only a tunnel of vegetation bored through the rain forest.

Rodriguez stopped and told the group to sit and rest. Javier reached into one of the daypacks and brought out more water bottles, which he uncapped and handed out. He thought about passing out more energy bars but calculated they had only two more miles to go, and no one except Vincent and Jack seemed fatigued.

About nine o'clock, which Tom guessed from the height of the sun, they entered a long, narrow clearing. At the far end was a low earthen berm with a small opening that led to another trail in the forest. Along the edge of the clearing, Tom spotted a series of long, open-sided structures with thatched roofs, as well as two small huts elevated above the ground on eight-foot poles; a small corral stood next to the huts. All the structures seemed to be unoccupied. At the center of the clearing were many three-inch ruts in the soil. When he saw the remnants of an airfield windsock on a pole on the ground next to them, Tom realized the place was a drug lab.

Boats brought coca leaves by river through Peru or Ecuador, loaded them onto mule trains, and hauled them to the clearing, where they were chopped and processed into unrefined paste and then flown out of the jungle on single-engine planes. Tom guessed the runway was only about a quarter-mile long, which must have made for pretty hairy takeoffs with a loaded plane and a hundred-foot canopy at either end.

He was impressed. The lab would be impossible to detect by river, given the distance and dense forest, and only accessible by well-hidden trails. And unless someone was directly overhead, it would be almost invisible by plane. Satellite imagery could detect it, but that would require a constant vigil to identify any activity. Tom also knew that FARC protected the cartels from nearby villagers, who were, more likely than not, employed as processors.

It was really a numbers game. The cartel hedged its bets by having many labs processing great quantities of cocaine. If the National Army of Colombia, supported by the US Drug Enforcement Agency, raided a few, well, that was the cost of doing business. Once the drugs and equipment were burned, the authorities left. A site would be abandoned for a few months, and then operations would resume. All the while, other sites were processing and shipping. There was safety in numbers.

Rodriguez led them past the open structures. These contained long makeshift tables milled from planks hewn from the trees that had been cleared for the runway. At one end of the structures was a low, cinder-block ring filled with ash from long-extinguished fires. They walked past the primitive corral and a row of fifty-five-gallon drums where the cocaine alkaloid was extracted through the addition of lime, kerosene, and sulfuric acid and then dried to a hard paste.

At one of the elevated huts, Rodriguez ordered the group to climb the wooden ladder, a task made only slightly easier now that their hands were bound in front. Still, Vincent and Jack required help to negotiate the rungs.

The hut was square and about twelve feet long on each side. It was empty except for a few plank-and-log benches and a table. Three hinged boxes at one side served as the larder for the cooking area. Tom had difficulty imagining any cooking in a hut, but the smoke-stained opening in the thatched roof suggested a chimney. He visualized the workers sleeping—crowded and uncomfortable—on the wooden floor.

Rodriguez arranged the hostages in a semicircle with their backs to the wooden railing. Javier tied their feet to one another's for additional security.

"Watch them," Rodriguez ordered Javier as he descended the ladder.

After walking past the opening in the berm at the end of the airstrip, certain no one from the hut could see or hear him, Rodriguez reached into his pack and pulled out a cinched nylon bag. He had hidden it for a reason. *No need for them to know I have this,* Rodriguez thought as he depressed the "on" switch, waited for the green light to illuminate, and dialed a prearranged number on the satellite phone Curruca had given him a few days earlier.

CHAPTER THIRTEEN
Saturday Morning, Verde Vista Ecolodge

By nine o'clock, Colonel Hernandez had heard back from the Natura Sucumbios headquarters in Quito and from Carlos's family in Lago. Neither had had any contact with the group. The Natura Sucumbios manager had been alerted and was calling the colonel for updates, but he had none to offer. Since dawn, his men had been driving the roads, hoping daylight would prove more fruitful than Malin's nighttime foray, but they had found nothing.

With options quickly dwindling, the colonel dialed the army outpost and was immediately transferred to the watch officer.

"Good morning, Major. You have been briefed on our situation?" he asked.

"I have, Colonel, and we are ready to deploy," Major Edison Sanchez replied. "I have ten trucks, but I can contact our base in Baeza for more, if you think we need them. But it will take several hours for them to arrive."

"Thank you, Major. I think we should wait to contact Baeza. Let's see how much we can cover by fifteen hundred hours and then reconsider our options. Please have your troops canvass the area between Sacha and Lago Agrio. Have them check the villages and particularly the old oil roads. I am told those are the preferred areas for these nature tour groups because of the easy access to the jungle."

"Yes. We'll depart immediately. You have my cell number. I'll lead the search. Sergeant Villa will remain at the communication desk if you need to contact me by radio."

CHAPTER FOURTEEN

Saturday Morning, Quito

Curruca instantly recognized the number of the incoming call; in fact, he had been waiting almost sixteen hours for it. A geosynchronous satellite orbiting above earth was transmitting a call dialed only a few hundred miles away. But the sat phone he'd given to Rodriguez provided coverage in areas that lacked cellular towers or landlines.

"Good morning. I haven't heard from you in a couple of days," Curruca answered in the prearranged code from his prepaid burner cell phone.

There was a slight delay as the signal traveled the forty-five-thousand-mile round trip from earth to the satellite and back.

"I'm sorry," replied Rodriguez. "I had an unscheduled trip with my family. But all is well. We are resting now from the long trip. I will have to leave the family here for a few days while I return for a business meeting, but they will be well cared for by some old friends."

"I am glad to hear you are well. When may I expect to meet with you?"

"Probably in two days. But I will call to confirm. Until then, *adiós*," Rodriguez said before terminating the call.

Curruca had ordered that all communications would be less than a minute—any longer and they risked detection by spy satellites.

From the call, Curruca learned that Rodriguez would hand over the group to his FARC contact, who would then make the ransom calls. From this point on, the tour group was no longer a concern. Nothing stood in the way of submitting the lab results to the court and its special master.

Leaving the office for a late lunch at the Hotel Colon, Curruca reached for a second cell phone and hit speed dial. "Señor Reynolds?" he inquired.

CHAPTER FIFTEEN

Saturday Night, Drug Camp

Unsure whether their captors were below the hut, Ben whispered to Jack that he had concealed a knife blade in his shoe.

"Do you think I can reach it?" Jack asked. The pounding in his head had finally stopped and he was more alert after a little rest. He just wished that Vincent would quit asking so many questions.

"I don't know, but let's try," Ben replied.

To reach Ben's right foot, which was tied to Marsha's left leg, Marsha and Ben had to move their tied-up legs onto Jack's lap. Jack grasped Ben's right foot with his bound hands and edged his fingers along the side of the welt, slightly separating the sole from the boot by a fraction of an inch. With no light except the glow from the embers in the fire pit below, Jack relied on his sense of touch to locate the small blade.

"It should be just below my big toe," Ben explained.

After a few moments, Jack's fingernail encountered the resistance of the metal blade. With his left fingers gripping the sole, he used his left thumb to separate the sole from the welt as far as he could. With his right thumb and forefinger, he grasped the slightest bit of the blade and, with a controlled effort, pulled the blade out about half an inch from the shoe. After repositioning his hands, he extracted the blade, which he held up for Ben and Marsha to see.

"Thank God you got it out. I was beginning to cramp," Marsha whispered as she brought her leg away from Jack's lap, straightening Ben's leg in the process.

Jack carefully palmed the blade for fear of dropping it on the floor. Then he thought long and hard. He could easily free his hands and feet as well those of his friends, but what then? Overpower the kidnappers—he'd already tried and failed at that? Escape to the river? Steal the canoe and motor downstream to the first village? Or should he try to sneak out alone and get help? It was probably wiser to leave in the night and try to reach the river in darkness. By the time he was discovered missing, he would be on the river. He didn't know whether the outboard motor had been disabled, but he did know he could at least drift downstream with the current and steer with a paddle. He also knew he had to do something; he was the only one with nothing to lose.

He weighed the unknowns. What if the kidnappers checked during the night and discovered he was gone? They would surely go immediately to the boat. He didn't like the idea of launching the canoe at night; there were too many risks involved.

Even if he untied his friends and made sham knots to deceive their captors, one of the two men was always outside. He couldn't envision a situation in which they could overpower both of the armed men.

And sneaking off the platform of the hut would have many risks. While jungle noises were persistent at night, they wouldn't mask the creaking of the boards as Jack crawled to the wall and lowered himself over the side. Maybe if he timed it to the bellows of a howler monkey? Maybe while both guards slept? Maybe by creating a diversion? But a diversion was equally likely to have the men check on the hostages, and he would lose precious time to escape.

He wasn't sure how his escape would affect the others. They would be restrained more severely and guarded more closely for sure, but would they be harmed for his actions? *Too many unknowns*, he thought.

Finally he inched closer to Ben and whispered in his ear, "I think we'll have a better chance if I go alone."

Ben thought it over; he wasn't sure whether Vincent could handle the rigors of trekking through the jungle. Tom wouldn't leave the group, even to aid their escape. And he and Marsha wouldn't leave each other. "You're right," Ben whispered back. "But when, and are you up for it? You took a pretty hard hit."

"I'm fine," Jack said, trying to ignore the slight dizziness as he shifted his position. If there was one thing he learned in his physical training it was to work through the pain; to get beyond the wall. "I'll leave before dawn and be at the boat at daybreak."

Ben nodded. "I'll pass it along to the others."

It was awkward to bend one hand over the other while trying to keep a firm hold on the blade and still exert enough force to sever the rope. But Jack's hands were free within ten minutes and his feet in less than two. And he had no self-inflicted wounds to attest to the effort. He was gratified that Ben took such good care of his gear. While it was a small blade, he had carefully honed it to a fine edge. He would have to commend him after this was over.

Jack lay on the hard floor and strained to hear anything from the kidnappers below—the slow breathing of a sleeping man or, better yet, a loud and masking snore. Unable to detect anything below, he quietly rolled onto his abdomen and lifted himself to his knees. He raised his head just enough to see the scene below. Illuminated by just the quarter moon and the remnants of the fire, the feet and legs of what he thought was Javier appeared directly below. Jack thought he must have been sitting against one of the poles that supported the hut. He couldn't see Rodriguez.

After several minutes he lowered himself to the floor and made his way on hands and knees across the hut, easing his weight between limbs to muffle any creak of the floorboards, all the while praying he wasn't visible through the gaps between the boards.

After an agonizing minute, his sloth-like crawl had him just below the window in the kitchen portion of the hut. He slowly raised himself again until could just peer out. He scanned the darkness for any signs of Rodriguez but saw none, which reinforced his suspicion that he, too, was under the hut—asleep hopefully.

As carefully as before, he retraced his route to his original position, where he began, in earnest, to formulate his escape plan. He would climb over the railing and hang over the edge, then drop the last few feet to the ground. To muffle his fall, he would remove his shoes and string them around his neck—a softer, quieter landing with bare feet, he imagined.

Jack looked for the best place to escape. The ladder wasn't an option; their captors had removed it. He would avoid the area where Javier's legs protruded from under the hut. The area between Tom and Vincent looked best, but for all he could tell, he might land directly on Rodriguez.

Now he had to wait and make his best guess as to when to leave to reach the boat at dawn. He had no real experience reading the stars but figured he would watch the moon. When it was over the opposite side of the hut, he would make his move.

He tried hard to focus on the moon and listen for noises from their abductors, but he tried even harder to stay awake.

After what seemed like half the night, Jack again rolled onto his stomach, lifted himself on his hands and knees, and slowly, carefully, silently crawled to the railing next to Vincent.

He removed his trail shoes, tied them together, and looped them around his neck. He raised his head over the railing to inspect his landing zone. Seeing nothing, he stood, lifted his right leg over the rail, then his left, and balanced with his forearms on the railing. He carefully lowered himself until his arms were fully extended and he was holding himself with both hands from the railing. He waited a few moments to determine whether his movement had alerted his captors. He heard nothing. He then released his grip and fell almost silently the last few feet to the ground. He immediately assumed a crouched position to minimize his profile and, again, waited to see if had awakened the captors. Grabbing his shoes in his left hand, he rose then ran from the hut to the sheds. By now the adrenaline was surging full bore. His head was pounding in tandem with his racing heart, and he could barely hear above the internal drumming. He stopped momentarily and glanced back at the hut. Seeing no movement, he sat on a bench, put on his shoes, then sprinted toward the river trail.

He turned frequently to look for lights or other signs of pursuit but saw none. After fifteen minutes he began to relax a little. He remembered the trek in from the river had taken a couple of hours, but that was because he had been groggy, and the pace was set for both him and Vincent. Jack figured he could run to the river in less than ninety minutes, but he was without food or water and didn't want to overtax himself. Fortunately the forest had cooled by twenty degrees, which would help conserve his energy.

Jack's tenacity and ability to overcome pain and fatigue had served him well in his athletic pursuits but also in his business life. His hard work as a design engineer at a small computer research and development company in Palo Alto had paid great dividends. He carefully reinvested in real estate in San Francisco's Mission District at the perfect time—just as the young techies from the Silicon Valley were escaping the South Bay doldrums. He continued to reinvest his real estate profits and even expanded into Marin County north of San Francisco, where he eventually settled into a two hundred-acre horse ranch near Point Reyes. It was there that he did his first birding trip and, like everything else, he was all in. His near-obsessive behavior, while useful professionally, was hell in his personal life. He had trouble opening up—showing any emotion, which made his dating life a car wreck. His relationships never lasted more than a year before his girlfriend at the time would run away at full speed, pulling her hair out at her inability to reach Jack. He wanted to open up and longed for a relationship, but it didn't happen and now, he knew, it never would.

Jack's eyes acclimated to the low light, and he had no trouble following the trail. At best he could see maybe fifty feet ahead, but that was all he needed. There wasn't much chance of his getting lost, since he couldn't remember any other paths branching off the trail.

As he advanced deeper into the forest, it darkened quickly and his initial excitement was supplanted by a nagging anxiety. He had been alone in the wilderness before and had relished the solitude. But then he knew where he was, he knew how to get back, and he knew the risks. This was different. He only knew the trail and not well. He knew the boat was ahead, but where would it be safe to land?

This was a land of unrelenting danger: jaguars, cougars, six-hundred-pound tapirs, and a plethora of poisonous snakes. He felt eyes watching him from the trees. With each footstep he hoped not to disturb a fer-de-lance hunting the trail for rodents and lizards. One swift injection of its venom would be lethal, especially with no chance for an antitoxin or even first aid.

He realized how totally exposed he was. He had no place to hide; he could only keep moving forward. He tried to assure himself that the animals were equally afraid of him. But at least they knew the terrain; they had their safe harbors.

It was now pitch-black, the thick canopy straining the anemic light from the waning moon. He felt his way one footstep at a time and had to be sure each step was on the path. He dared not venture off into one of the small side channels and oxbows scattered along the floodplain of the main river. When the rains raised the river, these backwaters flooded and remained inundated even after the floods receded. These swamps were the perfect habitat for the green anaconda. He willed himself to stay on the path.

Suddenly he stopped and stood motionless. Not more than thirty feet ahead he saw a dim yellow glow low on the trail. He squinted hard to focus, but it was impossible to make out the object in the dim light. He looked slightly off-center to take advantage of his low-light vision. He detected a form, a rough outline of a seven-foot object spanning the entire width of the path. Sweat streamed down his face and a shiver ran down his spine. He held his breath for fear that exhaling would give him away.

Jack sensed movement from the log-shaped figure and now he saw two yellow orbs reflecting the pale moonlight. A snort. The animal, too, sensed something—something foreign, another creature.

The animal turned slowly in the direction of Jack, stretching its three-foot long head skyward to capture more scent.

It lumbered forward, one clawed limb at a time gripping the ground; its head moving left as its sharp-scaled tail swung right,

Jack wanted to bolt. His brain was telling him to turn and sprint full speed to the safety of the kidnappers, but his body would not react. He was paralyzed from fear.

Jack could now see that the animal was staring straight at him. It rolled its head slowly side-to-side trying to triangulate his faint smell. Jack thanked God, all the Gods, the heavens, and anything else he could think of that he remained downwind from the creature and in its olfactory blind spot.

But the ten-foot-long black caiman, a cousin of the alligator, did see Jack. In fact, she saw Jack very clearly with her acute night vision. What she didn't know was whether he was a threat to her newly hatched brood in the oxbow channel off the path. She had seen these creatures before and they hadn't caused her harm, but this particular creature reeked of fear, and was unpredictable. She had to decide; attack or return to the nest?

In an instant, she raised herself from the ground on all four limbs, turned, issued a loud and high-pitched yelp and with a speed and agility that frightened Jack, galloped off the trail and into the forest toward the dark slough.

Jack exhaled and collapsed to his knees. Before, fear had been an abstraction, a vague tingling in his nerves; now it descended on him like a black shroud. He had to move forward—he had to—he wanted to run, but his legs were like lead. He remembered an old Mark Twain adage: "Courage is resistance to fear, mastery of fear—not absence of fear." He wasn't terribly reassured by this; it worked better on a motivational poster.

His body was tiring more from mental stress than physical exertion, but his senses were on overload. He smelled the mustiness of the decay surrounding him. He could hear the buzz of a single mosquito long before it was close enough to land on him. The hairs on his arms rose at the slightest change in the wind direction. He willed himself forward, step by careful step, occasionally brushing away a web that had been spun since their last passage.

It started as a distant, eerie glimmer. *Daylight*, he thought, and his spirits were boosted. It was directly ahead, which seemed strange because he thought he was walking south. The light increased as he continued, but it didn't seem right. He had seen sunrises and sunsets in blazes of red, orange, and yellow. But this light had a curious dim, pale cast as it flickered from the movement of the leaves in the light breeze.

Could the vegetation color the light that much? he wondered. *Is there something in the air obscuring it?* His focus was now exclusively on the light. It was very low in the early-dawn moments, but it seemed to fade rather than intensify.

Jack froze. To his left he saw the yellow halo of the morning sun through the trees; in front, the green glow. He took another dozen steps forward, and directly in front of him stood a grinning Rodriguez, armed with a revolver and illuminated by a propane lantern that hung from a low limb. Behind him was the faint outline of the bow of the canoe.

Rodriguez lifted his radio in his left hand. Before he depressed the "transmit" button to hail Javier, he looked at Jack and said, "I didn't think I was guarding the boat against *you*."

Totally spent of energy and hope, Jack dropped to his knees for the second time in an hour. He had a long walk back. At least he would see the trail this time.

Week Two

CHAPTER SIXTEEN

Sunday, Philadelphia

Douglas Reynolds's case now hinged on the water-quality tests underway. If they didn't find that the buried treatment pits continued to seep oily sludge into the streams, his pollution claim would be dead. Without detecting hydrocarbons in the waters, he had no way to link the health claims to Steator.

A few years before the suit was filed, Reynolds, at great personal expense, had sent teams of scientists to collect samples of groundwater, surface water, sediments, soils and plant tissue in and around all the areas vacated by Steator Energies. The samples were subjected to batteries of tests, the most important of which was gas chromatography / mass spectrometry (GC/MS), which identified the petroleum compounds in the samples.

Reynolds knew the real advantage of GC/MS was its ability to identify the thousands of individual hydrocarbon compounds in crude oil. Even better, because the compounds and concentrations varied considerably over time as the oil degraded, it was possible to determine when a crude-oil sample had been released into the environment from a district "fingerprint" on the GC/MS chromatograph.

However, his results were inconclusive. While hydrocarbons were found in elevated concentrations at certain locations, they were generally lower than international standards. And when petroleum was detected in higher concentrations, it was considered fresh oil—oil that had entered the environment within the past ten years and well after Steator had departed the area.

Reynolds had no physical evidence. All his lawyers had to present to the court was the testimony of thirty to forty plaintiffs who claimed they were harmed by Steator's pollution. His lawyers told him the testimonials were questionable because there were no medical records or histories, just anecdotal tales of mysterious growths and maladies. They were even more concerned about how the plaintiffs would hold up in court. Their testimonies had been enough to start the lawsuit, but he would need physical evidence to get the case to trial.

His only hope was that the current sampling would yield more favorable results. It had been a tough negotiation between Reynolds's lawyers and Steator, but the judge and the court-appointed master finally had approved the testing plan. Reynolds had no control over the sample collection or testing—they were in the hands of third-party laboratories. But he felt the pressure and knew he'd need a Hail Mary.

The plan he finally had devised resulted from a conversation he'd had months earlier with a chemist who explained the testing process for hydrocarbons. The chemist told him that laboratories routinely used spiked samples of a known concentration of a compound to calibrate instruments and to test and verify results. It didn't take Reynolds long to advance the "spiking" concept to his advantage.

But he had no idea where he could get the materials he would need until he talked with his drilling consultant, Matt Simmons, a retired petroleum engineer and grizzled veteran of oil fields from Texas to Nigeria and all stops in between.

"I need to know all you can tell me about all these well pads. I need to understand how they work and how oil could pollute the area," Reynolds said.

"Each well pad is about an acre in size, but most of it's taken up by two large pits to hold the water from the well," Simmons explained in his slow West Texas drawl.

"Water in the oil well?"

"Yeah, in the petroleum-bearing layers underground, the oil actually floats on a lake of water. When it gets to the surface, whew, it's a witch's brew. Oh, you got your oil, all right, but you also get a mess of water and gas. It's easy to deal with the natural gas—we used to just burn it off, but it's too valuable now, so we collect it and use it to power the drilling operations. But the water is a real problem. First, we have to separate it from the oil in tall tanks. The oil floats to the top and is pumped into pipelines. Ya don't want too much water in the pipelines because it will rust the hell out of 'em."

"What do you do with the water?"

"It's a major hassle and why we dig the pits," Simmons told him. "The water from the well is highly polluted with hydrocarbons, salts, and other chemicals, so it can't be dumped in the river—it would kill almost anything living there. So, the water is piped to the pits, where it's treated. The oil comes to the surface and is skimmed off and sent down the pipeline. But we rely on the high rainfall in the jungle to dilute any remaining oil and chemicals in the water until it's safe to release it into the rivers. There is so much water in the rivers that the concentration of pollutants is just about zero. You know the old saying: 'The solution to pollution is dilution.'"

"So how could the pits cause any pollution?" Reynolds asked.

"Well, the pits are very good in controlling pollution, but a small fraction of oil always remains, even after the pits are cleaned—'remediated' as we say."

"How so?"

"In the old days, after the well was drilled and all the equipment removed, the last of the water was pumped from the pit, and the pit was filled with soil, leveled, and planted with grasses," Simmons explained.

"What's done now?"

"You should know—it's all those environmental laws and regulations; they changed everything. Now the soil has to be cleaned before it can be buried, just like the old gas station tanks you used to clean. But I don't care how good the process is—there's always some dirty soil left. There isn't much risk of pollution because the levels are low and the pits are lined with clay so the soil is really in a tomb."

"Couldn't the rain get in and leach the contaminants to the groundwater?"

"Usually not. The clay gets wet and seals up tighter than a frog's butt. Nothing gets through, one way or the other."

"How does the pollution get into the groundwater then?" Reynolds asked.

"Sometimes the pits are poorly constructed. Not enough clay is used, or it doesn't cover the whole area. I heard about one farmer who tried to drill a well in an old pit and went right through the seal. I'll bet he didn't drink much of that water. But like I said, it's rare."

"Let me get this straight. Even after remediation, the pits will have some old polluted soil?"

"Yep, but unless there's a leaky seal, it ain't goin' nowhere."

Reynolds had his source.

***

Curruca had immediately gotten on board with Reynolds's plan, which was no surprise since he usually worked just south of the legal limit. But Muniz was a different case. He had come from a deeply religious family and a strong Catholic education, and what Reynolds proposed wasn't right; it was cheating. To Muniz, a sin in the battle for good was still a sin.

But Muniz was putty in Reynolds's hands. He trusted Reynolds, looked to him as an authority figure, and didn't want to disappoint him, but the plan was too dishonest. Reynolds knew it would just take time to mold and shape Muniz. He was sure he could convince almost anyone to do almost anything. He just needed to assure Muniz that they were working on the side of angels.

It was sometimes difficult by telephone, but Reynolds had evoked every emotion to convert the wavering Muniz. One day, Reynolds would break down in tears, shaming Muniz for not caring about the poor *indios* and *colonos* who had no one else on their side. Another day, he would sear with anger and guilt-trip Muniz, calling him a hypocrite for starting his organization yet not having the commitment to actually help anyone. After all, most of the money his organization got was through donations to the website Reynolds had started for Muniz. He convinced Muniz that showing a few furry animals and some sick children would bring in money from all over the world. And he was right. Now the NPFP donations were a significant source of funds for the lawsuit.

"What if we find out in twenty years that the pollution Steator caused is killing your children and grandchildren, and you could have prevented it if you'd had the money to clean up the mess they left? How would you feel?" Reynolds had asked. "Here you have this chance to get the money we'll need, but if we lose our lawsuit, we'll never have this chance again. I don't like it any more than you do, but sometimes the ends *do* justify the means," Reynolds said, hoping Lady Justice wouldn't raise her blindfold to see his thumb on the scale.

"I hope you aren't so naive as to think Steator doesn't own the laboratories doing the work. At the very least, they have a few people in the labs on their payroll," Reynolds lied to Muniz. "They will *never* play fair. Too much money is at stake for them. The only chance your people have is you and me—that's it. And now maybe they only have me because of your skewed sense of righteousness. I guess in your church it is permitted to kill the young, the old, and the weak if you have enough money."

Gradually, it had worked. Muniz finally capitulated and was convinced of Reynolds's commitment. He never would know that he was just a player in Reynolds's vendetta.

CHAPTER SEVENTEEN

Sunday, Lago Agrio

It was midafternoon when Major Sanchez's driver alerted him to the presence of a man ahead of them on the road. They had left a small Quichuan compound down the road about twenty minutes earlier, and the next village was five miles north. They weren't surprised to encounter people along the road, since this was the only route through this area, aside from the narrow, muddy river trail that connected the family compounds. What was unusual was to see someone walking alone. Even in the middle of the day, traveling in the jungle was safer in groups.

Not recognizing the jeep, the man darted into the forest—an unexpected and curious reaction, Sanchez thought. "Stop here," he ordered the driver.

The major stepped from the vehicle and walked toward the forest. After several seconds, the man emerged from behind a seventy-foot-tall moriche palm. "I wasn't sure who you were until I saw your uniform," the man said as he approached Sanchez.

Major Sanchez saw that the man was disheveled, but he was wearing good clothing and boots, unlike those normally worn by locals.

"Why did you hide?"

"I thought you might be the kidnappers returning for me," he said, at which point Carlos began to recount the events of the past thirty-six hours.

***

They drove directly to the lodge, where Colonel Hernandez awaited their arrival.

Malin whisked Sanchez, Hernandez, and Carlos to a small meeting room adjoining his office. As he passed the reception desk, he called for Maria to have a meal prepared for Carlos.

Adorned with colorful posters and photographs of local wildlife and plants, the room was an unlikely place for a debriefing. It was better suited for the evening slide shows and lectures presented by the resident naturalists it normally accommodated. But it had blinds on the windows and doors to preclude curious tourists, and it offered the privacy the colonel needed.

By habit, Colonel Hernandez took the chair at the head of the table and then motioned Carlos to the chair directly to his right. Major Sanchez sat next to Carlos, and Malin took a seat across the table.

Sanchez started to inform the colonel of what Carlos had said to him. On the return trip to the lodge, he had only radioed a cryptic message to the colonel about "retrieving the package."

"Thank you, Major," the colonel interrupted, "but I think it would be more valuable to hear it in Carlos's own words." He turned to Carlos. "Do you feel that you can talk to us now? Is there anything we can get for you? Do you think you need to see a doctor?"

"No, sir. I am fine. I am hungry and tired, but I am more worried about Tom and the group. Have you heard anything from them?"

"No, but we still have troops and the police looking."

Stopping only for a sip of water or a bite from the cheese-and-ham empanada Maria had brought, Carlos spent the next hour detailing the events at the pad two days earlier. His skill as an observer proved valuable as he accurately described the men and vehicle involved in the abduction, how he had escaped when one of the men had returned to find him, and how he had remained hidden and away from the villages. In response to a question from Colonel Hernandez, Carlos offered that he never had seen men in the Trooper before. One of the men appeared to be Quichuan, he said, but the other two were dressed like workers from the cities.

Carlos explained how Ben and Marsha had signaled him to stay behind, and from his vantage point, he got very clear views of the men through his binoculars. He described how the cell phones, wallets, and other valuables had been collected and how his friends had been bound and led into the minivan.

He explained that one of the men followed in the Trooper, which was missing its license plate but otherwise had no distinguishing marks.

Carlos said he thought that it wasn't a planned kidnapping and that the group was merely a target of opportunity—in the wrong place at the right time.

"Why do you think that?" the colonel asked.

"They left without even making an attempt to search for me. So they didn't know who or how many were in our group until after the first encounter."

Colonel Hernandez asked Malin to find Carlos a room so he could clean up, rest, and call his family to let them know he was safe. The colonel would continue the questioning later, but he wanted to alert Natura Sucumbios of the situation. He was particularly interested to know whether the kidnappers had contacted the company.

CHAPTER EIGHTEEN
Sunday Morning, Drug Camp

Except for Jack's ill-fated foray, the captives had been confined to the hut for most of the past day, save an occasional latrine break. Even their meals, such as they were—an energy bar, some hard-boiled eggs, and canned tuna—were served unceremoniously on the hut floor. Most annoying, however, was trying to sleep while being bound at the feet. Any movement had to be conducted with care so as not to disturb the others.

Although they were tired and bored, their mental states were improving. With each passing hour, the group felt less fearful. If their captors meant to harm them, they'd had plenty of chances to do so in the isolated camp. Jack had certainly provided enough opportunity. They believed they were needed alive and safe for ransom.

But in the past few hours, Ben had noticed impatience on their captors' faces. They too must have been feeling the strain. Ben wondered how they were contacting the authorities with their demands. How were the logistics being planned? When and where would they be freed?

Ben's thoughts were interrupted by Tom. "Did you hear that?"

"What?" Marsha asked.

"I hear voices—different voices—and at the other end of the field," Tom said.

All fell silent, concentrating, trying to isolate voices from among the myriad jungle sounds. From the hut, they could see nothing except the sky and canopy.

"I think they're getting closer!" Tom exclaimed.

Within a couple of minutes, they were certain that Rodriguez and Javier were engaged in conversation with others. While muted and indistinct, the discussion sounded more collegial than confrontational.

A figure emerged at the top of the ladder. Dressed in a sweat-soaked camouflage uniform complete with utility hat, the tall mustached figure flashing a wide and satisfying smile announced, "*Buenos días*, my friends. I am Comandante Flores, and I have come to liberate you from the hands of these despicable outlaws. You are now in the safe custody of the Revolutionary Army."

"FARC?" Tom said. "Why were you after us?"

"There are many things in life that we do not know. For you, this is one of them," the comandante laughed heartily. "Now, down the ladder, *por favor*."

Their hope for release now dashed, fear returned to the faces of the captives. Unbound, the group was led down the ladder to a line of four men armed with well-worn AK-47s, the weapon of choice for their unique enterprise.

In the distance, Rodriguez and Javier were heading down the trail back to the river. In ten hours, they would meet Tepe at the landing and drive twenty miles south to Lago Agrio, where they would head east on Highway E45 for 110 miles to the town of Baeza at the eastern foothills of the Andes. From there, they'd drive another fifty-five miles east on Highway E28, where they, along with the Isuzu Trooper, would disappear undetected into the urban throng of Quito.

Left behind was Rodriguez's sat phone and one of the daypacks, from which Comandante Flores removed the passports. He examined the photos and called out each person's name. Satisfied, he then reached into a cargo pocket of his pants, removed Tom's cell phone, and inserted the SIM card and battery.

"The lasting gift of the oil companies was all the cell towers. We now even have limited communication on this side of the river for some distance, sometimes three bars." He laughed as he dialed the number written on the business card he had removed from Tom's wallet.

Within moments, a phone rang at a desk almost two hundred miles due south.

"Hola. Verde Vista Ecolodge. This is Maria. How may I help you?"

"Hola, Maria," the comandante replied. "I am in the company of five of your guests. I am afraid they have been apprehended on our property. And I believe we will have to ask that a fine be paid to compensate us for this trespass.

I will call you on Tuesday, at which time we can make the appropriate arrangements. Is there someone in particular with whom I should speak?"

"Do you have Tom? Is he all right? Can I please speak with him?" Maria asked.

"I will let you speak with him on Tuesday. We have some travel ahead, but rest assured that he and his friends are in excellent condition and are being well protected."

With these words, he terminated the call, ripped open the battery compartment, pulled out the battery and SIM card, and crushed the phone under his bootheel. He then reached down, picked up the remnants, tossed them to one of his soldiers, and ordered him to bury them in the forest.

He turned slowly to face the group and, with a reassuring smile, announced, "We have several miles to travel today before we reach camp. I think it is advisable to leave now so we can arrive before dark. Any objections?" After a few moments of silence, he said, "Well, then, let us proceed."

In minutes, they were exiting the airstrip through the opening in the berm opposite the river trail.

CHAPTER NINETEEN

Monday, Early Afternoon, Miami

Charlene Bennett sat at her console at the Allied Analytics laboratory on the south end of Miami. Like clockwork, a new batch of samples arrived at her station shortly after lunch. Regretting the large cheeseburger she'd opted for an hour ago, she vowed to eat salads for the rest of the week.

She opened the box of twenty-four sample bottles and removed the first one in a row of six. She methodically checked the sample number against the chain-of-custody manifest accompanying the box. She noted that the first signature was dated three days earlier in Ecuador, and since then, it had been signed by four others, the last being Brent Wagner at Allied's intake desk three hours ago. It was Brent who had handed the box to her.

After signing her name to the manifest, she unscrewed the cap from the sample bottle and withdrew five milliliters of the fluid with a sterile syringe. She then attached the tip of the syringe to the intake port and injected the fluid into the Fostran 2600 GC/MS analyzer. Almost instantly, a series of spikes appeared on the LCD screen in front of her as a 750-degree flame vaporized the fluid into molecular fragments, which produced an electrical signal read by the analyzer. After a few seconds' delay, the chromatogram she saw on the screen was reproduced on an eight-and-a-half-by-eleven sheet of paper on an adjacent laser printer. The printed version provided more detail. In addition to the name and concentration of the compounds detected in the sample, levels of detection, normal limits, and permissible concentration limits allowed by the US Environmental Protection Agency, the printout identified the sample number, date, time analyzed, and the name of the technician conducting the analysis.

Charlene removed the sheet from the printer, initialed above her printed name, confirmed the sample numbers on the bottle and printout, and inserted the sheet into a blue file folder.

She then grabbed the second bottle and repeated the process until the file folder was filled with twenty-four data printouts.

After sealing the box of sample bottles with red-and-white tape, Charlene initialed the tape and placed the box, along with the manifest, on a stainless-steel cart bound for the secure storage warehouse in the laboratory. She walked from the lab and placed the file folder in the in-box of Sarah Green, the chief chemist, for analysis.

As Sarah carefully reviewed each chromatogram, she noticed one graph with a series of peaks considerably in excess of limits. *Interesting,* she thought as she examined the names of the compounds. *These aren't fresh oil components.*

Crude oil is a complex array of organic compounds. When exposed to the atmosphere, the lighter components—those with the shortest carbon chains—are volatilized, or evaporated. The heavier, longer-chain hydrocarbons slowly seep into the soil, where they remain until degraded by weathering and digested by biological activity. Over the course of several years, only the heaviest hydrocarbons persist. High rainfall can, over time, slowly transport these buried hydrocarbons into groundwater, which can resurface though seeps and springs into rivers and lakes. Knowing the degradation rate of crude oil in the environment, a scientist can estimate how long a water sample has been contaminated by the proportions and types of hydrocarbons identified.

By Sarah Green's reckoning, this sample was many years old and must have seeped slowly into the river. It certainly wasn't a recent spill, she observed, not knowing, or even suspecting, the activities of Muniz and his men just four nights earlier.

To verify her findings and to confirm there wasn't a problem with the analyzer, she checked the sample number and searched for the results of the second sample. Of the three samples collected in the field, two were sent to the Allied lab and the third to a lab in Canada. This quality assurance/quality control procedure (QA/QC) provided a safeguard for analytical accuracy and precision of the sample measurements.

Having located the results of the second sample, Sarah noted a similar series of spikes, which indicated that there was agreement, or precision, between the samples. If the results from the Canadian lab were the same, then the results were accurate among the three samples.

After reviewing the results of the samples and duplicates, at least two of which showed elevated spikes of hydrocarbons, Sarah satisfied herself that the instruments were working properly. She signed her name to the chain-of-custody sheet and the QA/QC page, and initialed each chromatograph.

She could now prepare her report.

CHAPTER TWENTY

Monday; South of Puerto Asís, Colombia

The group had walked about three miles from the landing strip along the deserted path to a small stream where three small boats awaited. Their hands were bound again from behind, but at least their feet were free. Before they entered the boats, the comandante ordered his men to tape the captives' eyes shut and cover them with sunglasses.

Having his eyes covered concerned Tom, and he surmised they likely would be passing recognizable areas or would encounter other vessels. The sunglasses provided the illusion of tourists enjoying a day on the river. This hadn't been necessary with Rodriguez and Javier because they traveled only at night. It also bothered Tom that the comandante wasn't concerned about traveling during daylight, which told him that they weren't likely to encounter the authorities or that the authorities weren't cause for concern to him.

Not seeing, however, actually helped focus Tom on his surroundings. Over the din of the outboard motor, he tried to identify every call, chatter, and screech from the surrounding forest. He was able to identify most of the birds and a few of the primates, but nothing was unique. He had heard many of the same calls in the Amazonia regions of Ecuador, Peru, Colombia, and Brazil. But listening helped him focus.

They motored up the Río Putumayo to its confluence with the Río Guamuez and then up the Río Guamuez for a few miles before turning into an unnamed stream. After an hour, the engines were shut down, and the boats drifted to the bank. Still bound, each hostage was escorted up the bank and led along a dirt path to a truck. When the tape was removed from Tom's eyes, he caught a glimpse of the river, where water lapped against the sides of the three boats.

It's a white-water river, he thought. He'd seen rivers like this before in the mountains where the high flow velocities carried huge sediment loads that turned the water gray. These rivers were different from the "black water" rivers in the lowlands of Amazon that had a dark, translucent, tea-like stain from decaying vegetation. Tom knew that they had traveled upstream.

When they were all seated in the bed of the truck, Comandante Flores removed his hat and wiped the sweat from his forehead and cheeks with a white handkerchief and announced, "We have a short drive to our camp, where we have a meal ready for you. I'm sure it's not the quality of what is served at the Verde Vista, but it will have to do."

They traveled overland for a few miles to a short road and then crossed a small river via a ferry to a narrow, deeply rutted cow trail of a road to a gate.

The group arrived at the camp within an hour.

Exiting the confines of the truck, Tom took a deep breath. The musty scent of wet earth, smoke from a fire, and a faint odor of diesel fumes lingered in the thick air. He noticed that is was quite humid but not as repressively hot as the airstrip. *We gained in elevation,* he figured.

He was looking around the camp, trying to get his bearings, when he heard it! There was no mistaking that call. He had studied it for days on end for a field trip that never quite materialized. Now he knew where he was. *At least within about thirty miles,* he assured himself.

***

The old farm was secluded and not on anyone's map. Its former residents had eked out a living, but the internecine warfare among the government, the drug lords, and FARC made it impossible to get products to market, and eventually, they had abandoned it. Formerly productive fields of manioc and maize were now overgrown with grasses and saplings as the forest reclaimed its dominion. The orchard still produced guavas, papayas, bananas, and oranges, but untended and unpruned, the branches competed for sun, and fruit production had suffered. Now it had become a reliable feeding area for the local wildlife.

FARC had immediately recognized the farm's strategic value and assigned troops from the comandante's brigade to guard it. The abandoned farm was isolated. There were no nearby villages or farms. It could be accessed by river and road, and the ferry limited vehicle traffic. It was on the way to nowhere, so no one would arrive accidently. Any unannounced visitor was suspect.

The comandante's men had fortified the perimeter of the compound with a fence, cut escape paths through the forest, improved the road to the river, and installed a generator to power the operation. The farm became an important transfer point for the processed coca, which arrived in bulk by water and was then distributed to numerous other storage areas or airfields. But now, like the old airfield, the compound had assumed a new function.

CHAPTER TWENTY-ONE

Tuesday, Verde Vista Ecolodge

Malin's office was small and cluttered, with barely enough room for a desk and three chairs. With the addition of several file cabinets and a credenza he had salvaged from an old oil-field office, it looked more like a storage locker. This was his working office; for meetings, he used the conference room. But his office had a speakerphone and a landline, and that was what he would need in the next few minutes.

Landlines were a luxury in the Oriente region. At one time, they were the only link to the outside world but a very tenuous connection at best. Maintenance was a constant effort, and because only a couple of lines spanned the distance from Coca or Lago Agrio to Quito, service was frequently out because of high winds in the Andes. Landlines also were very expensive; only oil companies, government offices, and successful businesses could afford the service. In the past, for the average citizen in the highlands, a call to relatives involved walking to the nearest government-owned EMETEL telephone call center, registering the outgoing telephone number with the receptionist, and waiting with twenty to thirty other callers until finally being directed to a row of booths, each with a plastic chair, writing platform, and single phone, to which the operator would route the call. Often, whole families lined up outside a booth to wait their turn to speak to Abuela and Abuelo.

By the mid-1990s, however, cell phones opened a communication revolution on an unprecedented scale. Erecting a network of cell towers was substantially cheaper than expanding the landline system. In less than five years, the EMETEL offices were virtually empty because of competition among providers, and almost all families had access to at least one cell phone. In Quito and other cities, the chic and urbane residents once seen strolling the sidewalks with dangling Walkman earbuds were now engaged in perpetual conversations on their cell phones as they navigated the metropolises.

Yet, even now, cell-phone service was sometimes spotty. And, in critical situations like this, Colonel Hernandez preferred to have both options available.

He and Carlos had arrived in the lobby at about 9:30 a.m. and were immediately escorted to Malin's office. Each had spent a frenzied few hours after the phone call Maria had received. The colonel had spoken with his superiors to determine whether he should alert the Ministry of Foreign Affairs. Malin had contacted Natura Sucumbios in Quito to apprise them of the contact. After both calls, it was decided to hold off on informing the families and respective embassies of the tourists—no one had yet uttered the term *hostages*—until more was known about the demands. Colonel Hernandez would serve as the local incident commander. Natura Sucumbios requested that Carlos serve as their representative until a manager from Quito arrived.

Malin was surprised that the authorities wanted to use the lodge as a command post because the army garrison was only a few miles away, but the lodge was the only link with the kidnappers. Besides, the kidnappers probably would figure—wrongly, as it turned out—that the army had access to more sophisticated tracing and recording equipment than the lodge.

The three of them, soon to be joined by Maria, sat in the cramped office and waited for the call from the kidnappers. The colonel said he would be the contact; the others would take notes and witness the conversation. While tracing the call was impossible, the colonel emphasized the need to keep the kidnappers on the line to garner as much information as possible.

***

Around 10:30 a.m., a guard opened the door to the wooden shed and escorted Tom out. He, Jack, and Vincent had been locked in a windowless shed since their arrival at the camp the day before. Ben and Marsha were confined in a separate shack.

The three had eaten a meal of rice, beans, and meat in the shed. Their collective best guess was that the meat was pork, but it easily could have been armadillo, tapir, monkey, caiman, or any number of jungle animals—not that it mattered; it was their first hot meal since their abduction at the oil pad, and they consumed all of it. They had a decent night's sleep since they weren't tied and had separate sleeping pads.

Squinting hard to acclimate to the bright morning sun, Tom surveyed the compound while flanked by two guards. The perimeter fence consisted of wooden planks on rails that were attached to concrete posts. The fenced area contained six small buildings, all of wooden construction with metal roofs. Tom could see one gate but nothing beyond the walls except the forest. The truck, a small van, and an old Land Cruiser were parked in the center of the compound.

The guard led Tom into the main house. Although still Spartan, it was much better appointed than the storage shed. A bare electric light bulb dangled from a wire at each end of the larger of the two rooms. A few kerosene lanterns were hung from the walls and sat atop tables for the evenings after the generator was shut down. The room had two shuttered windows, which were open and allowed a slight cross breeze. A wooden table with four chairs was centered in the room, and a sofa and upholstered chairs were set against the walls. A large frame covered by a white sheet hung behind the table, which Tom assumed to be a map or chalkboard with information not intended for his eyes.

Seated at the head of the table was Comandante Domingo Flores, buoyant and always smiling. His teeth looked even whiter against his tanned skin, two-day beard, and a tangle of wavy black hair. Tom saw him as a person of curious contrasts. His demeanor and language suggested a he'd had a refined education, not what he expected to see in a terrorist.

Like his hero, the infamous Carlos the Jackal, Flores was born into privilege in Venezuela. Although his parents weren't necessarily wealthy, they were certainly a well-to-do, influential, cultured family that traced its lineage to fifteenth-century Spain on his maternal side. Although many of his parents' former holdings had been sold, taken, or redistributed during land reforms by successive Socialist governments, his family's name had afforded him the best education.

His early life was idyllic, but his parents' separation when he was twelve changed everything. His grandfather on his mother's side never had approved of his son-in-law, believing that his daughter had married beneath her station.

The son of a local merchant of mixed heritage wasn't the line her father wanted propagated. But love trumped all, at least temporarily.

After the divorce, young Domingo seldom saw his father, whom the family had banned from their properties—not that his father didn't try; he just didn't have the resources or connections to fight for custody.

To make matters worse, his mother, after feeling tied down for so many years, wanted her freedom and to live the good life, but taking care of a nearly teenage son was a detriment to her new lifestyle. So it was off to boarding school—Domingo's second abandonment.

Fearing more rejection, he found it difficult to make friends or form any close relationships. His reserve was mistaken for shyness, which resulted in harassment. By the time he was fourteen, however, he was six feet two inches tall, with a gangly but athletic build. After pummeling an older classmate who had teased him incessantly, he was bothered no more. It took the considerable influence of his grandfather—and a healthy donation to the school's building fund—to rescind his expulsion.

While no longer physically threatened, he still resented his classmates for the wealth and arrogance of power borne by generations of indulgence. He took solace in his studies, in his books, and in the very few teachers who cared about the matters they taught. Unfortunately, these were of the revolutionary leftist movement so fashionable at the time. They had been brought up on the Che Guevara of T-shirts, not the real-life psychopathic murderer of women and children.

His mentors taught him to empathize with the underdog, which came naturally to him, even when it was the Soviet Union, which his teachers taught him had been repressed by the Western world. Why he gave up religion wasn't clear but probably had stemmed from the authoritarianism he had observed in the Catholic Church. This was ironic, since during his years in school, the church was the foremost champion of the poor in war-torn Central and South America. If he'd met the right priest, one of the many liberation theologists, he might have not made that fateful leap from social justice to terrorism. But that wasn't where his path had led.

"Please, Señor Steps, take this seat next to me," Comandante Flores said. "I am about to make a telephone call that I am sure will be of interest to you."

Tom pulled out the chair and sat. With his holstered pistol, two guards, and a locked gate, the comandante obviously had no worries about Tom.

"Who are you calling?" Tom asked. "Natura Sucumbios? They will pay you what you want."

When the comandante ignored his question, Tom immediately knew his role—he was the "proof of life." It would be his voice they would recognize. Almost as quickly, Tom understood what he had to do. It might be risky, but he had to try. He just needed the right opening.

As they were beyond the range of any cell tower, the comandante picked up the sat phone Rodriguez had given him the previous day and dialed Verde Vista Ecolodge. After three rings, the call was answered. As the sat phone was pressed against the comandante's ear, Tom could make out only a muffled voice.

"Hola. This is Colonel Xavier Hernandez of the Twentieth-Ninth Jungle Division of the Ecuadorian Army," the colonel responded over the speakerphone.

"Please call me Domingo, Colonel."

"Well, Domingo, would you please apprise me of the conditions of your guests?" the colonel asked, noticing the few seconds' delay in the exchange.

"Mr. and Mrs. Cales, Mr. Murray, Mr. Sinclair, and Mr. Steps are all comfortable after their long journey. They have been fed well and had a good night's rest."

At the other end of the line, the colonel nodded to the others in the office to confirm that the comandante at least knew the names of the hostages. He was relieved that Domingo had acknowledged the name of each person. This familiarity showed that he humanized the group, unless he was some sort of sociopath.

"I think you know what my next request will be," Colonel Hernandez said.

"Yes, Colonel, I anticipated that. I have Mr. Steps seated across the table from me."

"Señor Steps, there is someone who would like to speak to you," the comandante said as he handed the sat phone to Tom.

Expecting instructions but hearing none, he spoke slowly and quietly into the phone, "Hello. This is Tom Steps."

Immediately, Carlos nodded, affirming that the voice was Tom's.

"Tom, this is Colonel Xavier Hernandez of the Ecuadorian Army. I am sitting here with a few friends who are very worried and who will be helping us do all we can to get you back. How are you and the others feeling?"

This was the opening he needed. "We're all doing as well as can be expected. So please tell Mr. Greenthorpe to try to get our group home safely."

The comandante took the phone from Tom and signaled one of the guards to return him to his shack.

Carlos, brow furrowed, looked at the colonel; he didn't know anyone named Greenthorpe at Natura Sucumbios.

With Tom gone, the comandante's demeanor hardened. "You know who we have. I want an initial good-faith payment of two hundred fifty thousand dollars US. That's fifty thousand dollars each and certainly not too great a sum for a successful company like Natura Sucumbios."

The comandante had carefully calculated the ransom. Most kidnappers in South America assumed all *Norte Americanos* were wealthy or had easy access to large sums of cash. But large demands were far beyond the means of most tourists' families, and they had to involve many others to raise the money. This prolonged negotiations and inevitably involved the police.

In his risk-reward calculations, Domingo knew that demanding a ransom accessible to the hostages' families increased his odds of success because the money would be more quickly obtained by a loan from the bank or a second mortgage on a home. It also reduced the chances that the families would go to the authorities. He also knew the Colombian government; big demands equaled big responses. A fast payoff and hostage release minimized his exposure. Plus, this kidnapping wasn't really about the money.

Comandante Flores knew he held the trump card—the hostages—and he always could raise the ante if he suspected anything awry.

"I would like to speak to the others first," Colonel Hernandez replied.

"I will call you in six days with instructions. That should give you time to get the money," the comandante said, and with the touch of his right thumb, he terminated the call.

***

The colonel hung up and turned to face the others.

"Did you recognize Domingo's voice? Did you hear anything that can help us?" he asked.

Malin shrugged.

"That was the man who called last evening. I recognized his voice," Maria said.

All three turned to Carlos. "I don't know him, but I know where he is," he said.

It had struck Carlos just as Domingo was reciting his demands. He knew of no "Mr. Greenthorpe." So Tom was sending a code. Tom, not knowing Carlos was in the room, knew the authorities would first check with Natura Sucumbios. Each employee would be asked about Greenthorpe. If enough were asked, someone eventually would decipher it. Carlos knew the basic connection with all Natura Sucumbios guides was birds. In an instant, he understood the genius of the code. It was one that Tom's captors would have virtually no chance to comprehend but one that transmitted volumes.

"They're in Colombia!" Carlos shouted with excitement. "Actually, I can probably pinpoint where," he continued, with a satisfied grin—his first real smile in days.

"Why do you think that?" the colonel asked.

"Greenthorpe isn't a person, at least not anymore; he's long dead. It's the scientific name of a bird, a bush tanager, *Chlorospingus greenthorpei.* It's only found in one area—a remote watershed, the Río Guamuez near Puerto Asís in the Putumayo province in Colombia. Tom had been preparing for a tour to Colombia and was memorizing the calls of all the birds he'd hoped to encounter. He must have seen or heard the bird near where he and the other members of the group are being held. With some maps and a field guide, I might be able to better identify the range of the species."

"Can you get your maps and books and bring them here?" the colonel asked. "I have some calls to make."

***

Tom was returned to the shed, missing the business end of the telephone conversation.

"What happened?" Jack asked.

"I was their proof of life. They're negotiating our release with the Ecuadorean Army."

"Do you know what they want? Have they contacted our families?" Vincent asked.

"No. I was only able to identify myself and let them know we're all right," Tom replied. He was silent regarding his secret message.

"I guess all we can do is wait," Jack added, looking but failing to find a comfortable place to sit it out.

CHAPTER TWENTY-TWO

Wednesday; Hobart Lab; Baton Rouge, Louisiana

The water-quality testing results were couriered to the office of Dr. Stanley Hobart at the chemistry department at Louisiana State University. Dr. Hobart, "Stan" to friends and acquaintances alike, was an expert in environmental chemistry. His specialization was the breakdown of petroleum compounds, based on thirty years of study, numerous peer-reviewed articles, and two books that were the authoritative texts in the field. With his graduate students and colleagues, he had developed protocols for hydrocarbon analyses that had been adopted as standards by the US Environmental Protection Agency and, eventually, many foreign governments and international organizations.

Outwardly affable and a lighthearted punster among friends, he was driven by acute intellectual curiosity and strict adherence to scientific methods. Unlike too many in contemporary academia, quality, not quantity, of publications was his goal. If his hypothesis in a study was falsified by experimental data, he moved on; he refused to torture data to confess to a false result. He was driven by science, not policy. For his scholarship and standing, he was a distinguished fellow at a number of national and international societies and academies.

He had arrived at his present position by a curious route. His original intent was to study civil engineering, which he initially did, hoping to design spans like the Paris Road Bridge in his native New Orleans. But the death of his father in an automobile accident during the fall term of his sophomore year had forced him to find work to help support his mother and younger brothers and sister.

Through a family friend, he was hired as a laborer on Platform Zelda in the gulf, where he started as a gofer. The hours were long, the work tedious, the isolation suffocating, but the money was great.

He planned to work there for a couple of years, but providence intervened. One day, a drilling foreman instructed Stan to take a gravy-like sample of drilling mud to the lab two decks below. Upon entering the lab, Stan was struck by the contrast with the grimy working decks just fifty feet away. Here, everything was gleaming stainless steel, with a dazzling display of instruments, the quiet hum of sophisticated electronic equipment, and, best of all, air conditioning.

"What ya got there?" Terry Finley, the chief chemist and lab director, had asked him.

"Oh, it's a sample Harry King said you should check out."

"Can you leave it on the counter and fill out one of the lab request forms?"

"Sure. Can I see what you're doing?"

Over the years, Stan went from a lab assistant on the rig to a PhD student in organic chemistry and ultimately to a full professor and renowned scientist.

The previous spring, between a graduate seminar and a senior lab course, Stan received a call from a bailiff at the federal district court in Houston asking when would be a convenient time for him to speak with Judge Nancy Grant.

A bit taken aback, and conducting an instant inventory of past behaviors and misbehaviors that might have brought him to the attention of a federal judge, Stan inquired, "May I ask what this is about?"

The bailiff said only that the judge needed an expert in Dr. Hobart's field. Then they arranged a day and time that bridged the previous commitments of both.

One Thursday morning, promptly at eleven, Stan received the call from Judge Grant. After polite introductions, the judge requested that Stan keep their conversation confidential for the time being because of the nature of the case before her.

She explained, in general terms, the elements of the case between Steator Energies and the representatives of the Victims of Sucumbios Contamination. Both had presented highly technical, well-researched briefs, but each had a team of specialists providing seemingly contradictory evidence. She emphasized that because of the uncertainty and conflicting data, she was unable to render a decision whether to proceed to trial or dismiss the case due to lack of evidence of contamination.

"I'm a quick study on most matters," Judge Grant explained, "but the issues here are complex, and frankly, I would need an inordinate amount of time to fully vet them. With the concurrence of both parties," she continued, "I'm considering the appointment of a special master to assist me in obtaining and analyzing the scientific data independently. I would rely very heavily on the opinion of the special master. I need a person whose professional skill and integrity are beyond reproach. And, Dr. Hobart, I can't tell you how highly you were recommended by a number of your colleagues I contacted. I ask that you consider accepting this position."

A modest man, Stan was both embarrassed and flattered.

"Your Honor, I understand the situation, and I would, of course, provide any assistance you need. Do you have a timeline? I only ask so I can clear my teaching and research responsibilities with my graduate assistants and the department chair."

"I was hoping to make a decision within six months, but I realize many tasks need to be completed in that period. The first of which is the approval of your appointment by both parties," the judge said. "I propose you prepare a terms of reference report detailing sampling and testing protocols that need to be conducted. After that, we'll conduct our own independent assessment."

Since his appointment, Stan had been closely following the field collection and the laboratory analyses. He even conducted a surprise inspection of Xebec's field station in Sacha, accompanying a field team for a day during sample collection. His inspection of Allied's laboratory in Miami was logistically easier, and he was satisfied with its procedures.

But now the heavy lifting was on him. He had analyzed all the field and laboratory data. Just as Sarah Green's report had concluded, Stan detected an elevation in hydrocarbon levels at a couple of sampling stations. But unlike Sarah Green, Stan was able to see similar spikes in the samples analyzed by the Canadian laboratory. He had asked a couple of his postdocs to double-check the data. They too concluded that his samples had the precise signature of "highly degraded hydrocarbons with persistent long carbon chains" characteristic of highly weathered, aged oil.

The only plausible explanations for the lab results were either that the hydrocarbons had slowly leached into the groundwater and were entering the river through a spring or that high water flows had eroded a bank in which hydrocarbons had been spilled or buried. Either way, the hydrocarbons entering the water supply were most likely from Steator's days of oil-production activities. Recent spills wouldn't have the same chemical fingerprint.

He decided to allow the attorneys and scientists for the plaintiffs and defendants to offer their interpretations of the data. He had given himself at least three months to prepare his report for Judge Grant, as he wanted to be sure of his decision. Billions of dollars were at stake, and there was no hurry.

***

What seemed like due diligence to Hobart was just dithering to Reynolds. All he needed was a simple decision: that there was sufficient evidence to take the case to trial. It seemed like such a low hurdle, but the judge was resistant, and Reynolds was more than a little curious. He knew it might not even get to court and, if it did, it would never get to a jury—Steator would settle long before that. But to force Steator's hand, he needed a judge to green-light the case.

But for Judge Grant, this was a unique lawsuit—suing an American corporation for actions in another country when that country actually had approved the actions. Steator had documents signed by the highest officials of the Ministry of the Interior that all contractual obligations had been met. Overturning such a contract would set a precedent, and any careful judge would be hypervigilant.

CHAPTER TWENTY-THREE

Friday, Quito

"Please make sure your seat belt is securely fastened and your seat back is in its full, upright position," the flight attendant announced first in English and then in Spanish as InterAmerica Flight 147 made its final approach to Quito's Mariscal Sucre International Airport, named after Simón Bolívar's trusted lieutenant, Antonio José de Sucre y Alcala.

Gary Cales could see only the glimmering lights of the city below as he gazed from his window seat. He'd hoped to catch a view of the Andes, particularly the Cotopaxi or Antisana volcanoes, but the airport's 9,230-foot elevation required nighttime landings so the planes could be ready for morning departures when the fully laden aircraft had the proper temperature conditions for takeoff in the thin air.

He had been on the road or in the air for the three days since receiving the call from Natura Sucumbios. They had assured him that his parents, Marsha and Ben, were in good condition, and while most unfortunate, these abductions and ransoms were not uncommon and almost always safely resolved.

In the intervening days, he had met with his superior, the chief of detectives, and then the chief of police and was granted emergency leave. He drove to his parents' home outside of Detroit, where he met his brother, Russell. They arranged to secure the ransom money through their parents' attorney.

As directed, they wired the funds to a secure account arranged by Natura Sucumbios. Gary wanted to deliver it personally but didn't want to risk confiscation at customs for transporting currency in an amount that violated US and Ecuadorean laws. Nevertheless, he wanted to be there to bring his parents home.

Russell stayed behind to handle their parents' affairs in Michigan. Though both sons had studied Spanish in high school and college, Russell had a real gift for languages. Living in California, Russell could practice Spanish almost daily. But both agreed that Gary's law enforcement experience would be more valuable.

The wheels touched down gently, masking the 110 tons and velocity of the Boeing 757.

Gary was amused at the sight of four workers rolling an ancient portable stairwell to offload passengers from the sleek, ultramodern jet. As he uncoiled his cramped six-foot-three-inch, 220-pound frame from the seat, he cursed himself for not upgrading to business class. His back would have appreciated it.

Clearing customs was hastened by a waiting representative from Natura Sucumbios who was proficient in dealing with the airport's bureaucracy and navigating the gauntlet at the baggage carousel. Within minutes, he and his guide were in an old Toyota Corolla negotiating the nighttime city traffic.

"Señor, I will take you to the Hotel Quito. All the arrangements have been made. I will pick you up at nine a.m. to take you to the office. If there is anything you need, here is my cell number," he said, handing Gary a business card. "The hotel is very nice, and you can have a fine dinner before you rest for tomorrow."

Looking at the card, Gary said, "Thanks, Gustavo. You've been very helpful. I appreciate your assistance."

"*De nada*," Gustavo said. As he pulled into the covered semicircular driveway, a small battalion of porters and bellhops rushed the car to welcome the guest and retrieve his bags from the trunk.

The receptionist directed Gary to room 1207. It was all he could do to undress before he crashed onto the bed, forgoing dinner, opting instead for much-needed sleep.

CHAPTER TWENTY-FOUR

Saturday Morning, Quito.

Gary awoke at 5:30 a.m. without the aid of the alarm he had forgotten to set the night before. He pulled back the drapes to reveal the city beginning to come alive. Through the gray diesel haze, a hint of orange in the distance backlit the magnificent mountain crests ringing Quito.

He met with the Natura Sucumbios manager at his office early that morning, as planned. After less than ten minutes, he knew not much information had filtered up since he had left the States or the manager wasn't showing all his cards. The manager confirmed that the money he and his brother Russell had wired had been deposited and provided him the requisite assurances that everything that could be done was being done. When advised to stay near the hotel in case new information was received, Gary resisted; he needed to be closer to the action.

Realizing Gary wouldn't be easily placated, the manager had his staff arrange a flight to Lago Agrio and a driver to Verde Vista Ecolodge. Within a couple of hours, Gary had checked out of the hotel and was sitting in the domestic terminal awaiting Amazonian Airway's one o'clock flight.

Accustomed to a more orderly boarding process, Gary tried to dodge the chaos at the ticket counter as locals vied for the few unreserved seats on the flight. He was thankful Natura Sucumbios had insisted on an escort to see that he got his ticket and boarded the flight. Gustavo wasn't so much a driver as a fullback digging for a few extra yards. But Gary had his ticket and Gustavo a thirty-dollar tip.

The flight was shorter than forty minutes, and this time, Gary had an almost cloudless view of the Andes. The gray-blue mountains were topped with gleaming white caps of snow. A tendril of volcanic gas twisted slowly skyward from Mount Tungurahua ninety miles to the south. As the Embraer E-170 jet descended from the crest of the cordillera, the infinite sea of green that stretched beyond the horizon awed Gary. Nothing could have prepared him for the vastness of the Amazon. He struggled to take it all in and relished the moments before touchdown.

Gary was transported to the lodge and immediately escorted to Colonel Hernandez and the others at the makeshift command center in the conference room.

Colonel Hernandez gave him a fifteen-minute briefing regarding what had transpired over the past few days. He then indicated the next task was to get the ransom to the kidnappers.

"Have they provided instructions yet?" Gary asked.

"No," the colonel replied. "We know only the amount of money they are demanding." He didn't reveal the possible location of the hostages, which was known only to him and his small circle. "We are expecting another call shortly with more specific details. The abductors seem to have knowledge of the difficulties in acquiring the necessary cash."

"So are we dealing with professionals?"

"Yes. I believe they've done this before. In the past, it was not uncommon for foreign oil workers to be kidnapped. The oil companies even maintained contingency funds for such circumstances as well as special agents to handle negotiations. In the beginning, the police and army were involved, but it became almost a routine occurrence and was handled better by the companies. They would inform us only if problems arose."

"Do we know who they are or where they are?" Gary asked.

"No," the colonel responded. "We have a suspicion, but I won't divulge this until we have better intelligence from the next call."

"Can you tell me about the location of the abduction and how they were taken away?"

The colonel looked to Carlos and, with a slight nod, signaled him to elaborate.

"Señor Cales, let me first say that your parents are wonderful people, and they showed great courage," Carlos began. "Your father had a premonition of what was happening while we were on the trail and thought it best that I hide and try to elude capture. He knew I would have the best chance to escape and get help. But because of your mother, it was a difficult decision for him. We didn't know what the kidnappers knew. They didn't start looking for me until several hours after the encounter. I'm convinced they knew little of birding groups. Otherwise, they would have known that a local guide is almost always hired."

Gary eyed the smaller, wiry man, probably five years his junior, with a bit of unease. *Seems a little convenient that they didn't check out the trail,* he told himself. Although he thought the man seemed sincere, he had his doubts. About what, he didn't know. He wasn't suspicious by nature, only by experience. During his seventeen years on the Detroit police force, he couldn't think of a single day he hadn't been lied to, even for the simplest traffic citation. "But, Officer, I'm sure I was only going thirty-five. Have you checked your radar gun lately?" He hadn't lost faith in the goodness of human nature, but he did have to search longer and harder to find it.

"Do you think they just came upon you at the clearing?" he asked. "Just a target of opportunity?"

"It seems that way. What reason would they have for targeting this group?" the colonel offered.

"Has this happened to other groups? Could we be dealing with a gang that's targeting tour groups?"

"No. Nothing like this has happened in this area in many years."

"I don't know," Gary pondered aloud. "Three things suggest to me that this was planned. First, they were in the right place at the right time. So they know birders use the area. Second, they had the necessary weapons. I assume rifles and shotguns are common in the jungle, but handguns? Third, they knew to disable the cell phones that might have GPS tracking chips. Leaving Carlos behind was their only mistake, it seems. Have you examined the scene for any evidence?"

"Not yet," the colonel replied. "We're not sure how much more information we could extract. Carlos saw the men and the vehicles."

"What about the vehicles? Have you searched for them?"

"We have, but these are the most common trucks in this country. Carlos saw nothing special about the kidnappers' Trooper, and you probably passed thirty just like it from the airport to here," Colonel Hernandez said. "Given our limited time and resources, our focus should be on getting the ransom delivered and the hostages released. We'll get better information from them once they're returned."

"You're probably right," Gary acknowledged. "But perhaps Carlos would recall additional details if he returned to the site. I don't know—maybe something about their clothing, anything to stimulate his memory."

"Señor, it is only a one-hour drive. I can take you there," Carlos volunteered, looking to the colonel for approval.

"I have no objection," Colonel Hernandez noted. "But the next call could come in, and we may have to mobilize immediately. Be sure to take your radio and cell phones."

"Then let's go now," Gary said, trusting that his interrogation skills would get more information from Carlos as they drove.

***

From the rutted gravel employee-parking area at the rear entrance to the lodge, Carlos eased onto the road. The paved parking in front was reserved for guest vehicles and buses so the guests wouldn't have to walk through puddles on their way to the lodge. Ironically, by the time they arrived back in the late afternoon, they often were soaked and mud caked from the day's adventures.

"Was the site of the abduction supposed to be your last stop for the day?" Gary asked Carlos.

Carlos adjusted the car's visor against the bright glare off the windshield and shifted the car into gear. He never wore sunglasses and seldom wore hats, believing they restricted his vision and range of view.

"Yes, we were on our way back to the van for the trip to the lodge for dinner. Sometimes we'll wait until dark for owls, bats, and other nocturnal animals, but we were planning an early start the next day."

"You said you saw nothing unusual and didn't encounter other groups," Gary continued. "How about your schedule? Could anyone know of your itinerary? Did you leave information at the lodge, or would Natura Sucumbios know your schedule?"

"We have a general idea of areas to explore," Carlos replied, "but it changes day by day, depending on conditions, seasons, and which birds have been reported in different areas. We don't have a daily itinerary that is printed out. We often decide over breakfast which birds the group wants to see most. If someone needs to contact us, we have the cell phones. If we know we are going to be late, we call the lodge to hold some food for us. We made no call that day, and I don't believe Tom spoke to either Señor Malin or Maria."

"But you do go to that site often?"

"Yes, but not on any regular schedule. We would go there and three or four other sites in the same general area but not in any particular order."

"And the white Isuzu Trooper wasn't there when you arrived."

Carlos shook his head.

"And how many days had you been with the group?"

"Three."

"Did any of them make a cell-phone call while you were at the site?"

"You don't think that...No, no. I saw no one calling," Carlos answered, surprised at the suggestion that one of the birders might have been involved with the kidnapping.

As they drove, Carlos's attention was on the road. Gary could see the deep concentration on the younger man's face. His eyes slowly scanned the landscape before returning to focus on the road. Gary imagined that Carlos recognized everything and was searching for that one thing out of place—some disharmony that would cue him that danger was close.

After several minutes of questioning, Gary considered what he'd learned—or more accurately, hadn't learned.

Maybe the site will reveal something, he thought.

After an hour, they arrived. Even to his trained investigator's eye, the pad yielded little—just a series of tire tracks from many vehicles and tall grasses trampled from the recent vehicle activity.

Carlos traced his route from the site of the kidnapping. He showed Gary his vantage point behind the shrubs, where he had witnessed the confrontation. From the angle and distance, Gary was sure Carlos did have a good view, and his observations probably were correct.

They walked along the path to the river. Carlos pointed out the debris field that Gary's parents had left. Gary spotted the note and the now-dead FRS radio in the vine overhanging the trail and immediately recognized his father's handwriting. Continuing on, they found a water bottle, a tube of sunscreen, and pages ripped from a field guide.

Gary was proud of his parents' ingenuity; unfortunately, nothing they had done provided much more information other than to confirm what Carlos had told him.

None of the men came back here. If they had, they would have removed all this stuff, Gary thought. *Why? Maybe they didn't think anyone had time to leave anything, or maybe they just didn't care because they'd be long gone by the time anything was found. Maybe they couldn't spare the manpower or the time, which means they had just enough of both to do what they did.*

"Was there anything in the days before the kidnapping that seemed strange or out of the ordinary?" Gary asked.

"No," Carlos said, mentally reconstructing those days. "I can't think of anything. We encountered only a couple of *colonos* near their village and, of course, passed vehicles on the road. We stopped at a couple of bodegas for refreshments. We never saw anyone on the trails or at the pads in the evening. We did pass a fisherman in our van one night as we left a pad near another river trail."

"Anything unusual about that?"

Carlos tilted his head slightly and stared off in the distance trying to recall that evening. "It was getting dark, which is not a great time to fish. But I thought he was probably getting ready for the next morning."

"Why is that?"

"He was refueling. He had a couple of drums at the top of the bank."

"Fifty-five-gallon-type drums?"

"Yes. The kind the oil companies brought in with chemicals. When they disposed of them, the locals would clean them to use for storing gasoline. They also used them to store water, but sometimes, people got sick because the drums still contained chemicals."

"Maybe he was loading the drums into his boat."

"I don't think so. The bank was too steep and too high."

"Is that normal?" Gary asked. "I mean, is that a normal place to refuel?"

"No. There's a landing about two miles downstream, with a small wharf for loading cargo," Carlos explained.

"Why would he need two drums? That's over a hundred gallons if they were filled all the way. How big are the tanks in the fishing boats?" Gary asked. "Could that fisherman have been transporting chemicals for another purpose?"

"Maybe two ten-gallon gasoline tanks. They don't go very far either, up or downstream, to set their nets. They don't have refrigeration, so they need to be close to home. And if you mean drugs, I don't think so. Most processing occurs in Colombia. This area is too well patrolled."

"Did you see a pump or hose?"

"No, señor. We saw only a man near the bank, his small pickup truck, and the drums."

"Could he have been offloading the drums?"

"Maybe, but again, the bank is steep, and unless the drums were empty or nearly so, it would be difficult. Anyway, why wouldn't he just go to the landing?"

Gary shook his head. "I don't know. Can you think of any other reason for him to be there?"

"It didn't seem so strange at the time. But looking back, you may be correct. It is hard to explain why he was there since no village is nearby."

"Do you think you could find the spot?"

"Yes. It is not far."

They walked back to the car and headed east.

The interior of the car was stifling hot even though Carlos had jacked up the air conditioner to high. Thinking that a cross breeze would help, Gary rolled down the passenger window and was instantly greeted by a blast of sunbaked air. He turned to Carlos with the sheepish look of a kid in trouble.

"You'll get used to it in a few days." Carlos laughed.

***

Gary looked down to the small stream channel twenty-five feet below. The stream bank was very steep, but even on a near-vertical angle, plants had rooted tenaciously and almost completely carpeted the sheer slope. As they walked, Carlos tried to visualize the location of the drums and fisherman.

Ahead, they noticed a disturbed area. The vegetation had been trampled in a six-foot-wide swath. The top of the bank showed signs of damage and exposed soils.

"Are those the outlines of a drum?" Gary asked, pointing to oblong indentations in the muddy soil at the river's edge.

"Could be. They're about the correct length, and the deeper ruts look like they came from the ribs on a drum. And look, those are footprints."

"That means the drums were either offloaded from a boat and rolled uphill or rolled down the hill and loaded onto a boat. I'm guessing the latter," Gary said. "The drums would be too difficult to fill with water for the fish."

"This does look strange, but I can't see how it would have anything to do with the kidnapping."

"I don't know either, but we don't have anything else at this point. So let's think this through. If the fisherman, or whoever he was, was involved, how could he know who you all were?"

"We have a magnetic sign on our van. He could have identified our Natura Sucumbios logo as we drove from the road."

"So we have a man, a pickup truck, and some storage drums. There's also the possibility that he knew you were with Natura Sucumbios. Pretty thin," Gary said. "And why would he even be interested in your group?"

"I don't know," Carlos said, shaking his head.

"Where would someone get those drums?" Gary asked.

"They could have had them for a long time. They could have gotten them when the companies discarded them. There's a bodega that collects drums. They clean and resell them. It is not far, if you would like to go there."

"Why not?"

***

They pulled up to the front of a weather-beaten bodega just off the road. The rickety structure had a side door, a large open concession window, and a counter that faced the road. An old woman, almost oblivious to their approach, sat behind the counter.

Behind the bodega was a garage with a sign indicating tire repair. The ground surrounding the single bay in the garage was heavily stained with oil and grease, and spent tires and unusable wheels were strewn about. Stacked along the back of the bodega immediately adjacent to the garage were plastic and steel drums in all states of repair.

A middle-aged man with slightly graying hair in a grease-stained Air Jordan T-shirt, nylon swim trunks, and plastic flip-flops sat on a three-legged stool breaking the bead between a tire and steel wheel with a rubber mallet and wooden wedge. No pneumatic tire-mounting equipment was in sight, but a small compressor periodically hissed as its pressure-relief valve was actuated. Gary thought it incapable of pumping a tire to full pressure. Most tires in the jungle had tubes, however, because tubeless tires constantly broke their seals from traveling the rough roads.

Carlos introduced himself and Gary to the proprietor. He started in Spanish but quickly transitioned to Quichuan. The man stood and immediately offered his handshake to Carlos and then to Gary. Gary noted that his hands were muscled, blackened, and gnarled from years of hard work, but despite his diminutive stature, the man probably could have crushed Gary's hand.

Carlos asked the man who usually bought drums from him. The man explained that villagers sometimes purchased them to use as communal trash incinerators or as rain barrels. Sometimes farmers bought clean ones to haul produce to market. But most often, a truck came from the highlands a couple of times a year to buy barrels and sell them in the city. This had occurred more frequently when oil production was greater but had slowed the last five years.

Carlos asked whether anyone had bought drums from him in the past few weeks. "No," the man responded, "but I sold some to the man from the cooperative a month or so ago. And I sold one or two to some villagers recently. But that is all I can recall."

"Do you know if they're used by fishermen?" Carlos asked.

"Maybe, but they're too big for most fishing boats."

Carlos thanked the man, who returned to the half-mounted tire.

Still harboring reservations about Carlos, Gary asked, "Can you give me the English version?"

When Carlos finished explaining, he asked Gary, "Do you want to track down the drums he sold?"

Gary weighed the prospects of going from village to village on what was likely a fool's errand. "No, we probably should get back to the lodge."

***

Upon their return to Verde Vista Ecolodge, Gary and Carlos debriefed Colonel Hernandez and Major Sanchez. Gary explained his vague suspicion about the fisherman and the drums. "We pretty much hit a dead end and thought we'd be more useful here when the kidnappers call back," he said.

Sensing Gary's frustration, the colonel said, "It's the only lead we have. If nothing else, maybe the fisherman saw something. But this occurred the evening before the abduction and at a different location. So I have my doubts, but maybe Major Sanchez can have his men follow up as they canvass the area."

"Thank you, Colonel, but I wouldn't want to divert your men from anything more promising."

With that, they waited for the next phone call.

Week Three

CHAPTER TWENTY-FIVE

Monday, FARC Camp

The days following his brief phone conversation with Colonel Hernandez had amounted to stifling boredom for Tom, interrupted by seesawing emotions. Sometimes, he was depressed, not knowing whether his message had gotten across *and*, if so, what good it might have done. Other times, he allowed himself a little optimism, because at least negotiations were underway. He kept his doubts to himself and his outward spirits high for the sake of the others.

Communicating with Ben and Marsha in their separate shed was difficult. But Ben, relying on his military experience, had crafted a crude knock code. Tom was grateful the couple was together and separate from the others. It might have been too much for Marsha to live with four guys under these conditions.

At least she has privacy and her husband, Tom reassured himself.

To occupy the others, he planned a daily work routine, although it wasn't much. Because they were neither bound nor blindfolded, they were free to roam the shed. Tom had Vincent inspect each board for a screw, loose nail, or anything else with which to dig or bore. Jack was charged with trying to devise a way out of the shed. From their trips to the latrine, they knew the door was secured only by a couple of flimsy hasps and clip bolts, not a lock. But the door always seemed to be guarded, so Jack focused his efforts on the back wall. He could tell that the vertical wallboards were nailed into the timber frame. He first tried to push the boards outward, but he couldn't get enough purchase. Finally, he had Tom sit on the floor with his legs anchored against the opposite wall. Jack sat back to back with Tom for added leverage and used his legs to push against the boards, which were stubborn and well constructed.

Jack and Tom moved along the back wall, board by board, slowly and silently, trying to pry one loose. From the outside, they had seen that the exterior was cross braced with narrow boards. They tried to approximate where the bracing met the bottom of the wall, figuring that if they could move the bracing at that point, the board would flex more easily. Once they found the most vulnerable point, it really didn't take long to loosen a board. And once one was done, they worked on the next, Jack strained with all his strength against Tom's back. They just wanted them loose and ready for a final push if the opportunity presented itself.

Meanwhile, Vincent had coaxed a three-inch nail from an overhead board, which he used to scratch and scrape a series of pinholes into the soft wood planks. Not more than one-eighth inch in diameter, they were just large enough to see through with his face pressed against the board yet small enough to be mistaken for the work of insects.

It wasn't much, but it kept them active and cooperative. Better still, it diverted their focus from their plight. Tom was worried, however, about Jack. He seemed to spend more and more time on his mattress, and at times, he was listless and seemed confused. Vincent checked his condition as best he could under the circumstances but found nothing wrong. Tom hoped it was just temporary, maybe from the stress of confinement, and not from his injury.

CHAPTER TWENTY-SIX

Tuesday, Ransom Drop

As instructed by Comandante Flores during his follow-up call to the lodge the previous day, the boat departed on the Río San Miguel with only one man aboard, along with a canvas duffel bag with the $250,000 ransom in twenty-dollar US bills. The 12,500 bills weighed a little more than thirty pounds and nearly filled the bag.

The colonel selected Major Sanchez for the mission. Stripped of his uniform in favor of the more cryptic clothes of a local fisherman, he looked at home on the river. Sanchez had no idea exactly where he was going. The comandante's instructions were simple and not confusing—just to proceed downstream on the Río San Miguel to its confluence with the Río Putumayo and then travel upstream on the Río Putumayo.

After several hours, two larger boats overtook Sanchez from behind. Each had been hidden along the bank to observe any craft tailing Sanchez against the comandante's instructions. A third boat remained concealed to cover the hand-off and radio the other boats if trouble ensued.

The boats sandwiched Sanchez's boat. Each boat had two men—one driver and one gunman—and their faces were concealed under bandannas. One gunman grabbed the gunwales of Sanchez's boat and ordered him to cut the engine. He then boarded Sanchez's boat and grabbed the duffel bag. After inspecting its contents, the gunman tossed it into the boat on the right, which immediately accelerated up the channel and out of sight. The gunman in Sanchez's boat deftly unscrewed the motor mounts, disconnected the gas line, and dumped the forty-horsepower outboard into the river. Then he proceeded to search Sanchez for radios, phones, or weapons. Finding none, he stepped back into his boat and took the bow seat. The driver of the chase boat revved his engine, and Sanchez suddenly felt his own boat begin to turn. He saw that both men were holding on to the gunwales of his boat. When both vessels had turned ninety degrees, the larger boat accelerated and the men released their grip, flinging Sanchez's boat toward the west bank of the river.

The second boat then raced to cover the retreat of the ransom boat. The entire encounter lasted less than five minutes. One of the men in the ransom boat had tied a short, thick length of rope around the duffel bag and secured the rope to a stainless-steel deck cleat. He then tossed the bag into the river. It bounced violently in the wake created by the powerful motor until, saturated, it sank below the surface. Towing the bag underwater would jam any homing device hidden inside it. After a few minutes, the bag was retrieved. The duffel was then opened, and each stack of bills was searched for hidden devices.

Sanchez's boat drifted toward the bank. He had two oars but thought it would be better to wait to use them until the ransom boats were clear of the area. He also didn't know how far he'd have to row to the nearest village but assumed it would be hours in order to give the kidnappers time to get away. Sanchez felt a grudging respect toward the criminals. There was no way he could have expected to follow them; they had the river covered, and pursuit was fruitless. His best hope now was that the kidnappers would be true to their word and release the hostages unharmed.

When Sanchez no longer could hear the roar of the motors, he rose from the plank that straddled the gunwales, which he had used as his seat. While uncomfortable as a seat, it possessed one special feature. He slowly pried apart the two boards that had been glued lightly together to add strength to the seat. Once they were apart, he took a small, sealed plastic bag from a three-by-four-inch pocket mortise that had been crudely chiseled earlier in the day. The kidnapper had searched Sanchez and even felt beneath the seat, but he hadn't detected the joint between the boards.

As he took out Gary's smartphone, he hoped some battery charge remained, knowing that running the GPS app quickly zapped power. Seeing the 10 percent power warning and no reception bars, Sanchez immediately turned off the phone. At least the GPS was working and his position was well marked. Maybe with Carlos's map of the bush tanagers' range and the location on the river, they could get closer to the group. That was the thrust of the plan Carlos had hatched immediately after the second call from the comandante.

At first, Colonel Hernandez had balked at Carlos's idea of searching for the kidnappers by shadowing the ransom drop. He wouldn't condone the plan, but he wouldn't interfere either. He sympathized with Carlos and probably would do the same thing in his position. But there were risks—risks that the hostages would be harmed or worse, as well as risks to Carlos and Gary. He finally relented, largely because Gary was a trained police officer and Carlos knew his business. The colonel, however, insisted that Sanchez conduct the ransom drop because that was the most dangerous encounter.

Sanchez was relieved that at least he would be paddling with the current. He knew he would need to be judicious in his next communication, as little battery power remained on Gary's cell phone.

He drifted for about an hour, occasionally correcting the boat's course with a couple of light strokes. *Not a bad sailor for an infantryman,* he assured himself. He figured the farther downstream he floated, the sooner he'd have cell reception.

Satisfied that he wasn't being followed or observed, he maneuvered the boat to the bank. He again took the phone from the plastic bag and switched it on. After a few moments, the screen lit up with a request for the pass code. After entering the four-digit number, he focused on the upper-left corner and was relieved when two bars appeared.

Knowing he had limited battery life, he quickly accessed the GPS function and waited as the constellation of overhead satellites triangulated the position of his boat. A red dot appeared on a digitized map of the surrounding landscape. The map was merely a blotch of green bisected by a wide blue swath representing the river. No roads, no villages, nothing. He touched the red dot, and the coordinates of his position appeared, which he immediately highlighted and copied.

Sanchez entered the number to his personal cell phone, which he had left with Gary since his phone lacked GPS capability. Then he pasted his coordinates into a text-message box and pressed "send." After a few seconds, the audible "swoop" informed him his message had been sent. Then he waited.

A minute later, the message chime sounded. He opened the message icon and read, "Got it! On the way. Boatman 2."

***

Downstream, at the Puerto San Miguel landing just north of Lago, Gary punched the recently received coordinates into a handheld GPS unit. He removed his sunglasses to better read the dim LCD screen in the bright afternoon sun.

"Twenty-four miles," he said as he looked over his shoulder to Carlos and pointed downstream. Carlos shoved off from the bank, yanked the motor's pull-cord starter, and began the search for Major Sanchez.

According to the GPS, they were motoring at about ten miles per hour as they headed downstream on the Río San Miguel, but they slowed to just over six miles an hour as they moved upstream and against the current on the Río Putumayo.

"Carlos, I know why I'm here, but I can't figure out why you're taking such a risk," Gary said. "You aren't a soldier or a police officer. Why are you involving yourself like this?"

Carlos looked forward to Gary, taking his eyes off the river momentarily. "It was my plan," he replied matter-of-factly.

"The colonel could find others to help."

"Yes, but I know what to look for. I know the birds. I know Tom's habits. And I won't draw the curiosity of anyone," he said. "But most importantly, these are my friends. Your mother looked me in the eyes as she passed me hiding along the trail. She saw in me her only chance. She placed her faith in me. I was her only hope, and I will not let her down."

"How about your family? How about them? Do you have a family?"

"Yes. I'm married. Cecilia is her name, and we have two children, Carlito and Magdalena—we call her Maggie. The boy is nine, and my daughter is six," Carlos replied, as he gently adjusted the tiller to negotiate a sharp river meander. "They would not be happy if anything happened to me, but I could not live with myself if I didn't try to help my friends. I think that would make my family proud."

"Do you live in Sacha?" Gary asked.

"No, we bought a house in Lago. It was much cheaper when the oil people were leaving. I was lucky and bought a big house. After my father died, my mother moved in. It is wonderful for the children to be with Grandma. She also helps much with cooking and shopping. My younger sister and her daughter also moved in after my brother-in-law left them so that he could work on the fishing boats in Costa Rica."

"Must be a very big house."

"Cecilia and I have a room," Carlos said. "My mother and sister each have a room, and the children share the fourth bedroom. It is tight but comfortable."

"You support them all?"

"No, I make good money with Natura Sucumbios, particularly the tips from the birders, but my wife works a couple of days at the *supermercado*, and my sister works at a hotel. My mother has a small social security pension from the government. We are very fortunate. My mother and wife have turned the backyard into a farm. There is a vegetable garden, fruit trees, and a chicken house. We have eggs with almost every meal. Sometimes we cook a chicken when its laying days are over."

"It must be difficult to be married with the type of work you do."

"It helps to have a big family around when I'm working on tours for weeks at a time," Carlos said. "They all have each other to help with the work."

Carlos suddenly jerked the tiller, and the boat instantly listed hard right, almost capsizing the narrow vessel. Startled, Gary instantly heeled to the left, grabbed both side rails to steady himself, and glared back at Carlos.

"Sorry. We just missed a sandbar," Carlos explained.

"I thought I was going swimming." Gary laughed and continued, "How long are you usually gone on your guiding trips?"

"Usually less than a week but sometimes a couple of weeks. That's when I miss them terribly."

"At least you have a cell phone."

"Yes. Most of the time. I know your mother and father, but how about the rest of your family?" Carlos asked.

"Just my younger brother, Russell."

"Are you married?"

"Was. We were married for five years. But she left. Said I was married to the job. She was probably right. I mean, she *was* right. She got the short end of the deal. I was young. I wanted it all, and I wanted it fast. We're friends now. She remarried."

"Short end?"

"Yeah. It was harder on her than on me," Gary tried to explain.

"Anyone now?"

"I've been seeing someone for a few years. It's serious, but we've both been married before and aren't in any rush."

Gary realized that his initial impression of Carlos was wrong, and this didn't happen to him very often. A detective had to have good instincts about people. He was beginning to admire Carlos. The hard work, his devotion to his family, his dedication to his friends—these were all values Gary shared. *I'll have to work harder on that family thing next time,* he thought.

***

The trip took almost four hours, and it was late afternoon when they approached the position Sanchez had sent them. Carlos circled for a few minutes, knowing that if Sanchez had stayed put, they were close.

Sanchez remained hidden amid the brush along the bank on the boat's first approach. Then, recognizing Gary and Carlos, he shoved his boat free of the bank and signaled to them.

"What happened?" Gary asked when he saw the motorless boat.

"I'm pretty sure they didn't want to be followed," Sanchez replied.

"I guess so. But do you think you can get back?"

"Sure. Just give me my phone back and some water. I grew up on these rivers. With this current, I should be back at the San Miguel in several hours. I'll call the colonel to come pick me up."

Gary reached into one of the two duffel bags he and Carlos had prepared. He removed a couple of foil-wrapped sandwiches and two bottles of water and handed them to Sanchez.

"You will need this, too," Carlos said, handing Sanchez's phone back to him.

"Can you tell us anything about the men and boats?" Gary asked.

"I saw two boats," Sanchez said. "They came up from behind, so I must have passed them. If there were more, they stayed out of sight. Once they had the money, they took off upriver. There were four men—two on each boat—but only one boarded my boat for the money. The lead boat was light blue on the sides with no name on the bow or stern that I could see. The other boat had red or brown peeling paint. Both looked pretty typical of local fishing boats."

Sanchez then described the men, at least what he had seen despite the bandannas that covered their faces.

"Wait another thirty minutes before you head downriver," Gary said. "We'll call you and the colonel with anything we find."

"Maybe I should go with you."

"No. They already saw you. If they see you again, they'll know we're after them," Gary said.

Carlos slowly eased the hand throttle on the tiller and made a couple of wide-circle turns midriver.

"Which way?" he asked Gary, who was digging through a duffel bag, searching for the topographic maps Carlos had prepared for the colonel and Malin days ago.

Gary unfolded the map and located the river. He then used the GPS coordinates he had received from Sanchez earlier in the day to pinpoint their current position, which he marked with a small circle in pencil. Using his pencil as a rule and the scale on the map, he measured the distance to the two irregular polygons that depicted the range of the bush tanager.

"We're about seven miles downstream from the nearest location," Gary informed Carlos. "I can see only a couple of roads and villages on the map, but there are many miles of unmarked trails. I say we continue upriver and check out each tributary that's near a road and deep enough to access."

Carlos shifted slightly in his seat, adjusting his handhold on the tiller, and reached into his bag. He rummaged around until he found what he was searching for—two bright-yellow plantains at their peak of ripeness.

"Gary," he shouted over the roar of the motor, "try these."

Gary grabbed the fruits flung to him. He noticed again that Carlos's focus returned instantly to the river where he looked around constantly, reading the current, studying the forest, searching the sky for rain clouds, analyzing every call and squawk from the canopy, and at the same time, eyeing each passing boat driver who stared just a little too long.

"We have about two hours before sunset, so we should look for a spot to tie up for the night," Carlos said. "We can get a fresh start in the morning."

Gary agreed, and they found a small, cleared area that would allow easy access up the bank. Neither had any intention of sleeping anywhere other than the boat, especially since they didn't know how often caiman visited the area. But at least they could walk, stretch, and relieve themselves outside the confines of the boat.

Exhausted from the twenty-hour day, they slipped into their nylon-net sleeping covers and slept with the duffel bags as makeshift pillows. Not the best accommodations, but fatigue trumped comfort.

CHAPTER TWENTY-SEVEN

Tuesday, FARC Camp

The ten-by-fifteen-foot shed was claustrophobic and the heat oppressive. No air moved at all. The only light in the windowless shed came through the cracks between ill-fitting boards.

Ben and Marsha sat next to each other, their backs against the wall, and tried not to move. Any exertion sent rivulets of sweat down their faces and backs. Their clothes were soaked. Even breathing was more difficult in the heavy, moisture-saturated air. But they were together, and Marsha was thankful for that. She knew she could get through nearly anything with Ben at her side.

Ben had some experience with this type of situation—at least training. He knew the key factor in survival was hope.

He began by first talking about how they could make the best of their situation. He said it would be cooler as soon as the sun went down, so they could expect good conditions to sleep. He also assured her they were certainly worth more to the kidnappers alive than dead, so they would be fed and treated well. He pointed out that this wasn't any kind of political action. These men only wanted money, which they wouldn't get if any harm came to the group.

But Marsha was tough. She understood and appreciated what Ben was trying to do, but she was enraged at their situation. And she wanted nothing more than to exact a little revenge against her captors.

If I'm going down, she thought, *I want to take a few with me!*

Ben loved her attitude. She was a fighter and didn't need much coddling.

The first day, they mostly sat and talked—talked like they hadn't in many years, if ever. Of course, now they had more to talk about—a lifetime of shared memories—as well as nowhere to go and few distractions.

They talked about their family, their friends, their likes and dislikes, their favorite birding sites, their next trips, but mostly they talked about each other. How lucky they were that painfully shy Ben had mustered the courage after weeks of false starts to ask the beautiful brunette in the front row of freshman literature to the Michigan State football game. He had been a veteran of four years in the US Navy and two tours of duty in Vietnam, and yet he was deathly frightened of the pretty coed. The fear of course wasn't of Marsha but of rejection. Ben wondered how many great romances never happened for the same reason.

Ben hadn't been a typical college student. Like many returning veterans after Vietnam, he was older, focused on getting his education and moving on with life. Flying bullets had a way of expediting maturity.

Marsha, on the other hand, lived college life to its fullest. She studied hard but longed for the weekends and the endless parties. When she and Ben started dating, it was synergy. Their friends immediately saw that if two people ever complemented each other, it was Marsha and Ben. It was as if they were meant to be, and they were.

In Ben, Marsha saw what no one else did. Despite his pleasant demeanor, he was masking a deep hurt and sadness. The harder Marsha tried to open him up, the deeper he descended. There were things Ben just didn't want to remember. That worked OK most of the time, but when he slept, the memories flooded his dreams. Marsha was there for him. She was always there. When Ben finally opened up, Marsha's love and understanding slowly exorcised his demons. Eventually, the visions of the napalmed bodies of the Viet Cong and the memories of his dead buddies machine gunned in the rice paddies faded just enough to get him through the night. It was far too much for the psyche of a twenty-four-year-old to handle. All these years later, Ben knew Marsha had saved him from a lifetime of depression.

Whatever happened, they agreed now, they were truly grateful for all the blessings of their life, and really, if they went out together in the end, so much the better.

Ben put his arm around Marsha, and she nestled her head against his chest. They embraced despite the heat or perhaps because of it. They'd never been closer.

With something akin to the stages of grief, by the second day, they had quickly moved from the resignation stage to the rebellion stage.

On their thrice-daily trips to the latrine, they gathered all the information they could. They counted the steps forward and back and, adjusting for their different stride lengths, calculated the distance. They mentally mapped as much of their surroundings as was visible. They noted the location of their captors and tried to determine the number of men by hats, clothes, facial hair, and any distinguishing characteristics. They even gave them nicknames. "Fidel" had a full beard, while "Che" had only a mustache. "Bin Laden" was the tall, thin one. "Hugo" was the heavy one. They only hoped the monikers didn't fit their personalities.

Ben told Marsha they had to devise some method to communicate with the other shed. It was twenty-five feet away, so they'd have to shout to be heard, and the guards would overhear and stop the communication by merely gagging everyone. No, it had to be subtle. He remembered how the prisoners at the Hanoi Hilton had their own code, which he thought was based on Morse code. If he ever knew it, he certainly didn't remember it now. And did anyone in the other shed know a dot from a dash?

It couldn't have been simpler: "Blink once for yes, and two for no." He'd seen it in some movie. It didn't convey much information, but it was a start. Until they could pass basic messages to the others, no complex code was possible.

Each time Ben or Marsha returned from the latrine or had a meal, they rapped one time on the wall that faced the other shed, hoping the others understood that these were positive events and would associate the single rap with "OK." Midday, when it was really hot and uncomfortable or in pitch-darkness at night, they rapped twice, indicating "not OK."

It took several iterations, but at last, knowing one rap and two raps, the second shed followed with three raps, which was interpreted as "Message received." Crude, but it was a start, and at least the general condition of all could be communicated.

Almost simultaneously with those in the other shack, Ben and Marsha began to systematically search for flaws in the shed—any weak points to exploit. It might not have yielded great results, but it kept them occupied and focused on escape.

"I don't know if will be any help, but I still have this," Ben said, extracting the small file blade from his shoe.

Martha smiled as she looked around the shed. "Hmm…" she said, "with that and a hundred years, we'll scrape our way out of here."

"Maybe a weapon," Ben suggested.

"What are you going to do? Poke someone's eye out?"

Ben laughed. "OK, but I'm still keeping it, just in case."

"You do that, Mr. Boy Scout. I'll get you a merit badge when we get home."

"Plan B—let's check out the roof," Ben said, trying to change the subject.

With no furniture other than the mattresses on the floor, there was nothing to climb on top of to reach the roof, which was about ten feet high at the peak.

Ben bent down, and Marsha straddled his shoulders; then he boosted her up. They now had ample height. Marsha pushed up on the corrugated metal roof. It was solid at the shed's eaves but looser toward the ridge. Many nails missed the wooden frame, were neglected altogether, or had wormed their way out. Whatever the case, some movement was possible, and Marsha could lift the sheeting an inch or so in many places. Unfortunately, the metal sheets overlapped, making it difficult to create a gap to see through or to make hand signals.

At other times, they placed their ears flat against the wall to listen for any talking among the guards or from the other shed. This proved difficult during the day with the incessant low rumble of the generator. It was much quieter at night with the generator off, but there were also fewer people talking.

All their planning and spying broke the monotony of the long, hot days—but just barely.

CHAPTER TWENTY-EIGHT

Tuesday, Houston, Texas

"Hello. This is Joe Caldwell," the man answered from his office at the headquarters of Steator Energies in Houston.

"Joe, it's Stan Hobart. I received the results of the latest tests from the Sucumbios Province a few days ago. We've gone over them pretty thoroughly. I want to send them to you and maybe have a videoconference with Reynolds's team after you all have reviewed them."

"Anything in particular you'd like me to go over?" Caldwell asked.

"Well, there are spikes at a couple of the sites that concern me. I've verified that both labs are reporting consistent results."

"Sure. You want to e-mail them?"

"No. I think I'll send only hard copies overnight."

"OK. Let me know when you want to set up the call."

"Will do. Thanks, Joe. We'll talk soon."

Just what I needed, Joe thought. His life hadn't been the same since he had started the project.

One of the younger geoenvironmental scientists on Steator's staff, Joe had managed the entire remediation plan. He had been chosen for the Ecuador project based on his success in cleanup operations at refinery sites and abandoned well fields throughout the Southwest and Gulf Coast. He nearly always succeeded in reducing contamination to trace levels at his sites, and the levels were certainly below any federal, state, or local standards. In fact, the US Environmental Protection Agency's website had used one of Joe's projects as an example of innovative design.

Joe's contractors would excavate dirty soil from the pits and spread it out in a series of long hedgerows. The rows were then tilled to provide aeration; inoculated with a broth of bacteria, fungi, and fertilizer; and sown with specialized grasses. The mixture was allowed to ferment under the sun for several months. In a very symbiotic process, the roots of the plants provided nutrients, water, and attachment sites for the bacteria and fungi. This allowed the bacteria and fungi to thrive and digest the oil residue, breaking it down to carbon dioxide and water, which in turn the plants used to grow and to create many more minitreatment factories.

This process of bioremediation, specifically phytoremediation, reduced hydrocarbon concentrations by 75 percent to acceptable environmental standards.

Through trial and error—known in the industry vernacular as "adaptive management"—Joe found that intensifying the upfront treatment through multiple techniques actually saved money over the long term. It was like aggressive cancer treatment that used radiation, chemotherapy, and surgery to optimize results.

At first, his managers wanted only token cleanup efforts—just enough to pass the minimal standard. But over time, as more stringent standards were imposed, the company was responsible for meeting the new, tougher standards even on previously remediated sites because of strict liability. The cost of cleaning a site a second time was doubly expensive. The bean counters finally realized that once the staff and equipment were mobilized, it was more efficient to use Joe's holistic method.

He had conferred with experts around the world in developing his remediation strategy. It worked, and it became the gold standard for the industry, as well as the subject of numerous technical papers and presentations at professional conferences. At each stage, Joe's cachet with the company rose, and larger and more complex projects were assigned to him.

Joe considered his work on the Ecuador project as the pinnacle of his career. His budget and resources were huge but commensurate with the task.

Over a ten-year period, he had managed a staff of 120 people. Beginning with the environmental audits of each facility to determine the level and extent of pollution and through cleanup and five years of postremediation monitoring, he had maintained hands-on involvement. He even had employed two independent firms to sample each site to verify the results his team reported.

It was a celebratory day when the Ecuadorean Ministries of Interior and Environment finally signed off on the successful remediation of the old sites. Champagne corks popped in Houston and Quito.

Steator's remaining operational sites had been transferred to Andean Power, along with a ten-million-dollar contingency fund to compensate for any future work that might be necessary. Joe had closed the project and moved on—that is, until Douglas Reynolds and his parade of lawyers had entered the picture.

For the past few years, Joe's expertise had been diverted entirely from the work of remediation specialist to that of professional witness. He was unable to count the hours he had been deposed by attorneys from Steator's and Reynolds's teams, but he did know that each hour of testimony required days of data review and preparation.

As a consequence, he saw many of the best new opportunities going to others. While it was a team effort, he felt as if he had been assigned to a taxi squad or injured reserve. He wasn't quarterbacking anymore.

Now this, he thought, wondering what the new test results would reveal.

***

The air-express envelope reached Joe's desk the next morning around eleven. He had tried to put the subject out of his mind the previous evening, but he couldn't help worrying. Stan would call only if it was something serious. And so much was riding on the water samples.

He quickly ripped open the cardboard envelope and removed the four-page printout. The first two were folded eleven-by-seventeen-inch spreadsheet pages that displayed the sample information and results. The last two pages were copies of the chromatographs from the two laboratories.

Joe saw that all were within normal limits (WNL) except for two entries Stan had highlighted in yellow. Both entries were well over three times the permissible level. He noted the consistency between the results of the two testing laboratories. Then he noticed the compounds.

That doesn't make any sense, he thought. The two locations were showing highly degraded hydrocarbon compounds. *How did they get there?*

He reviewed previous samples from one of the sites. Samples had been taken within a half mile of the present site for a period of five years. This particular compound never had been observed. He checked the second sampling location and found the same.

He checked sampling stations farther downstream. Again, nothing.

OK, he thought, *what could account for this? The lab results were consistent, so that rules out equipment error. Maybe the sampling equipment hadn't been cleaned properly. But the odds of two sampling teams both having contaminated equipment are very low. Maybe it was a new source, but which processes along the river would generate weathered hydrocarbons? Could it be a slow seep from a buried hydrocarbon source? But what kind of activity would release it now?* There had been no ground disturbance that he'd heard off, such as a flood or an earthquake.

If it happened at one location, Joe could accept that the remediation and monitoring might have been sloppy. But two sites just didn't seem possible.

Could it happen again at other locations? He would need to determine the source and begin the remediation again.

He was totally lost in the technical aspects when the implications for the lawsuit suddenly struck him. The contaminated samples presented the worst possible situation now.

Joe called Morris Bennett, Steator's deputy chief counsel. He was glad he could go directly to Morris. Even with his high position, Morris was the attorney who always seemed to have time for others, and he took a special interest in Joe's plight. He had held Joe's hand through all the depositions, and he was a trusted adviser, who tenaciously defended Joe against opposing counsel as well as critics in the company. Joe especially admired Morris for his insight and compassion for others. Joe sensed he was a guy who was bullied as a child, but he had the humor and smarts to talk his way out of trouble—a trait that proved useful in his chosen career. As a result, he was empathic toward those under fire and quickly came to their defense. Although Joe and Morris seldom saw each other socially, Joe considered him a friend and confidant.

"This is a critical point in this lawsuit for this to come out. The special master is trying to determine whether enough evidence is available for the judge to take the case to trial," Morris said. "Could this be the result of a mistake or error in the process?"

"There's probably little chance for error. I just can't figure out how this could happen. With all the samples we've taken before, nothing like this has ever shown up. You'll need to be on the conference call. I am sure Reynolds and his lawyers will claim this proves the entire production block could be contaminated."

"Then we'll need to come up with some reason to delay going to the judge. Can you get a start on this? Maybe request a field check or run additional samples? Anything to give us time. I have a feeling the board of directors will want to settle, and settle fast, if it looks like the case could go before a jury. These results sure give Reynolds's lawyers more leverage in any settlement talks."

***

Over the next week, Joe researched all the past records of the sites cleaned by his team, taking special interest in those near Colibri-6 and Halcón-4. Then he met with his team, who also reviewed the data. They found nothing to suggest any contamination.

Morris came down to Joe's office from the "rampart"—which was what the working stiffs in the company fondly called the executive floor occupied by the corporate officers and the legal department—for an update.

"We aren't finding anything. We've studied reams of data but have found nothing. This has me totally baffled," Joe informed him.

"Look—it is what it is," Morris replied. "We just have to make our best case to Stan that the new samples were incorrectly collected, the analyses were wrong, or maybe that the results were from a more recent spill. We can't stipulate that we're at fault."

As the videoconference approached, Joe and Morris met daily. They planned to show the inconsistency of the new data with the earlier studies and hoped that Stan would allow another limited round of sampling to verify the results. If that didn't happen, they would request a delay to give them time to study the issue further. But what Morris really wanted was more time to negotiate a settlement.

Morris had briefed Jessica Bradon, Steator's chief counsel and his boss, as well as most of the corporate officers. The board encouraged him to make his best presentation at the videoconference, but if he didn't succeed, they would begin settlement talks immediately.

Morris had argued that waiting for the outcome of the teleconference was too late. Now was the time to sit down with Reynolds's team. If they sensed that Stan might recommend going to trial, the settlement number would skyrocket.

"Does anybody know this Reynolds guy?" Morris remembered Clark Royal, Steator's CEO, asking at a recent briefing.

"Have we got any history on him?" Royal asked as he shifted in his chair. For all his authority and power, he was uncomfortable around attorneys, even those at the table dedicated to the defense of the company. He felt more at home on a grimy oil derrick "shooting the shit" with the newest roustabout than sitting around a table of lawyers.

"Not really. He just parachuted in from nowhere," Morris said.

"Actually, it seems Bill Haller interviewed him for a job several years ago, for chief of regulatory compliance, I believe. He was rated pretty high but was beaten out by Rebecca," Bradon said, glancing down for verification at the single printed page in her leather portfolio that contained her summary of the relevant points regarding the case.

"Has anyone talked to Bill about him?" Royal asked, nervously tapping the conference table with the eraser of his number 2 pencil—his choice writing instrument rather than the pretentious Mont Blanc pen his wife insisted he carry.

"Yes. Bill thought he was a good guy, not at all unreasonable; he really wanted to hire him," Bradon said.

"Maybe Bill and Morris should talk to him and see if we can work this out," Royal suggested.

"Maybe, but I'm not so sure. He may view it as desperation on our part," Morris said.

"I have great confidence in your negotiating skill, Morris. But let's see if you can make any headway with the federal judge. That's our best hope. Plan B will be settlement talks. Just don't move to Plan C. No way this goes to trial, understand? A protracted lawsuit would tank our stock and encourage copycat suits," Royal said.

"What are you thinking would be an acceptable range?" Morris asked. "Their initial papers indicated damages to the tune of ten billion dollars and a bump of five billion for punitives."

"No fucking way. That would be more than we grossed in those fields," Royal said.

"Well," Bradon said. "I believe a dime on the dollar is too much. Maybe five percent, but that's with an airtight nondisclosure."

"I've got to believe that time is money to them, too. If we could speed the process, they'll have less sunk costs and settle for a reduced amount," Morris said. "And if we can reach a reasonable amount, I think we can spin this to our advantage."

"How so?" Royal asked.

"We don't want to look like we're conceding to extortion. Like you said, Clark, doing so would attract other suits. But what if we set this up as an endowment to fund a foundation for the study of—I don't know—maybe the health of indigenous people, maybe to study rain forest restoration? Something that gets the money to Reynolds and his cohorts to use as they see fit. But we'll make it look like it was our initiative so we can look real good. PR could go pedal to the metal spinning this. We would be paragons of corporate virtue, the Jolly Green Giant. You know, Charlie Rose, NPR, the whole enchilada. The shareholders would love it."

"Did you have a lemonade stand as a kid?" Royal laughed. "You know, I like it, but it galls me to pay for something we didn't do."

"Yeah, if we didn't do it. But what if we can't prove that. Worse yet, what if we actually did it?" Morris asked.

"I thought you had great confidence in Joe and his team?" Royal said.

"I do. He does a great job, and he has saved us billions. But he's not perfect. How many dry holes has this company drilled? Ten percent, twenty percent, despite having the best geologists, engineers, and equipment?"

"That's about right."

"Well, so far, we've only had a challenge on one of Joe's projects. That's close to ninety-five percent. Not bad in anyone's book."

"It'll be expensive PR, but I'll discuss it with the board. Jessica, keep me updated. I've got to talk with the boys in finance."

CHAPTER TWENTY-NINE

Wednesday, on the Rio Putumayo

The cool night air created dew high in the canopy, and water droplets condensed on each leaf. The droplets, drawn together by molecular cohesive forces, coalesced into larger drops until they overcame the surface tension of the leaf and fell to the ground. Created from the tens of millions of leaves that made up the dense canopy, a cascade soon soaked everything below, including the two contorted figures in the boat.

Carlos was the first to awaken, a habit formed through years of early morning field trips. He doffed the insect netting, pulled his dry boots from the duffel bag, and put them on. He eased himself from the boat and onto the bank, where he eliminated the better part of a liter of water he had consumed the evening before.

Relieved, he walked back to the boat just as Gary stirred.

"Your choice is chocolate-marshmallow or oatmeal-brown-sugar breakfast bars." Carlos laughed. "I'd serve coffee if I had some."

"Tempting offer. I'm a marshmallow guy."

They got underway almost immediately. Again, Carlos was at the tiller as Gary pored over the topo maps that identified tributary streams.

"Is there a place to refuel?" Gary asked, looking at the map of the sparsely inhabited jungle.

"Yes, Puerto Asís is a large town, and there is much river traffic. We can resupply there. But first, we'll both need to check in at the immigration office."

The long boat ride left plenty of downtime for Gary. Some of it he spent in conversation with Carlos but most in reflection. He began to realize how much he missed his parents. It had been almost two weeks since the abduction. Other than dropping them off at the airport, he hadn't spent any real time with them in a long time. In their busy lives, it didn't seem to matter. But now it meant something. That thing you cherish, yet take for granted, can be gone in an instant. Gary knew this. He had seen it throughout his career. Teenagers—raised with such care, love, and pride—had been taken away forever in a blinding freeway crash. The parents were left with the perpetual guilt of having allowed them to take the car. Gary had seen it. He had felt it, and he had secretly shed tears for their suffering. But it was different when it was your own family, and this fact now weighed heavily on him.

***

Carlos had known they would have to register with customs when they arrived at Puerto Asís, Colombia. Although border-crossing stations were few and enforcement was lax, they still would need visa stamps to get rooms and or rent a car.

Anticipating this, he'd had to get papers quickly. Gary couldn't use his own US passport in case the kidnappers had a mole at the immigration office who recognized his surname. And Carlos didn't want to be identified with Natura Sucumbios in case anyone checked their backgrounds.

The colonel was more than helpful in orchestrating the preparation of a lost-passport letter with a fake name and a bona fide photograph for Gary. It was even stamped by the local magistrate in Lago Agrio. Carlos was given a fake passport. The documents, along with a carefully palmed twenty-dollar bill, would be sufficient for a visa stamp in Colombia.

"We'll stop at the wharf and ask about local guides," Carlos said. He had figured the best cover was also the easiest—he was Gary's guide, and they were in pursuit of the bush tanager. It would give them a reason to search many areas. "Hiding in plain sight" was how Gary described it. They had all the gear and experience to pull it off.

"Do many birders visit this area?" Gary asked.

"More now since drug activity has decreased but not like in Ecuador. People are reluctant to travel farther inland here."

They arrived at the municipal wharf at about ten in the morning. It was evident that the whitewashed concrete-block building that fronted the river with three tall poles and proudly flew the city, provincial, and national flags was a public building.

After securing the bow and stern lines to a wooden pier, Carlos approached a worker who was busy manicuring the small lawn in front of the building. "Can you direct me to the immigration office?" he asked.

The worker looked up and pointed at the front door.

Gary unloaded the duffel bags from the boat and caught up with Carlos. Then they went inside. The waiting area was dominated by a long, imposing counter that separated a series of desks from the chairs and tables.

A rather young-looking clerk rose from one of the desks and hurried to the counter. "May I help you?" he asked.

"We just arrived from Lago Agrio and would like to get our visas," Carlos replied.

Reaching under the counter for a bound ledger and a stamp and ink pad, the clerk asked about the nature of their visit to Colombia.

"I am leading this gentleman on a nature tour. We are in search of birds unique to this region," Carlos responded.

The binoculars around Gary's neck, the camera at his side, and his floppy sun hat were the perfect affectations and enough to convince the clerk.

"May I see your passports, please?"

Carlos handed his worn document to the clerk, along with an envelope with the letter regarding Gary from the magistrate in Lago.

The clerk thumbed through Carlos's passport, looking for any partially blank area to stamp. "You've traveled much," he murmured. He opened the envelope, unfolded the two-page letter, and saw the two twenty-dollar bills.

"I wasn't sure of the visa fee," Gary volunteered, as the clerk perused the letter.

With a quick stamp, he said, "That should be enough," and handed the letter and envelope back to Carlos.

"Perhaps you could recommend a local guide?" Carlos asked, while folding the letter and inserting it into the envelope.

"I don't know of one, but Roberto, the wharf manager, may know. He sees and talks with everyone who regularly visits on the river. Just ask anyone down there to point him out. He seldom leaves the area. If he's not there, check at El Riendo Loro on Calais Street."

"Muchas gracias."

"De nada."

Carlos exited, with Gary two steps behind.

The two walked to the wharf where they had tied up the boat. They eyed the few people along the wooden dock; all appeared to be loading or unloading their boats.

"Stay by the boat while I ask around," Carlos said.

Gary observed a couple of people shake their heads while speaking with Carlos. A third pointed in the direction of the main road that led out of the wharf area. Carlos signaled for Gary to follow, and they walked toward town.

At the corner of Calais and Bogotá Streets was El Riendo Loro, and true to its name, a six-foot carved wooden parrot with a painted grin stood beside the doorway. It wouldn't have been Gary's first choice in cantinas, but he wasn't planning on staying long. It was a one-story wooden structure on the street corner with newer, more modern two-story buildings on either side. It seemed that when the street was renovated, the cantina's owner wanted nothing to do with it. It had been there eighty years and had survived the rubber boom, the drug boom, the oil boom, and now the tourist boom. For him, no change was good.

Inside was a hodgepodge of tables and chairs of all vintages and conditions. Only the long bar at the end of the room looked like it always had been there. The walls were covered in a jumble of posters—comely beauties advertising cerveza, billboards of *fútbol* stars in contorted airborne postures making or saving a goal, and political banners from bygone elections. Fortunately, they blanketed most of the dingy, smoke-stained wallboards. The lighting was miserly. Even near high noon, the sun barely penetrated the single window in the front, and the wall and ceiling fixtures were better suited as night-lights.

But, Gary admitted to himself, the place had its charm. It reminded him of the old taverns that dotted the lakes in Northern Michigan, where he had spent many summers as a child, particularly on Friday nights for the perch fries—the jars of pickled bologna and pigs' feet on the bar, the huge muskie or northern pike mounted on the wall, the smell of stale beer infused in the wood floor, and, of course, the same low cloud of smoke permeating everything. The cheap laminated tables were arranged and rearranged as the night progressed. Behind the varnished bar top were rows of every imaginable liquor, which were more for show since 90 percent of the sales were the Stroh's and Carling Black

Label taps. Once in a while, his folks ordered a highball, a Manhattan, a pink lady, or—for him and his brother—a Shirley Temple or Roy Rogers. But beer was king. It was cold, cheap, and plentiful—perfect for those hot, muggy summer nights. The jukebox blared the latest top 40 hits and an occasional standard from the war. Mostly, he remembered the gut-busting laughter of hardworking people playing even harder on the weekends. Yes, El Riendo Loro was a place for regulars, not tourists.

Carlos approached the bartender and asked if Roberto was there. The bartender pointed to the man at a table in front of the picture window, watching as the street life unfolded just beyond the glass.

They walked over, and Carlos introduced himself and Gary. He explained that they were looking for a local guide who was knowledgeable about the area's birds and wildlife.

Roberto, middle-aged, was weathered from long days on the river managing the constant ebb and flow of commerce in the harbor. "A few groups come here from Bogotá and Cartagena. They usually stay at Hotel Chilimaco, not in town," he offered. "You should check there."

After getting directions, Carlos thanked the man, and he and Gary departed.

It was a short distance—maybe three miles—to the hotel, but burdened with the duffel bags, they opted for a cab. In ten minutes, they were dropped off in the semicircular driveway to the hotel.

The old, white, hacienda-style building stood as a graceful reminder of the slower, more staid colonial period. A wrought-iron trellis entwined with jasmine surrounded two large, ornately carved mahogany doors. The purple-blue flowers of the two large jacaranda trees and the brick-red roof tiles contrasted with the stark whitewashed building. Small mosaics of colorful ceramic tiles dotted the stucco walls. A single doorman in white shirt, pants, and hat greeted the men.

"Do you have a reservation?"

"No, we just wanted to speak with someone at the desk," Carlos said, and they entered the lobby.

They walked across the highly polished floor tiles to the imposing counter. The heavy masonry of the building, along with four slowly turning ceiling fans, created a respite from the heat outside.

On their approach, the desk clerk looked up and asked if he could provide assistance.

"Yes," Carlos said. "Roberto at the wharf suggested you might know a local guide we could hire to assist in locating birds and wildlife in the area. I understand that nature tour groups sometimes stay here at the hotel."

"Why, yes," the clerk answered. "Santos Jobim has been requested by several tour groups. It is said that he is very knowledgeable about the area and its animals. He is part *indio* and grew up in the forest. He isn't an employee, but he has family working here. Perhaps I could have them contact Santos and ask him to meet you here?"

Carlos and Gary looked at each other, realizing they had no place to stay other than their boat. "Do you have a room available for a few nights?" Gary asked the clerk. "We were in such a rush to get here for the birds that we didn't secure any accommodations."

"Certainly," he replied. "We have a room with two single beds off the patio that is available. How long will you be staying?"

"Two, maybe three nights. It depends on how well we do in the field," Carlos said.

"Let me have the porter take your bags to the room while you register. I will have someone contact Santos and have him meet you here. May I have your passports?"

They handed the clerk their freshly stamped papers, and Gary reached into his wallet for cash. They had decided earlier against using credit cards. "Do you mind if I pay in advance?" he said. "Sometimes we leave very early in the morning, and it's much easier if I don't have to check out."

"Cash is always welcome, sir. Please fill out the register, and I will inform you when Santos arrives."

Gary signed the register with their new names.

***

When they reached their room, the porter had arranged the duffel bags on luggage stands in the closet, turned on the ceiling fan, and opened the French doors to the garden.

After the night in the boat, Gary availed himself of the nearest bed and unceremoniously flopped down. "I just need fifteen minutes," he pleaded to Carlos. He was out in two.

The phone jarred him to consciousness. His short nap had progressed into a full slumber. He'd slept for an hour and a half, he realized, glancing at his watch.

"Hola," Carlos answered.

"*Sí. Espera diez minutos.*"

"*Gracias*," he finished and hung up the phone.

"Señor Jobim is waiting in the lobby. I told him we would meet him there shortly."

"That was a good nap," Gary said as he rose from the bed. He walked to the lavatory, opened the cold-water faucet to full, and splashed his face and neck to wash away the sleep-induced fog. He toweled off and headed for the door, just behind Carlos.

As Gary and Carlos entered the lobby, the desk clerk pointed to the waiting area along the front wall.

Seated on a brown leather chair was Santos Jobim. Slight in build with a shock of gray hair, he easily could have been mistaken for a retired clerk rather than a wilderness guide. Even his clothes belied his profession: a starched white collarless shirt, a pair of stiffly creased brown trousers, and polished brown shoes. Not what Carlos was expecting, but maybe he was dressed for an interview.

Santos stood to greet them. Carlos, speaking in Spanish, introduced himself and Mr. Gary Wright of New York, the name the colonel had arranged for the new papers.

"I speak pretty good English," Santos said.

Gary, who had been trying to keep up with the conversation, was relieved.

They sat opposite one another, and Santos opened with, "How can I assist you?"

"Mr. Wright has come a long way to observe birds in the area. For the past few weeks, I have been guiding him through Ecuador," Carlos said. "He decided that since we were so close, he should spend a few days searching for birds in Colombia as well. We came upriver yesterday and were told that you know this area very well. Mr. Wright would like to hire you to guide us through the region."

"I'm particularly interested in seeing the rarer species," Gary said. "I understand this is the area where the Greenthorpe bush tanager is found. I've seen many similar species on this trip, but encountering the Greenthorpe would be special."

Testing Santos's local knowledge and expertise, Carlos inquired whether he knew the breeding period of the species.

"Yes. We are fortunate that the males typically set up territories at this time, so they are very vocal as they try to attract the females. In a few more weeks, they will be in their nests and much more difficult to detect as they hide from predators during this vulnerable period," Santos explained,

Carlos noticed that Santos sat ramrod straight, his back not even touching the chair back. He sensed the man was trying to relax, but was ill at ease in the plush surroundings. Carlos easily imagined Santos was more accustomed to sitting hours in a tree branch one hundred feet in the canopy than in the soft leather chair in the elegant lobby.

"Have you found any recently?" Carlos asked.

"No, not this year, but there are three areas where I have found them in the past. They have a very strong urge to return to the same areas year after year."

"Are these areas difficult to access?" Carlos inquired. "We only have our boat at the wharf."

"No. We can reach at least two of the locations by nearby roads. We will have to do moderate hiking but less than a few miles," Santos replied. "The third location is in a valley a little farther away, but it isn't an area that is very safe to travel."

Feigning ignorance, Gary asked, "Why is that? Rough terrain?"

"No, señor. It is an area inhabited by an indigenous Indian tribe that is not friendly to outsiders—particularly after the government appropriated some of their lands for mineral exploration."

Gary cast a glance toward Carlos, who nodded slightly.

"But you've been there before?"

"Yes, once. I made arrangements with the local shaman but was allowed to stay only a few hours. Fortunately, the other areas are no problem."

"What is your availability? Could you take us to the first two locations?" Carlos asked.

"Yes. It would not be a problem. I would very much like to take you. I have access to a truck. We can visit both areas in one long day, but it would be best to go out for two days and return here at night."

"We would like to start tomorrow," Carlos said.

"I can be here at five thirty a.m."

"Do we need any special equipment?"

"No. Just boots, cameras and optics, and rain gear. I will have food, water, and other refreshments in the truck."

"What is your daily rate?" Gary asked.

"Seventy-five dollars a day. We have a good chance to see the bush tanager, but it would not be difficult to observe maybe one hundred to one hundred twenty-five other species in this area."

"The more the better," Gary said excitedly. "We'll see you here tomorrow morning."

Santos leaped to his feet when he sensed the meeting was over—almost as if he were sneaking out before the management saw him. But this was only in his mind; the staff and patrons who knew of him had great respect and admiration. It was Santos's youthful poverty and feelings of inferiority that he had never fully overcome. He said good-bye and left the hotel.

Gary and Carlos headed toward the hotel restaurant and were quickly seated.

Both were underdressed for the elegant setting and drew a disapproving glance from the maître d', who sat them in a darkened corner.

"We better just get room service next time!" Gary laughed.

Carlos just stared in disbelief at the table setting. On the crisp white linen tablecloth sat two place settings, each with a full array of forks, knives, and spoons in different sizes and shapes.

Gary saw the perplexed look on Carlos's face and said, "Just use whatever one you want. We're paying for it."

"What do you think about Santos?" Gary asked.

"He knows his birds, but I think he doesn't want us to visit that third site. I haven't heard of any particularly dangerous tribes in this area. I think it *is* dangerous but for other reasons. Santos doesn't want to scare us off with tales of drug runners and guerrillas."

"How do we get him to take us there? If we push, it'll raise his suspicions. If we find the bird at one of the other sites, we'll have no reason to continue. Our only chance is to have no luck at the first sites."

"Maybe we don't want him to lead us. Maybe we just want the location," Carlos contemplated aloud. "If we can have him show us the location on the map, we can go ourselves. It will be more risky, but we don't know if we can trust Santos."

"We'll need to get him to reveal the location casually, and only after we've been with him awhile so he'll trust that we won't go on our own and short him on his fee," Gary offered. "If we pay him up front, he probably won't be too concerned. Let's eat and then get our gear ready for tomorrow."

"Good," Carlos said. "I am now very hungry."

***

Later that evening, after the lobby was clear, a policeman carefully copied all the names and passport numbers from the register as the clerk pretended to busy himself with other tasks. The names didn't make it to the police station. Instead, they were handed to a man in a green Nissan Pathfinder, along with names from all the other hotels in the area. They were checked against the names supplied by the immigration office and the information Roberto had provided. The comandante's network was wide and deep—much better than the government's. Sometimes, they were one and the same.

CHAPTER THIRTY

Thursday, Puerto Asís

The blue Ford Ranger pulled into the driveway of Hotel Chilimaco just a little after 5:15 a.m. As was his habit, Santos arrived early. He had heard numerous stories from his clients about how late other guides often were. Santos thought this was a sign of disrespect and vowed, as a representative of his country, to give a good impression, one that would reflect well on his people. So he dressed nicely, arrived early, had good meals and transportation, and most important, knew where all the clean bathrooms were.

They drove an hour or so before Santos pulled off onto a wide area on the roadside. "The trail is off to the right," he said.

They grabbed their gear from the truck bed and headed up the path.

Gary fiddled with his binoculars, first adjusting the focus on his right eye, then the left, just as Carlos had instructed him the prior evening. Gary had accompanied his parents on their trips when he was a child, but he hadn't birded in many years. He'd always told his parents, "I have too many interests to be very good at any of them." But Santos couldn't know this, so Carlos had given him a crash course.

He never had really appreciated why his parents did what they did. In just a few years, what had started as a quaint hobby—admiring birds in the backyard, setting up feeders on the deck, and participating in local bird counts—had morphed into an all-consuming hobby. More than once, he had worried that their passion had crossed the line into obsession. Their formerly tidy den had become a command center fitting for an invasion of a small country. Bookcases overflowed with field guides from all corners of the planet; special publications on warblers, gulls, ducks, flycatchers, woodpeckers, shorebirds, and raptors;

ornithological treatises; scientific journals; and binder upon binder of field notes and lists. Maps were strewn over coffee tables and hung by pushpins in the plaster walls. There was always a new spotting scope, lens, or sound-recording gear. And the trips! Tanzania and Nepal one year. New Guinea and Guatemala the next. Brazil and the Pribilofs in the coming year or two. Gary and Russell joked that any inheritance they were expecting probably had been consumed counting penguins off Patagonia.

"Just follow me," Carlos had instructed Gary while in their room. "You won't be able to identify any birds, so don't try. I'll tell you what to look for when we are in the field, like color patterns, beak size and shape, behavior, and habitat. While we're in the field, I'll point out the birds to you. All you need to say is, 'Yes, I have it.' Sometimes say, 'I don't have it. Can you point it out?' I'll describe where in the brush or tree to find it. If Santos asks you a question about a bird, let me handle it. When Santos or I stop along the trail, it will be because we have seen or heard something. I want you to freeze. Don't move, and don't talk until one of us says something and has the bird in view. Most important, always be writing in your notebook. Even the most inexperienced birder maintains daily lists, country lists, and a life list of all the birds seen on their trips."

As they headed along the trail, Gary took up the rear, allowing him to better mimic the actions of the two experienced guides. It wasn't long before Santos stopped to scan the trees. Dutifully, Gary did the same, not having a clue as to what he was looking for.

"We'll see a lot of birds along the way, but I will only stop if there is something unusual. It is more important that we get to the bush tanager habitat to give us plenty of time to search. We will return on the same path and have another chance to see the more common species on the way out," Santos explained.

Carlos nodded. Gary was relieved. He wouldn't be tested for a while.

They continued on for a short distance when Santos slowed and searched the low shrubs.

"Did you hear a call?" Carlos asked.

"No, but this is the area where I found a nesting pair a few years ago."

Santos reached into his field vest and pulled out an old, scratched iPod. From another pocket, he pulled out a small plastic box about the size of a pack of cigarettes. With a short length of wire, he connected the iPod to the portable speaker. Holding the speaker at eye level in his left hand, Santos carefully manipulated the dial of the iPod until the appropriate title appeared on the screen. He pressed the "play" button, and the territorial song of a male bush tanager in desperate search of a mate blared from the small speaker. The song played for fifteen seconds before Santos hit the "pause" button. Silently, the three waited for a response from a live male who would be agitated that an interloper was intruding into its territory. A male works hard and long to establish and defend its territory and doesn't tolerate competitors.

Nothing. Santos repeated the call, this time after pivoting his body ninety degrees. Again, no response. Once more and still nothing.

"Let's move farther up the trail," he said, repacking the audio gear.

They repeated this several times while advancing only about a mile. Around noon, Santos said they should stop to eat. "I would have expected to have heard them by now if they were in this area," he explained.

Waiting for such a chance, Carlos said, "How much farther to the other site? If we see the bush tanager today, we'll have all day tomorrow for more leisurely birding."

"About an hour to the truck, then another hour on the road. We have about six hours of good light left," Santos said.

"I like that plan," Gary replied, as if on cue. "We can eat on the way."

They retraced their route back. Upon arriving at the truck, Carlos unfolded a topographic map of the area that he had prepared for the colonel. Large circles in pencil showed the areas where the bush tanager had been reported to nest. He placed the map on the hood of the truck and asked Santos to locate their current position.

Santos studied the map, noting the roads, trails, and rivers, and traced their route from the hotel. He counted the number of stream crossings and then followed an elevation contour line.

"The trail is not shown on this map, but I know we are very near this position," he said, pointing with the tip of a pencil Carlos had provided.

Carlos marked a "1" at the location and scribbled the date immediately below.

"I like to keep records of the places I've birded," he said. "Is the location of the other site on this map?"

Santos again perused the map, following the road, again reckoning with streams and contours. At a spot about twenty-five miles northeast of the first mark, he placed a "2." "It is next to this river," he said.

Not wanting to seem too obvious about the third site, Carlos tucked the map away.

"We should go if we are to have any more chances today," Santos said.

The trip to the second site was quicker than Gary had expected. He sat in the rear seat, fiddling with his GPS unit to track their route, pleased at the strength of the signal, even under the thick canopy.

In the front seat, Santos and Carlos exchanged war stories about guiding tour groups, often lapsing into frenetic Spanish, and Gary couldn't keep up with what was being said. Carlos explained that he used to work as a guide and driver for a large US tour firm, but he found it was much easier to work on his own and set up tours through various lodges. This was partially true, except the large US firm was actually Ecuadorean, and he wasn't really working on his own now. But the story was plausible, and Santos wasn't an inquiring sort, other than about good places to bird.

Santos explained that he had gotten into guiding by accident. He had worked for a surveyor when the oil companies were exploring sections of southern Colombia near where his family lived. He had grown up within the protected area of his tribe. Even as a child, he appreciated the diversity of the wildlife, particularly the birds. There were only one or two names to describe what he knew to be many distinct species, and it wasn't until he worked with the surveyors that he ever saw pictures of the birds. They were in an early edition of Hilty and Brown's *A Guide to the Birds of Colombia*. He immediately recognized many of them from his region. But now the birds had Spanish names, English names, and most importantly, scientific names. The Indian, English, and Spanish names were quaint and descriptive, but the scientific name truly defined a bird. It took Santos time to remember the new names, but he already knew exactly what they looked and sounded like. When he encountered his first pair of binoculars, courtesy of the chief surveyor, that was it—he was hooked.

They arrived at the second site and headed toward the trail. Once out of sight of the road, Santos pulled out the iPod and again called for the male bush tanager. For the first three stops, they heard nothing. But after the fourth, just after the recording stopped, they heard a faint echo.

"Did you hear that?" Santos asked.

"Yes," Carlos replied.

"I'm not sure," said Gary.

"I'll try to bring him in a little closer," Santos said, repeating the call. At each play, the bird moved in closer, scolding the invisible Lothario.

"I don't see him," Gary said.

"He is hidden in the branches to our right. Wait. I will try to point him out," Carlos said. He reached into his pocket and pulled out a small pen-size laser pointer. Then he turned it on and carefully aimed the small red dot at a branch to the right of the bird, just twenty-five feet in front of them.

"Can you see the red dot?" Carlos asked.

Gary looked through his binoculars for a few seconds and then said, "Yes."

"OK. Follow the dot as I move it to the left," Carlos instructed.

He moved the dot about two feet until it was it at the bird's feet.

"I see him!" Gary exclaimed quietly but enthusiastically.

Carlos then turned off the pointer, careful not to shine it into the bird's eyes. For birding groups with an array of sighting skills, tour leaders had found laser pointers invaluable in getting all members of the group "on the bird" for a good sighting. It was a much superior approach to "It's on the third branch on the left of the second tree at about ten o'clock in the canopy."

Santos silenced the iPod as the bird moved even closer. To his right, just above eye level on a thin branch, the agitated bird flared its wings, wagged its tail, and dipped its head in a display of extreme machismo. *This territory is mine, and you'd better get out,* it scolded. Frustrated that it couldn't find the intruder, the bird flew to another perch for a different vantage and sang fiercely again.

All this time, the three silent, motionless birders thoroughly enjoyed the show.

Finally, sensing it had successfully repelled the unseen trespasser, the bird disappeared back in the foliage to its sentry perch to await the next challenge.

"What a great sighting. I clearly saw his eye ring and buff underbelly. There was no doubt about that bird. And his call—just as it was in the recordings," Carlos said.

"Wow!" Gary exclaimed in exhilaration. "He was one angry bird. He didn't even know we existed."

"When they're that agitated, their total focus is finding and scaring away the other male. During the breeding season, the males have high levels of testosterone, which triggers belligerent behavior when another male enters his territory," Carlos explained.

Gary pulled out the map to confirm the location. He penciled in the coordinates from his GPS. Then he looked up at Santos. "Where is that third site you mentioned? Is it in the Indian preserve territory?"

"It's along this river, past that third road. The protected lands start here," Santos said, pointing.

Careful not to raise any suspicions, Gary made no notations on the map but memorized the landmarks as he folded the map and handed it back to Carlos.

"I'd like to get a little more time here to see what we can see," Gary stated. "Now that the pressure is off, we can work a little more leisurely."

They did, and after an hour and a half, Gary had added another thirty species to his life list—overall a very satisfying day for him. He had recorded fifty-five species, gotten an excellent view of the bush tanager, and most important, thanks to Santos, knew his destination for tomorrow. All without tipping his hand.

They arrived back at Hotel Chilimaco a couple of hours after dark. Carlos asked Santos if he would like to join them for dinner. He declined gracefully, noting his family was waiting for him.

Gary thanked Santos for a great day. He told him that he and Carlos had decided to go upriver the next day and wouldn't need him. Gary vowed to look Santos up on his next trip and handed him a sixty-dollar tip. Santos helped them haul their gear back to the room and said good-bye.

Santos went to the front desk, looked around to make sure no one could hear, and then reported his uneventful day to the clerk. He knew this, along with other scraps of intelligence, would be reported back to the comandante. It was a wide and deep network indeed.

As soon as Santos had left the room, Gary sprang for the map from Carlos's pack. He had to relocate the site Santos had pointed out before he forgot the details. He traced the route from the annotated "2" and followed the road to its second bifurcation and then to the river crossing. He made a small circle, which partially overlapped the breeding range of the bush tanager that Carlos previously had drawn on the map.

"It's a long shot," he said.

"Long shot?" Carlos asked quizzically.

"A figure of speech. It means something with a low chance for success. It's easier to hit a close target," Gary continued, mindful that as fluent in English as Carlos was, idioms could be troublesome for nonnative speakers. "*Cómo se dice en Español?*"

"Ah." Carlos laughed. "It is '*Es un tiro largo*' in Spanish. I will have to remember—long shot. But not from a gun." He returned his attention to the map. "It looks like the area is accessible by boat or by auto. The road leads to the river, and this is the symbol for a ferry crossing." He pointed to a dashed line through the river. "There would not be much need of a ferry if there wasn't a road on the other side."

Carlos had a great deal of experience crossing rivers using cable ferries. There was usually a raft that could accommodate two or three vehicles plus a few passengers. The ferries were simple plank structures on drum or pontoon floats and were propelled across the river by men who pulled on two thick nylon or sisal ropes that spanned the channel. For these primitive versions, it was "all hands on deck." On each bank was a small landing ramp, typically constructed of thick wooden beams, similar to railroad ties. Since the road on the opposite bank didn't appear on the map, Carlos figured it was a dead end, and the crossing benefited only the local tribe.

Other than the road, there were no signs of villages or settlements on the map. But it was an old military topographic map from the 1960s, and there were plenty of areas that even the most intrepid cartographers had avoided.

"Do we have Internet access here?" Gary asked.

"I saw some computers and printers in an alcove off the lobby."

"No, I mean Wi-Fi in the room."

"I didn't ask. Let me check," Carlos said as he looked through the service directory and information pamphlets on the desk.

"Yes, they do. I need to call to get the password."

Gary walked over to his duffel bag and took out a soft neoprene case that contained his laptop. He powered it on, waited for the Wi-Fi icon, and logged in with the access code Carlos had obtained. In seconds, he was scrolling through an online geographic information program.

Having no towns or distinct geographical features to enter, Gary asked Carlos for the coordinates they had recorded on the GPS at the second site earlier in the day.

"Zero degrees, thirty-six minutes, fourteen seconds north latitude, and seventy-six degrees, thirty-six minutes, fifty-three seconds west longitude."

As Gary entered the position, the image of the earth from space slowly zoomed in until a carpet of green filled the screen. He zoomed out slightly and panned to search for signs of the road, which was obscured in most areas by the canopy. Finally, a patch of brown appeared, and Gary zoomed in. "I think that's it," he said.

He switched from aerial-satellite view to map view, and there it was, the thin line of the road they'd followed most of the day.

Four eyes focused intently on the eight-inch screen.

"Can you move the map to the northwest to locate the third site?" Carlos asked.

"What was it? About eleven miles from the last site?"

Carlos went back to the topographic map and scaled the distance with his pen. "Yes, between ten and fifteen miles to the outside limits of the breeding range. The location Santos pointed out is closer to ten."

Scrolling with the touch pad, Gary dead reckoned to the approximate location. He panned east to west and then west to east, starting from the south and working northward, searching for any signs of civilization.

He switched back to the aerial view since it had much more recent satellite imagery. Then he zoomed out to get a better overall view. Following the segments of the main road that were visible, they located the river crossing. As Gary zoomed again, they discovered that Carlos's assumption about the ferry was correct—it was a blurred image of a primitive raft that could probably hold only a medium-size truck, certainly nothing as large as a semirig, which were rare off the main roads anyway. The road on the opposite bank appeared considerably narrower and less used.

"I guess it's used only by locals," Gary speculated. "They pull it to the side of the bank they're on, ford the river, and leave the ferry there. The next person has to pull it back and repeat the process."

"Keep following the road on the other bank," Carlos urged.

Gary did. The road, maybe even just a trail, was visible only through small breaks in the canopy. After a few seconds, a larger clearing appeared. It contained a handful of structures and was surrounded by forest toward the river and on two sides. They saw a field dotted with trees on the side farthest from the river.

"Looks like a small farm," Gary said.

When he zoomed in, they saw what looked like a small house and a few smaller structures. In the center was a cleared area where a couple of trucks were parked. It seemed to be fenced, judging by the way the vegetation stopped abruptly at the perimeter, but the camera view was straight down.

"Is that some kind of orchard?" Gary asked.

"Maybe coffee."

"Does it seem like the type of farm that indigenous Indians would use?"

"No," Carlos replied. "Those people usually live in villages."

"Maybe we should get a closer look."

Gary moved the cursor to the center of the buildings and clicked the touch pad. The latitude and longitude displayed. He wrote down the coordinates and repeated the procedure for the site of the ferry crossing.

"Can you put these coordinates into the GPS unit?" Carlos asked.

"Sure. How should we get there? Boat or truck?"

"Boat," Carlos answered. "Otherwise, we'd have to rent a truck and maybe hire a driver. We would be less obvious if we blended with the normal river traffic. The kidnappers, if they're there, know what they're doing. They will have guards and lookouts posted along the river and road. There is only one way into the compound. If the army or police pursue them, their only escape with the trucks will be on the road. Of course, they could abandon their equipment and escape on foot or by boat, but they would leave a lot behind. Lookouts would give them enough warning. On the river, we would be less conspicuous and have a better chance to slip through. Maybe we should disguise our intentions. We could fill the boat with sacks of manioc, maize, and anything else."

"But some people already think we're here for birding. How can we suddenly become river traders?" Gary asked.

"Or we could make a point of heading farther upstream, wanting to find more birds like I told Santos."

"I like that idea better. If anyone questions us, we'll say decided to explore the river more."

CHAPTER THIRTY-ONE

Friday, FARC Camp

By the third week, Comandante Flores had left the camp and the conditions of the hostages quickly eroded. First, their meals were cut back to just rice and beans; the guards took the extra rations for themselves. Discipline among the guards broke down as well. No longer were they changed regularly, and the captives heard the bickering and shouting as one guard arrived late to relieve the other. The guards also became less responsible with the prisoners. A couple of times, Jack and Tom had been slapped around for not returning to the shed fast enough.

Worst of all, the formerly cooperative hostages had begun to get on one another's nerves, which was understandable in the hot, cramped, dark confines. Jack became openly hostile and confrontational with Tom. He resented any suggestion Tom made and let him know in no uncertain terms that he didn't take orders from anyone. It was a side of Jack neither Vincent nor Tom thought existed. Whenever Vincent tried to reason with him, Jack sulked and sat in his corner, ignoring the other two.

"What's with him?" Tom asked when Jack was at the latrine.

"It must be the stress. Jack is a very physical person, and he's wasting under these conditions."

"What can we do? He's really pissed at me, like I'm trying to dictate to him. I just want to keep us together and focused until we're released."

Vincent shrugged. "I don't know. I'd normally recommend that you give him some space, but that's quite impossible here. Let me talk with him when you're gone."

"That may not be such a good idea. I don't want him paranoid, thinking we're scheming against him. It's better if he puts all his bad feelings on me and sees you as an ally. Give him a chance to confide in you."

Jack, however, became more sullen and distant. Vincent wondered whether he'd had bouts with depression in the past.

It all came crashing down one day. Jack had all he could take with Tom and Vincent's incessant planning, the barely tolerable conditions, and the increasing cruelty of the guards. His mind was a pressure cooker. With only the slightest provocation—a "hurry up" shove from a guard—Jack snapped.

He turned and threw a right jab that grazed the guard's cheek. He followed with a flurry of lefts and rights, but few landed and none was effective. The guard was armed only with a large club, which he swung hard at Jack, barely missing his shoulder. Jack lurched to tackle him before he could swing again. When they tumbled to the ground, Jack seemed to have the advantage. Out of his mind with rage, he climbed on top of the guard and strangled him. His eyes were wide with anger, and his face was distorted in a maniacal grimace. His total focus was to destroy the man; he was so blind to his surroundings that he never saw the blow coming from a second guard behind him.

He didn't remember much after he came to in the shed. He just wondered why Tom and Vincent were hovering over him and staring at him so intently.

"You sure are a scrapper," Vincent said.

"Yeah, and maybe you'll win one of those scraps one day," Tom said.

The following days proved to be a disappointment for Tom. He had hoped the fight would change Jack's attitude, but it didn't. Jack remained contemptuous of Tom, maybe more so because of the embarrassment of the drubbing by the guards.

The guards hadn't taken kindly to Jack's rebellion, and the entire group had to pay for it. Trips to the latrine were substituted with a couple of buckets. This, however, lasted only a day or two because it proved inconvenient for the guards. But physical abuse increased, particularly for Jack, who became the personal piñata for one guard in particular.

Tom wondered what was taking so long with the negotiations and how much longer even he could hold out.

***

The situation was a little better in the smaller shed, but Ben and Marsha were also feeling the effects of isolation and deprivation. Ben wasn't concerned about their safety until the day "Fidel" shoved Marsha forcefully through the threshold and onto the earthen floor.

Ben rose to help her to her feet. "You OK?"

"Yeah, but they're starting to get a bit rough."

"Have they tried anything with you?"

"No," Marsha said, "but who would want an old, washed-up hag like me?"

"Me and maybe a billion other guys."

Marsha smiled a little. "You're such a charmer, but your eyesight is failing fast."

"You underestimate yourself. Just be careful around those guys. Don't give them any reasons to harm you."

"I won't."

Ben sensed a certain desperation among the captors, though his interaction with them was limited—never more than a few words in a mixture of Spanish and broken English. Most communication was done by pointing. He figured they must be concerned about the ransom. Maybe they had expected a faster payoff. He was worried; things were definitely getting worse.

CHAPTER THIRTY-TWO

Friday, Puerto Asís

The desk had arranged for a taxi to pick up Carlos and Gary, along with their gear, and transport them to the wharf. Along the way, they made a brief stop at a bodega to purchase supplies.

When they arrived, Roberto was standing on one of the docks, engaged in a heated discussion about docking fees with a couple of local boatmen. They were visually estimating the size of the load since the nearest scales were several miles away.

"Señor," Carlos called out as they approached Roberto, "we wanted to thank you for referring us to Hotel Chilimaco. We were put in touch with Santos Jobim, who was a great guide and directed us right to the birds we wanted to see."

Trying to recall these men, Roberto scratched his head. After all, how many did he see on any day? "Oh, yes," he finally said, remembering their short encounter at El Riendo Loro. "I will remember Señor Jobim when next asked about a guide."

"We are heading upstream. But we may stop on our way back," Carlos added. "There is so much to see in this area, and we have just begun."

"Good luck," Roberto replied, as the two men set about loading and organizing their gear.

***

Before they headed further upriver on the Rio Putumayo where service would be spotty, Carlos pulled out his cell phone and placed a call to Colonel Hernandez to inform him of their plan.

Carlos manned the outboard, while Gary tried to maintain a low profile by sitting on the damp floorboards with his head just above the gunwales. Self-assigned to the role of navigator, he only needed to make sure Carlos remained in the main channel and continued upstream for the next few hours. He occasionally checked the GPS, but with its low-range scale, their preprogrammed destination wasn't yet on the screen.

As day turned to night, the river remained alive with traffic, mostly laden boats heading downstream to be the first at the market in Puerto Asís and other downstream ports. Although traveling counter to the flow, Carlos and Gary didn't move at a speed or in a manner that would attract attention. In fact, they motored at such a moderate pace that they were overtaken by some of the boats moving upstream.

At its confluence with the Rio Putumayo, Carlos steered the boat east into the Rio Guamuez. Gary pulled out his small night-vision scope from his duffel and slowly scanned the river. The oncoming boats were easy marks, their engines revealed by small white-hot images. The hazy-gray images of people in the boats weren't visible until they were within about five hundred yards. As they approached, Gary, amazed by the resolution, was able to discern the number of people in each vessel. He figured he would get even better images at a slower speed.

After several more hours, they were less than a few thousand feet from the tributary that led to the ferry and encampment.

"We should slow down and move along the east bank to get a better view of the confluence," Gary suggested.

Carlos slowed the engine and gradually veered to the right until he found a spot to pull up to along the bank. Then he cut the engine and grabbed an overhanging branch to steady the boat. Even with the smidgen of moonlight, Carlos couldn't see the tributary, but with the night-vision scope, Gary clearly saw the opposite bank and the accreted sandbar just downstream from the entrance.

The new generation of thermal night-vision equipment was considerably more powerful at detecting low-resolution, low-contrast targets than the older light-intensifying units. Rather than the green-cast images produced by the older units, the new thermal systems produced high-contrast, black-and-white images. Not dependent on moonlight, starlight, or other low-level illumination, the thermal units read heat, not light, and the hotter the subject, the brighter the image. They also were unaffected by rain, smoke, fog, or haze. The thermal units were so powerful that the heat signature of a vehicle could be detected from more than three miles away, while a human could be spotted from a distance of a mile.

"We should figure that these guys could have equipment as good, or better, than ours," Gary said. "This is totally off-the-shelf gear, so if we can see them, they probably can see us."

Gary again raised the scope and scanned the area. He detected small, dim splotches of heat, particularly in the canopy, which were likely small mammals and birds, but nothing the size of a human. On the river, it was a different story. Although only four or five boats were in their vicinity, the heat from the outboard engines lit the scope like headlights on a truck. When Gary turned toward the stern, the emission from their motor was like a burst of sunlight on the scope.

"We'll have to ditch the motor once we're in the tributary," he said. "There's no way they won't see us coming if they have night-vision. Plus, the engine is loud."

Reasonably confident that no guard was posted near the mouth, Gary instructed Carlos to proceed across the river to the tributary. Once they were on the smaller river, Gary used the scope to inspect the bank for a landing.

"Pull up over there, and cut the engine," Gary instructed Carlos as he pointed to the bank.

The boat turned ninety degrees, and Carlos gave it a little burst of throttle to propel them the last few yards to the shore. Then he cut the power. They drifted until the bow bottomed out, and Gary jumped to the shore with a tie line. He quickly secured the bow and pulled the boat parallel with the bank.

Carlos unscrewed the two motor mounts that fastened the outboard to the stern. He disconnected the gas line as well as the safety chain clipped between the motor housing and an eyebolt on the stern. He grabbed the handles on the motor's cowl, while Gary lifted the lower unit and propeller. As the motor weighed two hundred pounds, it was a struggle to haul it onto the high bank.

"Let's find a place nearby to hide this," Carlos said, bending under the strain.

They walked fifty feet into the forest and placed the motor on its back with the propeller up and the fuel intake off the ground. Carlos covered it with one of the mosquito nets and tried his best to camouflage it with fallen branches, twigs, and leaf litter.

Gary returned to the boat and retrieved the two fuel tanks, one full and the other half full, and then returned to where Carlos stood next to the motor. He placed both tanks under the netting next to the motor.

"If anyone finds this stuff, all they'll need is a boat," he said.

Back at the boat, Gary checked the GPS. While there were many side channels, he was reasonably sure this was the correct one. It was large enough to require a ferry crossing, and the straight-line distance to the marked location seemed correct. *Only one way to find out,* he thought.

As Gary grabbed a paddle, Carlos pushed off from the bank and then jumped into the stern. They paddled along the right-hand bank, which had calmer water, although the current on the tributary wasn't nearly as strong as that of the Río Guamuez.

"We have about a mile to the ferry," Gary noted. "But we should pull out a little downstream of here to check the area."

CHAPTER THIRTY-THREE

Saturday, FARC Camp

Shortly after midnight, Gary scanned the banks with the scope and spotted the ferry landing about a quarter mile upstream. He clearly made out a stationary object and a moving figure ahead. He signaled Carlos to remain quiet and pointed to a spot along the bank to land. Quietly, they maneuvered the boat toward the bank, hoping the drone of the cicadas would mask their approach.

They removed the duffel bags and paddles and hauled the boat onto the bank and out of sight from the river. From behind the buttress roots of a large palm, Gary motioned for Carlos to look through the scope.

Carlos slowly panned from left to right. When he found the location of the ferry crossing, he stopped and concentrated on the two bright spots. He raised two fingers toward Gary, who nodded. In barely a whisper, Carlos said, "One person. Also a vehicle, which is not as bright."

"Probably means the engine has been off for a while and is cooling," Gary said. "Let's get away from the bank."

He had barely finished the sentence when an outboard motor roared to life. The formerly dull blur now glowed white in the scope. Moving gingerly into a thicker stand of trees, Carlos said, "Do you think he heard us?"

"No, but let's get farther away."

Within a minute, the boat passed at a good clip. It traveled beyond their position and continued downstream for five minutes until it was barely audible. The boat then turned and started back upstream. The driver had a small spotlight, with which he alternately illuminated the left and right banks, back and forth, in a systematic manner. He then turned off the light, traveled a bit farther upstream, and repeated his spotlight search. Fortunately, the lookout didn't spot the signs of Carlos and Gary's haul out. Otherwise, he would have seen the disturbance on the bank and maybe even the boat itself. The lookout continued upstream past the ferry crossing.

"He's gone. Let's move in closer," Gary said.

They hid their duffel bags in a dense thicket, which now contained only clothes, extra water, an old tripod, and a spotting scope—things they wouldn't need. If caught, they could maintain their cover by saying the equipment was too cumbersome in the forest, so they left it. Instead, they carried two daypacks with food, water, the GPS, headlamps, the night-vision scope, field guides, notepads, mosquito netting, and all the other gear a well-equipped guide and birder would carry.

They checked the GPS for the direction to the compound. Carlos grabbed his headlamp from his pack and switched it on low. He held the unit in his hand to better control the direction of the beam. Gary used the night-vision scope to scan ahead. Seeing nothing, they set out toward the compound.

It was rough travel: crossing over fallen trees and branches, ducking under lianas and vines, slipping on greasy soil, and stepping into hidden puddles.

Gary was impressed with—yet a bit jealous of—the speed and grace with which Carlos negotiated these hazards in near darkness. Gary lumbered, almost out of breath, trying to keep pace. He found walking in high rubber boots cumbersome and uncomfortable. But Carlos walked as if he were born in them.

Gary also encountered the many defenses deployed by rain-forest trees. Trying to steady himself, he grabbed a limb only to feel the sting of a small spine pierce his hand or the attack ants that swarmed to protect their tree against invaders. Carlos, on the other hand, merely dipped his head slightly or tilted his body a bit left or right and avoided all hazards. And always Carlos's hands remained at his sides. Carlos hardly even sweated, while Gary was soaked. The effort, coupled with the heat and humidity, was draining Gary, and they had just started. It took all his ego and self-respect not to plead with Carlos to slow down.

And I thought I was in shape, Gary thought with a laugh. *Well, maybe in Detroit.*

After they had slogged several hundred yards in a near-crawl posture, Carlos stopped and signaled to Gary. He moved a few paces forward and shined his light to the left and right. Gary strained to see what had halted their progress.

Carlos walked back and whispered, "There's a path ahead. It leads in the direction of the compound."

Gary handed the night-vision scope to Carlos, who returned to the side of the path, crouched, and scanned the path in both directions. Gary joined him a few moments later.

"I don't see anything. How far is the camp?" asked Carlos.

Gary pulled out the GPS. "Maybe fifteen hundred feet."

"There's a curve in the path," Carlos said. "You stay here. I'll try to get a little closer."

Gary nodded. This close, he had expected to hear some noise or see some light, but there was nothing. He looked at his watch: 2:30 a.m. *They probably turned off the generator*, he surmised.

Carlos proceeded slowly and cautiously, checking each step of the path for anything that might creak or snap under his weight. Fifty yards out, he saw the compound, at least its back wall. A propane lantern illuminating the area sat on a small table with an empty chair next to it. He saw a crude plank wall with a tall chain-link gate. He stepped back a few feet behind a tree and pulled out the scope. The glow of the lantern was the only thing visible on the screen, but as he panned to the right, a large moving figure appeared. Carlos watched as the figure approached the gate, walked past it, and then continued in the other direction for about fifty feet before seating himself in a chair.

Having seen enough, Carlos returned to the spot where he'd left Gary. "It's right up ahead—very close—and a guard is by a gate."

"Is he armed?"

"I could not see well enough, but why have an unarmed guard?"

"Do you think we should get closer?" Gary asked.

"Too risky. What if they patrol the trail? But I have an idea."

Carlos crossed the path to a strangler fig that towered over the jungle floor. "If I can climb high enough, I might be able to see over the wall and into the compound," he said.

"But you'd be a sitting duck up there!"

"Sitting duck?"

"I'm sorry. Another phrase. It means you'd be vulnerable. It's easier to shoot a duck that's on the water than in the sky," Gary tried to explain. "But the point is you'll have to stay very quiet and out of sight."

"*Ah, una presa fácil.* I will climb up now while it is still dark and stay on the side away from the compound. I will be still if I see anyone approach after the sun rises. I will stay concealed and promise not to quack."

"That's a hell of a climb! Can you do it?"

"Oh, yes," Carlos replied. "I climbed many such trees when I was young, and I still do when I need to collect eggs or photograph a nest. The strangler fig has many good handholds and footholds."

On this last point, Gary agreed as he eyed the mass of intertwined branches, actually roots, that clung to the trunk of the underlying kapok tree. The fig started as a germinated seed deposited in bird droppings in the canopy of the kapok. There, it started as an epiphyte, technically a hemiepiphyte because the nascent fig sent out roots that crawled down the trunk of the host tree until they reached the ground. Once on the ground, they penetrated the soil and took root. Eventually, the roots grew and totally encircled the host tree. The leaves of the fig climbed higher than the host leaves and eventually starved the kapok of light and nutrients. Over time, the host tree died, but the superstructure of the fig remained and thrived.

It was the latticework of branches that Carlos ascended. With a daypack containing his binoculars, the night-vision scope, water, and energy bars and with his headlamp clenched in his teeth, he scrambled to the canopy in only a few minutes.

Gary had nothing to do but serve as lookout. He found a hummock well hidden from the path. He sat down, pulled the last mosquito net from his pack, and wrapped it around himself to stave off insects and, he hoped, prying eyes from the path.

Carlos, exhausted from the climb, eased himself onto a sturdy eight-inch-thick limb. Using his belt and a small length of rope, he improvised a crude safety harness that he secured around his waist and the trunk of the fig. He promptly emptied a sixteen-ounce bottle of water to sate his thirst. Suddenly, and with some urgency, he was sorry he hadn't planned better before the climb. But nature calls at the most inopportune times. He stood, unzipped, and, with a sigh, relieved himself. *I hope Gary is out of range,* he thought with a laugh.

Now, it was time to wait. He slung his binoculars around his neck and pulled the night-vision scope from the daypack. The scope had only a hand strap, so he tied it to his safety line with a bandanna. *I'd hate to lose that,* he thought.

Relaxed and more comfortable than in the boat, simply because he could stretch and dangle his legs, he took in the sights and sounds of the jungle. He thought about his days as a young boy on the hunts.

Although Carlos was from a *colono* family, he grew up near an Indian village and had become great friends with Gustavo, a boy about his age. Like most children, both were fast at adapting to each other's culture. Gustavo stayed with Carlos's family and Carlos with Gustavo's. Carlos even accompanied Gustavo's father, grandfather, uncles, and the other men from the village on their hunts. While most relied on .22-caliber rifles, some were proficient with blowguns and darts. Carlos had sat in blinds with them for hours, waiting for a troop of monkeys, a sloth, or best yet, a tapir, to come into range. He learned patience, quiet, and the joy of solitude—so different from the constant commotion of village life. But hunting demanded a special skill set, and he had learned it well.

It was during the hours spent in trees that he began his study of birds. There were so many. They were so different, and each one was a curiosity. He found that most of the life in the forest existed in the canopy. He also was blessed with abilities to exploit the experience. He had sharp vision and a practiced ear to discern songs and calls. He also could remember and mimic the vocalizations. As he matured, so did his skills. He occasionally wondered whether they were acquired traits or somehow genetically based. *Maybe both,* he thought.

The quiet splash of a tree frog escaping into a small pool of water accumulated in the crotch of a branch caught Carlos's attention. He heard the incessant buzz of insects and smelled the fragrance of bromeliads and orchids rooted into the bark of the fig.

In this moment of reflection, he thought of his family. He'd barely had the time in the past few days for such a luxury. Before he had left, he had made a last-minute call from the lodge to tell Cecilia that he had a client and would be back in a few days. Yes, he would call when he could. Yes, he would spend some time at home soon. No, she shouldn't try to reach him.

He felt a sense of mission. He owed this to Tom, Jack, Ben, Marsha, and Vincent.

There but for the grace of God, he thought. *Also, who better? Gary is enthusiastic and resourceful, but he's so out of his element. The colonel and the soldiers have the jungle skills but never would fool anyone about how and why they were here. Fortunately, or unfortunately, I'm the perfect person for this.*

He picked up the scope and turned it on, realizing its usefulness was now counted in minutes, at least for today. He scanned the compound; not much was happening. The structures were visible as they emitted heat stored during the day. Three brighter but smaller objects in the center of the compound were probably vehicles.

The corrugated roofs showed the most heat, probably indicating people inside, but one small structure was particularly bright. *Probably the generator,* Carlos thought. Toward the front of the compound, he saw a concentration of medium-hot objects moving about and even smaller objects on the ground. He suspected, correctly, that these were livestock pens with goats and cows, along with chickens in their roost.

The guard at the back gate was clearly visible and appeared motionless in the chair. *Sleeping,* Carlos guessed. The front gate and the road that led to the ferry crossing were obscured, but he was fairly sure another guard was posted there.

He put the scope away and waited for the camp to revive.

Week Four

CHAPTER THIRTY-FOUR

Sunday, FARC Camp

Slightly after dawn, Carlos noticed the faint smell of smoke. He looked through his binoculars and saw a figure walking around the compound.

The cook.

He then heard a call, very faint at first but enough to draw his attention. He heard it again, slightly louder this time.

This is a good sign, he thought. *There's a Greenthorpe bush tanager here! Maybe the one Tom heard.*

Gary, a hundred feet below, somehow had managed to find a position comfortable enough to actually sleep for an hour or two. But he also smelled the smoke. Still hazy from sleep, he took a few seconds to reorient himself. He looked around, determined he was alone, and sat up. The sunlight was dim but brightening by the minute. This was his first good view of their accommodations. *Not bad,* he thought. Even in the dark, without the help from the night-vision scope, he had found a well-concealed location. Although he was only twenty yards off the trail, he would be difficult to detect unless he were particularly noisy.

He stood, stretched, and looked skyward to see whether he could find Carlos in the canopy. He was thankful he couldn't; it meant probably no one else could either.

Concerned that someone could monitor radio chatter or hear them conversing, he and Carlos had set up a code for their FRS radios. With their radios preset to a little-used channel and set on the Morse code function, each depression of the "transmit" button would elicit a click. They had agreed to send one click to hail each other. If no response was received, another click would be sent after one minute. If the signal was heard, the other would click twice. After that, they would look for each other and rely on hand signals. If either sensed danger, he would click three times in rapid succession.

Gary hit the transmit button and waited. He looked up, and Carlos made himself visible and flashed the OK sign with his thumb and forefinger. He then lifted his index finger, pointed it downward, and rotated it in a circle, indicating that one person was moving around the compound.

Gary signaled back that he understood. He grabbed a bottle of water and two energy bars and settled down for a less-than-satisfying breakfast. A few minutes later, he heard a click. He looked up, and Carlos signaled that three people were in the compound.

Through his binoculars, Carlos saw one man standing near two sheds, while two other people walked in tandem to a smaller building. As their backs were to him, he didn't recognize them.

After a few minutes, the two figures returned to the sheds. This time, he saw faces—one person was a stranger, but the other was Marsha!

The process repeated, and on the second round trip, he saw Ben.

They're being taken to an outhouse one at a time, Carlos concluded.

He had to tell Gary. He clicked the radio, and Gary immediately looked up. He saw Carlos furiously flashing the OK sign with both hands.

He sees them! Gary thought.

Carlos had thought long and hard about this moment and how to signal Tom. Taking Tom's cue, he had devised a solution, but he didn't have much time. A couple of minutes had passed since Marsha and Ben had been returned to the shed.

He reached into the daypack and pulled out his iPod and speaker. He scrolled through the directory until he highlighted a particular audio file. He played it once, on low, to calibrate against the noise level of the forest. *Don't want to be too obvious,* he thought.

Then he waited. The guard escorted an older man from the second shed.

Vincent, Carlos thought.

Then another. *Jack.*

Finally, a fifth person was taken out.

Has to be Tom.

Carlos waited until Tom was on his way back from the latrine. When he was sure it was Tom, he hit the "play" button.

A call emanated from the small speaker. It wasn't much different from the hundreds of other calls that could be heard, except this species of bowerbird was found only on the east coast of Australia eight thousand miles away.

With the speaker between his knees and the iPod on his lap, his hands were free to steady the binoculars. Carlos stared intently into Tom's face for any sign of recognition. Nothing.

He hit "play" again. Nothing. And again. This time, Carlos saw Tom's eyes look ever so slightly skyward.

Then, a few seconds later, confirmation: a smile.

***

Understanding Carlos's signal, Gary wondered, *What do we do now? It's like the dog finally caught the car. We can't storm the camp—we have no weapons, but they do. We don't even know how many men they have.*

While preparing for the trip, they had paid special attention to ensure their clothing and equipment would be that of a birding group. This didn't prove difficult for Carlos because that was all he had, but back in Michigan, Gary hadn't packed for a birding trip, and he had to scramble to beg, borrow, and steal—but mostly buy—what he needed from other guests at the lodge. Most critically, they had taken no real weapons of any kind—only pocketknives, a multitool, and one machete.

Malin and Maria had spread the excuse that Gary's luggage had been lost and he was desperate to get into the field with his tour. It worked. By the following morning, he had what he needed. Most of it was well worn, adding authenticity. Fortunately, the lodge had a selection of rubber boots because there was almost zero chance of finding size twelves in the area. Even the duffel bags had been salvaged from the lodge's lost-and-found bin—again, worn and without identification. Gary had written his "new" name and address on them with a permanent marker and then abraded the information with a sandstone knife hone to age it. This had proved particularly convincing to the housekeeping maid at Hotel Chilimaco when she had searched the room while

Gary and Carlos were out with Santos. Her observations had been duly noted to the desk clerk and reported up the chain later that evening.

***

Carlos saw some of the men were in villagers' clothing, while others wore military fatigues. Domingo's brigade was a disparate group.

Most had been recruited from the slums of Bogotá and Cali and saw this as a way into the money and life that the cartels offered. At least in the past decade, few had any political alliance to the revolutionary politics of FARC. Most just wanted into the drug trade for the money. Cash, not ideology, motivated them.

A handful of old revolutionaries who saw themselves as soldiers and dressed as such remained. These men disdained the close relationship with the cartels but knew money was necessary to further their political goals. Castro and Che had never had to rely on drug money, but that was a different time, when the USSR was more generous. Now it was adapt or die. So the old guard did their job and tolerated those less dedicated to the cause while hoping for their eventual conversion.

Most of the new recruits were ill suited to jungle life. They didn't know the forest; they knew the streets, where their weapons of choice were blades because they couldn't afford guns. Although they were furnished with AK-47s, their training on the care, the handling, and most important, the firing was limited. After a few months in the jungle, most longed to return to the teeming streets. To bolster unit cohesion, the comandante was lenient with his leave policy, for he too needed his nights away.

Loyalty was typically achieved through a combination of bribery and intimidation. The old guard was the most reliable, followed by the recruits from the city. The least committed were the local villagers indentured by guns or money. However, they were the ones who knew the jungle, where to walk, where to hide, what to eat, and when something was out of place. They were the least trusted, were seldom armed, and made up the bulk of the working crews. As often as not, they sneaked out in the middle of the night to return home. Not your typical guerrilla fighters.

Fortunately for the hostages, the camp guards were city boys who didn't know a parakeet from a marmoset. Their tracking and hunting skills were nonexistent. Seldom did they stray from any trail, afraid of what they might encounter. At least they could feed and guard a few unarmed hostages while the more dedicated old guard and more skillful locals tended to the important tasks of guarding and processing the drugs.

***

Tom had been returned to the shed. He waited until he thought the guard had moved on and then told Jack and Vincent what he'd heard.

"What does it mean?" Vincent asked.

"First, my message over the phone got through. Second, someone who knows me played that call."

Thinking of all the guides at Natura Sucumbios, he knew the only logical candidate, the one most intrigued by the birds from Tom's homeland. He was sure. "It has to be Carlos," he said with a wide grin.

"You think he brought help? Do you think the police or army are on the way?" Vincent asked.

"I don't know, but let's prepare just in case," Tom said.

"What about Ben and Marsha?" Jack asked, finally exhibiting some interest in their situation.

"I think it's time we test our work," Tom said. "But first we need to let Carlos know where we are."

***

Carlos stayed in the tree for several hours. He regretted not having brought more water, but he could only carry so much. At least he had found a branch that was well shaded. Still it was hot, and he was sweating.

He took note of the activity within the compound, which wasn't much, only a few men walking across the open area. He wasn't sure how many men he had seen in total, maybe five. A guard no longer was posted at the back gate. He figured the kidnappers felt more confident during the day. In fact, he had seen only one man with a firearm, and that had been the guard at the back gate. He saw no activity at or beyond the front gate.

***

The hostages weren't sure how closely they were guarded at night. During their trips to the latrine, one guard would lead them, while another stayed at the shed. In the morning, a single guard usually opened the shed, and the cook brought in food. Tom figured only one man guarded the camp at night.

Earlier, they had decided to test his hypothesis. Late one night, Vincent knocked on the door to signal the guard. After less than a minute, the door opened slightly, and a flashlight caught Vincent in its beam. Vincent motioned that he needed to use the latrine. The guard pointed to the night bucket. Vincent shook his head, pointed to the latrine, and doubled over with his arms around his abdomen. The guard, sympathetic to the old man's plight, nodded and allowed Vincent to exit. The guard closed and secured the door before leading Vincent to the outhouse.

Vincent, with just a glimmer of light from the flashlight, took note that the compound was empty. No one else was outside, and no second guard was posted at the other shed. He entered the latrine, made a few gratuitous noises to dramatize his condition, waited a couple of minutes, and then stepped outside to be led back. He couldn't see whether either gate was guarded, but he assumed that if they were, it was from the outside.

He entered the shed and thanked the guard, who closed and locked the door.

From the moment Vincent had left the shed, Tom had pressed his ear tightly against the rear wall to detect any sounds at the back of the compound. He also slowly counted the seconds, since they no longer could rely on their watches, which had been confiscated.

Tom, Vincent, and Jack had decided to defer discussion of this newly acquired intelligence until the next morning, when noise from the camp would drown out their conversation.

***

The next morning, the hostages were brought breakfast and allowed a trip to the latrine in the same sequence as the previous morning. Just before dawn, Carlos had reclimbed the fig after a needed respite on the ground from the confined limb. This time, he noted that Jack and Vincent also looked in his direction and made big smiles as they exited the latrine—the message had gotten through.

When Tom appeared, Carlos repeated the bowerbird call. This time, Tom signaled back. As he walked back slowly, he casually opened and closed his left fist six times. He stopped and repeated the six clenches, followed by six more. Although he was using his binoculars, Carlos didn't notice right away, but when he did, he counted.

What's he trying to say? he wondered.

***

Carlos remained in the tree until dark. He scrambled down the vines for what he hoped would be the last time, careful to remain hidden from the compound.

Gary closely monitored his progress, keeping a sharp eye out for any activity along the trail. It had been a long and tedious lookout. He tried to remain quiet and confined to his blind, but the heat and insects were maddening, and he moved about more than he should have.

He greeted Carlos with a water bottle, and they moved a safe distance from the tree, deeper into the forest.

Carlos briefed Gary on the day's activity and his assessment of the number of men in the camp. "I sure didn't see anyone doing any farming activities or anything other than an occasional patrol around the camp and to escort the group," he said.

He then told Gary about Tom's signal.

"Six, huh? Not eighteen?"

"No, I think he was just repeating the six," Carlos said.

"But six what? Six guards?"

"Maybe, but how would he know since he's locked in the shed?"

"Six days? No, that means nothing to me," Gary said. "Six o'clock? What would that mean? They're led somewhere at that time, maybe to eat?"

"Could be, but he knows I would see that," Carlos said.

"Maybe it's an alphabetic signal. You know, the sixth letter, F, three times. F-F-F," Gary speculated.

"Maybe he's telling us six o'clock but in terms of direction. If twelve o'clock is north, six could be south," Carlos offered. "Maybe it's the camp. Twelve is the front, and six is the back."

"Yeah, like I've got your six covered, meaning I've got your back."

"Does he mean the whole camp? I don't think he's had enough freedom to know the whole camp," Carlos said.

"But what he does know is his shed. Maybe he means the back of the shed. But why the left hand? Is Tom left-handed?"

"No. Maybe he means the left building or the back of the left building."

"That makes sense, but what about it?"

"Maybe they're working on their own plan?" Carlos suggested.

***

Under the cover of night, Gary and Carlos moved slowly and quietly toward the rear gate with all eyes focused on the guard. Earlier, through binoculars, Gary had seen the guard take a key from his pocket to unlock the gate. He told Carlos he couldn't tell whether the gate had been relocked, but he assumed it had been. This complicated their plan. Now Carlos might have to climb over the gate, and while there was no barbed wire, it would certainly make more noise than he wanted. There was only one way to find out.

Carlos waited until the guard walked past and had his back to them. He darted from the brush, crossed the fifty feet to the gate, and then pressed himself tightly against it. He had to act fast. He would be in plain sight once the guard turned to walk back.

He grabbed for the lock. It was open. He quickly and quietly removed it, lifted the handle, pushed the gate open, and entered the compound. He then took a thumb full of dirt and pressed it into the lock case so the shackle couldn't be engaged. He reached his hand through the fence mesh to replace the lock and sprinted silently to the sheds.

Reaching the rear of the left shed, Carlos gently tapped on a board. He pulled his iPod from his daypack, played a muffled call of the bowerbird, and waited for a response.

It didn't take long. He heard a slight creak as one of the wallboards was pushed out two to three inches from the bottom of the shed. He crept closer and saw a familiar face through the crack.

"Glad you could make it," Tom said in a faint whisper.

"I've been a little busy," Carlos replied.

"Can you get us out?"

"Maybe, but I don't know if there are any other guards."

"Stay here, and be very quiet for the next few minutes. We have a plan of our own," Tom said.

The plank slowly moved back into place as the shoestring that was looped around the bottom of the board was pulled.

After several moments, Carlos heard a knock on the door of the shed. As he had a few nights before, the guard escorted Vincent to the latrine. Within seconds, the board, along with two others, was pushed out. Tom squirmed out and told Carlos to stay put as he moved to the front of the second shed.

Tom unclipped the hook, opened the door, and slipped in unseen. Having heard the tap code and prepared for something to happen, Ben and Marsha rose and quickly followed Tom from the shed. Tom closed the door and reattached the clasp, hoping no one would notice the vacant shed for several hours.

Jack helped Carlos into the shed and explained their next moves. "Vincent will be gone for another two minutes," he said.

Ben and Marsha appeared and crawled through the back of the shed. Only Tom remained outside. Jack instructed them to stay low and told them what to do in the next few minutes. With that, he positioned himself against the wall on one side of the door, while Carlos took the other side.

Then they waited.

They heard the metallic clink of the hasp being unlatched, followed by the opening of the door.

Their timing had to be perfect. And it was. As soon as Vincent crossed the threshold, Tom dashed from the side of the shed and shouldered the guard in the back, pushing him and Vincent through the door. Jack jumped from the side and wrapped his hands around the guard's mouth and eyes. But the guard, still on his feet, was able to swing the butt of the rifle squarely into Jack's right temple. He staggered and fell.

Carlos grabbed the AK-47 before he could swing it again, and Ben knocked the guard to the ground. Vincent shut the door and added his weight to the back of the struggling guard. With both arms tight against his back, Tom sitting on his legs, and Carlos twisting his head and neck nearly 180 degrees, the guard finally gave up.

Carlos saw Ben struggling to tie the guard's hands with a short shoelace. "Check my pack," he said.

Ben opened the pack and pulled out a roll of thin nylon cord.

"There's a knife in there, too," Carlos said.

Ben began with a couple of half hitches and a bowline to secure the guard's hands behind his back and then tied similar knots around his ankles. Marsha used her bandanna as a gag.

It was over in less than two minutes; six on one was a decided advantage.

Carlos patted the guard down and grabbed his radio, a pack of cigarettes, a lighter, a flashlight, and a pocketknife. "You should read the label, señor. These could endanger your health," he whispered to him. "Maybe we can use these. Now follow me," Carlos told the group, while heading for the eighteen-inch opening at the rear of the shed.

He stopped suddenly as he saw Jack thrash violently on the floor next to the guard. After several seconds, the seizure stopped, and Jack's eyes rolled back as he slipped into unconsciousness. Vincent knelt beside him and slapped him hard on the face to rouse him. He lifted an eyelid to find a large, nonreactive pupil.

Seeing no chest movement, Vincent placed his ear against Jack's sternum. He heard nothing. He slammed his fist hard into Jack's chest and blew three quick breaths into his mouth. He began to pump his chest but stopped when a thin rivulet of blood ran from Jack's right ear. Vincent listened again.

"He's dead," was all he could say.

"Oh, my God. This can't be happening," Marsha said, her eyes filling with tears.

"What should we do?" Ben asked.

"There's nothing we can do," Vincent replied.

In an instant, Tom was on top of the guard. His hands gripped his throat, crushing his larynx. All the pent-up anger, degradation, and fear exploded in an adrenaline-fueled rage at the sight of his dead companion. He had a target. *Now who's the victim?* he thought. Payback. To the edge of sanity.

Gagged, the guard couldn't scream, but his eyes bulged in panic. He couldn't fight back or defend himself.

With all the force he could muster, Ben lowered his shoulder and slammed into Tom's chest. Now there were four men on the floor—one dead, the others writhing for advantage.

Ben was followed a second later by Vincent. "Stop! You can't do this. We're making too much noise," he pleaded.

Tom eased his grip on the guard's throat. Then he grabbed him by the hair and slammed his head as hard as he could against the floor. "You fucking bastard. Look at what you did," he said as he lifted himself from his knees and took his first breath in nearly a minute.

"We don't have much time. We have to leave," Carlos ordered.

"What do we do with Jack?" Marsha sobbed.

"We have no choice but to leave him," Carlos said.

"What about *him*?" Vincent asked, pointing at the semiconscious guard.

"Let's put him out front in case someone comes around," Ben suggested.

Vincent and Carlos lifted the guard by his arms, and Ben lifted his legs. Marsha opened the door. They tied the guard to his chair with his back to the camp. To all but the most observant, he appeared to be guarding the sheds diligently.

Tom closed the door and secured the hasp as Marsha covered Jack's body with a blanket.

"Good-bye, my friend," she said, gently stroking his forehead.

"This way," Carlos instructed, and they all quickly exited through the opening in the back wall.

***

Gary's task was to subdue the armed guard at the back gate—alone—and be silent in the process.

He had apprehended many suspects but usually with an armory at his disposal—in order of decreasing lethality: mace, Taser, nightstick, German shepherd, 9mm Glock, Remington 1100. But now, he had only a pocketknife and a club that was really a fallen branch. He scoured the area for something—anything—solid.

What he did have was the element of surprise and his bulk. He easily outweighed the patrolling guard by fifty pounds. But it had been a while since he had roiled the ground with a less-than-compliant combatant. And anyway, fists were among the worst options. Not only was he likely to stun the guard only momentarily, but he also could just as easily break bones in his hands, and then who would be vulnerable?

He waited, watched, and timed the guard's paces. Just then, Gary saw Carlos at the gate. Carlos, in turn, saw the guard still patrolling.

Gary had waited long enough, and he timed his sprint almost perfectly. He jumped the guard from behind and wrapped his legs around the man's torso, pinning his arms against his chest, while his hands covered his mouth. The guard tried mightily to repel his assailant but without success.

Gary whispered in his ear, "Stop struggling." He repeated it in Spanish, as Carlos had taught him. He then said, "Look at your chest. If you don't quiet down, you're dead."

The guard looked down and saw a small red laser spot slowly circling his chest.

"Move again, and my man will shoot," Gary said.

The guard froze. Gary jerked the man's head back so violently that he lost his balance and fell to the ground with Gary breaking his fall.

Carlos put away the laser pointer and bolted through the gate. He dropped his full weight, such as it was, on the guard, partially pinning his right arm. He wrested the man's AK-47 free so he couldn't fire a shot and arouse the camp.

The others followed Carlos, and in moments, they dragged the guard to a concealed spot where Ben made magic with the nylon cord.

"Ever try calf roping?" Gary whispered.

Carlos removed the guard's radio but found nothing else, not even a smoke.

Marsha immediately leaped for Gary and gave him a hug that far exceeded the reach of her arms.

"I thought I'd never see you again," she said, with tears streaming. Ben joined in, and they held one another tightly.

"Everyone, this is Gary, our oldest son," Ben whispered with obvious pride. "How did you find us?" he asked, wiping his eyes too.

Gary looked at Carlos. "There's your answer," he said, wondering how he ever could have had any doubt about him.

All eyes turned to Carlos, who, in his usual understated manner, said, "We're not out of here yet. Let's get going."

They tied the guard to a tree, not bothering to stage him like the other guard, since no one would be able to see him from a distance inside the compound. Using the guard's belt and a piece of cloth ripped from his shirt, Martha made another gag.

They exited through the gate and walked a few hundred feet from the compound until Gary stopped. He looked around, confused. "Wait. We're missing someone," he said.

"I'm afraid the guard killed Jack," Vincent replied. "He struck him with his rifle during the struggle."

Knowing they didn't have time to elaborate, Carlos said, "Gary, you take Marsha and Vincent to our boat, and get downstream to where we hid the motor. Tom and Ben can help me at the landing."

Gary shouldered one AK-47. Carlos had the other.

"Do either of you know how this works?" Carlos asked Tom and Ben.

"Let me have it," Ben replied.

***

Gary and his team headed down the trail until they reached the makeshift path he had scouted the day before while Carlos was tree bound. To ensure he would find it at night, he had paced it accurately. He also had left a few signs along the trail, mostly branches, which to the uninitiated would look like they had just fallen on the path.

When they reached the fourth marker, Gary led them to the nearly invisible path. He stopped and turned to Marsha. "Mom, can you see the path we made yesterday?" He shined the light to show the bent grasses and footprints.

"Yes," Marsha replied.

"Take this light, and you and Vincent go ahead. You'll have to crawl through some brush and under some branches, but it isn't that far to the river. I'll be right behind you, trying to cover our tracks."

Marsha and Vincent headed down the trail.

Gary put on his headlamp and kicked up the laid-over vegetation at the intersection of the trail and path. He did that for about thirty feet until the path turned, where it couldn't be seen from the main trail during the day. He then pulled out what remained of the roll of nylon cord and strung it across the path. He did this at several locations, varying the height from ankle to neck level.

Won't be much use after dawn, but it could help until then, Gary thought of his trip wires.

***

During his time in the canopy, Carlos had thought hard about the rescue; it was risky but necessary.

There was no way to get all seven in the boat—now six—but that hadn't been their plan originally. It was just to locate them and go to the authorities. But something in the compound had raised the hairs on the back of his neck. He knew they had to try the rescue themselves because help wouldn't be coming—at least not from the police, whose pickup truck had left the camp midday. Another of the comandante's minions.

"Where are we heading?" Tom asked.

Carlos took out the GPS and pointed to the red circle that depicted the location of the ferry crossing. "This is where the kidnappers cross the river with the trucks and where they keep their boats. I thought maybe we could borrow one," he said, laughing quietly.

He figured that the easiest way out and, the best hidden, would be along the bank and maybe in the river itself. So, like Gary's group, but farther upstream, they were heading off the trail to the river.

As they slogged through chest-high grasses and reeds, sometimes sinking up to their calves in mud, Carlos was glad to be with Tom and Ben. Both men were used to hiking through such conditions and wouldn't slow him down.

He used his headlamp sparingly, only illuminating the area ahead ten to fifteen feet at a time. When they reached the river, Carlos explained to Ben and Tom that their captors had a boat patrolling the waters. "We have only a short time," he warned.

He and Tom worked their way up the bank to the ferry, leaving Ben to deal with the boats hauled out on the bank.

The steel cable that spanned the seventy-five-foot-wide river looped through large pulleys that were secured to massive trees on each bank. *There's no way to cut the cable,* Carlos thought, needing to figure out another way to disable it, even for just a few minutes to give them valuable lead time. He reckoned that the pulley was the most vulnerable point. He shimmied up the tree for a closer look. The pulley was secured by another steel cable girding the tree trunk. *Can't cut that cable either.*

He examined the pulley. The sheave—the center wheel around which the cable was wound—was on an axle that freely turned on bearings. One side of the pulley housing was solid, but the other was open. The sheave was held in place on the axle by a large washer and cotter pin through the axle.

Carlos pulled out his multitool and, using the needle-nose pliers, straightened the cotter pin. He tried to pull the pin out of the axle shaft to free the sheave, but the tension was too tight, and he couldn't get a firm grip. He signaled to Tom, who climbed the tree. Carlos motioned for him to pull on the cable to release tension. He did, but because of the weight, the cable barely moved. They tried it again, but the pin was too tight. Instead of trying to pull the pin through the eye with the pliers, this time, he tried to push it through from the bottom using the flat side of a knife blade.

Seeing what Carlos was attempting, Tom motioned for him to stop. He spat on the pin, thoroughly wetting it. He grabbed the cable, and Carlos pushed his knife blade, using all the strength he could muster. Finally, there was a little movement. Tom pulled again. After four more attempts, the pin was free.

With both of them pulling, the pulley separated, and the cable fell to the ground. Tom climbed down, grabbed the fallen sheave, and heaved it as far as he could into the river. *Even if they find it,* he thought, *it would take hours to reassemble the pulley.* For one last bit of insurance, he threw the cotter pin, which made a barely noticeable splash midstream.

***

Two boats rested on the bank, tied off to trees. Ben noticed plenty of slack in the lines to allow for the rise and fall of the river during the rainy season. Both were powered by outboards, the larger of which had a key ignition but no key; fortunately, the other had a pull-cord starter. Both had fuel tanks and oars but not much else.

Even though he preferred the larger, faster boat, Ben had no way to start it. *Sorry, old girl. You look like you'd be a hell of a ride,* he thought as he began his work.

He removed the engine cowling from the larger motor and yanked out the spark-plug wire. He then replaced the cowl. He thought about cutting the fuel line, but that would be too obvious. Instead, he disconnected the line at the engine and crammed river mud into the fuel-intake fitting. Then, with some effort, he reattached the fuel line. Next, he grabbed the fuel tank, removed the filler cap, and submerged the tank in the river, topping it with about two gallons of water. He screwed the cap back on and placed the tank back into the boat. He took both oars and put them in the smaller boat.

Carlos heard it first and alerted Tom. "Listen. A boat is coming."

They signaled Ben, who joined them next to the tree with the cables.

"Get into the trees fast," Carlos commanded.

As the boat approached the ferry landing and slowed, the driver shined his spotlight and scanned the shoreline. It took him a few seconds to register that something was wrong, but it was dark and the light of the spotlight was limited. Then he saw it—or actually, didn't see it.

The cable's down, he told himself.

The cable had broken before; it was usually because of a heavy load, but he noticed that the ferry was still on the landing. He shined his light on the cable ends. Nothing unusual across the river. Then he saw the disassembled pulley hanging from the tree.

How did that break? he wondered. *I'd better get someone on it.*

He maneuvered the patrol boat next to the two tied-up boats and got out. He went over to the tree and inspected the pulley in the better light. *That's good. The cable is still on the bank,* he thought. Then he grabbed a length of line from his boat and tied the loose end of the steel cable to the tree so it wouldn't sink into the river.

That done, he thought about radioing the camp, but it was about time to change guards. He decided to return to the camp, wake his replacement, and alert the mechanic about the cable. He headed up the road from the landing.

Seizing the opportunity, Tom, Carlos, and Ben ran from their cover in the trees to the small boat with the pull-cord starter and pushed off—but not before Carlos had loosened the mounts on the guard's patrol boat motor and dropped it into the river.

"A little payback," he said with a laugh.

Three paddles silently plied the river.

***

It was half an hour before the mechanic and the relief guard got down to the river—not exactly the military precision or dedication the comandante tried to instill. But they were the bottom-feeders—the "harvestable surplus" that wouldn't be missed from the population, which was why they'd been assigned to such a low-priority camp. All the important men had returned to the headquarters after the ransom money had arrived. The six remaining men could leave in a few days after the hostages were dropped off. In the meantime, they alternated in twelve-hour shifts guarding the hostages.

It was a few minutes before they recognized the sabotage. The relief guard first noticed a boat was missing and then a motor. *The cable couldn't be an accident. Pulleys don't just fall apart,* he thought. *What's happening?*

"Someone's been here!" he shouted to the mechanic and pulled out his radio.

"Jaime, Jaime. Over," Pedro called to the guard stationed at the sheds.

In possession of Jaime's radio, Carlos responded, "*Sí*," as he pressed the squelch button to distort his voice.

"Are the hostages secure? We've had an intrusion at the landing. One boat is missing, one motor gone, and the cable is down!" he shouted.

"All is well here. I just checked them. You stay there, and I will send help."

"That should buy us a little time," Tom mused.

***

Gary, Marsha, and Vincent had made it to the boat and dragged it into the water.

They had made good time in the predawn hours, aided by the fact that the path was still fresh. Gary worried that his mother and Vincent would slow them, but his concern was unmerited; their pace was crisp and fluid. Many years of slogging through fields, forests, and marshes had its dividends. However, the three made quick work of the water Gary had cached in the duffel. With any luck, he figured, they'd be able to resupply downriver.

They pushed off with Vincent and Gary manning the paddles. They had a ways to go to retrieve the motor, but they were moving with the current. Fortunately, Carlos had recorded the coordinates of the motor's location in the GPS. Unfortunately, Carlos had the GPS.

I'll call him to arrange a rendezvous, Gary thought.

"We had to risk getting you out. We didn't know if they planned to release you or drag this out for more money, and when Carlos saw the police are in the camp…well—how are you all doing?" Gary asked.

"We're fine, except for Jack," Vincent said. "But things started to get bad when the Colombians took us."

"What I want to know is how you met Carlos," Marsha said.

"Carlos has been incredible," Gary told her. He went on to explain his meetings with the colonel at the lodge, the plan Carlos had hatched after he had figured out where they were being held, their days on the river, and how they had ultimately pinned down the location of the camp. "These weren't the guys who originally took you?" he asked.

Vincent told him they had been apprehended by what seemed to be three Ecuadoreans and then taken by boat—blindfolded and bound—to an airstrip. A second group of men, paramilitary types, had taken over for the Ecuadoreans. This group had taken them by boat and then by truck to the compound.

"I don't think they thought much of each other," Vincent explained. "The groups barely spoke to each other, and the Ecuadoreans left as fast as they could."

A little less confused about events but still anxious about their situation, Gary said, "Look, we're not in the clear. We may be ahead of them, and they can't pursue us right now. But all they have to do is radio ahead. So remain on alert. We'll find a place up ahead to hide until Carlos can catch up and take us to the motor."

They paddled for a while before Gary pulled off next to a heavily vegetated section of bank, where they hid behind a screen of overhanging branches and vines.

"We'll wait here for Carlos," he said. "I won't be able to find the motor without the GPS." He pulled out his cell phone. Still no service. He grabbed for the FRS and, using the code they'd used earlier, tried to contact the other boat.

Carlos heard the clicks coming from his pocket and pulled out his radio. Fortunately, they hadn't started the motor for fear of making too much noise. "It's Gary calling. They must be close."

He switched the radio to channel 11-22 and called Gary.

"Tanager-one. Over," Carlos said.

"This is Tanager-two. Go ahead. We will wait for you from our current position."

"*Claro.* Will be there shortly."

***

With hundreds of possible combinations from fourteen channels and thirty-eight privacy codes, one might think there was little chance of their transmission on channel 11-22 being intercepted, particularly since the radios had such a limited range. But with a good scanner, one could instantly detect and record FRS frequencies. The comandante's intelligence team had scanners on frequencies used by the police, immigration control, boatmen along the rivers, and air traffic controllers. Only military channels and proprietary frequencies used by the telecommunications companies couldn't be monitored. What prompted the concern of the radio operator was that this transmission was in English. He would report it later to the comandante.

***

Unlike the short-range FRS radios used by birders, the comandante's men used high-powered General Mobile Radio Service (GMRS) radios. Years earlier, before the construction of cell towers, there was no communication among the comandante's far-flung camps other than word of mouth. Walkie-talkies were limited to a range of a few miles. To remedy this, and to give his men a heads-up when raids were expected, the comandante had set up a series of stationary and mobile repeater stations at strategic locations. Now his radios had effective ranges of twenty to thirty miles, well within the reach of the comandante's headquarters. But there was no security, so anyone with a receiver could overhear conversations. So they implemented a strict code system, to which Jaime and the others at the compound often failed to adhere.

When the men at the landing tried again to hail Jaime, Carlos and Gary didn't respond on Jaime's radio. The men at the landing then radioed the other guard. Nothing. Finally, they radioed the house, figuring by then they'd been alerted.

"Rico, Rico, can you read me? Over!" the relief guard shouted into his radio.

Rico, who had returned from his shift patrolling the river, was on his cot when he heard the radio from the other room. Trying to decide whether to ignore or respond, he figured they probably just needed help with the cable, but he was too tired to help them after a night on patrol.

"What is it?" Rico snapped.

"No one has come down yet," Pedro responded.

"What do you mean?"

"I called Jaime and told him someone had been at the ferry landing and had taken a boat and also taken a motor from another. And it looks like they took down the cable."

"What? Who was supposed to go down there?"

"Jaime was going to send someone. He said the hostages were secure."

"He didn't tell me. I'll get right back to you."

"I've heard that before," Pedro mocked.

Rico put down the radio and ran from the main house to the sheds. From a distance, in the dim light, he saw Jaime sitting on guard. It wasn't until he got closer that he saw that Jaime's chest and legs were tied to the chair.

The adrenaline kicked in as Rico sprinted the rest of the distance in seconds, passing right by Jaime, directly to the sheds. He opened the first one. Empty. Then the second. He saw Jack's body and a gaping hole in the back wall.

He ran full speed to the back gate. No guard. He turned and headed back to Jaime. He removed the gag from Jaime's mouth and asked what had happened as he pulled out a knife and cut the restraints.

Because of the damage Tom had inflicted upon his throat, Jaime explained in a barely audible, raspy whisper, "I was jumped from behind and wrestled down by at least seven people, two I'd never seen before."

"Your radio and rifle—" Rico started.

"They took them."

"What about Ortega?" Rico asked of the other guard.

"I never saw him."

Rico got on the radio and called Pedro back at the landing. "They're gone!" he informed him. "Someone came in and tied up Jaime, and we can't find Ortega."

"But I talked to Jaime on the radio," Pedro said.

"*Estúpido*, it was one of them! They have Jaime's radio and rifle," Rico shouted. "Come back to camp, but leave the mechanic there to see if he can fix the cable."

"*Claro*" was the last thing Rico heard from Pedro as he scrambled to assemble anyone remaining in the compound.

Rico began to understand his situation. They had no boat. They had trucks but no way to cross the river. The only thing he could do was radio Comandante Flores to send help. That was a call he didn't want to make. Maybe the comandante wouldn't care since he already had the money and was going to release the hostages anyway. But to have them escape, worse yet, to have someone enter the compound and rescue them—no, there would be a price to pay. He just didn't know how much or by whom.

Sooner or later, he's going to know, Rico told himself.

Believing that bad news didn't get any better with age, he reluctantly radioed the comandante.

CHAPTER THIRTY-FIVE

Monday, FARC Headquarters

The comandante sat in the lumber mill that served as his headquarters on the Río Putumayo in the small community of San Gabriel ten miles northeast of Puerto Asís. "They what?" came his incredulous response. His anger swelled as Rico elaborated.

What a bunch of utter incompetents! he thought. He knew these weren't the best of his men, but hell, allowing unarmed, helpless civilians to escape was too much. And who had found the camp? He made a mental note to speak to his intelligence chief about who might have been operating in the area. He certainly had spread enough money around to collect that information.

Rico tried to remain calm as he related the events of the past few hours, but now, he and the others were in for it. He was fighting the urge to take off like the hostages. But he knew, sooner or later, he would have to deal with the comandante.

"Which way did they go?" Comandante Flores asked.

"I think downriver because a boat is missing."

"How would all of them get into one boat?"

"They must have brought their own boat to get here."

"Could they not have come by truck, crossed the river by raft or canoe, gotten the hostages, and returned across the river with our boat to the truck?"

"Yes, Comandante, but we didn't see any boats on the other bank."

"They could have hidden them. Send someone across and let me know what you find. In the meantime, try to see which way they went to the river after they left the camp. And find Ortega. Maybe he saw something."

"Yes, sir," Rico said. "But could you send a boat so we can get out in case the police come?"

"Tell me what you find. Then maybe we'll get you out!" the comandante shouted as he slammed the microphone down, knowing full well the police wouldn't raid the camp and jeopardize its steady flow of income. He worried about the Colombian Army, but he hadn't heard that they were working in the area. But maybe his intelligence wasn't as thorough as he'd been led to believe.

Comandante Flores was enraged, but he didn't know precisely why. He had no use for the hostages. He already had the money. It hadn't even been his plan; he was merely accommodating the need of an associate. And it seemed they had held the hostages long enough.

So why his anger? He wondered how this ragtag group could come into his territory and undertake such an operation. Perhaps his control in the area was waning. Certainly, his network hadn't reported any suspicious activity. Maybe it was an inside job. Were his men paid off, unhappy with their share? One of his camps had been compromised, but he had many more, and this one was almost inconsequential. He blamed himself for not being there. He had lost his focus. He had his mind on other things. He had succumbed to her temptation.

They had met months ago. It was an early May morning in the plaza at the Fiesta Aniversário, at a celebration of the founding of Puerto Asís.

Señora Camilla Martinez, the wife of a very successful businessman, was shocked and dismayed when she learned the comandante's true identity. But something about him excited her—maybe his charm or the lure of the illicit.

The comandante was instantly captivated by the elegant raven-haired beauty, her self-assuredness, her grace, her poise. It wasn't long before initial attraction led to a furtive, passionate affair. They stole the moments they could, those days when Señor Martinez was away on business—a business that the señora thought was suspicious.

The comandante waited impatiently, sometimes days on end, for her call and their short but torrid nights together. When they parted, the comandante longed for the next time. He thought of her constantly and desperately wanted to call just to hear her voice, but he knew he couldn't. Never had he felt such a deep love; his fear of abandonment would not permit it. Now this love consumed him. His heart ached at their separation. He agonized until the next call. He could think of nothing else. He even envisioned a new life, an escape from the jungle. He would take her anywhere she wanted. Suddenly, the very reason for his life—everything he had worked so hard for—meant very little. He couldn't concentrate on his work, and his men could see his distraction. He had taken his eye off the ball, and this was what had happened. He knew he had to focus now. He had to exorcise the señora from his thoughts—at least for a few more days.

***

Comandante Flores now had to contact Quito and inform them that the hostages were loose. He didn't relish the thought of failure, of being ridiculed. It was his job to ridicule others. What was it he once had heard someone say? "I don't get ulcers. I give them!" But he knew it was coming and, more important, deserved. In his line of work, once you failed, your reputation was lost. Those who once feared or respected you did neither.

I haven't failed yet, he thought. Not if he recaptured the hostages only to release them on his schedule. Even better, if he remedied the transgression, he surely deserved to reopen negotiations—and possibly with two additional hostages.

Maybe I will wait a day before calling Quito, he thought.

"Sergeant, get in here!" the comandante shouted.

CHAPTER THIRTY-SIX

Monday, FARC Camp

It took fifteen minutes to find the bound and gagged Ortega. As soon as the gag was released, he was peppered with questions. Dazed from his ordeal, Ortega could only say he saw the hostages and maybe two strangers, but he was sure there were others out there. They'd had a sniper scope on him, after all. They left down the trail, but he wasn't sure how long ago. They took his rifle and one clip, but more important, they got his radio.

"Nobody use their radios," Rico ordered the men at the camp. "They can hear everything we say."

He communicated the latest bad news to the comandante.

***

Carlos started the pirated boat on the third pull after priming the engine. It had been light for a short time, so any chance for stealth was lost. Speed and distance were their best hopes now.

"Keep watch for Gary's boat!" he shouted over the engine's roar.

They found the other boat and towed it until they reached the location of the hidden outboard motor and fuel tanks. Within minutes, both boats were under power and heading downstream. Unlike the Río Guamuez, the tributary had very little traffic, and the two boats filled with gringos occasioned long stares and second looks from passing boats and people standing along the bank. They would blend in much better in the larger river just miles ahead. It was a race; they weren't sure if they were being pursued, but they assumed the worst.

But it wasn't so much the threat from behind that concerned Carlos as what might lie ahead. When they reached Puerto Asís, they would have to decide whether to continue downstream or take the chance of flying out. The latter was definitely preferred, even if they had to charter a plane. But it also meant they would have to identify themselves, and their lack of passports or other identification could raise questions and delay their departure. But to make it back to Lago Agrio by boat would take many more hours, and they'd have to stop at the port for fuel, which would expose them.

Carlos pulled out his cell phone but still had no service. *We have a ways to go before we're closer to the cell towers. Might as well enjoy the ride,* he thought, as he watched the sharp bow cleave the deep-green water into a frothy foam.

They made it to the confluence without incident and merged onto the Río Guamuez.

Only a few hours, Carlos thought, briefly questioning his judgment to travel by day rather than holing up until night. But they needed to refuel and the municipal wharf in Puerto Asís was closed at night. The line of fishermen queued early in the afternoon to fill up, anticipating the morning crowd. *Better to be there midday,* he thought.

The two boats pulled off to the bank just upstream of the port. Carlos and Gary got into their boat and grabbed the tank from the purloined craft.

While the others stayed back, hidden, Carlos and Gary motored into the port to resupply but not before one more attempt to call Colonel Hernandez.

***

The comandante dispatched a crew to dispatch a crew. Rico and the other men stood at the ferry landing when the boat the comandante had sent arrived. The driver turned the boat toward the bank as the second crewman tossed a line to Rico. As the men were about to board, four quick, accurate bursts from a hidden Uzi by the comandante's HR department ended the personnel problem.

***

Roberto was in his customary spot at the Puerto Asís wharf when they pulled up.

"Good to see you again," Carlos said.

On this, their third encounter, Roberto finally recognized him. "Hello to you," Roberto said. "How was your trip? Did you find the birds you were searching for?"

"We did, but we're glad to be heading home. We just need a little fuel and food."

Roberto assisted as Carlos lifted the nearly empty tanks to him on the dock. He noticed the folding stock of the assault rifle barely sticking out under the large duffel on the bottom of the boat. He hadn't remembered seeing them with a weapon before.

They refueled, grabbed a few provisions at the bodega, and left the marina, heading downstream. After a few minutes, they reversed course, hugging the opposite bank, to meet up with their friends.

CHAPTER THIRTY-SEVEN

Monday, FARC Headquarters

Roberto's call was welcomed. In minutes, two boats shoved off from a concealed location near the comandante's headquarters north of Puerto Asís. These were boats built for speed. Long and wide, they had minimal draft. They were strange crafts for these waters, with modifications seldom seen. All but the pilot's seat had been removed from the open-bow vessels. The propellers had been replaced by jet drives. The shiny red, yellow, and gray factory paint jobs were now a combination of matte green and black. The chrome wakeboard towers were wrapped in green camo tape and festooned with an array of running lights and spotlights, all in blackened housings. The dashboards were sparse and efficient. The radar units had been replaced by a second, more sensitive forward-sounding fathometer to accurately gauge depth to within about six inches. Engine gauges, a GPS, and radios completed the dashboard instrumentation.

These boats had been repurposed to haul cargo—to haul cargo fast and in very shallow waters. If they couldn't outrun police boats, they certainly could outmaneuver them in the shallow side streams.

Eight men, four to a boat, took their places, along with an impressive cache of hardware. While their quarry had a two-hour lead, their outboard motors would be good only for a sustained speed of fifteen miles per hour, which the fast boats could triple. They could make up the distance in a little more than an hour, if conditions were right.

***

With all the fuel tanks topped, the two boats headed south toward the Ecuadorian border, Gary and his parents in one boat and Carlos, Tom, and Vincent in the other.

Sitting in the bow and facing the stern, Tom saw them first. "Look!" he shouted, pointing behind the boat.

Carlos turned, as did Vincent, to see the boats fast approaching.

"This doesn't look good," Vincent said. "Could they be military?"

"I don't think so," replied Carlos. "The army uses gunboats, and these do not have turrets." He throttled up until he was even with Gary in the lead boat. "Look back. They're after us. Separate and try to evade!" Carlos yelled over the roar of both outboards.

The chase boats were now within a couple of thousand yards and closing fast. Gary jerked the tiller hard to the left and made a run for the right bank. He realized there was no outrunning the fast boats; their best chance was to flee on land. At least they could try to hide.

"Hold on!" he shouted to Marsha and Ben as he headed directly to the bank. At the last second, he cut the engine, but that didn't help, as the keel and the motor skeg ground deep into the soft mud. The abrupt stop threw them all forward, ejecting Ben from the boat. Ankle-deep in mud, he quickly rose and grabbed for Marsha's hand. With one hard pull, she was out of the boat and scrambling up the bank ahead of Ben. Gary jumped out, keeping himself between his parents and the dark-green boat that was quickly approaching. Almost as an afterthought, he reached into the bottom of the boat and grabbed the rifle.

He followed his parents up the bank. There was no way to run through the thick brush. Gary shouted for them to get in deep and hide. On their hands and knees, Ben and Marsha crawled, clawed, and snaked their way into the green mass, barely aware of the thorns and spines slicing their flesh.

Gary turned, engaged the bolt of the AK-47, and took careful aim. He could see the men in the boat now. These weren't police or soldiers; there were no uniforms. He sprayed a three-shot burst, which was too low and hit the bow near the water.

Immediately return fire from at least three weapons riddled the bank near Gary. He knew he was outgunned and leaped up the bank for cover.

The boat slowed, turned, and moved downstream, where one man jumped out. The boat circled and headed upstream, where a second man was dropped off.

Hemmed in on three sides, Gary and his parents could only scramble deeper into the jungle and hope to hide.

***

Carlos had headed to the opposite bank, weaving between smaller boats and canoes, barely eluding the second fast boat.

"There's no way to outrun that boat, and they're heavily armed!" Carlos shouted. "I think we have only one option." Because of the risk involved, he explained the plan to the others. "The only other thing to do is surrender."

They all agreed. Any option was worth a try.

Carlos turned sharply to the midchannel, allowing plenty of space between his boat and the others, and opened the throttle wide with a quick twist of his wrist. Although Carlos's boat was at full speed, the fast boat pulled alongside effortlessly. Carlos saw weapons drawn. He turned the tiller quickly away from the other boat, but the fast boat also made the course correction. Carlos repeated this a couple of times. Finally, he shouted, "Hold on!" He again turned away from the fast boat, but just as it corrected its course, Carlos jerked the small craft almost ninety degrees toward the fast boat and rammed it.

The combination of the force of the collision and the hydrodynamics of the small boat caused its bow to lurch up and over the side of the larger boat, balancing the small boat precariously on one gunwale and knocking the driver from his seat.

A little more speed, and I may have cleared the boat altogether, Carlos thought, as he tumbled backward into the violent wake, but not before he heard the loud screech of davits and rails being ripped away as the keel of the smaller boat plowed deeply through the fiberglass skin.

The fast boat was surging downstream at a high speed, unpiloted with a second boat dangling across its beam. The propeller of the small boat's outboard motor was fully out of the water and rotating at 6,500 revolutions per minute in a ghastly whine.

Tom and Vincent lay in a crumpled pile at the stern, where Carlos had been sitting. Tom recovered his balance first and leaped into the larger boat, his hands and arms flailing in an effort to neutralize one of the pursuers.

With Tom's exit, the center of gravity of the small boat shifted, and it quickly spun counterclockwise, slamming its propeller into the third pursuer at the rear of the larger boat. A rain of tissue and blood showered the others as the blades ground through the man's torso, not stopping until they smashed against the plywood-reinforced stern of the larger boat. The pursuer slumped dead as blood filled the hull.

The propeller seized when it struck the deck of the larger boat. The power of this momentum shift caused the bow of the smaller boat to rise and expose its keel to the full velocity of the larger boat's slipstream. As the small boat cartwheeled into the river, Vincent was catapulted from the deck. In the last second, he was able to grab the side rail of the larger boat with just one hand as the small boat vaulted over him. The turbulent current and erratic course of the careening boat forced Vincent's body underwater, where he took in what seemed like a gallon of water. Barely able to hold on and unable to breathe or raise his head from the river, Vincent pondered just letting go.

It won't be a peaceful death, he thought, *but it'll be over.* He had little fight left. *Just inhale. A lungful of water, and I'll gently sink to the bottom, and it'll be over. It would certainly be easier than holding on.* His hand and arm were locked in a painful cramp from his death grip on the rail. He knew he couldn't last much longer. His strength was quickly ebbing, and the force of the river was tumbling his body like a ragdoll. Besides, he was seventy-nine, and what did he have to look forward to? Not that many years ahead, and they could be filled with pain and suffering as age and disease exacted their toll. *Just let go,* he told himself. *Let go.*

In the same instant, he envisioned Jack's lifeless body on the floor of the shed, and anger enveloped him. *No way,* he thought. *There are scores to settle.* Then he thought about Betty, and as lonesome as it had been since she died, she would want him to live. And with that, he mustered his reserves. He kicked both legs with a fury to get his body out from under the water. He was just barely able to grasp the rail with his free hand. Almost spent, he rested for a moment. *Take some breaths,* he told himself. *Only a few more feet.* Vincent kicked again while lifting himself on his elbows over the gunwale. Exhausted from the final push, he fell into the boat.

He saw that Tom was engaged with the pursuers and looked around to see what he could do. He crawled to the console and grabbed the steering wheel. He centered the boat in the channel and pulled back on the throttle, slowing the boat. As he did, a pursuer broke free of Tom's grip, grabbed a 9mm pistol from his holster, and demanded that everyone freeze.

Vincent thrust the throttle forward in hopes of knocking the man back to the deck, but the man held tight and demanded that Vincent cut the engine. He complied.

Another pursuer regained his legs and grabbed his weapon. With an AK-47 trained on them, Tom and Vincent were ordered to the stern. With no choice, they sat next to the slumped corpse in a pool of blood on the deck.

"Where's Carlos?" Tom asked.

"I didn't see him," Vincent said. "He must have gone over."

They saw that the fast boat was also shy a driver.

***

In a classic pincher movement, the men from the first boat were slowly closing in on Gary, Ben, and Marsha. As hard as they tried to mask their movements, there was no way to advance through the tangle of vegetation silently. Eventually, after twenty minutes, and totally exhausted from the combination of heat, humidity, and exertion, the three were an easy capture.

They started back to the boat, where only the driver had remained.

With any luck, the other boat will be at the bank too, the lead man hoped. *That way, we can get the hostages back to camp.* He was certain the comandante would be very pleased. When they finally broke into the clearing by the bank, he saw the other boat was indeed there. But a stranger held a rifle to their driver's head.

At almost the same instant, he felt the hard steel of a barrel against his spine, a feeling shared at precisely that moment by his two colleagues.

"Drop your weapons," Major Sanchez ordered.

Comprehending the futility of their situation, the three men complied.

"I see you had cell service," Gary said.

Sanchez grinned. "Three bars. We'd been waiting at the mouth of the Río Putumayo when the colonel radioed. Thankfully, we had a fast boat."

Ben and Marsha were confused, but their initial fear about their second capture was eased as they sensed the rapport between Gary and this stranger, whom they first thought was another kidnapper. They were further relieved when they saw Tom and Vincent sitting in Sanchez's boat.

Gary saw their confused looks and said, "It's OK. These are friends."

"We have to get out of here," Sanchez said. "We created quite a commotion, and we still have a few miles to the border. We don't need an international incident with the Colombian government. Can you drive that?" Sanchez asked the group, pointing to one of the boats that had pursued them earlier.

"We'll figure it out," Gary said. Then he looked around. "Hey, where's Carlos?"

"We think he went over when we collided with the kidnappers' boat," Vincent replied. He explained the entire sequence of events, including how a boat that was hauling manioc upriver turned out to be Sanchez and four of his men, who quickly overpowered the pursuers before turning their attention to the other large boat on the opposite bank.

"We have to find Carlos," Gary insisted.

"We looked," Sanchez said. "We couldn't find him."

"We have to look again," Gary pleaded, his gut tightening in a strangling knot. "We have to."

"If we had time, we would. But we don't. We have to get out of here. We're here illegally. I'm in the military. Do you know how that could be construed in Bogotá?"

Resigned to the necessity of the moment, Gary merely nodded. *This isn't right,* he told himself. *I owe everything to him. I can't just abandon him. What about his family?* He was overwhelmed.

"Tie up those four and leave them here," Sanchez ordered. Pointing to the two leaders, he said, "We'll bring these two with us."

The four men were zip-tied with their hands behind their backs and placed into one of the small boats. The other two were similarly tied but placed in the undamaged large boat along with Tom and Vincent and two of Sanchez's men.

Gary, his parents, Sanchez, and two of his men boarded Sanchez's boat.

They towed the boat with the zip-tied men for a few minutes until it was in the main stream of the river.

With any luck, Sanchez thought, *maybe they'll drift into my waters.*

The throttles of both boats were opened full for the ride to Puerto Putumayo, the nearest port in Ecuador.

Gary sat pensively, searching the waters, hoping against hope for signs of his friend, knowing tears and sleepless nights were ahead.

CHAPTER THIRTY-EIGHT

Tuesday, Lago Agrio Army Base

Technically, it wasn't a kidnapping. The two men were considered pirates—more likely terrorists—internationally and by the Colombian government.

Colonel Hernandez wasn't too upset by Sanchez's actions. While he could never condone such a cross-border incursion, the initiative shown by the major would be amply recognized. And providing the colonel with plausible deniability was, well, just another reason for personal reward. *Lieutenant Colonel Sanchez,* the colonel thought. *Yes, that has a pleasant sound to it.*

The two captives proved to be a trove of intelligence. They provided names, locations, equipment, command hierarchy, and further details regarding the strength of the comandante's organization.

A few days later, a small boat drifted into Ecuadorean waters with four sunbaked, dehydrated, exhausted aliens. These men, upon transfer from the local police to the colonel's custody, yielded even more information. The information was shared with the national police in Bogotá, which quietly and quickly launched a full-scale raid on the comandante's headquarters and camps.

***

Comandante Flores had eluded capture by pure luck rather than a tip from the network of informants he so generously paid. His network was wide and deep but less than helpful lately. He had decided to spend an evening with the lovely Señora Martinez since her husband was "away on business" again.

As the comandante approached his headquarters after an evening of passion, he saw the trucks and troops milling about. At the last second, he ditched his car in the forest and fled on foot before the soldiers caught sight of him.

CHAPTER THIRTY-NINE

Wednesday, Baton Rouge

As was Dr. Hobart's practice, the videoconference started promptly at 1:00 p.m. in his office in Baton Rouge, which was in the same time zone as Houston and only an hour earlier than Philadelphia, Miami, and Ecuador. Stan had a graduate assistant there who was more adept than he was at manipulating documents on the videoconference website. Judge Grant had decided to rely on Stan's expertise and not participate in the call.

At Steator, Joe had Morris come to his office so they would have better access to the binders and files on the project. Morris had been more involved in the details of the case than Jessica Bradon, and she had assigned him to handle the day-to-day operations.

Joe had a thin manila folder in front of him with all the pertinent information he felt he needed to convey to Stan. He also had loaded the data onto his computer so he could show it to the other participants.

Reynolds called in from Philadelphia, with his technical consultant online from Maryland, as well as Curruca in Quito.

"I can see from my screen that a number of us are now online. Joe, is all your whole team on board?" Stan asked.

"Yes we are."

"Doug?"

"I have Luis Curruca online from Quito; he is our legal representative, and Dr. Jill Shepherd of SAMS Consultants from Landover, Maryland," Reynolds responded.

"Good. I have James Belfry, Xebec's project manager in Ecuador, and Sarah Green of Allied Analytics in Miami online also to respond to any concerns you may have," Stan said. "Before I do my spiel, let's all introduce ourselves. Try to speak slowly, as I have a graduate assistant taking notes. As an academically indentured servant, he may not work at a lightning pace." Stan laughed and smiled at Cameron.

Immediately donning a fake frown, Cameron said, "Well, Professor, you've always told me you get what you pay for."

Laughs could be heard through the speaker.

"I am Stan Hobart," he said. "I am the special master working on behalf of Judge Nancy Grant to review the case. And with me is Cameron Ferrell, my graduate student who you've already heard from but won't again, I trust."

Everyone else on the call introduced him- or herself as well.

"Anyone else?" Stan asked after hearing from the last participant. "Anybody? Anybody? Going once, twice—OK, let the meeting begin. I hope you had sufficient time to review the data I sent out last week, and I want to emphasize that this is an informal meeting. You're free to take notes, but a formal transcript will not be prepared since this is not a legal proceeding. This is really a fact-finding exercise for me. It's my intent to review the latest sampling results with you and to solicit your views. This is an opportunity for you that I am extending. Ms. Green, if you wouldn't mind, please tell us about your testing results."

Over the next five minutes, Sarah summarized the results of the testing, noting that all but two samples were within normal limits. She explained that the two outliers were from channels that drained a watershed in which production wells Colibrí-6 and Halcón-4 once had been located. She went on to explain that the results had been checked and rechecked at Allied's lab and further verified by the second independent laboratory. "Both labs reported similar results within five percent," she said.

"Can you explain your QA/QC process?" Dr. Shepherd asked.

"We follow the protocols established by the USEPA," Sarah replied. "Before each analytical run, we calibrate our GC/MS with a mixed hydrocarbon sample with known concentrations that we acquire from the National Institute of Standards and Technology. We repeat the standard after every twenty-five samples to ensure our instruments are within sampling tolerances, which in this case is plus or minus two percent. We also run a blank of double-deionized water after every sample to flush the line of any residue and to establish a proper zero reading."

"How often is your equipment repaired or serviced?" Dr. Shepherd inquired.

"We service our machines in accordance with the manufacturer's recommendations. The machine in which the samples were run was serviced about ninety days prior to the testing and isn't scheduled to be serviced for another six months."

"When was the last time the lab was certified?" Stan asked.

"We received our renewal certificate from the EPA just last year," Sarah said, "and from the Florida Department of Environmental Protection the year before. Both are issued for three-year periods but can be revoked if spurious results are reported or for noncompliance with sampling and testing protocols."

"Joe, do you have any questions for Ms. Green?" Stan asked.

"Has anyone lodged any complaints against your company, or is your firm involved in any litigation regarding testing results?" Morris asked.

Joe was relieved that Morris took the lead. He was a quick study and could handle the other lawyers. He also was glad they were only using the computer screen and not the cameras for the conference. Short, balding, and bespectacled, Morris just didn't look the part of corporate litigator. Despite spending considerable money for his wardrobe, Morris's physique could make any three-thousand-dollar suit look like it was off the rack at Target.

"No," Sarah said. "I would know as the quality control officer."

"Mr. Belfry, could you please inform us of how and when the samples in question were obtained?" Stan asked.

"We followed the sampling protocol specified in our contract with the court," Belfry explained. "Both of these samples were collected by our field technician, John Lacker, who is very experienced in the streams at the project area, having sampled there in the past. He was directed to the sites on the morning of the testing and returned with the samples at about four p.m. The samples were duly logged in at our intake desk, placed in locked and sealed shipping containers with blue ice, and sent along with a shipping manifest and chain-of-custody form to the airport in Coca. The samples were then flown to Quito, where our representative walked them through customs and placed them on a flight to Miami. In Miami, our technician collected the sample cases from the airline, walked them through US Customs, and drove them to Allied's laboratory, where he logged them in and transferred custody."

"About how long was the time between collection and testing?" Dr. Shepherd asked.

"We are allowed a ninety-six-hour window under our terms of reference, which is the industry standard for hydrocarbon samples, but we have never taken more than eighty hours," Belfry explained. "In this particular case, the samples were processed within seventy-two hours of collection."

"Was the seal on any case broken by customs in either country?" Morris asked.

"No. We're a bonded and insured company and have permits from both the United States and Ecuador to transport samples. So, they generally don't inspect our samples. However, we have a contingency for such an occurrence. If either country breaks the seal during an inspection, it occurs in the presence of our representative. The customs agent then signs the chain-of-custody form and attests that the case was resealed and records the number of the new seal. Our representative would then cosign the entry. But like I said, this did not occur with the samples in question," Belfry explained.

"Is it possible for someone to tamper with the samples on the aircraft or in the luggage claim area?" Morris asked.

"I guess it's possible," Belfry said, "but we would know about it by the broken seal, at which point we would dispose of the samples per the terms of reference and report the incident to Dr. Hobart. It would be virtually impossible for anyone to tamper with the case and then reseal it," Belfry said. "What are the odds that they would have the sealing tape with the correct alphanumeric sequence?"

"I want to give Steator a chance to respond. Joe, is there anything you want to discuss?" Stan asked.

"I would like to show everyone a couple of figures," Joe said as he opened the files on his computer. "The first figure is the location where the two samples in question were collected—they're depicted by the two red circles. Now, please notice the array of blue circles. There are eleven of them located up and downstream of the two red circles. These represent sites that were sampled in the past by both Steator and Reynolds's group."

Joe opened a new file and a spreadsheet appeared on the screen.

"I hope you can all see this OK?" he said. "The text was reduced to get it on one screen. The top row represents the different sampling dates, and the first column describes all the chemical constituents that were tested. You can see that the second and third columns are the latest samples, which were represented by the red circles on the previous map. As you move to the right, you have the next sampling episodes, which are the blue dots on the map. I've highlighted in yellow the hydrocarbon species that Allied found in excess of standards. But if you follow each of these rows to the right, you will see that in none of the other samples were the concentrations even close to the latest results. This is very curious because over the course of ten years, the concentrations should, if anything, go down, not spike so significantly. We should have seen some evidence of this contamination in the past."

"Anyone have any ideas on how this could occur?" Stan asked.

"I suspect one of the drilling sites wasn't adequately cleaned and recent rains have eroded the cover from a pit, allowing a pulse of contaminated material to wash into the river," Reynolds said. "We aren't testing the water constantly, just taking snapshots in time. This is probably happening all the time, which would account for the health condition of the locals."

"Let's say your hypothesis is correct," Stan said. "How could the concentration be so high? Wouldn't it be diluted as it flowed over the surface of the land before entering the stream and then be further diluted in the stream? It seems that the initial concentration at the pit would have to be—what? Twenty to forty times the concentration at the sampling site?"

"It could be a pit that wasn't cleaned up, only covered with dirt. The contents leached into the groundwater and have made their way to the rivers," Dr. Shepherd offered.

"I find that even more implausible," Joe said. "The concentration would be reduced even further before migrating into groundwater and then diluted in groundwater, then diluted even more again in the river."

"Frankly, I don't know what the hell the difference is or even if it matters," Curruca exclaimed. "Somehow, it's in the water, and that's what matters. My people bathe in the river, fish for food, and water livestock. They drill wells for drinking water and cooking. So, either way, surface pollution or groundwater pollution, it is there. Look, Dr. Hobart, the purpose of this entire procedure was to determine if there was sufficient evidence of contamination to proceed to trial. What more could you possibly need?"

Out of camera range, Reynolds smiled widely at Curruca's impassioned response. *He's learning well,* he thought.

"Wait a minute," Joe interjected. "This doesn't make sense. You've seen the results of the past testing, and there's nothing there—absolutely nothing. All of a sudden, we have significant contamination? I think we need to take another look at those sites. Don't you still have teams down there, Mr. Belfry?"

"More sampling? You want more sampling?" Curruca shouted through the speakers. "That was the whole purpose of this process. I didn't think it was necessary in the first place. We had plenty of evidence already—look at all the sick people. I only agreed to participate because there would no longer be any questions as to the veracity of the results—they weren't mine; they weren't Steator's. Now, Joe wants to change things yet again."

"It sure seems like a scientific mulligan to me, and only because something Joe doesn't like has occurred," Reynolds said. "Would he have been so eager to retest if the result had been within limits? I very much doubt it. He's been told to draw out the process in order to bankrupt Luis's clients."

"This sounds like one of those stalling tactics I hear they use in US courts. We do not tolerate such behavior in my country. No, I will not agree to more testing. Either the results are right, or they're wrong. Either the sample collection was done correctly or it wasn't. I see no evidence that anything wrong occurred during any of the procedures," Curruca said.

Reynolds laughed to himself. He realized that Stan was unaccustomed to the courtroom theatrics and the feigned belligerence between arguing attorneys. He didn't want to make him angry and changed the tone instantly.

"Stan, I think we can all appreciate the situation in which Joe and Steator find themselves, and I want you to know that Luis and our other attorneys have worked tirelessly with Steator to avoid the confrontation in court. After all, time and money spent on litigation could be much better used to help the poor Indians in the forest. But we haven't been able to reach a reasonable accord, which is why we are here today. It is my feeling that any further delay is punitive against the poor native peoples we represent," Reynolds said.

"Joe, Morris, I am tending toward Doug's position," Stan said. "This was the unbiased sampling and testing by a highly qualified and reputable third party. Unless there is a procedural or technical error, which frankly I don't see, then I have to make my recommendations to Judge Grant."

"It would take—what—an additional three days to collect and process new samples? That's nothing. Billions of dollars are at stake here," Morris said.

"And the health and well-being of thousands of people the more we delay," Curruca added.

"Look, I understand what you're saying, Morris, but where do we draw the line?" Stan replied. "At best, I could present your request to the judge, but she'll ask me what my opinion is, and I'll give it to her. Let me offer this. I suspect it will take me at least a couple of months to complete my report. If you can provide any firm evidence disputing the laboratory findings, I'll include those in my report. But we can't rely on speculation. We must have something firm."

"I don't know if an objection is in order, but I don't like this. We never said anything about a minority report," Curruca said.

"Mr. Curruca, my purpose is fact-finding. If I get credible facts from either side, it is my duty to evaluate them and report to Judge Grant. I offer you the same opportunity. This is the fairest way I know to proceed," Stan said. "Unless anyone else has something to add, I think we've pretty much accomplished what I wanted. I'd like thank you all for your participation. Again, eight weeks before I submit."

With that, Stan signaled Cameron, who terminated the videoconference.

"Whew, that was like watching King Solomon in action," Cameron said.

"No, it's the judge, not me, who'll do the baby-splitting," replied Stan.

***

"What do we do now?" Joe asked, looking at Morris as he disconnected the call. "None of our arguments worked. They had an answer for everything. It's like they could read my mind."

"You have to realize that he had quite a stable of experts at their disposal. I am sure they 'red team/blue team' everything. They were just ready. They probably had us checkmated with whatever argument we had. These guys are good. We just have to be better," Morris said. "I have to take this to corporate, and they're going to have to make some heavy decisions. I need to contact our outside counsel too. They need to be ready. Is there anything you can provide in the next few weeks to counter the lab results?"

"I pretty much delivered all I had in that salvo," Joe said. "Short of going down and collecting and sampling again, it'll be difficult to dispute the results. Even if we collected new samples, who'll believe our results? All we could do, maybe, is introduce them into court during trial and try to convince the jury of their credibility."

"Give me the odds that Stan will change his opinion."

"Less than ten percent, at best."

"Well, we have a little time, but not much," Morris said. "Why don't you think this out, confer with your colleagues and brainstorm the issue? See if there's any way to discredit or even discount the lab's report. In the meantime, I have to do a damage assessment. I need to make a recommendation on a settlement. Given this new information, it would be much too risky to take this to a jury. Unless you find something we can use, I have a feeling I'll be sitting across the table from Curruca and Reynolds and handing them a big fat check."

"I will. But tonight, I think I have a date with a bottle of Jameson's to clear the cobwebs," Joe replied.

***

Reynolds had arranged a follow-up call with the members of his team immediately after the videoconference.

"I don't think it gets much better than this," he told them. "I don't like it that Steator has another bite at the apple, but I really don't know what they can say. Any ideas on how they'll likely proceed, Dr. Shepherd?"

"No, maybe just more of what they already did. It looks like the sampling and laboratory work is rock solid. I see no chinks in the armor."

"Luis?"

"I agree."

"I can't wait for this to get to trial," Reynolds said with great exuberance. "Steator can't risk an adverse decision. And once they see our lawyers in front of the jury, they will scramble to cut the check. Luis, I have some matters to discuss with you about the court filings. Can you stay on the line after Dr. Shepherd leaves?"

"Yes."

"Dr. Shepherd, thank you again for your expert advice. I'll be in contact very soon."

With that, she hung up.

"Are you on a secure phone?" Reynolds asked Curruca.

"Yes," Curruca replied.

"You were great, and we didn't have to involve the US lawyers and their twelve-hundred-dollar-an-hour billing rates. As you heard, we are now in the most critical stage. If Stan recommends that a trial go forward, I have been alerted that Steator will be at the table immediately. We'll have all the leverage we need. They don't want a trial. I am hopeful we can start at five billion dollars."

"Why not more? I thought you said something greater than ten billion," Curruca said. He was worried. On Reynolds's advice, he had cultivated a relationship with the deputy minister of justice to obtain additional funding for the lawsuit. As usual, he had overplayed his hand and was sorry he had even mentioned the fifteen-billion-dollar amount to entice the minister. He had assumed, wrongly, that the deputy minister would understand that such a large figure was but a negotiation gambit and any settlement would be less. But the deputy's experience with civil lawsuits in the United States was nonexistent, bordering on naïveté, and now the larger figure was etched in his brain.

"Look," Reynolds said, "our lawyers in the US have told me if we demand much more, Steator might as well risk the trial. They need an incentive to settle, and something less than five billion may be it. Also, think of how long a trial could last. With a settlement, we could begin to see payouts in months, not years. As you know, our financiers are beginning to waver. They based their risk analysis on a settlement. They won't be happy going to trial, with the expenses they'll incur. Also, we have no idea who'll say what during depositions or cross-examinations."

"This could be trouble for me," Curruca said. "I have been telling our friends in Quito that ten billion to fifteen billion dollars was likely. They have that number in their heads and have been making plans accordingly. Is there anything I should do now?"

"No. Stay low-key. I'll have to see what kind of latitude we have in a settlement."

Curruca, like the other lawyers, had been a constant headache for Reynolds. The lawsuit had been his idea; he'd done all the research; he'd made all the contacts; and he'd literally mortgaged the farm to finance the plan—it was actually a second mortgage against his grandmother's property. But each lawyer eventually tried to take control, treating Reynolds more like he was an employee than the boss.

The first lawyers were very enthusiastic and immediately saw the potential of the lawsuit. They worked at very reduced rates—a fee for day-to-day expenses and a percentage of any recovery. But because they weren't drawing much pay, they demanded more control. Reynolds didn't tolerate that. After all, he provided them with everything in a neat package; all they had to do was the lawyering.

As the suit progressed, Reynolds learned more and more of what really was required and became his own best counsel. He finally found a couple of attorneys who were better suited to his style. For their chance to participate in the suit, the new lawyers were required to obtain a certain percentage of operating expenses through a litigation financing entity—they needed to have skin in the game. But everyone knew that the potential rewards would be immense.

Even with the right team, the burden on Reynolds was heavy. The machinations of the lawsuit were complicated, and no one, not even Curruca, could be trusted. Everyone was just a hired hand. Reynolds exerted his power by controlling the data and, more important, the money. Curruca knew little about lawsuit financing in the United States, and the American lawyers had no idea about the secret funds from the Ecuadorian government. Everyone took for granted that Reynolds had some personal wealth.

Reynolds thought it ironic that everyone was in it for the money except maybe Muniz and himself. For him, the money was secondary; it was his ticket into the club.

***

The next morning, Morris and Jessica sat stiff and upright, just like a couple of students at the principal's office. Neither wanted to be there, but relaying bad news was most of their job. Their anxiety increased as they waited for the CEO to finish his call.

"Sorry about that," Clark Royal said from the glass-and-chrome desk in his forty-second-floor office. The floor-to-ceiling windows provided a 270-degree panorama of downtown Houston. "A little problem in Scotland."

Royal rose from his desk and walked the thirty feet to the conference table, where he sat at his chair at the head. He had removed his suit coat and rolled up his shirtsleeves to signal to everyone around the table that he was ready for the hard work ahead.

Looking directly at Jessica, he said, "Give it to me."

"Not good. The judge's special master probably will recommend that the suit go forward."

"That's it? No chance to retest? No reevaluation?"

"No, but he did give us a few weeks to present our arguments, which he'll provide to the judge. But it would be highly unlikely that the judge would disregard her own expert," Morris said. At this news, Morris felt Royal's discomfort. He noted that rather than looking at them as they spoke, Royal's eyes darted back and forth as if looking for some secret door to escape the meeting.

"Jessica, it's up to you," Royal said. "Get these guys to the table. If you need help, call me. I'll see if I can charm Reynolds and his attorneys down a few billion."

CHAPTER FORTY

Wednesday, Verde Vista Ecolodge

The group arrived at the lodge late in the evening. Malin and Maria were waiting to welcome them with a meal that they dispatched with great exuberance. Next were showers and sleep.

The next morning, their elation at being free was tempered by the sadness of the loss of Jack and Carlos.

Carlos had been a kind, funny, helpful guide they had only known—and not truly appreciated—for just a few days. But with Jack, they had shared much pain and anguish.

For Tom, the losses were profound. Carlos was a friend, a colleague, and a part of his life he could never—and didn't want to—replace. He thought of the days, weeks, and months they had hiked and talked, discussing family and their futures. He recalled all the shared adventures, the endless packing and unpacking, the care and feeding of clients, the complaints. Things he shared with no other he had shared with Carlos. Friend? No, he was a brother. Tom also felt a strong sense of despair over not being able to protect Jack, whose safety ultimately had been his responsibility.

For Gary, the loss of Carlos also was devastating. It was like losing a friend in the line of duty—someone you trained with, joked around with, but most important, went into battle with; someone who had your back—a brother-in-arms. And when that loss happened, however noble, a piece of you was lost. Only a select few answered the call, donned the armor, and fought to the end. Carlos was one of them.

CHAPTER FORTY-ONE

Thursday, Verde Vista Ecolodge

It had been a full day: taking long, hot showers, laundering clothes, making travel arrangements, calling family and friends, and packing for the flight out of Coca in the morning. Earlier in the day, Tom had the sad task of calling Jack's brother, his only living relative. The manager of Natura Sucumbios had expected to make the notification, but Tom insisted.

Tom called Jack's brother, Rich, and informed him of Jack's death.

"He told me this would be his last trip, but I didn't expect it to end quite this way," Rich said. "Can you tell me how it happened?"

Tom explained the blow to Jack's head from the fight and the earlier hits he'd taken.

"That sounds like Jack," Rich said. "But I am not surprised."

Tom was confused, and Rich sensed this by the delay in any response.

"I need to let you know something," Rich said. "Jack had starting having severe headaches about two years ago. By the time I convinced him to see a doctor, the tumor had grown too large to remove. His neurosurgeon had been blunt and honest. He said if it was him, he'd avoid all treatment, all of which would inevitably result in memory and cognition loss."

"He should have let me know in case of an emergency," Tom said.

"There is nothing you could have done. Other than his doctor, his lawyer, and me, he had told no one. He didn't want anybody worrying about him—it made him feel very uncomfortable, very vulnerable, and maybe even weak. The last thing in the world Jack wanted was pity," Rich said.

"But if I'd known, I would have—"

"What? It was a death sentence, but he died doing what he wanted to do and with the people he wanted to be with," Rich said.

When Tom said good-bye to Rich, he was sad and conflicted. On one hand, he felt guilty about his unwarranted feelings about Jack's aggressive and irrational behavior. It wasn't Jack's fault; it was from the tumor. On the other hand, there was a modicum of relief in the fact that his trip and his leadership wasn't the real cause of Jack's death. But it was still painful losing a friend regardless of the cause.

Tom was too emotionally drained after talking with Rich to call Carlos's family. He needed a little more time—and maybe a few more drinks—before he could muster the nerve. The call to Rich was painful, but it wouldn't compare to calling Cecilia. He'd be better prepared tomorrow morning.

The group planned a final dinner at the lodge for that evening—part celebration, part remembrance—not sure when or whether they would see one another again. They had thanked Colonel Hernandez, Major Sanchez, and all their soldiers. They also thanked Malin and Maria. But they saved their most heartfelt thanks for their departed friends.

Tom felt he owed it to the group to explain his call to Rich and Jack's condition.

"He knew he was dying, yet he tried to save us at every chance he had," Marsha said, wiping her eyes.

"If only we had known," Vincent said. "We wouldn't have—"

"We didn't know, Vincent," Tom said, "and Jack didn't want us to know. We have to respect that. Like his brother said, we should all take comfort that Jack died doing what he loved, and he always tried to help us."

Tom raised his glass, which was immediately followed by the others. "To our lost friend," he said.

Gary cleared his throat, clearly affected by Tom's explanation. "I'm sorry that I never got to meet Jack, and I only knew Carlos for the better part of two weeks," Gary began. "While some of you have known him for years, I quite possibly saw in him something you never may have. I saw a man who knew no boundaries when it came to ensuring the safety of his friends, and you truly were his friends, not just clients paying for his services. When you were in Carlos's circle, you were his family. He would go any distance, overcome any hurdle to see to your safety and happiness. I saw in him what I hope to see in myself someday. I ask you to also raise your glasses in tribute to our friend, that we never forget that we're here because of him. To Carlos."

A mix of "*Salut!*" and "To Carlos!" came from the group as they stood and sipped from their glasses.

"If I might have a word," Tom said. "As Gary pointed out, I've known Carlos for about fifteen years. I met him on my second tour to Ecuador when he served as a driver and cook and set up field camps. Even then, he had that mischievous sense of humor that lightened everyone's day. Even the most demanding clients—those insisting on being the first in line for all views, complaining that they hadn't seen enough birds, grumbling that the food and accommodations weren't as advertised or that the days were too long or too short—were putty in this gentle soul's hands. With a quick quip and light laugh, he'd fix any problems they imagined. It was a quality he never lost."

Tom's voice began to break and tears welled as he continued, "It wasn't until later trips that he revealed the depth and breadth of his knowledge and his capacity to learn more and more on every trip. I gave him countless books, tapes, and scientific journal articles, which he devoured, often asking me to explain a series of technical terms. But he got it and got it fast. He would isolate himself in his tent or take a solo walk in the forest. I'd say, 'If you have questions, just ask me.' He'd respond, 'Some things can be taught; others must be learned.' And that's what he did—learned. Under different economic circumstances, I would say he easily could have become a PhD and taught at a university. But that wasn't home; the jungle was. University professors are turned out by the thousands each year, but a guide like Carlos is truly unique. I know Natura Sucumbios and I will always see that Cecilia and the kids are well—"

"He's on the telephone!" Maria yelled from the front desk. "He's on the telephone! It is Carlos! He's calling from Lago!"

Tom turned, saw the mixture of elation and slack-jawed shock on Maria's face, and raced to the desk. Maria handed him the phone. "Carlos, we thought you were dead!" he exclaimed. "We searched the river, but we couldn't find you. Where were you? How did you get back? There's a roomful of people here with huge smiles on their faces."

"I was tossed from the boat and could not swim fast enough to keep up," Carlos said. "I was running out of energy, so I floated on my back downstream, always angling toward the bank. After a few minutes, I got close enough so I could swim hard through the current and reach the bank. I was exhausted and saw I had a large laceration on my left arm. I hadn't even felt it. I covered it with my shirt as best as I could. I just lay there for several minutes, trying to catch my breath, but you had all motored downstream and out of sight. I had no idea if you'd been captured again.

"Within a couple of hours, a boat heading downstream saw me flailing my good arm and picked me up. I told them my boat capsized with all my belongings. They took pity on me and took me all the way to Puerto San Miguel. I walked to the small clinic. It only had a nurse, but she was able to sew up my arm. I wanted to leave, but she insisted I stay overnight. She was afraid I'd lost too much blood. The next morning, I rode in the back of a pickup truck to Lago and my family. I wanted to call earlier but was too afraid of what I might hear over the phone—that maybe you'd been captured again, and it would be my fault for attempting a foolish rescue."

"No, remember our call to the colonel from Puerto Asís? Well, his men got there just in time," Tom explained. "We've got much to talk about, and several members of the group are leaving in the morning. When can you get here?"

"I'll be with you and our friends in the morning when we say *adiós*."

CHAPTER FORTY-TWO

Friday, FARC Headquarters

The sat phone was the first domino to topple. It had been an expensive purchase but well worth it in terms of access and security. The phone provided a link to areas totally inaccessible by any other communication method save smoke signals. And the 128-bit encryption key guaranteed that no call could be intercepted, monitored, or tracked unless locked on and processed by the US National Security Agency. Even then, the use of codes Comandante Flores had developed would disguise the true nature of his calls.

What he hadn't expected was the loss of his sat phone. The comandante had failed to follow his own procedures. But such was the cost of hubris.

The Colombia Special Forces raid on his headquarters had been lightning fast—no time to erase hard drives or memory cards. The weapons cache was valuable to the authorities—at least getting it out of the wrong hands—but the intelligence was invaluable.

Because of the tip-off, the Colombian government asked few questions about an alleged incursion into its sovereign land, satisfied with a wink and nod that the information about the FARC camps had come from four guerillas who somehow had been captured in Ecuador. Truth be told, the Colombian government had its informants well distributed in Ecuador too.

As a sign of mutual cooperation in these times of international terrorism, the Colombian government shared much of the data it had collected from the FARC operations, especially any information that directly affected Ecuador. This information included a series of telephone numbers retrieved from the SD card of a sat phone, all to or from the 593 country code: Ecuador.

Week Five

CHAPTER FORTY-THREE

Monday, Lago Agrio Army Base

It took the entire weekend, but Colonel Hernandez had his analysts map the location of all calls from the sat phone recovered at FARC headquarters. Fortunately, the comandante hadn't thought to delete the call log or remove the SIM card, both of which had recorded the GPS coordinates, numbers called, and call durations during any uplink or downlink to a passing satellite. There were only a few calls, and all were from remote locations in the Oriente or Colombia. But all were to and from the same number.

With assistance from the telephone company's GES (ground earth station), the analysts were informed that the telephone receiving the calls was a prepaid burner cell phone that could not be traced to an individual.

The company was, however, able to triangulate the approximate location of the calls based on the cell towers used in connecting the sat phone through the GES. Because multiple calls were made to and from the cell phone, the phone company was able to pinpoint the location to a small two-story office building in Quito.

The analysts were unable to identify from which office the calls had been placed and received or even whether the calls had taken place inside rather than outdoors. If they'd occurred outdoors, anyone could have made and received the calls. But the analysts figured the calls probably had taken place indoors. Colonel Hernandez knew the building needed a closer look, but he couldn't authorize his men to conduct an illegal break-in, even if it was for the best of reasons. And he knew he had zero chance of obtaining a search warrant from the Ministry of Justice—he didn't trust them. But the colonel had an idea.

After the birders had left for home, Carlos was a bundle of raw nerves. He paced back and forth and often woke in the middle of the night. It was driving Cecilia crazy. She was used to not having Carlos around, but when he was there, he was usually recuperating from a long trip. He was too distracted right then to return to guiding. He was outraged over Jack's death, and he wanted to do something about it.

He walked to the army base every day, trying to get more information from the colonel. He pleaded with him to let him help. He'd do anything; he had to do something. The colonel was patient and tolerant of Carlos and understood his angst.

"There may be something you can help me with," Colonel Hernandez said. "It is something I cannot do myself because of political implications."

"What is it? I can help. I was successful last time. Please let me try again," Carlos told him.

"I need more information on these telephone calls from Quito. There's some involvement with the Colombians."

"Maybe I could take a look. What kind of information do you need?"

"Mind you, this is something I cannot endorse," the colonel said. "You're a civilian, and it may be a dangerous situation."

"The rescue in Colombia was dangerous too, but we got it done."

"That is why I am concerned," said Colonel Hernandez. "You weren't supposed to confront the kidnappers, remember—only collect information."

Carlos shrugged. "We had to improvise."

"And you did well. Because of you, five people are alive and sleeping soundly this evening. Check with Sergeant Rosales. He will tell you what we need."

***

Around noon on Tuesday after the long drive from Lago Agrio, Carlos entered the office building in Quito and wrote down the names of each company in the lobby directory. No listing seemed to be of obvious significance, such as an import-export company, an equipment supplier, or even a travel agency. Most were small insurance firms, real-estate offices, and a law office—all commercial, no retail. None, it seemed, would have an obvious need to call a sat phone.

Upon his return to his hotel room, Carlos checked the names of the owners of each company in the city phone book and conducted Internet queries. Again, not much. He discovered that Luis Curruca, *abogado*, had defended a couple of drug smugglers in the past, but so had many lawyers in Quito. Digging a bit deeper, he found that Curruca also had tried cases in Lago Agrio.

So he knows the Oriente, Carlos concluded.

Deciding he needed a further look, he returned the next day and entered Curruca's first-floor office. A small waiting area had a couple of cushioned chairs, a sofa flanked by end tables with aged magazines, and an unoccupied desk that he figured was for a receptionist. A frosted-glass door embossed with Curruca's name and title led to an inner office.

As Sergeant Rosales had instructed him, Carlos searched the walls of the reception area for signs of an alarm system: a keypad, motion detectors, heat sensors, et cetera. Seeing none, he figured that only the exterior of the building was wired. He would check on his way out.

He went to a window in the waiting area, looked out, and saw the adjacent alley. He unlatched the window, raised it, and found a magnetic contact embedded in the sill. Then he reached into his pocket and pulled out a thin steel slug, about the size of a coin, which Rosales had given him. He placed it on the magnetic contact to complete the low-voltage circuit. He then placed a thin strip of duct tape on the metallic lead in the window frame, short-circuiting the alarm. Finally, he closed the window but left it unlatched. He was out of the office in less than a minute and didn't have to recite his prepared speech on the benefits of his company's "latest building alarm systems," since no one had confronted him in the waiting room.

As Carlos was leaving the building, he spied the alarm pad on a sidewall with all LEDs illuminated in green.

He returned at about seven in the evening after the building had been vacated. He saw no lights that suggested any late-night activities. He looked for indications of a night guard, such as a flashlight beam or movement in the windows, but saw none. He waited an additional hour in his car to see whether the building was patrolled by a security service.

Carlos exited his vehicle and walked to the side window he had cased hours earlier. To his relief, the window hadn't been locked; it remained as he had left it. He took out a thin pry bar and gently and slowly lifted the window a few millimeters. No alarm sounded; the metal slug was still attached to the magnetic contact.

He raised the window, hoisted himself up, and entered the office. Then he closed the window, making sure the false contact remained in place, and drew the blinds shut.

He switched on a penlight. With a roll of duct tape, he sealed the cracks around the office's front door to prevent any light leak if a security guard made rounds. He then entered the main office. Certain the blinds were completely closed, he turned on the overhead light and went to work.

He began by looking in all the desk drawers for a cell phone. He then checked the file cabinets and credenza. Next he paged through paper files, flipped the Rolodex, and examined business cards. He pressed the memory button on the telephone and wrote down the numbers of past incoming and outgoing calls. He switched on the Gateway desktop computer and knew he'd have no problems with a security code when the old Windows 98 logo appeared. Carlos was surprised that the vintage version would still support today's functions. Immediately, he got into the "Contacts" file and scrolled through the entries; everything appeared to be legitimate businesses and contacts.

There were far too many, so he constrained his search. First to any entry in Colombia. Nothing. Then to Lago Agrio. Then Sucumbios. Finally Coca. These were all areas where the birding group had visited, either voluntarily or by force. With his cell-phone's camera, he photographed the information on the screen.

Discouraged by not finding anything definitive, Carlos carefully removed any evidence of his search. He turned off the lights, removed the tape from the front door, and exited through the window. He wanted to remove the steel slug to erase all evidence of his intrusion, but he couldn't chance setting off the alarm.

He returned to his hotel room to get a few hours' sleep before reporting back to the colonel.

CHAPTER FORTY-FOUR

Wednesday, Lago Agrio Army Base

The names Carlos brought to Colonel Hernandez were first organized by geographic region and then evaluated for possible links to drug trafficking. Few fit the category. A couple of names were of locals in Lago who had worked as low-level mules for the cartels and had been caught transporting drugs into Colombia. They were placed at the top of the list. Those remaining were somehow related to Curruca's work in a lawsuit against Steator Energies.

"It's not much to go on," the colonel said. He hadn't expected a smoking gun or flashing neon sign, but he would have preferred something more tangible. "Sanchez," he continued, "you take the first six names. They're all near Sacha. Sergeant Gutierrez, you take the next five along the Río Aguarico, and Sergeant Rosales, the next four."

Colonel Hernandez knew he had to tread carefully. This was really a matter for the National Police of Ecuador, but he didn't trust them. Their reputation for corruption was well deserved. At the same time, he was encroaching on their territory. But now this was personal. He knew the victims, and the abductions had occurred in his province and on his watch. He saw it as an armed incursion orchestrated by FARC and the cartel into his country. It was all the justification he needed to exert and maybe extend his authority.

He knew that any investigation he pursued would have to be done quickly and under the radar.

Besides Sanchez, Colonel Hernandez included Gutierrez and Rosales, two of his best intelligence analysts, who were most often squeezing their contacts for information. Fishermen, merchants, boatmen, Indians—anyone regularly venturing up and down the river between Colombia and Ecuador, even as far east as Peru—provided useful nuggets of data that these men would assemble, disassemble, and reassemble to get a snapshot of the river's activities. They even had a source in the cartel, a couple with the Colombian police, and a few in the National Police.

The colonel's analysts were comfortable driving up and down the roads and river, working odd jobs on boats, driving trucks, tending fields, and talking to everyone they could. They always hoped to be selected to do some job for the cartel, which would yield the jackpot of intelligence. All the while, they were dressed as civilians, and Colonel Hernandez insisted on long hair and beards. Few people, if any, knew they were military. They even lived off base, returning only when absolutely necessary and then under the guise of making a delivery.

"We need a good cover story—something to deflect suspicions—for the people you visit. We don't want anything getting back to Curruca," Sergeant Gutierrez offered.

"Maybe request to use their phone because your cell battery is dead, or ask to recharge using an electrical outlet," the colonel suggested. "Anything to get them engaged about phone service. How often do they call Quito? Do they use landlines or cell phones? But stay away from any discussion of the cartel. If they're innocent, we don't want them running to the police and impeding our investigation."

For the better part of the day, the three worked up the telephone cover story and added another. They were looking for legal help for their cousin, who'd been arrested for a minor drug-possession rap, and they'd mention that Curruca had represented the cousin in the past. Mostly, though, they would look and listen, relying on their instincts, which was what they were trained to do.

They left that afternoon.

CHAPTER FORTY-FIVE

Thursday, Sacha

It was late in the day when Sanchez approached the small farm outside Sacha that was next on his list. It was the headquarters of the Native Peoples Forest Project, which seemed like a strange client for Luis Curruca. But the address was on the contact list Carlos had photographed a few nights before.

Sanchez drove up the narrow dirt road to the small house, which was shaded by large *Otoba* trees. He exited his truck and knocked three times on the front door. After waiting for a response, he decided to check in the back in case Señor Muniz was tending to his farm. He found no one. There was nothing but an old lean-to, a poultry coop, and assorted rakes, hoes, and other farming tools in progressive stages of disrepair.

This land hasn't been farmed in a while, Sanchez thought.

He knocked at the back door but again got no answer. He walked around to the opposite side of the house. There, lying on their sides, were four fifty-five-gallon drums. All were without lids and empty. Sanchez had seen these used before as rain barrels to collect water for livestock and washing, but these weren't being used for either. He continued to his truck and drove to the next address on his list.

***

Upon their return, Gutierrez and Rosales reported about as much success as did Sanchez, and it seemed that Carlos's foray to Curruca's office was a dead end.

"The calls were probably to someone else," Sanchez surmised. Still, they needed to report to the colonel, who was expected soon.

***

His analysts' reports were thorough and methodical but fruitless, the colonel thought, while considering the next possible course of action.

"And the house was occupied, but no one was home when I arrived. Nothing of note other than it looked like the farm had been idle for a few years," Sanchez continued. He then recited the inventory of what he had seen.

"Wait," the colonel said. "You saw storage drums?"

"Yes, on the ground beside the house. They weren't being used for anything."

The colonel remembered that Gary and Carlos had mentioned something about drums. What was it?

"Sanchez, can you contact Gary Cales and ask him about the drums that concerned him?"

"*Sí*," Sanchez responded, and completed his debriefing.

After the others finished, Sanchez walked to his desk. He checked his watch. *Five thirty p.m. here, and Detroit is an hour behind,* he thought. *Not too late to call.*

It had been a week since Gary, along with Marsha and Ben, had left Ecuador for home. But with all the activity of settling his parents, he hadn't returned to work. He was in decompression mode and trying to make sense of the past few weeks.

He heard the phone ring. He had left his cell phone in the kitchen of his two-story, two-bedroom condo. He recognized the number immediately, at least the three-digit country code.

"Hello," Gary said.

"Hi, Gary. This is Major Sanchez in Lago Agrio. I was hoping to ask you a few questions."

"I was planning to call to find out if you had anything new."

Sanchez went on to explain the information that had been retrieved from the sat phone and their follow-up on some of the numbers. He didn't get too specific, even though he knew Gary wouldn't discuss their conversation with anyone other than Marsha and Ben.

"The colonel said you were concerned about some drums, but he couldn't recall the details," Sanchez said.

"Carlos remembered seeing a man by a truck when they left a birding site the night before the kidnapping. He had a couple of fifty-five-gallon drums at the top of the bank, which seemed strange. We thought maybe he was refueling, using the drums to unload fish, or was transporting them."

"But there are drums everywhere around here. The oil companies have many uses for them."

"I know, but after we revisited the site, it didn't seem logical that the man would be loading them or using them to refuel," Gary said. "There's a fueling and loading dock just downstream, and the bank is high and steep. Not the kind of location you'd use for a transfer, unless you wanted to be inconspicuous. It was just a strange feeling Carlos had."

"What about the truck? Do you remember what Carlos said about it?"

"Not much. Why not give him a call?"

Sanchez did just that.

CHAPTER FORTY-SIX

Friday, Sacha

"That could be it," Carlos said, pointing to the pickup truck as he drove Colonel Hernandez and Major Sanchez up to the farmhouse.

"It wasn't here yesterday," Sanchez added.

"Look," the colonel warned, "all we know is this man may have been at the river the night before the kidnapping, but we're not sure about that. There's no evidence he was involved. Do you think you'd recognize the man who was there that night?" he asked Carlos.

"I don't know. It was dark, and I didn't pay that much attention."

They exited the car and approached the door. Dressed in fatigue uniforms, the colonel and Sanchez hoped their aura of authority would be intimidating but not threatening.

Thanks to Rosales's quick analysis, they had learned of the man's activist background, but nothing suggested involvement with drugs. And Sanchez's brief inspection of the property found nothing in that direction, other than the drums, for which there were a million possible explanations.

The door opened almost immediately after Sanchez's knock. Palumbo Muniz, dressed in jeans, a T-shirt, and sandals responded, "The army? How can I help you?"

"Señor Muniz, my name is Major Sanchez, and this is Colonel Hernandez of the Twenty-Ninth Jungle Division. Our driver there is Fernando," Sanchez said, pointing to Carlos. "We have a few questions, if you don't mind."

"Please come in," Muniz said, motioning them into the house.

They took seats in the front room. Carlos sat behind Muniz so his observation of him wouldn't be too obvious.

"Señor Muniz, we've been investigating a drug operation in the area. Our intelligence unit in Quito has uncovered a number of calls from a satellite phone that was recovered in a raid," Sanchez said, launching their newest cover story.

Muniz shrugged. "There certainly is much trafficking through the province, but I don't see how that would involve me."

"No, we don't think you have any involvement. We've checked your organization and see nothing but community service," the colonel said, attempting to ease Muniz's anxiety.

"But this phone had many numbers, and we are obliged to check them all," Sanchez explained.

"Was a call placed to my phone from this satellite phone?" Muniz asked.

"The satellite phone had a number in its call history—the office of a lawyer in Quito," Sanchez continued. "And we see that you've also called this lawyer. Have you needed an attorney recently?"

The colonel could see Muniz was conflicted, which was the point of the cover story.

Curruca had called him—and he had called Curruca—but Muniz wondered how that could have anything to do with a drug ring.

"I have been employed by a Señor Curruca, a lawyer in Quito, to assist in a lawsuit, but we haven't spoken in weeks. I was responsible for providing affidavits from local residents. Señor Curruca would drive in on occasion to collect them and also to conduct personal interviews."

"As I mentioned, Señor Curruca's office was called with the satellite phone," Sanchez said. "Do you think he could be involved in the drug business? Maybe worked as an attorney for traffickers?"

"I am sure he could have. He is a good lawyer, but I do not know about his practice or clients other than the case I am involved in."

Sanchez casually looked in the direction of Carlos, who sat just behind Muniz. Carlos shrugged his shoulders a fraction, indicating, "Maybe." He saw that Colonel Hernandez had also witnessed the interchange. They had set the trap; now it was time to bait it.

"We normally do not investigate local drug operations," the colonel explained. "But a group of foreign tourists was kidnapped here in Ecuador and transported to Colombia. So we became involved."

Until the instant that the colonel had finished his sentence, Muniz appeared relaxed, at ease, knowing he had nothing to do with drugs. That changed with the mention of the kidnapping. He had known Curruca was planning something after he told him about the van full of tourists, but he'd never considered a kidnapping.

Muniz's stomach churned. His heart pounded faster and faster as adrenaline coursed through his system, activating his fight-or-flight reflexes, all in a matter of seconds. He kept a calm demeanor, but his microexpressions—rapid eye movement, forced stare, narrowed lips, forced swallow, nose scratching—were all tells the colonel had been trained to spot, and they hadn't gone unnoticed.

Pull yourself together, Muniz willed himself. He drew a deep breath. "Where did this happen? I haven't heard about it. I had no involvement."

"We don't think you did. We are not accusing you," Sanchez said. "We would like to know those people who would know both you and Curruca. Someone called both of you," Sanchez continued, further coloring the story.

"I can't think of anyone at this moment. Can I call you if I think of anything?"

Sanchez fished out a card from the cargo pocket of his utility trousers. He reached over a small table and handed it to Muniz, noticing his clammy palms. "You can call me at this cell-phone number at any time. If I don't answer, leave a message. Any information you can provide, regardless of how trivial you may think it may be, could be useful to us."

Muniz nodded. With that, the colonel rose, followed by the others.

"Thank you for your time and cooperation," Colonel Hernandez said as he shook Muniz's hand.

"I hope I have been helpful," Muniz lied.

***

In near panic, Muniz watched as the car drove off the property. He didn't know what to do. He couldn't believe Curruca would have the tourists kidnapped. There was little chance they had seen what he, Jorge, and Raul were doing. Even if they had seen the men or the drums, they would have had no idea what was going on. They could have been dumping anything. How in the world could they ever associate it with the water testing?

Muniz wondered whether they were even the same tourists he had seen. He had read nothing about a kidnapping in the papers, although these situations usually were kept quiet until the hostages were released.

Each question cascaded into ten more.

He began pacing, thinking, talking to himself out loud, trying to sort things out but becoming more confused and scared, working himself into a mental frenzy.

The authorities know something. They know I am somehow connected, and what is Curruca's involvement? I need answers.

He was reacting as the colonel had anticipated. The set and baited trap would now be sprung.

Muniz reached for his cell phone and began to dial but stopped, realizing his phone could be monitored. He hesitated for a moment and then put the phone in his pocket, grabbed his keys, and headed for Raul's truck.

***

As they drove down the road, Sanchez said it first. "He's lying."

"How long before he tries to contact Curruca?" Carlos asked.

"Soon, if not now. I wish we could tap his phone or plant a bug," the colonel said, thinking how good it would be to have the resources of larger militaries. "We now have two lines of evidence: We have a sat phone number to an office. We have a number of contacts from that office. On the second track, we have a man and steel drums that may have been in the vicinity of the group the night before the kidnapping—that could be Muniz. I don't know what it has to do with the kidnapping, but it is far too coincidental."

As soon as they turned off the farm road onto the main road, Sanchez said, "Slow down. Maybe I can find something out."

Carlos came to a near stop out of view of the house, and Sanchez exited.

"Drive down a mile or so, out of view, in case someone comes along."

Sanchez turned and headed back toward the house under the cover of the neglected orchard. Fortunately, there were few windows, but he stayed low as he approached the house. He passed the drums at the side and peered into the window next to the back door. He couldn't see Muniz. He tried the doorknob. It was unlocked. He carefully turned the knob, trying to minimize any sound, and did the same as he pushed the door open. He heard a little squeaking of hinges that needed oiling but not enough to arouse anyone. He closed the door quietly, and with his back pressed against the kitchen wall to minimize his profile, he advanced slowly toward the entrance to the front room.

Muniz paced frantically, too distracted to see or hear anything.

As Sanchez had hoped, Muniz picked up his phone but stopped and ran out to the truck.

We got to him, Sanchez thought, smiling. He took out his cell phone to alert the colonel.

***

Muniz, in the pickup truck, sped by the colonel and Carlos while they were parked off the road in a dirt driveway.

Carlos chuckled. "Someone's in a hurry."

"We know where he's going, so stay back," the colonel said.

Carlos slowly pulled onto the main road to follow Muniz, who was now out of sight.

As expected, Muniz made a beeline to downtown Sacha. They had spooked him about his phone, so he was heading to the EMETEL office to make a call. The receptionist wouldn't recognize him—she probably would barely look up—and he could pay for the call with cash. Any trace would die out like a wave crashing onto a beach.

Muniz was justifiably paranoid—he was being followed. Constantly looking over his shoulder, he parked his truck a block from the phone office.

The colonel and Carlos observed this from their car. Once Muniz entered the building, Carlos drove closer to the office and then jumped from the driver's seat. "I'll be less conspicuous than you," he said, looking at the colonel's uniform.

The colonel slid over and drove the car out of sight.

When Carlos entered the building, Muniz was already in one of the booths facing away from the front door. The thin cloth curtain at the front of the booth was drawn tightly.

The receptionist, the patron saint of bored sinners everywhere, casually looked up at Carlos, who gestured that he and Muniz were together. She returned to her magazine as Carlos slipped into an empty booth next to Muniz.

The thin plywood partitions that separated the booths weren't made for privacy. Perhaps you couldn't see the person next to you, but you certainly could hear his or her conversation. In fact, when the place was full, such as on a Saturday night in the old days, the volume would amp up as each person tried to outshout the other. Those on the other end of the line would have to hold their receivers at arm's length to avoid permanent hearing loss.

But Muniz was talking quietly, and Carlos could hear only snippets.

"The army was investigating…"

"Came to my house…"

"Satellite phone…"

"Your phone number and mine…"

"A kidnapping…"

"What's this all about?"

"We'll talk on Sunday."

The call ended. Muniz exited the booth, walked to the receptionist's desk, and paid her for the three-minute call.

Carlos stayed in his booth until Muniz left the building. Then he walked to the receptionist and, without asking, grabbed her clipboard with the telephone log. He knew she wouldn't voluntarily show him and would recite some company privacy policy. As she was about to protest, Carlos handed her a twenty-dollar bill, which assuaged her concerns.

He memorized the number she had placed for the man in booth four. Then he tossed the clipboard onto her desk and left. As he stepped out of the building, he looked both ways to make sure Muniz was out of sight. He returned to the car and told Colonel Hernandez what he had overheard.

"Muniz doesn't know we're on to him yet. We'd better pick up Sanchez," the colonel said.

***

Muniz drove back to the farm thinking about what Curruca had said. *He's probably correct,* he thought.

Muniz had nothing to do with any kidnapping, so he needed to just keep saying so if questioned again. He was telling the truth. All they had were a couple of phone calls between them, and all they ever had talked about was a lawsuit. Curruca assured him that none of this had to do with him and that he and Reynolds would make sure to keep him out of it.

Muniz was relieved, yet he was more than a little concerned that Curruca didn't express any surprise about a kidnapping occurring. He didn't think it was possible that Curruca was involved. He remembered his telephone call to Curruca about being seen at the river but didn't think the call could have led to an abduction.

CHAPTER FORTY-SEVEN

Friday, Quito

"Satellite phone?" Curruca asked, eliciting more information.

"Yes, they said that they had telephone numbers from a satellite telephone and that it was confiscated during a drug raid. The telephone had a call to your phone, and they traced calls from you to me," Muniz explained. "They said the satellite phone was somehow involved in a kidnapping."

"A kidnapping? Who was kidnapped? And what does that have to do with our phone calls?"

"They didn't say. They said they were just following up on telephone numbers from your phone since a satellite call had been made to you."

"I don't know anything about a satellite phone call, and I certainly don't know anything about a kidnapping," Curruca said, in a convincing tone perfected through years of deceit. "How could they know the phone call was to me? I don't recall receiving any calls from a satellite phone. Surely phone company records would prove that."

Curruca sensed the fear in Muniz's voice and knew it was critical that he reassure him. Muniz knew enough to compromise the whole operation. If he was intimidated by the police or army, he could be a terrible liability. So much was at stake. If they kept it together a little longer, Reynolds was sure Steator would settle, and all this would disappear.

Curruca said in a calming manner, "Don't worry about anything, Palumbo. I'll handle any questions from the army. If they contact you again, just stay with the truth. You know nothing about a satellite phone or any kidnapping. Tell them I call you on occasion about a lawsuit that you're working on, but they should talk to me if they want more specific information because you aren't allowed to divulge confidential client information because of court orders. I'll call you in two days, but don't say or do anything until we have spoken. "Do you understand?"

"*Sí.* We'll talk on Sunday."

"OK then. *Adiós.*"

Curruca was concerned. He hadn't heard from Comandante Flores for a couple of weeks, but that was expected because they were limiting their sat phone calls to emergencies only.

Muniz's call was troubling. He wouldn't have known about the sat phone. Curruca kept very separate compartments. Muniz didn't know about Rodriguez or the comandante. The comandante had been free to demand whatever he could extract in ransom, but they had agreed that the hostages weren't to be released until Curruca ordered it.

And what of the hostages? he wondered. *Are they now free?*

Curruca suppressed his impulse to call the comandante, figuring he might be under surveillance. He began to assess his vulnerability.

Who knew of his involvement? Reynolds for sure. Rodriguez, but probably not his men. The comandante, but again, not his men. Reynolds wouldn't know of Rodriguez or the comandante. Reynolds knew the purpose but not the mechanics, and Rodriguez and the comandante knew only part of the mechanics but none of the purpose.

CHAPTER FORTY-EIGHT

Friday; Otavalo, Ecuador

Curruca had to contact the comandante, but he wasn't about to do it on any phone he had. He hadn't thought his phones could be traced, but apparently, he was wrong, and it wasn't going to happen again. He would contact the comandante from another phone and in a different town. This time, he would text a message to the comandante's personal cell phone, which they originally had used.

Curruca walked out of his office building and hailed a cab to the Terminal Terrestre bus station. He purchased a ticket to Otavalo.

With all the stops, the thirty-mile drive took almost two hours. Curruca had been too impatient to wait for the express bus, but now he was having second thoughts. Once there, he headed for the Plaza de Ponchos, which, even midweek, teemed with tourists, mostly from Europe and North America, busily negotiating with artisans for fine textiles, blankets, leather goods, *zamponas* (pan flutes), and all manner of trinkets.

The Otavaleño women donned intricately embroidered blouses and long skirts. The men wore the characteristic long braided hair, woolen ponchos, white pants, and sandals. They paraded the grounds as the aromas of pork, chicken, guinea pig, and banana wafted from the open-air grills through the plaza.

Curruca found the vendor he was looking for and purchased two prepaid cell phones with cash. He figured the five hours of cell time and two-hundred-text-message allotment would be sufficient.

He cut the plastic wrapping from one phone and discarded all but the phone and charger. He turned the phone on to find that it had a courtesy charge. He entered the comandante's cell number and selected the text option. "Need information about guests. Text this number in twenty minutes. Búho." He pressed the "send" button and waited for the "Message sent" response. Then he removed the lithium battery, looked at his watch, and waited.

***

The comandante heard the notification sound on his cell phone. Unlike the sat phone, his cell was with him always; it was his lifeline to the señora.

In a small village north of Puerto Asís, the comandante had been eluding the authorities for several days. He had paid the villagers quite well over the past years, so his situation was safe. But it was difficult to reconstitute his brigade with only a single phone and a couple of loyal bodyguards at his side. The village was just within range of the cell towers servicing the port. A few more miles to the north, and service was gone.

The comandante thought himself fortunate that he hadn't been at the headquarters on the night of the raid, which was only because Señor Martinez had more meetings in Cali that week. But he had lost some equipment, and some men had abandoned him. Fortunately, only a few were captured. These were the men who had tipped off the police about the other cartel camps that FARC was guarding. While only three camps were revealed, it would take months for the comandante's organization to recover.

He didn't recognize the number, but the signature was unmistakable: "Búho"—the owl. He had wondered how long it would take for Curruca to contact him. He was certainly in no hurry to tell of his failure to secure the hostages.

As instructed, he waited twenty minutes and then sent his reply: "Friends left. I have moved to a new neighborhood. Need new phone for better service. Vacation delayed. El Gato."

***

Curruca read the message immediately upon hearing the notification sound. He began to interpret. *The hostages are gone. Flores had to relocate. He lost the sat phone and won't be coming out of hiding for a while.*

This confirmed the story Muniz had pieced together from his interrogation by the army. The most important information to him was that the hostages were free and likely in the hands of the authorities.

He would have to communicate this to Reynolds.

Walking back to the bus terminal, he erased the comandante's number from the phone, removed the battery, and pried open the sealed back cover of the phone to remove the memory chip. He crushed the phone under his foot and tossed it into a trash receptacle. The battery and chip were similarly disposed of at different locations.

***

"Why didn't you contact me by e-mail?" Reynolds asked.

Curruca sat on a bench at the far end of the plaza. Overly paranoid, he looked around before he spoke. "There can be no record of this matter. That is why we acquired these telephones. You know what to do with it after this call," he responded. "I took the precaution of disabling the location-based-services (LBS) function, so this phone can't be traced."

He went on to explain to Reynolds the information he had learned from Muniz and his contact in Colombia.

Reynolds knew Muniz but not the anonymous contact in Colombia, which was the way Curruca had set it up and the way he liked it—plausible deniability.

"Are you sure your Colombian contact is trustworthy?" Reynolds asked.

"Yes. Even if the authorities capture him, he knows absolutely nothing about you. There is no way he would talk. He is a zealot, and his silence is a badge of honor. I am more worried about Muniz. He is not a man of such strength."

"Do you think he would he talk to the officials? If so, what damage could he do?"

Curruca related his concerns. "He knows nothing of the abduction, but he knows everything about the testing. I'm worried he will figure out that the tourists he saw that evening were the ones taken. If he does, I don't know if he can be trusted to remain silent. I can't be sure he won't fold under pressure."

"He must remain silent. Do you understand?"

"Yes," Curruca responded. "What about the American lawyers? What do they know?"

"They know nothing. They get the laboratory results and your affidavits from our plaintiffs. From these, they build our case. They see nothing else. If they need something from Ecuador, they go through you. Everything is sanitized before they see it—I can't rely on privilege. If they knew what we were doing, they'd be required to inform the court. It's not exactly the way things work in your country."

That's for sure, Curruca thought, as he disposed of yet another phone.

Week Six

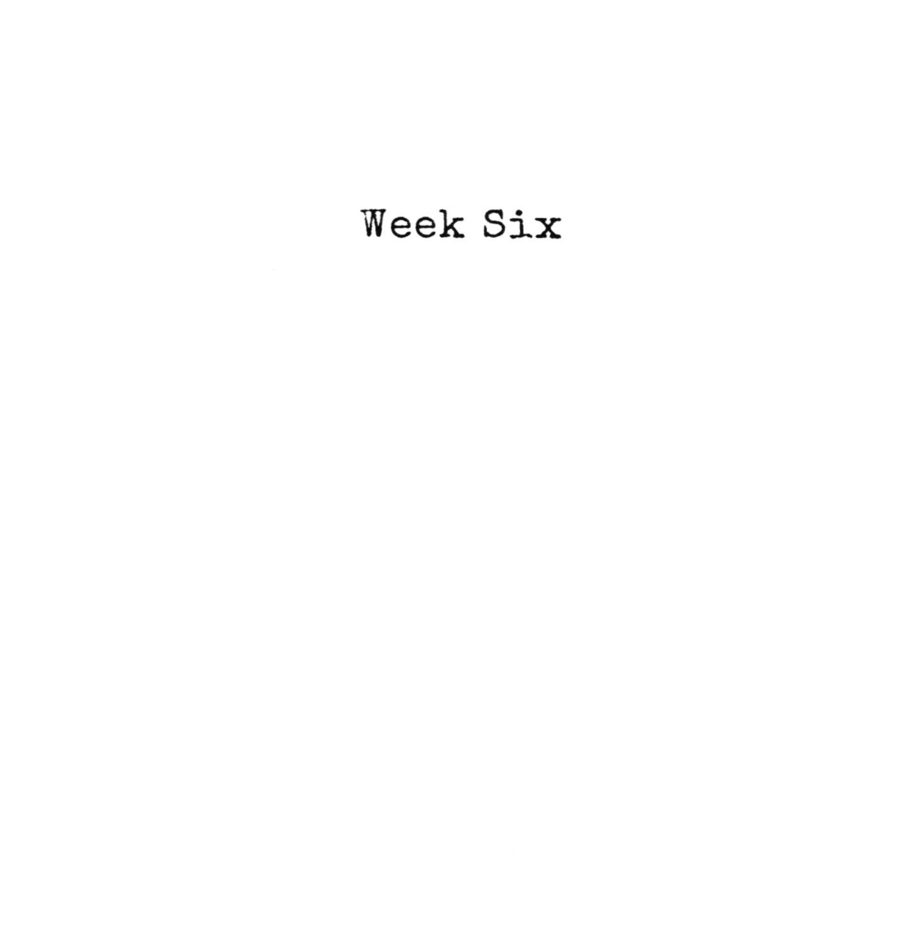

CHAPTER FORTY-NINE

Sunday, Quito

For security, both men called from EMETEL centers, but it hadn't gone well. Curruca heard the trepidation in Muniz's voice. He was nervous and talkative and jumped from "what if" to "what if" despite all of Curruca's reassurances—not the coolness and detachment Curruca had hoped he would hear. Curruca could tell Muniz was having doubts.

No, Curruca thought, *this is not a strong man.* He knew midconversation what had to be done.

With his most contrived empathy, he tried to soothe Muniz's concerns, to keep him calm at least for a few days. "Remember, you refer all questions to me. If the police, the army, or anyone else wants to speak with you again, agree to it, but schedule a time so I can be there to represent you. You have done nothing wrong, and you have very good legal representation. We will not let anything happen to you. You are too important to the people of Sacha. I think this is a veiled attempt by the oil company to tear apart our team. We cannot let this happen. So many people need you. Do you understand?"

"Yes, I do. Thank you," Muniz replied, temporarily boosted by Curruca's confidence.

"Get out of Sacha," Curruca said. "I want to meet with you in Baeza. There's a hostel there. I have a court date in Lago the day after tomorrow," Curruca lied. "We'll discuss this matter in more detail to better formulate a plan. It is an easy bus trip from Sacha."

Muniz agreed.

It was the next call that sealed Muniz's fate.

"Hola," Rodriguez answered.

"Meet me at El Ejido Park at three p.m. today," came the response from the other end of the phone.

"*Sí.*"

CHAPTER FIFTY

Monday, Baeza, Ecuador

It had been a very difficult drive. While the road was well traveled, maintenance was haphazard. Throw in the slow, serpentine path up, over, and down the Andes, and fatigue from constant vigilance resulted.

But Rodriguez arrived at Baeza about noon. He was tempted to check into the hostel for a few hours' rest or even a meal, but he didn't want anyone to see him.

The instructions in the park had been simple. Who, where, and when were dictated. Rodriguez was to determine how, but it had to look like an accident or a permanent disappearance.

He thought about a traffic accident but figured his truck was incapable of inflicting much damage. Also, it would leave too much evidence. Falls weren't uncommon in steep mountains. *Maybe a mugging gone wrong,* he thought. *Worst case, the twenty-two is under the seat.*

In the meantime, he would wait and watch from the truck parked across the road from the hostel. *Get a few minutes of sleep,* he hoped.

***

The bus dropped Muniz off at the terminal in Baeza. The town was located at the junction of Highway E45 to Lago and Highway E20 to Coca, and if Curruca had commitments in Lago, it was the logical place to meet.

Muniz walked the few blocks to the hostel, which was a familiar stop for many traveling to and from the Oriente in the lower eastern foothills of the Andes. For those traveling east, it was an appreciated respite after driving the treacherous mountain road. For those traveling west, it was the last chance for fuel, food, and rest before Quito.

During the boom times, it had been a stop for oil workers and truck drivers. There were still a few trips by maintenance crews, but they largely had been replaced by tourists heading into the jungle.

At the cantina, it wasn't unusual to see groups of students from Europe, the United States, Australia, and Japan devouring meals of beans, rice, chicken, and for the more adventurous, roasted llama. The latter was a tough—literally—taste to acquire. It was a rite of passage for these adventurers to partake of exotic meals in exotic places—their chance to "go native." A small percentage had intestinal flora ill adapted to the rapid lifestyle change. They were usually back on the trail after a short regimen of Cipro and intravenous electrolytes, after which they tended toward more familiar fare.

Accommodations at the hostel varied from one-person rooms to group bunk rooms favored by students for the camaraderie and cheap price. Muniz chose the former so he would have a little privacy during his meeting with Curruca. A room was certainly preferred to the crowded cantina.

While the hostel's exterior was worn and weathered from the constant battering of rain and wind, the interior was well kept. Rooms were painted frequently and fastidiously cleaned between guests. Linens and towels were fresh and crisp. The furnishings had been produced by local artisans in a rustic but pleasing style. Artwork adorning the walls also had been obtained from resident artists. Overall, the hostel provided well-run, pleasant accommodations suited for the discriminating tastes of tourists and was a welcome luxury for the locals.

Rodriguez hadn't met Muniz, but Curruca had given him a photo at the park. Rodriguez easily identified him walking the grounds of the hostel near the gas station that fronted the complex. He had decided to introduce himself and inform him that Curruca had sent him to drive him to Quito because of an unavoidable change in Curruca's plans. Once Muniz got into the vehicle, his options would increase. He planned on disabling him and then disposing of him in a deep ravine.

I'll inject him if I can, but a swift blow with the twenty-two, followed by a head bash against the doorframe will work too, he thought. If not, the more conventional use of the pistol was an option. But first he had to get Muniz into the pickup truck and away from witnesses.

"Señor Muniz!" Rodriguez shouted as he exited the truck.

Muniz turned in curiosity. As Rodriguez approached, he responded, "*Sí.* How do you know me?"

"Señor Curruca hired me to meet you and drive you to his office. He was delayed in Quito by a change in the trial schedule in Lago, so he won't be coming this far east. He asked if I could drive you to him, and he will get you on a bus back to Sacha tomorrow."

"Maybe I should call him to reschedule."

"I believe he wants no phone calls. He is afraid they might be bugged. That is why he sent me."

"I understand," Muniz said. "I need to get my bag from my room and check out. Maybe they will refund my room."

"I will wait for you at my truck across the road."

Bag in hand, Muniz was at the truck in less than ten minutes. "They wouldn't refund my room," he said as he pitched his bag into the bed of the truck.

"I am sure Señor Curruca will cover all your expenses," Rodriguez said as Muniz climbed into the passenger seat.

"How long to Quito?"

"Normally five hours, but with this truck, add an hour or so. I have to pull over frequently to cool the engine. I've been saving for a new truck for years, but the wife and children need more and more. So I take longer and longer to get where I am going," he said, laughing.

"Maybe I could get a little sleep until you need me to drive."

"Please, relax and sleep. Señor Curruca told me how important you are to him. So you are a VIP. I'm only sorry I don't have a limousine," Rodriguez said, all the while thinking how much easier his task would be with a sleeping, unsuspecting victim.

***

They drove only twenty minutes before Muniz was in a deep sleep, evidenced by his thunderous snoring.

That should keep me awake, Rodriguez thought.

He knew the location he wanted. It was a small road that led to a cellular tower and relay station. The road made a few turns as it switchbacked up the steep slope, and much of the road was obscured from the highway. Rodriguez's only concern was whether the station was manned full-time. If so, a chance encounter with a vehicle was possible. He would just have to play it carefully. But first things first—he had to disable his passenger.

With one hand still on the wheel, he took the ketamine cocktail from under the seat. He removed the needle sheath with his teeth, jammed the sixteen-gauge needle into Muniz's left thigh, and rammed the plunger, injecting the anesthetic deeply and quickly.

Muniz awoke with a start. In confusion, he looked at Rodriguez from the fog of sleep, saw the syringe embedded in his leg, and was about to ask what had happened when a warm wave of euphoria washed over him, and he returned to sleep, albeit a much deeper one.

Rodriguez saw Muniz slump, his head forward, his body restrained by the seat belt. He figured it would be hours before he regained consciousness. He removed the syringe and tossed it from the vehicle into the grass along the highway.

He slowed as he approached the turnoff. No vehicles were in view in front or behind. As he turned, Muniz's body shifted against the passenger door. He drove farther, gently ascending the first switchback. He turned a curve from which the highway was no longer visible and then drove a little farther to find a spot wide enough to turn around so he could make a swift exit.

Rodriguez shifted the truck into park, engaged the hand brake, and turned off the engine. He exited the vehicle and walked to the edge of the road, still well out of sight of the highway and the relay station. He looked down. It was a sheer drop of at least 1,500 feet into a ravine thickly wooded with shrubs and dwarf trees, the only species that could survive the extremes of heat, cold, wetness, and dryness of this montane environment.

No chance of survival and, better yet, no chance of discovery, Rodriguez thought, priding himself on his initiative.

He walked back to the truck and opened the passenger door; if not for the seat belt, Muniz would have fallen out. Rodriguez reached over and released the buckle, and Muniz fell partially to the ground.

It took more effort than Rodriguez had expected to pull Muniz from the truck. Though a smaller man, Muniz was deadweight. He grabbed Muniz under the arms and, walking backward, dragged him to the edge of the road. Then he aligned the body so he would roll sideways down the slope.

Rodriguez placed his left foot on the supine Muniz and was about to exert the force necessary to propel him to an anonymous death when a voice shouted from the road just at the curve.

"Don't make another move, or I'll shoot," Rodriguez heard. Startled, he pivoted in the direction of the voice to find himself in the sights of a 9mm military-issue Beretta pistol.

Rodriguez attempted a sprint to the truck and his hidden .22, but a well-placed shot that landed three feet from his left foot erupted into a plume of dirt and gravel and convinced him otherwise.

"My next shot will be on target," Sergeant Rosales promised.

***

It had been Sanchez's idea. Muniz's demeanor told them that he was hiding something, that he was somehow involved with the kidnapping, but they had nothing more to go on.

"Let me follow him for a few days," the major requested of the colonel.

"I need you here. Let Rosales follow him," Colonel Hernandez had said. "Maybe Carlos could help out."

Despite Curruca's warning, Muniz hadn't been very careful. He'd look back occasionally, but he was too worried and distracted. This worked well for the trackers. Dressed in civilian clothes, they had to be cautious only when trailing Muniz near the farm because there were few places to conceal their car along the road. It was easier to follow him once he had arrived in Sacha and boarded the bus. Rosales, whom Muniz hadn't seen before, occupied a seat near the rear of the bus to keep watch. Carlos followed from a considerable distance in the car. They weren't sure where Muniz was heading, so Rosales bought a ticket to Quito, the bus's final destination before it turned around and returned to Sacha.

As on most bus trips, the passengers were a jumble of indios, colonos, tourists, farmers, and suitcases, as well bags of produce bound for the market. Everything but livestock was on board, although a few chickens may have been stashed out of sight.

Once the bus arrived in Baeza, Rosales exited after he was sure Muniz, bag in hand, wasn't getting back on.

From the car, in the parking area beside the hostel, Carlos had watched the interaction between Rodriguez and Muniz. Rosales stayed in the cantina, watching through the window, and then joined Carlos in the car.

They remained back, totally out of sight of Rodriguez's truck because of the sinuous mountain route.

It was by sheer luck that Rosales spotted a small dust cloud as they passed the access road to the relay station. "I think they pulled off," he excitedly told Carlos.

They found the turnoff and drove slowly, both by choice and circumstances of overdue maintenance. They approached each turn carefully. Rosales would exit the car to look around before signaling Carlos to proceed. At one point, they thought they saw another dust cloud ahead and above them but didn't see another vehicle.

After his third scouting foray, Rosales finally saw Rodriguez standing over Muniz's dead-still body. He reached into the waistband of his jeans and pulled out his pistol. Carlos immediately exited the car and sprinted to Rosales's side just as the shot was fired.

Rodriguez, outnumbered and outgunned, offered little resistance. In seconds, Carlos and Rosales had him spread-eagled on the ground before Rosales cuffed his hands.

Carlos was surprised when he bent down to examine Muniz. "He's alive."

He and Rosales dragged Muniz from the cliff edge into the passenger seat of the truck and placed a blanket from the car under his head. Seeing no external signs of trauma—no lacerations, no blood—Rosales glared at Rodriguez. "What did you do to him?"

As would be his modus operandi for the next few days, Rodriguez said nothing.

Carlos and Rosales muscled Rodriguez into the backseat of the car. He was placed on his back with his cuffed hands pinned under his body—probably not the most relaxing position, but Rodriguez's comfort wasn't their concern. They tied his legs together to further immobilize him.

"You lead in the truck, and I'll stay close behind in the car. Hit your brake pedal repeatedly if Muniz gives you any trouble," Rosales said.

"*Sí*," Carlos replied.

Muniz slowly regained consciousness as Carlos drove toward Lago, but he remained lethargic for several hours. He finally turned to Carlos with a look of total confusion. "I know you. You were at my house. Why are you here? What happened to the driver?"

Carlos began to explain, but it required too much of Muniz's concentration, and he was soon back asleep.

Must be powerful, whatever it is, Carlos said to himself.

***

The three-hour drive to Lago was uneventful, but Muniz was semiconscious and demanding explanations when they arrived at the base. Rosales deferred until they reached the colonel's office.

"We have the man in custody who drugged you, and when Sergeant Rosales found you, he was about to push you over the side of the cliff," Carlos explained. "How do you know him?"

Still suffering the effects of the drugging, Muniz was hearing but not believing the words. But the pieces were slowly coming together.

I was set up, Muniz thought. But by whom? *The police? Curruca? Only Curruca knew I was going to Baeza. Maybe the police were listening to my calls.*

"His name is Rodriguez. He's a driver who was hired to take me to Quito," Muniz explained.

"Why a driver? You could have taken the bus all the way there and not checked into the hostel," the colonel said.

"There was a change of plans. Wait. How do you know I arrived in Baeza by bus? Maybe I should speak with my attorney. Please call Señor Curruca in Quito."

Knowing they needed Muniz's cooperation, the colonel agreed to his request and allowed the call.

"Señor Muniz, I'm going to get a meal sent over and allow you to rest before we resume our questions," the colonel said.

CHAPTER FIFTY-ONE

Tuesday, Quito

Curruca telephoned his contact and arranged to have dinner with him that evening.

Years earlier, Reynolds had explained to Curruca that the Ecuadorean government's support was crucial, and he wanted to include the government as a plaintiff because it had legitimacy. Reynolds would have the government establish accounts to pay out the proceeds from the settlement, and it was from these accounts that both the government and Reynolds's team would receive their rewards.

Curruca had used his contacts at the Ministry of Justice to support the lawsuit. He even had convinced them to help fund the suit in return for a portion of the settlement. He explained that the government could justify its involvement by arguing that former governments had been corrupt and in bed with international corporations. The previous president had been duped into agreeing to sign off on the final cleanup of Steator's holding. The new government maintained that it was deeply concerned about the people living in the jungle who had been hurt the most by the pollution and the settlement could help rectify these old damages.

Promptly at 8:00 p.m., a black Lexus pulled in front of La Fiesta restaurant. The rear door opened, and the deputy minister of justice emerged. He closed the door, and the driver drove off to find a parking spot.

The deputy minister entered the restaurant to find a frightened, nervous Curruca seated in a red leather booth at the far end of the dining room. Few pleasantries were exchanged as the maître d' seated the deputy minister and summoned the waiter for drinks.

"May I offer you a cocktail before dinner?" the waiter asked, as he handed each man an embossed one-page menu of the evening's offering.

"Yes, I think we'll need more," said Curruca, already into his first bourbon.

"Make mine a gin martini, straight up," the minister said.

A second server appeared and carefully filled two water glasses from a cut glass pitcher.

"This had better be urgent," the deputy minister said as he carefully placed his napkin on his right knee.

"Well, if you mean the possible loss of billions of dollars—dollars that would fund many of your favorite programs, as well as the lifestyle to which you and others in your party have grown accustomed—then I'd say, yes, this is urgent."

The waiter arrived and placed the martini in front of the minister and the second bourbon in front of Curruca.

The minister waited to speak until the waiter had left. "Is it the lawsuit? I thought you assured us that everything was going well. Is that American and his lawyers still trying to settle for that paltry amount? You did express our concerns to him, didn't you?"

"Yes and no," Curruca responded. "Our plan worked well. I've been informed that the samples showed contamination in the river, and our American attorneys believe Steator is being advised to settle quickly to avoid a trial. It is probably a matter of weeks, not months. I am trying to convince them that a large settlement is required."

"So what is the *no*?"

"We had a situation with some tourists who may have observed one of our operations. We had to temporarily detain them with our friends in Colombia. Well, they somehow got back in the country. The problem is that the colonel of the Lago Agrio garrison has been investigating the situation, and he's getting a little too close to some of our colleagues," Curruca said, explaining his telephone call from Muniz the previous day.

"The army? What the hell? Why involve the army? They have no business in any investigation and certainly no jurisdiction. Should I be alarmed or just concerned?"

"I would be concerned. We need to put a stop to the colonel's investigation before he actually learns anything. He claims that because a cross-border crime occurred and could be related to *narcotraficantes*, he has the authority to investigate. That may be true if he is dealing with foreigners, but I am not so sure he can interrogate Ecuadoreans, at least not without the consent of the Ministry of Justice. I believe it is a police matter, not a situation for the military."

"Seems you have researched this," the deputy minister said, "and you may be correct. What do you think should be done?"

"Stopping his investigation would raise too many questions, particularly if this colonel has the ear of the opposition press. I think it would be better if your office led the investigation. You can assign a cooperative investigator, and we can determine exactly what is known and try to change the direction. The best scenario would be to lay the blame on the cartel and completely wall off any suggestion of Ecuadoreans having played a part in the kidnapping."

"It would seem much more plausible, even to a hostile media, that the kidnapping was related to drug traffickers or terrorists." The deputy minister paused for a few moments and then continued, "The downside is that the incident hasn't yet reached the press or even the government. Your plan certainly will make it a much higher-profile situation."

Curruca shrugged. "Yes, but it would probably be a two- or three-day story. Besides, you have many friends in the press."

"Maybe, but we have to make sure no one—absolutely no one—who was involved will talk."

"Actually only I have all the facts. You are well insulated. No one knows of your involvement or the government's payments. But two men, the ones in custody, have enough knowledge that a skilled investigator could piece their stories together and get a pretty good idea. That's why your intervention is absolutely necessary now before they talk."

"How do I handle the army?" the deputy minister asked. "Won't they claim interference?"

"You know sympathetic generals in Quito. Go to them. Tell them you're concerned that the local army investigators aren't well versed in these civilian matters and could very well jeopardize the investigation and any subsequent judicial proceedings. Extol the competence and initiative of the army, and be sure the praise is provided to the press. But explain that this phase of the case is beyond the expertise and ability of the local command. Thank them for their good work. Maybe arrange a medal or a promotion—I don't know—something to satisfy them. Knowing their normal reaction, good press is more valuable for promotion than solving some minor drug-trafficking or kidnapping case."

"I'll make some calls right away," the deputy minister assured Curruca. "And I know the best investigator for the job."

"He must take custody of the two men at the Lago Agrio army base tomorrow. I'll head there this evening to consult with my clients and advise them of their rights, but one is very unreliable and quite vulnerable to pressure. He also might redirect the investigation from the kidnappings to our enterprise."

"What are they holding them on?" the deputy minister asked.

"One is just a potential witness. The other is being held for attempted murder."

"Murder of whom?"

"The witness. I had to make sure he didn't talk, but Rodriguez, the murder suspect, failed, and the army's investigators caught him in the act."

"What possible defense could he have?"

"I'm working on that. But as long as Rodriguez remains quiet, I have a couple of options."

"I'll get my man down there on the first flight. In the meantime, I have some calls to make to the Ministry of Defense."

The deputy minister remained for a few more minutes while his car was retrieved. He was concerned—deeply concerned—that the proposed settlement was considerably less than planned. Perhaps the entire enterprise was in jeopardy, if Curruca was to be believed.

CHAPTER FIFTY-TWO

Wednesday, Lago Agrio Army Base

Curruca arrived at the sentry gate at 7:00 a.m. He demanded to see Muniz, his client. After several failed attempts by the guard to reach the colonel's office, Major Sanchez finally answered. A few minutes later, Sergeant Gutierrez was at the gate and accompanied Curruca to Sanchez's office.

"How may I assist you, Señor Curruca?" he asked.

"I have come to see Palumbo Muniz. I understand you are holding him. I am sure he advised you that I am his attorney."

"Señor Curruca, we are not holding Muniz for any crime. He is in protective custody because an attempt was made on his life."

"Then he is free to go?"

"That is up to him."

"I would like to speak to him—in private, please."

"I will bring him to my office, and you can see him," Sanchez said.

"Alone, please."

"*Sí.*"

Muniz was lying on a cot in a small cell when Sanchez arrived. He was still fighting off the lingering effects of Rodriguez's cocktail.

Sanchez opened the unlocked cell door and entered. "You have a visitor. I believe he is your attorney."

"Señor Curruca?"

"Yes."

Muniz was conflicted. The army investigators said the man who drugged him and tried to kill him was probably sent by Curruca. But Curruca was his friend and had worked so hard to help his people. It wasn't conceivable that Curruca would harm him. Still, the seeds of doubt had been sown.

"Is he coming here?" Muniz asked.

"No. Follow me. You can use my office."

***

Curruca immediately rose and gave Muniz a strong hug. "I've been so worried about you. I drove to the hostel in Baeza, as we planned, but you were gone."

He then looked toward Sanchez and asked that they be allowed privacy. As Sanchez closed the door, Curruca directed Muniz to a chair next to him and pulled out a yellow legal pad. He furiously wrote, "Room probably bugged," and then asked Muniz how he was being treated.

"I am OK. I am still drowsy, but I have eaten well and am not hurt."

Curruca flipped the page on the legal pad and pointed to a message he had written earlier.

Muniz read the note: "Army is setting you up. The man who drugged you is working for them. If they really wanted you dead, you would be. They're trying to trick you and separate us."

"Would you like me to drive you home, maybe stop and see a doctor?" Curruca asked, flipping the next page.

"That would be good because I am very tired," Muniz said as he started on the next line of text: "American friends concerned. Need us in the States soon."

"I will talk to the major. If they need more information, they can see you in Sacha," Curruca explained.

***

Sanchez had nothing on Muniz, just suspicions. So he put up token resistance to Curruca's demand to let Muniz leave.

"We're concerned for your safety," Sanchez said to Muniz as they left.

Curruca drew a deep breath of relief as they drove off the base and south to Sacha.

One down, one to go, he thought.

***

Rodriguez would be more difficult. The investigator from the Ministry of Justice would take him into custody, and Curruca, against his better judgment, had to involve a second attorney over whom he had limited influence. It was paramount that Rodriguez be advised to reject any plea deal. He just needed to stay silent. Rewards would be forthcoming.

All they had on him was the drugging of Muniz, which was a minor assault charge. They could try him for attempted murder, but what proof would stand up in court? There could be many explanations for what he was doing at the ledge. Curruca just had to be sure Rodriguez would keep to the story.

He had a trump card: the charges against Rodriguez the ministry would bring and any sentence a judge would impose. Here, Curruca knew he had much more control. A second critical factor was getting Muniz to corroborate the story.

***

"You have to understand—these guys are playing with you. They're trying to break you down. Tell me what happened in Baeza. Who was this man they say was trying to kill you?" Curruca asked on the drive south to Sacha.

"He said he came to pick me up because you had changed plans. He was going to drive me to Quito," Muniz said.

"Why didn't you call to check with me?"

"He said you told him that we should not call because you suspected the phones were tapped—that was something only you and I knew."

"And the army!" Curruca exclaimed. "You must see they're trying to drive a wedge between us. Have you ever thought that all this is a hoax? The alleged kidnapping, the telephone records, the attempted murder?"

"But why?"

"Ask yourself, 'Who would benefit if our team broke apart? Who has the money to buy a small-time army colonel and a few of his men?'"

"Steator?"

"Exactly! They spend—what—one million, two million to set up this charade, and what do they save? Billions! And who loses? The people. I must say it's ingenious. We must find out who is behind it. Then we'll have a chance to discover the truth."

"So, what do I do?" Muniz asked.

"Just as I said before, tell the truth. You don't know this Rodriguez fellow. You don't have any idea why he drugged you. You know nothing of any kidnapping. But you must insist that I'm with you during any questioning."

"But how will you find out who's behind it?"

"I know the attorney who represents Rodriguez. He owes me."

***

Damon Rivera arrived at the army base in Lago within hours of Muniz and Curruca's departure. Two police officers and a provincial prosecutor accompanied him.

The call had come earlier in the morning from the Ministry of Justice, informing the colonel of its concern about an unauthorized investigation it had been alerted to by a local attorney. That call was followed shortly by one from the Ministry of Defense.

Seems I've disturbed the wasps' nest, the colonel thought. He knew Curruca was behind the first call. It was going to happen sooner or later anyway.

"Colonel Hernandez, I'm Prosecutor Rivera. We have been informed that you are holding an Ecuadorean citizen, yet neither the provincial police nor the national police were informed. Can you tell us the charges against this individual and whether he has had any legal representation?"

Tall and gaunt, Rivera wore thin wire- rimmed glasses and bow tie. His bookish demeanor belied a very aggressive and even more ambitious prosecutor. While only in his late twenties, the minister of justice had seen the young man's potential and had groomed him for a bright future. In return, Rivera worked tirelessly for the minister and took on the most challenging cases—the cases with sensitive political overtones where prudence was critical.

"Señor Rivera, I see Señor Curruca has been in contact with you," the colonel replied. "Indeed, we are holding an Arturo Rodriguez on the charge of attempted murder. It is also possible that he was involved in the kidnapping of a group of tourists and the possible murder of one of them. I have asserted jurisdiction because the kidnapping occurred in Ecuador and the hostages were taken across the border to Colombia. As you are well aware, any such cross-border incursion falls within my purview."

"I believe your jurisdiction is for apprehension but not for prosecution," Rivera countered. "I appreciate your efforts to begin the investigation, Colonel, but do you have any evidence that Señor Rodriguez was involved in a kidnapping or even a conspiracy to kidnap? Certainly, the attempted murder is wholly outside your authority. Don't you see how it would compromise any investigation if your men, as witnesses, also were investigating the alleged crime?"

"I'm not exactly sure what you are requesting," Colonel Hernandez said.

"I am afraid it is beyond a request. The Ministry of Justice is demanding you turn over the man to the civil authorities along with any investigative reports and notes you have compiled."

"And if I refuse?" the colonel asked, already knowing the answer.

"Well, I do not want to involve the Ministry of Defense to relieve you of command."

"I don't think that will be necessary," the colonel said, feigning capitulation. "I will have Rodriguez brought to you immediately. It will take a while to complete our reports, but I will try to have them to you soon."

"I appreciate your cooperation. We will certainly be in much closer coordination as the investigation proceeds."

***

Rodriguez was escorted from his cell to the custody of the provincial police, who directed the handcuffed prisoner to a waiting police car.

The colonel and Sanchez watched from the front door of the administrative headquarters. "Well, I guess that pretty much ends our investigation," Sanchez said disappointedly.

"I don't think so," the colonel said.

"Why is that?"

"This action tells us much. First, Curruca is quite influential. Second, the speed and attention with which the Ministry of Justice and Ministry of Defense responded indicates that this is no mere civil rights issue—the fair treatment of an alleged attempted murderer. And it is much more than a simple kidnapping case. Third, it extends higher in the government, and we are getting very close to the answer, whatever that may be."

"So you really were testing Curruca?" Sanchez asked.

"Yes. I had to see how he would react. Now we know. We no longer have to speculate regarding the phone calls. His current actions tell us much more."

"What about our reports? How much do we want to turn over?"

"I guess since we weren't the jurisdictional authority over the attempted murder, we should merely provide the eyewitness accounts of what Carlos and Rosales observed while driving up the road to the cell tower for that 'breath-taking view' they were hoping to photograph," the colonel said. "And because there's no connection between Rodriguez and the kidnapping, those reports fall into our military-surveillance files, which the Ministry of Justice would have to request from the Ministry of Defense. With our shortage of clerical staff and the abysmal condition of our record-holding procedures, I wouldn't be surprised if they were misfiled or even missing from the base."

"Yes," Sanchez replied. "I once recall a file being found months later. It had inadvertently slipped under the seat of a vehicle that later left the base."

"It is unfortunate these events do happen, even on the hard drives of the most secure computers."

"By your leave, sir. I need to meet with Sergeant Rosales about dinner arrangements tonight. He and Gutierrez will need to have food brought in as they prepare their reports."

"Dismissed, Major," the colonel replied, returning Sanchez's sharp salute.

***

Rodriguez was transferred to a holding cell in the provincial courthouse. It was far more private than the city jail, with fewer inmates and police to observe him.

Rivera explained that it was for his safety. Rodriguez wasn't at all concerned. He knew the wheels were in motion and Curruca had a plan. He also knew his most important asset was his silence, which assured his safety. It would be very difficult to explain any harm that came to him if he didn't talk. It would point directly at Curruca. If he talked, well, Curruca had other resources. Best to keep quiet and let Curruca work his magic.

Around noon, a visitor was escorted to Rodriguez's cell. He introduced himself as the lawyer appointed to represent him. He explained that he was "fully aware of his situation" after having consulted with a fellow defense attorney. He said Rodriguez should trust his judgment regarding how to proceed. While speaking, however, he surreptitiously passed a sealed envelope to his client. Rodriguez tore it open and read the handwritten message from Curruca that read, "Stay silent. Man overdosed in your vehicle. You were trying to resuscitate him. Soldiers misinterpreted your actions. You were rolling him over on his back. The man will back up what happened. This is all your attorney will know."

Rodriguez wadded the message and placed it into his pocket. After his lawyer's visit, it would be flushed away.

"This is what happened…" Rodriguez began to explain to his new attorney.

***

"We must deter the authorities from any further investigation into his matter," Curruca explained to Muniz as he drove from the army base. "I have it on very high authority that the government does not want to pursue any investigation of either you or me. But in order for them not to investigate, it is necessary that we close this matter of the alleged attempted murder. I think it is just Steator Energies trying to compromise you in order to dismiss our suit. We must stop all investigations. You can never determine what someone will find when they start looking."

Muniz stared out the side window but was not really looking at anything. It was all too confusing for him. He just wanted to go home, to be rid of the whole thing.

"How can we do that?" Muniz asked.

"First of all, we stop the sham investigation about this Rodriguez character. Somehow, they are using it as a diversion to open a broader investigation. We must, somehow, put an end to it."

"How?"

"I am working on a plan," Curruca said. "But if there was no attempted murder, they'll have no case. This would work in two ways. First, if you can convince the authorities that it wasn't a murder attempt—that somehow you accidentally took too many allergy pills—then they'll have no case, and the investigation will end. If, somehow, they convince this Rodriguez guy to confess, it would make no sense since it will stop their own investigation. And what good would that do? Nothing. All he could say was he was working with the army to do what? Kill you? That wouldn't convince the prosecutors of anything. No, the best way is for you to actually defend Rodriguez. It takes all the cards out of their hands."

Curruca knew he was doubling down on Muniz, but it was his only chance. To prevent any backsliding, they would have to be constant companions from here on out.

He looked over at Muniz until he captured his eyes in a cold stare. "This is very important. I need to know who you talked to about the Steator plan. They all must be contacted and instructed to remain quiet."

"Only you, Jorge, Raul, and my cousin Clarita. That is all. I haven't even talked with Señor Reynolds in the past few months."

"Only Jorge and Raul know about the drums?"

"Yes. Clarita provided only the time and location information. I didn't tell her anything about the plan. She thinks we were trying to secretly monitor the scientists to make sure they were sampling correctly."

"We have to contact all three of them, but it must be discreet. I don't think the army will bother us again, but we must remain very careful," Curruca warned.

CHAPTER FIFTY-THREE

Thursday, Lago Agrio

"But we must remain very careful" was the last thing Colonel Hernandez heard before several minutes of engine noise and then blank-tape hiss. He finally pressed the "stop" button of the small digital recorder.

On the colonel's hunch the day before, after receiving the calls from the ministries, he had instructed Sergeant Gutierrez to hide the recorder under the seat of Curruca's car. The colonel was gambling that Curruca would be driving Muniz from the base. The bet paid off. The only difficulty was recovering the recorder. Fortunately for Gutierrez, Curruca stayed just long enough at Muniz's farm for him to sneak up, jimmy the lock a second time—this time the passenger door, outside the view of the house—and retrieve the recorder. He also was grateful the car didn't have an antitheft alarm, since he didn't have the time or tools to disable one. Gutierrez was pleased the unit was still recording, true to its advertised eight-hour battery life.

***

"Any ideas who Jorge and Raul may be?" the colonel asked, looking directly at Sanchez, Gutierrez, and Rosales.

All indicated no.

"I can check on Muniz's cousin, Clarita," Gutierrez volunteered, being the most savvy with electronic searches. "She shouldn't be too hard to find."

"Well, since we've been ordered off the case, I can't tell you what to do on your free time," the colonel said. "In fact, let me order you *not* to talk with Curruca or Muniz. Is that clear?"

"Yes, sir," they answered.

***

As Gutierrez had expected, Muniz had a large family. It took a few days of perusing provincial records, but he learned that Muniz's mother, Estella, had a sister, Clara, who had married a local *colono* named Felipe Ruiz. In time, they had six children: four girls and two boys. The second eldest daughter, who was about the age of Muniz, had been named "Clara" after her mother and maternal great-grandmother. It was no great leap in logic for Gutierrez to surmise that the daughter was affectionately called "little Clara" or "Clarita," to distinguish her from her mother.

Tracking her location wasn't difficult because she wasn't married and had retained the Ruiz surname. He learned that she was employed as a secretary with a company located just outside Sacha. This prompted a quick, quiet recon of the facility. Gutierrez saw only a small logo taped to the window of the front door. XEBEC ENVIRONMENTAL, it read.

Through an Internet query upon his return to Lago later in the day, Gutierrez discovered Xebec was an environmental-consulting firm headquartered in the United States with subsidiary offices throughout the world. Its main emphasis was environmental sampling and assessment. Their "highly professional team of experts" investigated and remediated contamination in the environment and was heavily involved with the petroleum industry.

While Gutierrez found no mention of an office in Ecuador, the "Xebec in the News" tab on the company's website contained a press release from several years earlier about how Xebec had been selected to conduct environmental sampling in the jungles of Ecuador for the US district court in Houston.

A deeper query revealed that the district court in Houston was the location of a civil trial: *Victims of Sucumbios Contamination v. Steator Energies.*

Whoa! Gutierrez knew he had uncovered the first connection between Curruca and Clarita. *So Clarita works for the company conducting the testing, which will be used in the lawsuit involving Curruca and Muniz. This is a little too convenient,* he thought. Did Xebec know of the relationship between Clarita and Muniz, and if so, did it really matter?

Since he was on his own time, Gutierrez decided to return the next day and talk with someone at the Xebec office to see what more he could learn.

CHAPTER FIFTY-FOUR

Friday, Sacha

Gutierrez, dressed in dusty tan trousers, a sweat-stained shirt, and leather work boots, sat on the wooden steps that led into the bodega. It was nearly three o'clock, and he thought people would be leaving the building across the road around this time. Most people in the area began work early in the morning, usually before 6:00 a.m., to avoid the midday heat. With any luck, maybe one would stop at the bodega for a Coke or cerveza.

A security guard opened the chain-link gate where a few exited in autos. Most, however, walked out the side gate. Gutierrez noted about twelve people leaving on foot. They looked like locals, and a few were heading toward the bodega.

"*Por favor,* señor," he addressed a man as he passed by.

"*Sí.*"

"I am looking for a job and was wondering if you could tell me about that company across the road. Xebec, is it? I can't find anyone going into the forest soon for trees, and I need money."

"Oh, it is a company from the United States that is testing water in this area," the man replied.

"What kind of work do you do for them?"

"I am a driver and a guide. They send me out with the scientists to collect samples."

"Are they hiring anyone now?" Gutierrez asked.

"Sorry. I don't think so. They are just here temporarily. Most of the scientists are from the States or Quito, and the work is coming to an end. Some already have left."

"You just drive for them?"

"No. I also help gather samples from the rivers and streams."

"Do you know what they are looking for?"

"Mostly oil in the water," the man said.

"Oh!" Gutierrez exclaimed, feigning concern. "Are you finding any? That could be dangerous, no?"

"A little, in some areas. But mostly, no."

"That is good. I will worry less. And if I wanted to ask about work, who should I ask for?"

"The manager is Mr. James Belfry. He hired me and most of the locals."

"Thank you, and have a good day," Gutierrez said.

"And you also."

***

The colonel sat transfixed during Gutierrez's debriefing.

"Clarita Ruiz is working for the company that's involved in testing water quality for a lawsuit against an oil company. And her cousin is working for the attorney for the plaintiffs in the lawsuit. I agree—this is more than a coincidence," he said. "Good work, Sergeant Gutierrez. I think I'll give this Mr. Belfry a courtesy call about potential dangers to foreign visitors."

***

"Yes, Mr. Belfry. It was very unfortunate, but the hostages were released unharmed and are back in their homes—all but one that is," Colonel Hernandez explained. "But I am, of course, concerned that it could happen again since we've been unable to apprehend the culprits."

"How does this concern me?" Belfry asked.

"It has come to my attention that you employ several US foreign nationals in your operation and that they may travel to or near the location where the kidnapping occurred. I am concerned that they may be quite vulnerable, and I want to provide you the necessary security to keep them safe."

"Our people always travel in teams of two and are accompanied by a local driver who knows the area very well."

"I am afraid that was also the situation with the tourists," the colonel stated. "They had a local guide, but that was not enough. I think we should discuss the possibility of having my men accompany your teams or at least be in radio contact with them when they are in the field. Maybe you could provide me with a schedule and locations, and I can make the appropriate security arrangements, at least until we apprehend the kidnappers."

"Colonel, your help would be greatly appreciated. But because of our sampling protocols, which we are bound by contract to follow, we aren't allowed to provide the sampling locations until the morning we dispatch the teams. It's a matter of sample integrity."

"I understand. That should not be a problem for us as long as we can have the locations in sufficient time to send out our patrols. Is there someone who could call or radio us with that information?"

"Only two of us have that information, and it is kept in a safe," Belfry said. "I make the assignments in advance but don't provide them to the dispatcher until a few days before so she can compile the necessary paperwork."

"Is that who would contact us?"

"Yes."

"And who is this person?"

"Clarita Ruiz."

***

How could Clarita help Muniz? Colonel Hernandez assumed the purpose of the testing was to determine whether there was oil in the water. If there were, people could be exposed and harmed. If that were the fault of the oil company, it would bolster Luis Curruca's case.

But is Clarita in a position to influence this? the colonel wondered. *Maybe. She's a secretary and could type out the wrong results, but the samples are tested in Miami, so she never would have the opportunity. Could she tamper with or even swap the actual samples before they're sent for testing? I'll have Sanchez follow up on that. But if she knows when and where the sampling is taking place, how could that help Curruca? She doesn't determine that; she just prepares paperwork for the field teams. Could she misdirect teams to areas she knows are contaminated? Maybe, but surely there must be some GPS location for the samples assigned at Xebec's headquarters, and they would see any inconsistencies in sampling locations.*

How could this advance information aid Curruca?

Suddenly, the hairs on the back of the colonel's neck stiffened, and a chill coursed up his spine.

If she can't adulterate the samples in the office, maybe she can have it done at the source. But how? They'd have to spill oil at the sampling site but avoid being seen by the sampling teams. How much would be needed? A quart? A gallon? A drum? A drum! Maybe several drums. Maybe several drums like those seen at Muniz's farm. Maybe like those barrels Carlos saw at the river!

The colonel now was putting it together, at least a rough framework—something he could share with Sanchez and the others. Let them shoot down the theory. Let them find the holes in his logic.

Week Seven

CHAPTER FIFTY-FIVE

Tuesday, Houston

The weeks after the videoconference had been hard on Joe, but not as hard as he'd been on himself. The company was in this situation because of him. It had been his job to clean up the wells, and he had failed. While the probability was low, there was a chance that the health of the people in the oil fields was in jeopardy. This fact hung heavily on him because his mission had been exactly the opposite.

His friends—particularly Kim, his girlfriend—found him distant, almost despondent, and because of the confidentiality surrounding the case, he could speak about it to no one except Morris, who had his own problems. Morris was pushing hard to settle to avoid a huge payout and the accompanying bad publicity. But a settlement would be a personal defeat for Joe.

Joe had heard a theory that there were two kinds of successful people: those who strived for and basked in the glory of success and those who succeeded out of fear of failure. He was sure he fit the latter category.

He constantly pondered how it could have happened. Did he miss a pit? Had a pit been illegally closed without his knowledge? Did the contractor short-cut procedures? All his questions led back to this inexplicable lapse and the absence of similar results earlier.

He had taken Morris's advice and set up an emergency-response team. They worked day and night reviewing all remediation data and monitoring reports. They reviewed contractor records and interviewed Steator's on-site construction representatives to see whether it was possible that errors had been made. They reviewed all the scientific literature and technical reports they could gather in the limited time they had. They found nothing. It was maddening. It just didn't make sense.

It's like the oil fell from the sky into the river, he thought.

CHAPTER FIFTY-SIX

Friday, Lago Agrio

"Look," Colonel Hernandez told Sanchez, "we're boxed in. I can't go to the Ministry of Defense because they want no part of anything this political. I can't go to the Ministry of Justice because, as we've seen, Curruca is protected. Plus, if I'm correct, they're a party to the lawsuit, and our information would harm their case. It is too risky if I contact the judge in the United States or Steator because that information would surely get back to the government. I see no way to get our information out."

"There may be a way," Sanchez volunteered. "You're correct. We'll risk too much if we provide this information ourselves. But we know someone in a better position, someone with a real interest in this situation, someone we can trust to keep our involvement quiet. We should contact Gary Cales. Tell him all we know. Give him our theories, and let him approach the judge or Steator. He certainly has his own motivations."

The colonel, assessing the risk, considered Sanchez's suggestion. "I think that may work," he said. "He certainly would have good reason to follow up because of his parents. He could emphasize that he spent a good deal of time in Ecuador, which is where he learned the details and developed his theory. And he's a detective—this is what he's paid to do. If he can get a sympathetic ear, all that needs to be determined is whether there's any relationship between the dates and location of sampling and the location where the tourists saw the man and the drums at the river. If nothing can be found, then, well, at least we did our best. And who knows? Maybe Muniz will come around someday."

***

Sanchez spent most of the day preparing the report. It needed accuracy and a little nuance, and he had the best English skills of Colonel Hernandez's analysts. He didn't mention it in the report, but in the accompanying e-mail, he would identify which information to keep confidential, so that it couldn't be traced back to the colonel, and which information Gary might have learned during his stay in Ecuador.

Using an anonymous account and the Wi-Fi at a local café, Sanchez sent the e-mail and attachment to Gary. Sanchez scrubbed the e-mail, the attachment, and browsing history from his laptop, obliterating any trace back to him. But Gary would know where it came from.

***

It was by sheer luck that Gary read Sanchez's e-mail. Two-thirds of the e-mail he received on any given day was junk mail, which was typically caught in his spam filter, particularly ones with such cryptic subject lines. He rarely checked the spam filter. But this day he did. Nestled amid the messages pitching Viagra, weight-loss pills, and cheap insurance, one caught his eye. It simply read, "Bush Tanager."

He read the e-mail and immediately knew who "Boatman-1" was and then opened the attachment. It was too much to take in, so he printed it out. He spent the next three hours reading, rereading, highlighting, and scribbling notes.

On the first read, he thought it had to be a bad joke. Why would anyone go to such an extreme to cover up such a simple fraud? But the more he read, the more compelling the case became. The potential money involved was incredible, and he knew people kidnapped and killed for far less.

First, he needed to know more about the lawsuit. The attachment provided a brief background, just enough detail to make the case. But he would need much more.

The e-mail had its intended effect; Gary was on the case.

Rather than reply directly to Boatman-1's e-mail, Gary sent an original—"Subject: Bird Tour," with a simple message: "Hmm, sounds like an interesting trip. I think I will attend."

Boatman-1's e-mail was a welcome diversion. It had been a few bad weeks for Gary since he had brought his parents home—especially in regard to his father. His mother was the first to notice. In the beginning, she attributed Ben's sadness and remoteness to Jack's death. Their initial elation over their escape and return home was short-lived. Within days of their return, Ben began to have terrible nightmares. He awoke in a cold sweat, trembling with fear, and all Marsha could do was hold him and gently rock him until he slipped back to sleep. Then he avoided going out to dinner. Next, he made excuses to skip their weekend birding trips. The curtains were drawn during the day, which was totally out of character for a man who relished sunlight. He'd have a bout of rage over the most meaningless trigger, followed by deep remorse for how he had treated Marsha. He avoided friends and gradually withdrew deeper into a dark solitude. Spending hours alone in their bedroom, he'd stare intently at the television, regardless of the program, just to avoid conversations. Gary or Russell would call to try to boost his spirits, but they'd only get a polite, distant hello before he passed the phone to Marsha.

Marsha's worries increased. Their family doctor assured her that Ben was adjusting to having gone through a difficult situation and encouraged her to be patient and allow him some space. The doctor prescribed a mild antidepressant, but Ben became even more reclusive. Any confined space or the sight of a stranger induced panic; he shivered with fear and hyperventilated until he almost fainted. Marsha could only hold him and pray until it passed. It got to the point that she was afraid to leave him just to go to the grocery store. She felt helpless as Ben continued to decline.

It was Gary who suggested a therapist. He'd known friends who had returned from Iraq and Afghanistan and experienced similar symptoms.

In just one session, the psychologist diagnosed it: PTSD. All the fears Ben had sublimated during the kidnapping now surfaced, along with the ghosts of Vietnam. At least they had an answer—a reason for his behavior—but they knew that what lay ahead was a long, long recovery. This, Marsha didn't mind; she would do anything to get Ben back. He was her everything.

Gary took it harder. While Marsha was too busy with therapy and keeping all the other balls in the air, Gary grew angrier and felt helpless to do anything about it—until Boatman-1's e-mail, that is.

Week Eight

CHAPTER FIFTY-SEVEN

Sunday, Detroit, Michigan

It wasn't how he had expected to spend his day, especially a Sunday, but in six hours, Gary had downloaded a binder full of information on the lawsuit.

Ya gotta love the Internet, he told himself.

Court filings identified the principal attorneys handling the case and Steator's technical staff who had been deposed for the case. Gary found repeated references to a Joe Caldwell, project manager for the company's in-country operations. Steator's website had an employee directory, which Gary used to obtain Caldwell's contact information.

The next day, Gary phoned him.

"Hello. This is Joe Caldwell."

"Mr. Caldwell, my name is Gary Cales. If you have a few minutes, I would like to talk to you about some questions I have regarding the recent water testing that occurred in Ecuador."

"Whom do you represent?"

"I'm not a party to the lawsuit," Gary said, "if that's what you mean. But I'm interested because the case may be related to an incident that involved a group of tourists, including my parents, several weeks ago, in which one man was killed."

Caldwell was silent for several seconds. He thought he had fielded every conceivable question about the project from an endless chain of lawyers, but to this, he didn't know how to respond. His suspicions were raised. Was someone out to scam the company?

"Look, Mr.... What was it?"

"Cales."

"Mr. Cales, I've been advised by our attorneys not to speak about the case to anyone unless they're also present. I'm afraid I won't be able to help you."

"Actually I think I can help *you*," Gary said. "I understand your dilemma, but maybe you and the attorneys could look over some information I've put together. I'm sure once you've seen it, you'll want to talk."

Joe's interest was piqued. "Can you e-mail it to me?"

"Yes, I have your address. I'll send it today. It won't take long to read, and you'll find it interesting."

***

Gary was right. It was more than interesting, but could it be true? He had provided contacts for Natura Sucumbios and the Verde Vista Ecolodge, including the guide from the trip. There was information about sat phones, cell phones, and the surveillance on Muniz. None of the information could be traced back to Colonel Hernandez. The connection between Reynolds's team and the secretary at Xebec was intriguing, to say the least. Joe thought it was a bit of a stretch that the man spotted by the river with the drums actually could have been salting the water. But with the location of the drums and the sample locations, it would be relatively easy to find any correlation. As farfetched as it might be, it was the only explanation that made any sense.

***

"I don't know. This is pretty wild," Morris offered, after reading the pages Joe had sprinted over to his office.

"Can you think of anything else? I know I can't. We should at least consider the possibility of water tampering."

Morris shook his head in frustration. "Even if I thought the theory had merit, this isn't proof. It's only speculation. We need evidence—*physical* evidence—or an eyewitness."

"I agree, but it wouldn't be that difficult to correlate the time and location of the tourists' encounter at the river with one of the sampling points. Let me do that and see if I find something."

"OK. Let me know what you find out. Maybe then we'll talk to this Cales guy."

***

Joe pulled out his map of the Sucumbios province. He plotted the location of the two sampling sites and marked each with a black felt-tip marker. He used a red marker for the location where the drums were spotted. Gary and Carlos had found the GPS coordinates by retracing the route the tourists had taken before they were kidnapped.

This can't be a coincidence, he thought, feeling a slight tinge of excitement. Then he began to question it. It was too good. *Could this be a false-flag tactic by Reynolds to divert us?*

Joe did the calculation anyway. It was conceivable. The timing and location worked out. He'd need more information to accurately calculate the initial concentration of the hydrocarbon source and then the river's flow rate and dilution factor to confirm the water-quality testing results, but it could be done.

If it was me, he thought, *and all I needed was the presence of hydrocarbon in the water downstream, I'd dump barrels of it. Most would remain in suspension and could be detectable downstream. Yes, I could easily do this!*

All he needed was a source of aged hydrocarbons.

Maybe something from the pits at Andean Power, he thought, *because plenty would be needed.*

***

"Morris, it's more than plausible. In fact, it would be easy," Joe explained over the phone from his office. "But they had to get the material from somewhere—and enough to do the job."

"Any ideas?"

"Probably from some open pit used by Andean Power."

"Well, you and Mr. Cales tell a good tale, but Stan Hobart is going to need more. Like I said, he's going to need physical evidence or witnesses."

"But you agree it's worth pursuing?" asked Joe.

"Yes. Right now, it's all we've got," Morris said. "But it would be better if this fishing expedition was on your own time, using your home equipment, and away from the office. Remember, almost everything you obtain, verbally or in writing, may be discoverable. Joe, you have to work fast. I'm concerned about any delays. If we go to trial and lose, I'm done. My job is not to win or lose but to minimize losses. I need to push for a settlement."

"But what if we can win?"

***

That evening, Joe left the office in a much better place than he'd been in when he'd come to work in the morning. For the first time in weeks, he felt a hint of optimism. He knew he probably was grasping at straws, but at this moment, even a meager handhold was welcome. At least he had something he could do. He might ultimately be disappointed, but for now, his burden was lighter.

He decided to work from Kim's apartment and use her computer, or even better, her roommate's—anything to shield the company in the event things didn't pan out. He convinced himself, correctly, that he wasn't doing anything illegal; he just didn't want his activities known by the parties to the suit.

***

"Look, Mr. Cales..." Joe said over Kim's phone from her apartment.

"'Gary,' please."

"Gary then. The information you gave me checks out, and your scenario provides a possible explanation for some curious findings we've had. But I'm going to need evidence. Something tangible. Some written record or a witness that can corroborate the story."

"Frankly, I don't much care about the water sampling or the lawsuit. I want to get the people responsible for the kidnapping and murder."

"If you're correct, one may follow the other."

"I have a couple of ideas," Gary said. "If I were to come into possession of such documents, who should get them?"

"I'll send you an e-mail address. The documents should be safe there, but send them anonymously. And Mr. Cales—er, Gary—thank you."

"Like you said, we need each other," Gary replied before hanging up.

Gary thought a lot about his father. His condition tormented him. He knew what had to be done, but he couldn't do it himself. After all, he was a cop, and now too many people knew of his involvement in what had happened in Ecuador. Fortunately, he knew a guy.

CHAPTER FIFTY-EIGHT

Thursday, Philadelphia

Douglas Reynolds answered the front-door intercom.

"Who is it?"

"Sixth Gear Delivery. I have a package for you."

"Hold on."

Reynolds walked over to the window, looked down, and saw a man standing on the stoop in spandex shorts and shirt, a cycle helmet, and wrap-around sunglasses. A nylon satchel was slung over his left shoulder, and a beat-up bicycle was chained to a tree at the street.

He buzzed him in. "On the fourth floor."

He usually received deliveries twice a day, mostly from UPS, FedEx, and more rarely, DHL from overseas. But a bicycle delivery was even rarer because little of his work involved local firms.

He opened the door on the second knock. The messenger held a large envelope in his left hand, which he handed to Reynolds. Before he could read the envelope, the messenger handed him a small clipboard and pen and asked for a signature. As Reynolds signed, the messenger pulled a blaze-orange plastic wand from the back of his shorts, shoved it into Reynolds's chest, and triggered fifty thousand volts of low-amperage direct electrical current. His nervous system in a state of chaos, Reynolds fell backward into his apartment, writhing in pain and confusion. The messenger stepped over his body, dragged him into the center of the room, and shut and locked the door.

He then grabbed two long plastic zip ties from his bag and bound Reynolds's hands and ankles. From a roll of duct tape, he ripped two strips—one to cover Reynolds's mouth, the other his eyes. This was difficult because the tape kept adhering to the blue nitrile gloves he wore under his half-finger bicycle gloves and Reynolds was coming to and beginning to resist.

Satisfied the downed man was secured and neutralized, the messenger whispered to Reynolds, "We have some work to do."

He immediately went to the desktop computer. His timing had worked. The computer was on, which he had expected during working hours. He wouldn't need to resort to more extreme measures to coax the password from the struggling figure on the floor. But he had been prepared to do so.

He searched the directories on the desktop and then mapped any network drives Reynolds might use. He figured Reynolds used an external data storage service to provide an extra layer of security and was surprised to find a network server and backup drives in the hallway closet where the apartment's cable raceway entered. Upon reflection, the messenger figured Reynolds was too paranoid to trust anyone with his data.

It took a little more than three hours, and the whole time, Reynolds lay silent, helpless, and fearful that the intruder would kill him. Just past six o'clock, using Reynolds's computer and e-mail account, the messenger e-mailed the last of the thousands of files he had compressed from the hard drives. On his way out, he removed the tape from Reynolds's eyes and left the front door slightly ajar. With a little effort, Reynolds could worm his way into the hallway—but not before the messenger was lost in the early evening Center City crush.

CHAPTER FIFTY-NINE

Friday, Houston

"Joe, you'd better get over here quick. Denise is really pissed! She's been trying to use her e-mail, but all these huge files are coming in, and she can't send anything," Kim said over her cell phone.

"Hey, I don't mind helping your roommate, but why the attitude? I'm not her personal IT guy," Joe replied, slightly agitated by the imposition.

"Joe..." Kim sighed loudly. "They were sent to Denise's account, but they're addressed to you from some guy named Douglas Reynolds."

"I'll be right over."

Joe took a portable hard drive to Kim's apartment. It took an hour before all the e-mails were downloaded onto Denise's computer. Joe then copied them to his portable hard drive and erased the files, links, and history from Denise's computer.

He apologized to Denise for the inconvenience and asked that she keep it quiet for a few days. He explained that the e-mails might be related to a project he was working on. He also promised her a dinner anywhere she wanted.

In his living room, Joe pored over the documents. He knew where they had come from, and it wasn't from Reynolds, at least not voluntarily. The documents were interesting but nothing more than you'd expect. He wasn't a lawyer, but he didn't see anything that would benefit Steator's case. There was nothing about sabotaging the water-quality testing and certainly nothing about a kidnapping.

Maybe Morris can make something more of these, he thought.

The sheer volume began to overwhelm him. He'd need another three or four people to review all the documents, particularly considering Stan Hobart's impending deadline.

I need to get organized, he told himself. *What do I really need?*

Then it hit him. He opened the file he had prepared for the videoconference with Hobart and checked the dates the samples were collected. "May 17," he saw. He then went to the zipped e-mail file Denise had received.

He unzipped the file, and more than 1,500 e-mails from the previous year opened. He sorted the e-mails by date. Then he highlighted the ones received by Reynolds in the two weeks prior to the sampling, since that was the time frame when the field manager and his staff in Sacha would have known of the sampling locations. This narrowed his search to fewer than thirty e-mails. He scrolled down the subject lines. Most had some reference to Steator, Ecuador, or the lawsuit. But one simply read, "Sampling."

He opened it. It was a short, terse note from a man named Curruca from Quito: "Sampling scheduled near Río Aguarico this week (Colibrí-6 and 7 on Thursday, Halcón-4 and 6 on Friday). These are our best chances."

That's it, Joe thought. Reynolds had advance knowledge of where and when sampling was to be conducted. But why would he need this information, and where did he get it?

He was on the phone with Morris immediately.

"I just received a bunch of files from Reynolds's office," Joe said.

"They were sent here, too, and they've created quite a crisis. How did you get them?"

"They were e-mailed to my home account."

"Who would know that address?" Morris asked. "Why not send them to your office?"

"I don't know who sent them, but it wouldn't be hard to know that I was the project manager in Ecuador," Joe said. "Maybe they sent them to me as a backup in case someone in the company didn't know what they meant. Were they sent directly to you?"

"No. They came to the general e-mail address, and someone in IT saw a file mentioning the lawsuit and forwarded them to me. I don't know if anyone else got them. Were they also sent to your office?"

"I don't know," Joe said. "I'll check later. But I've been going through them. I found a very interesting e-mail from Quito. I'll forward it to you now. Check out the date it was sent."

"No. Don't send it to the office," Morris cautioned. "We don't know where any of this information came from. If it was hacked, or stolen from Reynolds, we could be in receipt of illegally obtained information. I've advised everyone not to open any documents and to reply to the e-mail sender that files were sent to the wrong recipient and that we've deleted all the files from our system."

Joe was disappointed and puzzled. "Why would you do that?"

"We have no idea who sent these e-mails or why they were sent to us," Morris said. "What if Reynolds sent them to put us on a false trail, instead of focusing on our problem at hand? It seems a little too convenient that we're contacted by this Cales guy and then receive these e-mails. Worse yet, what if we're being set up? Maybe Reynolds had these sent to us to try to discredit us with Hobart and the press. I can read the headlines now: 'A New Watergate—Steator and the Break-in.' He probably embedded Trojan-horse software in there somewhere."

"You mean like a virus?"

Morris sighed. "I wouldn't put it past him. And he might have put some data in there that we couldn't resist using but that would be demonstrably false. Maybe he even set it up to look as if we generated the data ourselves and made it look like it was sent from him to us. Look…I don't trust any information from him that we don't get through discovery. We have no cover. In fact, I'm about to compose a letter to Reynolds and his attorneys with a copy to Dr. Hobart, informing them of our receipt of the information and the fact that it was destroyed. I advise you to destroy the information so there's no blowback to the company. It'll only increase our liability."

Joe was silent for a few moments. He knew exactly who would benefit with this information out. He knew who sent it or had a pretty good idea, but he would keep that to himself.

"You're probably right, Morris, but it sure is difficult. I'm running out of time and ideas."

"I know it's tough for you, Joe, and I really do understand your position. But I have to look out for the interests of the company. Those have to trump any personal vindication for you. I'm sorry, but that's how this has to play out."

"I understand."

"We'll talk at the office tomorrow."

Joe knew he had to proceed carefully—very carefully. If anyone suspected his involvement in the Reynolds data dump, the negative publicity would trump any benefit. Reynolds would spin the matter at dizzying speeds—how Steator had hired mercenaries to steal his data because they were about to lose a huge lawsuit. The publicity alone would force Steator to settle fast.

On the other hand, Joe thought, *is Reynolds clever enough to fabricate and bury one little e-mail to set us up? And what could he gain if we found it? Why would he even want us to suspect that the samples were tainted?*

It didn't make sense to Joe. He was well aware of his limitation as a linear thinker—chess and strategy weren't his strong suits. For that, he relied on Morris, who was always three moves ahead, balancing competing scenarios and searching for trapdoors in every argument. But this wasn't logical—and it would be so easy to verify. One or two little samples would show definitively who was correct. There was no way Reynolds would risk this. Joe knew his next move was risky. He'd be working without a net. He wouldn't have legal to provide any cover.

***

"I found something," Joe said as he discussed the e-mails from Reynolds's office and his search of the files with Gary over the phone. "Somehow, Reynolds knew the locations and times of the samplings in advance." He read Gary the e-mail Curruca had sent to Reynolds.

"Interesting. I wonder why Reynolds would send this information to you," Gary said.

"Well, the company wants nothing to do with it and is deleting all the files from our network. They think Reynolds might have sent them to trip us up. They're even writing a letter to him, telling him what happened."

"So why are you calling me?" Gary asked. "Do you feel the same way?"

"No. It doesn't make sense that Reynolds would send them."

"Well, if I were you, I would trust your gut."

It was all Joe needed. He knew. How the files got to Joe and Steator would never be mentioned again.

"Assuming the e-mail is authentic, no one but Belfry and the secretary knew this information at that stage. It was kept in a safe in Belfry's office," Joe continued. "I doubt Belfry is in on it. That wouldn't make sense. There are surer ways he could adulterate samples."

"So if you can't rely on the e-mail, you're going to need more?" Gary asked.

"Yes. We need a witness to corroborate the e-mail."

Gary believed the weakest link in the chain was the secretary, Clarita, in Sacha. *If she's involved, it's minor, but she can lead us up the chain,* he thought. *As with any investigation, you start with the minnows and work up to the sharks.*

But who could approach her? Colonel Hernandez and his men had done much but could do no more. His second thought was really his first choice—the best choice. *I just hope he's not on any birding trip,* Gary thought.

"I think maybe I can help," he told Joe. "We'll talk soon."

"Real soon, I hope. I need more information before Steator capitulates."

"I've got a flight to book," Gary told him, before hanging up.

***

Joe got word back to Morris to hold off any decision for just a couple more days, three at the outside. He explained that his contact was trying to get the secretary in Sacha to confirm she was the source and to whom she had provided the information.

"If she verifies the information in the e-mail, I don't see how Stan wouldn't at least give us more time, maybe even new tests. I'll keep you posted," Joe said.

"Please do that," Morris told him.

***

Morris had a problem. So far, he'd been able to handle the inside game and contain the damage. He had handpicked the law firm and even the litigators to work Steator's case. It had worked like the proverbial Swiss clock. What he couldn't control was the outside game. That was Reynolds's responsibility. And that was the division of labor they had agreed upon in the back booth of the Palm Frond Grill during the annual International Natural Resources Law Conference six years earlier in Belize.

It had started out innocently enough. The two were seated next to each other at a talk on environmental liability—a subject dear to both but from opposing angles.

They struck up a conversation and agreed to meet for drinks later in the evening. That led to a guided scuba trip to the Blue Hole, followed by sharing more meals and chasing a few coeds at the clubs—Morris being relegated mostly to wingman status. Reynolds thought it a stroke of genius to schedule a conference during spring break at the primo destination for the students. Fueled by ethanol and testosterone, Morris and Reynolds confided in each other. Reynolds talked of trying to grow his own small consulting firm and Morris of his stalled ascent to authority in a corporation dominated by cowboy engineers.

To Morris, Steator's leaders might be PhD geniuses, but they were still "flyover" country, which was too much for the native Manhattanite. He just had no way to buddy up the system. The connections between a Yalie and a Texas Tech or even UT graduate were tenuous to nonexistent. Nepotism and fraternity connections meant nothing with Steator. The thing that mattered was the ability to find, produce, and distribute petroleum and at a reasonable return.

Morris had sought a career with Steator because most fortunes were made in the energy industry. But somehow he had missed the pipeline. He had drilled a dry career hole.

Reynolds had sensed vulnerability in Morris during their first encounter over depositions even before that fateful meeting in Belize. As the lawyers argued over some procedural issue, Reynolds sat quietly taking it all in. He could not miss how Steator's chief counsel had relegated to Morris duties better suited to a paralegal. Reynolds felt Morris's anger seething just under the surface—his reddened face, his bulging neck veins, the forced smile, and the almost contemptuous tone in his voice.

Not a happy camper, Reynolds thought at the time. He was confident it was a vulnerability he could exploit.

What Reynolds didn't know was the office politics—how Morris had been passed over for the position of chief counsel. What made matters worse was that Morris had lobbied to have Steator hire Jessica Bradon from an outside firm early in the Ecuador case. On top of that, Bradon was taking credit for the work plan and strategy that Morris had developed. The executives knew Morris was the brain, but in their world, PR was critical. Jessica was the new, young, hip, and cosmopolitan image the company was trying to foster. She had the looks, the composure, the self-assuredness that Morris would never have. He would continue to be the man behind the curtain.

So Morris was in the throes of dejection, depressed, and more than a little angry when he attended the conference where he encountered Reynolds. He knew he had hit his own glass ceiling. Oh, salary increases, stock options, and bonuses would make him, if not a wealthy man, at least very well off, but he'd always be second chair. His disappointment simmered into a stew of resentment, and meeting Reynolds at the conference was like being thrown a life raft.

It began with a mojito-infused "What if…?"

Morris was every inch the silent partner. No direct or indirect connection telephonically or electronically, by mail or otherwise, could ever be detected.

A diligent investigator might have noticed the two attended the same technical conferences, but so did hundreds of other attorneys, scientists, and regulators. And unless one of the hotel rooms was bugged, any gumshoe would have no inkling of the elaborate planning that had taken place. They even avoided the same lectures so as not to be seen at a refreshment table during breaks. Over the last couple of years, as the suit had progressed, Morris had skipped the conferences but still visited his aging grandmother in Queens periodically.

It was with great trepidation that Morris broke protocol. He had to—they were getting too close. Morris still bristled over the kidnapping decision. A perfect plan is only as good as its imperfect practitioners. But this one might still be salvaged.

Morris left for lunch on time. He walked briskly to an Internet café a few blocks from Steator's headquarters. He pulled out a twenty-dollar bill, asked for a coffee—black—a blueberry scone, and a half hour of computer time.

He perused the lead news stories for a few minutes. Then he sent an e-mail to Reynolds via two e-mail accounts they had set up for such an emergency. The message was short: "Will call Grandma at five."

***

What now? Reynolds thought.

At 4:50 p.m., Reynolds stood outside a bodega two blocks from Morris's grandmother's brownstone. It was one of the few remaining public phones in Queens. It had been a hurried and stressful three hours. To cover his tracks, he had parked his car in Jersey City after the drive from Philadelphia and taken the ferry to the World Financial Center and then the N train to the Ditmars Station in Astoria.

He was relieved that no one was on the phone when he arrived. Reynolds picked up the receiver and pretended to be on a call in the event someone came to use the phone. He glanced over his shoulder and, through the store-front window, could barely see the short, burly man, almost certainly of Middle Eastern descent, behind the counter. With the interior fluorescent lights and dim exterior lighting, Reynolds was certain he couldn't be seen. Nonetheless, he kept his back to the storefront. The few people walking by saw nothing but a man engrossed in conversation, his face obscured by the aluminum phone enclosure.

Take no chances, he thought. A few seconds before five, he replaced the receiver.

The phone rang.

"Hello."

"Hello."

"You know the situation you had a while ago? Well, your colleague from south of the border apparently sent you an e-mail that detailed certain times and locations," Morris explained in vague terms. "They think they know who provided the information. Could that information or that person who provided it cause any problems?"

"More than a little. How much time do I have?"

"Maybe a couple of days. I'll try to get corporate into settlement talks, but I can't seem too aggressive."

"OK," Reynolds said and hung up the receiver.

"Fucking Curruca," he cursed.

Week Nine

CHAPTER SIXTY

Monday, Sacha

On Saturday, Gary had e-mailed Carlos and arranged to meet him two days later in Sacha.

That afternoon, Clarita Ruiz stood in the side doorway of Xebec's field station and momentarily watched the afternoon downpour drench the parking area before she took her first tentative steps leading home. She opened her cheap plastic umbrella before stepping outside—it was far too hot for a rain jacket. Her long, drab sleeveless dress contrasted with her bright-yellow rubber boots, which she always wore for the two-mile walk home. Even when it wasn't raining, the road was pocked with water-filled puddles and ruts. As she turned onto the road, she was met by two men. The smaller man asked to speak with her.

Initially startled, she realized that with all her coworkers huddled around her, she was in no danger. "I don't know you," she said.

"Would you mind if I walked with you a ways?" he asked. "My name is Carlos Serrano, and this is my friend Gary from the United States. I have a paper I would like you to see."

He pulled the folded sheet from his back pocket and handed it to her. A few raindrops moistened the page as she brought it under the shelter of her umbrella.

"Don't worry. I have copies at home," Carlos assured her. He noted that her long black hair was parted symmetrically in the middle and drawn back into a neat ponytail. Even obscured under the umbrella, he could see that while she was short and muscled from the burdens of farmwork that awaited her each evening after her secretarial chores, she was very attractive. Her eyes were large and brown and imparted warmth and innocence. He saw that her tanned face was absent of makeup save for a hint of red on her lips.

She began to read the short note. "What does this mean?" she asked.

"Señorita Ruiz, these are the locations and dates for the water-quality samplings your company did several weeks ago," Carlos explained.

"Yes. That is what we do here."

"Please take a look at the date of the e-mail and the dates proposed for the sampling," Carlos said. "Do you notice anything?"

Clarita shrugged. "No. Should I?"

"The e-mail was sent four days before the sampling. Who would know that far in advance about the schedule?" Carlos asked. "As it was explained to me, only Señor Belfry and you would know this information. Is that correct?"

"Why do you want to know this? Why are you asking me these questions?"

"It may be related to a couple of crimes that were committed. A kidnapping and murder."

"I know nothing of this!" Clarita exclaimed. "Who are you? Are you with the police?"

"No, I am not with the police, but that will be our next stop."

"I had nothing to do with this e-mail. I did not send it, and I do not know who Curruca is or who Reynolds is," Clarita said, speaking more loudly as she became more nervous.

"Oh, that is easy. Curruca is an attorney in Quito who is working with Señor Reynolds in Philadelphia. Do you know what they are working on?"

"I have no idea."

"Well, Señor Reynolds represents the Victims of Sucumbios Contamination against Steator Energies. What I find more interesting is that Xebec is also working on that lawsuit," Carlos continued. "But the most important piece of information I was able to learn is that your cousin Palumbo Muniz works for Señor Curruca and is also associated with the Native Peoples Forest Project, which is also a party to the lawsuit."

"I think the police will find this very interesting," Gary interjected. "It's an easy connection between Curruca and Reynolds and between your cousin and Curruca. I'm guessing that Palumbo probably got these sampling dates and locations from you or Belfry. I'll have to ask him. But if I get better information from you, maybe I can avoid telling the police about you. I'm not a lawyer, but what you've done can't possibly be legal."

Carlos could see that Clarita was shaken by Gary's comments. Gary was an experienced interrogator. He knew when to press hard and when to soften to gain someone's confidence.

"We believe you were only trying help your cousin, and you had no way of knowing what would happen with the information. I think we can convince our friends in Quito and Washington to help you if you'll agree to help us," Gary said.

They walked another couple hundred yards. The only sounds were rain pelting the umbrella and rubber boots sloshing through puddles on the road.

Clarita walked with her head down and eyes focused on the ground. Carlos thought he saw tears running down her cheeks, but it easily could have been rain. He couldn't get a read on her. As they continued to walk, their silence was begging release.

Clarita finally looked up. There were tears, and her childlike face was twisted with torment. This wasn't what she had expected. She could hold back no more and broke down. "I didn't want to do it. The company has been so good to me. Mr. Belfry trusts me and gives me more and more important work. I knew they would be leaving soon, but his recommendation would help me get another job. I never thought until today that I was betraying him. I'm so sorry," she cried.

"Did you give the information to your cousin?" Carlos asked.

"Yes. He was going to use it to monitor the samplers. That was all. Palumbo promised that he just wanted to make sure that all the testing was done correctly and that Xebec's crews sampled where and when they were supposed to. He said there was nothing to worry about and our secret was safe. But he told others. I never thought he'd do that."

"There's been more than enough betrayal here," Gary said. "But you have the opportunity to do the right thing, to correct your error before anyone else gets hurt. We'll talk to Mr. Belfry. We can't promise anything, but we can show that without your cooperation, his firm would have a bad reputation."

"What do you need from me?"

"I would like you to write down exactly what happened. We need exact dates, times, and contacts. We need the whole story—what Palumbo asked for and what he got. We need you to write it out by hand in ink, and we need you to sign and date your statement," Gary explained.

"Can I give it to you in the morning? I have to get home to my family."

"I'll pick it up from you tomorrow on your way to work," Carlos said.

***

Gary and Carlos walked the mile back to Xebec's lab and retrieved their vehicle. Then they drove to Carlos's favorite cantina for a long-delayed meal.

"We often stop here for lunch with tours," he told Gary. "It's very delicious."

Carlos ordered the ceviche, formerly a luxury in the jungle, but seafood was now transported daily from Esmeralda and other fishing towns. Gary, less adventurous, opted for rice and beans with grilled steak.

"Do you think Clarita will come through?" Gary asked.

"Come through what?"

"Sorry. I mean will she do what we asked?"

"I think so, unless someone else talks to her before the morning. I think she's influenced by who speaks last to her."

Gary nodded. "I think we should talk with Muniz. Get to him before she can contact him. Maybe we can pressure him with what we have from Clarita."

***

It was still light out when they reached Muniz's farm. They parked alongside a blue sedan in the front.

Gary knocked at the front door and waited. No response. He knocked again. Then he tried the door. It was unlocked. He opened it carefully and, without crossing the threshold, called out, "Señor Muniz." He heard nothing.

Gary entered, followed closely by Carlos. They looked around, but Muniz wasn't in the front room.

Gary signaled that he was heading outside.

Carlos moved toward the back bedroom. As he opened the door, he was shocked to see Clarita, even more so to see her splayed across the bed, her mouth taped shut, her eyes darting frantically about. When she recognized him, she jerked her head to the right. Her wrists and ankles were bound. As he stepped across the doorway, he sensed someone else in the room. Turning slightly to his right, he felt a dull thud. Actually, he heard it more than felt it, and a sharp pain followed. Carlos's knees buckled. He tried to steady himself, but he sank. He tried to focus, but he was losing consciousness. As he collapsed, his mind went blank. His last vision before darkness was Clarita's dark-brown eyes wide with fear.

Curruca stepped over Carlos's body to the window. He moved the shades slightly to see Carlos's partner walking toward the field. Rather than confront the tall, intimidating man, he made his escape through the front door. He jumped into the blue sedan and took off down the road.

Muniz wasn't in the field behind the house. Gary scanned the trees and sky. Above him, flying low, was a flock of black vultures. He walked toward the clearing, frequently looking skyward to center himself under the circling scavengers. None of them was on the ground yet. He noticed a trail of freshly trampled grass stalks and a slightly more open area ahead. As he approached, he saw a body facedown on the ground—that is, except for the head and neck, which were suspended inches above the ground. It was then that he saw the tines of the pitchfork protruding through the neck and head of the man.

Gary bent down and searched the man's back pockets. He found a wallet. It had a voter registration card and a provincial driver's license, both with photos of a somewhat younger Palumbo Eduardo Muniz.

He couldn't see Muniz's face clearly and considered rolling him over. He hesitated. It was a crime scene, and his instinct was to preserve it at all cost. But he doubted Sacha had CSI resources, so he gambled. The face was bloodied and locked in a twisted grimace, but it was the man in the photographs.

He also saw the handle of the pitchfork under the body.

It looked as if Muniz had been walking with the pitchfork, tripped, fell forward, and impaled himself—at least that was what it was made to look like.

This isn't right, Gary thought. *Why would he carry a pitchfork into the field? Not exactly useful for anything other than baling, and I don't see anything to bale.*

He knelt again. This time, he examined the back of Muniz's head. He moved some hair from the base of the skull and saw a reddish mark about three inches long and an inch wide.

He was hit from behind, maybe with the handle, and posed to look like an accident. With no rigor mortis and a warm body, Muniz clearly had been dead a short time. *Those are some lucky vultures,* Gary thought, as he heard the distant rumble of an engine.

***

It wasn't as hard as Curruca had thought it would be. Instead of remorse, he felt a sense of relief. No, it was more than that. Satisfaction. Maybe even excitement. It was the adrenaline rush that numbed his conscience, and he might feel regret later. After all, Muniz had been a colleague, maybe even a friend. But all he could focus on now was how much easier it would be not to hold his hand constantly. Muniz's usefulness had waned long ago. He had become a liability.

Curruca checked his rearview mirror to see whether he was being pursued. His real worry now was Clarita. She had seen him. With Muniz dead, Steator wouldn't know the details of the plan, but they already had linked Clarita and Muniz. It wouldn't take them long to piece everything together. They would, at the very least, be extremely suspicious of the lab results.

As he drove, desperation overtook him. Settling the lawsuit was next to impossible. Worse yet, it was only a matter of time before someone—probably that interfering army colonel—would further link Muniz with him and him to Rodriguez, who, under pressure, wouldn't hold out any longer. With the chance of exposing the government's involvement, the deputy minister of justice would turn on him fast to cover himself. Curruca knew too much. They could never let him talk. Even if he turned himself in, he never would get out of the holding cell alive; the deputy minister would see to that.

Curruca realized he was totally exposed. He had money stashed here and there, so his only option was to run. He still had friends north of the border. He'd have to get to Lago Agrio and across the river fast. He didn't have much of a go bag, but he had what he needed: money. With that, and a few friends, he'd get a new identity, a new passport, and an escape. Extradition would be unlikely even if they could find him. He just had to elude the authorities for a few more days. Curiously, not even a remote thought or care for Reynolds crossed his mind; he was on his own.

***

Gary ran back to the house to get Carlos. He found his friend lying on the floor, with a small pool of blood forming from the oozing, two-inch gash at the back of his head.

"Can you hear me?" he shouted, but Carlos was unresponsive. Gary was relieved he was still breathing.

He stood and walked to the bed and removed the tape from Clarita's mouth. "Are you OK? What happened?"

"I'm all right—just scared. A man, a friend of my cousin, hit him from behind. He left a couple of minutes ago," she explained. "Is he all right?"

"I think so," Gary said as he opened his pocketknife to cut the tape around Clarita's ankles and wrists. "Are there any bandages? I need to stop the bleeding."

Clarita, rubbing her wrists to restore circulation, sat up on the edge of the bed. "I don't know. I will check the cabinets."

"How did you get here?"

"He and my cousin were waiting at my house. They said they needed to talk about something. We drove to the farm."

Unsure as to the extent of the injury, Gary lodged pillows at either side of his head and covered him with a blanket. He considered rolling him onto his back but thought it better not to move him. He grabbed Carlos's wrist and felt for his pulse—it was slow but strong. As he had learned in his emergency training, he counted Carlos's respirations. They also were slow but regular. Carlos didn't appear to be in distress, but Gary knew he had to get him medical treatment soon.

Clarita returned with first-aid supplies. Gary unwrapped gauze pads and dabbed the wound on Carlos's head to remove some accumulated blood. He took a gauze bandage and held it tightly to stem the bleeding. After a few minutes, he applied another clean bandage and secured it with an elastic wrap.

Clarita was mostly silent as Gary worked. Finally, she asked, "Where is my cousin?"

"I'm afraid he has been killed. I found him out in the field. I think the man was going to kill you also, but Carlos must have interrupted him."

"It is my fault," Clarita said and began to cry quietly.

"Why is that?"

"The man got very angry when I told him and Palumbo that I had spoken to you earlier today. He told Palumbo that he needed to discuss something in private, and they walked to the field. When the man came back, he tied me up and said he needed to take me somewhere. That is when he heard your car approach, and he brought me to the bedroom."

"Do you know the man?" Gary asked. "Had you ever seen him before?"

"No. My cousin said they worked together; that was all."

"I don't know who that man is or whether he's coming back, but I need to get you somewhere safe," Gary said gently. "And I need to get my friend here to a doctor. Where's the closest place?"

With help from Clarita, Gary was able to get Carlos over his shoulder, and he carried him to the car. They carefully eased his unconscious friend into the backseat. Clarita got into the passenger seat, and they headed to the clinic in Sacha.

***

The doctor examined Carlos. Although still unconscious, he had good pupil reactions, and his limbs responded to pain stimuli, which the doctor explained were hopeful signs.

"He's had a major concussion, but I can't tell yet if he's sustained any permanent damage. We won't be able to fully assess him until he regains consciousness," the doctor explained.

"How long do you think that will be?" Gary asked.

"In a few hours, I suspect. In the meantime, I'll suture the skull laceration, get a couple of X-rays, and put him on IV fluids. I'll want to keep him under observation for twenty-four hours, maybe longer. You're welcome to spend the night here, but there's nothing you can do right now."

"Thank you, Doctor. I need to go to the police station for a couple of hours on another matter," Gary explained.

***

Gary and Clarita arrived at the canton police headquarters in the center of Sacha, about three blocks from the clinic. It was a squat, concrete-block building without any ornamentation other than a sign and two light fixtures that bordered the reinforced-steel entry doors. The facade was plain and utilitarian, without the enduring grandeur of public facilities in Quito or other major centers. Sacha was an outpost, still the frontier.

Clarita explained to the desk officer that her cousin had been killed. While homicide wasn't unknown in the canton, it was rare enough to warrant the attention of the entire force. Despite the late hour, within minutes, Clarita was explaining what had happened to a growing crowd of officers. The event broke the monotony of bar fights, stolen equipment, and the occasional drug deal gone awry. A murder was a real crime and something they all longed to investigate. Usually, the Orellana provincial police in Coca would take over the important cases, but until they did, this was a local matter.

Gary introduced himself as a police officer on vacation with a friend who was injured by the suspected murderer. He didn't want to get into the details about his parents, the kidnapping, or the lawsuit. He wanted the police to focus on one thing and only one thing: apprehending the suspect.

He described the car and suggested they radio nearby cities, such as Coca and Lago Agrio, to have matching vehicles stopped. Clarita provided a description of the suspect but didn't know anything about his name, where he was from, or what he did, other than he had worked with her cousin on a legal matter. Gary explained that the man was at least an hour, maybe two, ahead.

At the direction of the captain, the desk officer radioed other police stations and provided a vague description of a blue sedan with a middle-aged man possibly heading north or south, maybe even west toward Baeza.

The information was thin, and Gary knew it. Luck—and a lot of it—would be needed to catch this guy.

CHAPTER SIXTY-ONE

Tuesday, Sacha

Clarita led the police to Muniz's farm, and the investigation began. Gary stayed in Sacha to tend to Carlos.

As Curruca had figured, it didn't take long for the others to piece together the puzzle. Gary had called Colonel Hernandez from the clinic, informed him of Palumbo Muniz's murder, and provided Clarita's description of the suspect.

"It has to be Curruca," the colonel said. He passed the information on to the police in Coca and Lago, and now they had a name and photograph to go with the blue sedan.

Yet by the time the manhunt was underway in earnest, Curruca had abandoned the car, made his way to the river, and paid for passage to Colombia on a small cargo boat—but not before making one last call on his cell phone and then tossing it into the river. Somehow, he felt he owed Reynolds that much.

CHAPTER SIXTY-TWO

Tuesday, Philadelphia

"Fucking Curruca!" Reynolds shouted to an empty apartment as the realization finally hit him that the lawsuit was a lost cause. Steator could now surely demand retesting, and unless, by some miracle, the samples showed signs of contamination, there would be no reason, no evidence, for the case to go forward. What motivation would Steator have to settle if the Sword of Damocles wasn't dangling quite so precariously? No, now was the time to get out but in a manner that preserved his options. He didn't want to get tied to any fraud investigation. But he would need help extracting himself.

Perhaps he could get Morris to attest that some renegade lawyer in Ecuador was the responsible party. Who could argue against it? Clarita would have no clue. Muniz, even if he knew, wasn't talking to anyone now, and Curruca—*fucking* Curruca—was in the wind. Probably never to be heard from again.

He thought about his lost files. What was in there? Anything incriminating? He couldn't remember.

Then it dawned on him. *Morris has a copy of everything. He can let me know. Besides, I have things on him, too.*

***

Using the e-mail account through which he had contacted Morris before, Reynolds sent an emergency message to him and then made the three-hour trip to the phone booth outside the bodega in Queens.

When Reynolds explained about the situation in Ecuador, Morris was beyond furious. He was so angry that he had to exercise every fiber of self-control not to blurt out what he was feeling about Reynolds's incompetence and the utter stupidity of Curruca. He took deep breaths, trying to compose himself, which only marginally lowered his stratospheric blood pressure.

"This whole thing is falling apart!" he exclaimed. "If anybody finds out about our involvement, we're looking at serious federal time. I don't care what they say about Club Fed—I'm not ready to be Bubba's plaything. Not to mention the civil liability. If Bubba doesn't screw me, I know Steator can't wait."

"Calm down. You really worry too much. I have this thing totally contained."

Sure you do, you arrogant bastard, Morris thought.

"This is something better discussed in person," Morris said. "I'll be in Manhattan in two days on business. Book a room at the Hyatt, but don't tell anyone where you're going. We'll figure out what to do."

But Morris already knew what he had to do.

CHAPTER SIXTY-THREE

Tuesday, Sacha

It started with a low moan, but soon, there were head movements, and finally, Carlos's eyelids began to flutter. Gary watched this from his uncomfortable plastic chair across the room—the chair that had been his sentry post and bed for the past several hours.

"How you doing?" he asked, as he walked to his friend's side. "Don't move too much. You have a pretty nasty head wound."

Carlos looked up at the smiling figure. "Where am I?"

"You're at the clinic in Sacha. Do you remember anything?"

Carlos grimaced slightly as he tried to sit up. "My head really aches. I remember Muniz's house. I went into the back room, and I think I saw Clarita. After that, nothing."

"Do you know what day it is?"

"Monday?"

"No. You've been out for a day. It's Tuesday. That's pretty good, though. I was worried that you'd have some long-term damage. There was a man behind the door at Muniz's who hit you. He also killed Muniz."

"How about Clarita?" Carlos asked.

"She's OK, but only because you got there in time. We went to the police, and she went back with them to Muniz's farm. I think she's safe for now. I spoke to Colonel Hernandez. He thinks the man who attacked you was Curruca. The colonel e-mailed some photographs of him to the police. They want you and Clarita to identify him."

"I won't be much help. I didn't see him. Where is he now? Have they caught him?"

"No, he's on the run. We disrupted his plan, which I think was to get rid of any witnesses."

Carlos looked at his hand and saw the IV tubing. "What's this?"

"The doctor said it's just a precaution. Don't move around too much. I'm going to get him. He'll want to check you out some more."

"But Cecilia, my—"

"Don't worry," Gary said. "I've been calling her with updates, and the doctor has told her you're OK but need rest. We can call your family when you're up to it."

Carlos settled back into the bed, hoping someone would remove the daggers penetrating his brain.

CHAPTER SIXTY-FOUR

Thursday, New York City

Morris half carried Reynolds back to his room. He reached into Reynolds's pocket and removed his key card. He swiped the card, and the lock disengaged.

He struggled to get Reynolds on the bed. Half passed out, he muttered something about another bourbon.

"You had quite enough for tonight, my friend. Better to sleep this one off," he said as he bent down to lift Reynolds's legs onto the bed.

He removed Reynolds's shoes and socks, unbuttoned his shirt collar, and asked if he wanted any water.

Reynolds mumbled something unintelligible.

Morris sat in a chair near the window and waited. Thinking.

It didn't take long before Reynolds was in an even deeper drunken stupor, but Morris waited a little longer.

Finally, when he figured Reynolds was out, Morris rose and walked to the bed. He pulled a pair of leather gloves from his overcoat pocket and put them on.

He placed Reynolds's arms at his sides. He walked over to the opposite side of the bed and pulled the cover over Reynolds and tucked it in under his left side. He then took the other side of the cover and tucked it tightly under Reynolds's right side. He took the bottom end of the cover and wrapped it around and under Reynolds's legs until he was completely swaddled except for his head. Reynolds didn't move, except for making long, deep snores.

Morris then removed his wallet from his back pocket. Reynolds's mouth was partially open, and Morris carefully tilted the man's head back slightly.

When his mouth gaped sufficiently, Morris shoved two fingers of his gloved left hand down Reynolds's throat. With his right hand, he wedged his wallet into the side of Reynolds's mouth to prevent him from clamping down.

Reynolds immediately retched violently and tried to rise, but his bound arms and legs couldn't move. He thrashed side to side but immediately began to vomit, at which point Morris removed his fingers and the wallet and shoved a pillow over Reynolds's face.

Reynolds tried to scream, but the pillow muffled the sound. He tried desperately to breathe, but as he inhaled, the acrid stomach contents filled his trachea and were drawn deeply into his lungs. He struggled violently for that impossible breath but only filled his lungs further. Morris held his grip on the sides of the pillow to make sure he did not apply any direct pressure that could cut Reynolds's lips or break his nose. After a few minutes, the gagging stopped, as did any movement under the covers.

Finally, Morris released. He lifted the pillow, which was saturated with vomit, but no blood. He placed the pillow under Reynolds's head and turned it to the side so Reynolds's mouth was on the pillow. There was only a small spattering of vomit on Reynolds's face, most was still trapped in his mouth and lungs, but a small amount drained when his head was repositioned.

Morris then unwrapped Reynolds from his death cocoon and carefully straightened the bedcover to its original position. Because of the tight constraint, Reynolds's body would show no lacerations, no bruising, no signs of a struggle.

Morris checked Reynolds's face and mouth once more. No broken teeth, no bitten tongue, no blood. He did have a dilemma. *Do I close his eyes or not?* He decided against it.

He opened the door to leave the room. In case someone was in the hall or he was videotaped from a security camera, he turned back to Reynolds's lifeless body and said, "Get some sleep, Doug. You've had a big night." But there was no one in the hall, and Morris climbed the three flights to his floor.

***

The autopsy was pro forma. The coroner ruled the death as accidental asphyxiation by pulmonary aspiration induced by alcohol intoxication.

Morris was interviewed because he was the last person seen with Reynolds that evening. He explained that they were a couple of adversaries mending fences after a protracted legal battle by celebrating a night on the town. They both had drunk way too much, but Morris, being the soberer one, had taken Reynolds back to his room and put him to bed. He said he was too blitzed, so he took off only the man's shoes before leaving him to sleep it off. He explained how sorry he was that he had left him there so intoxicated and vowed if he could have done it again, he wouldn't have left.

The police examined the room when the hotel management called them the next morning. But it was never considered a crime scene—the security video confirmed Morris's story. By midafternoon, the room had been scrubbed, polished, and remade for the next guest.

The only evidence of what really had happened was in Morris's head, and the deep molar impression in his goatskin wallet.

Morris had no further tracks to cover.

***

It was never his "A" plan, but it wasn't a "B" plan either. Let's just say, "A-."

If the A plan had succeeded, he'd have had his secret share of the settlement, and Reynolds never could have revealed his involvement. Morris and Joe would have shared in the failure at Steator and their support from the company would have eroded. After a time, it would have been more comfortable for all if they just left voluntarily, which Morris would have done—maybe to start his own firm.

But if that plan went south, Steator would avoid costly litigation and settlement, and all because of the legal strategies so ably formulated by Morris. Even the oil cowboys would have to recognize Morris's achievements, which eventually, they did.

Week Ten

CHAPTER SIXTY-FIVE

Monday, Lago Agrio

Rodriguez contacted his attorney, only to be told the attorney had withdrawn from the case. It seemed several invoices to Curruca had gone unpaid, and repeated attempts to contact him had yielded no results. With great apologies, Rodriguez's lawyer wished him the best of luck.

Rodriguez himself had tried numerous times to contact Curruca by telephone and even sent letters to his office. He too had no success.

Slowly, the story emerged through the jailhouse grapevine that Curruca was on the run after killing Palumbo Muniz—the same Palumbo Muniz that Rodriguez had failed so miserably to kill. Even the once sympathetic prosecutor, Damon Rivera, had turned on him, which was also understandable, since Rivera also wasn't getting his promised stipend. Rather than risk exposure as a co-conspirator with Curruca, Rivera decided the best course of action was to come down hard on Rodriguez—part payback, part self-preservation. He figured a tough law-and-order stance was his only fig leaf now.

The deputy minister of justice, like the prosecutor, needed to distance himself and the government from any association with Luis Curruca. He had devised a plausible reason the government had helped advance the lawsuit, in case their involvement surfaced. But it had hinged on the legal case that had been presented to them by Curruca, which they now realized was untrue. The deputy minister concluded that Curruca had to be discredited at all costs. It would be necessary to portray him not only as the mastermind behind the fraud against Steator Energies but also as the perpetrator of the kidnappings of the tourists and the murder of Muniz.

For this, however, they needed Rodriguez to talk. But Rodriguez knew the government's case against him was weak since Muniz, the alleged victim, was dead.

All the prosecutor had now were the eyewitness accounts of the soldier and his companion, Carlos.

***

"Yes, sir. I will send them over tomorrow," Colonel Hernandez said and hung up the phone. He pressed the intercom button. "Please get me Sergeant Rosales and Carlos Serrano," he said.

Within an hour, the three were seated in the colonel's office.

"It seems the Ministry of Justice now needs our help," the colonel said.

"Why is that?" Carlos asked.

Colonel Hernandez went on to explain that Curruca was suspected of killing Muniz but hadn't been found. Muniz's cousin, Clarita, had identified him.

"Suddenly, they believe your story about Arturo Rodriguez trying to kill Muniz," he said. "They now want our help or, more precisely, your help. They need your eyewitness accounts and sworn statements so they can confront Rodriguez. Prosecutor Rivera wants to pressure him to testify that Curruca was behind the kidnapping of the tourists and, therefore, also responsible for the death of Jack Sinclair. I have a bad feeling that the corruption may go even higher up in the government than Rivera, maybe even to Quito."

"You think if they can prove that Curruca was the mastermind, it will end any further investigation?" Rosales asked.

"Yes. Unless Curruca is caught and implicates others."

"Well, what should we do?" Carlos asked.

"Let's give them what they want. We know Curruca is guilty, and this is what we wanted from the beginning. We just have to be aware that for us the investigation may not stop with Curruca."

"Why is that?" Rosales asked.

"We know the underlying reason for the kidnappings and murder was one thing—the lawsuit against Steator. I wouldn't be surprised if the government, or certain ministries, would have benefited from any judgment or settlement. I think only Curruca can tell us that. But if he's indicted for the crimes of kidnapping and murder, his credibility is shredded. And unless he had solid evidence against someone in the government, his accusations will be seen as the desperation of a cornered rat—that is, of course, if they find him. Maybe he's already dead."

***

Confronted with the testimony of Carlos and Rosales, it wasn't long before Rodriguez was convinced he would be taking the fall. Rivera was silent on the fact that the case against him was fairly weak without Muniz, instead emphasizing how any judge and jury would believe the testimony from a respected soldier and citizen over that of a career criminal.

Rivera left Rodriguez alone for a few days to stew on his fate. Without the funds to hire an attorney and no support from Curruca to grease the system, Rodriguez knew he was headed for prison. That was something he had done before and knew he'd be able to tolerate. The last thing Rivera told him, however, truly scared him. Rivera said Ecuador would not fight any extradition order from the United States, and Jack Sinclair was from California, which, unlike Ecuador, still had the death penalty for murder.

So when Rivera returned and informed Rodriguez that it was Curruca, not him, they were really after, Rodriguez jumped at the chance of a plea deal in exchange for evidence against Curruca.

Rodriguez dropped a dime on the whole plan, at least his involvement in it. He knew next to nothing about the water-sample scam, but he knew enough to explain that the tourists had been targeted for what they had seen.

His confession made it to Colonel Hernandez, who wasn't a bit surprised. This development only verified the information his men had pieced together. There was more than a little satisfaction that the Ministry of Justice now knew he had been correct all along. He and his men would have a little celebration over their success. While the colonel realized all wasn't yet known, it was enough for now.

He was the one who started the information cascade. He contacted Gary Cales with the Rodriguez confession, and Gary informed Joe Caldwell.

CHAPTER SIXTY-SIX

Tuesday, Baton Rouge

"Stan, I was hoping you'd heard the news," Joe Caldwell said over the phone.

"Yes. I never would have considered anything like this in my wildest imaginings. I thought our protocol was foolproof, but the only fool is one who thinks anything is foolproof."

Ten days later, John Lacker returned to the Colibrí-6 and Halcón-4 sampling sites, but this time with a small entourage that included Joe Caldwell and Stan Hobart. Hobart had tried to recruit someone from Reynolds's legal team, but since Douglas's untimely death, no one had responded.

This time, Stan carried the samples back from Ecuador to Allied Analytics and watched as they were processed, analyzed, and compared against the standards.

His report to Judge Grant would read that he had found no credible evidence to suggest any reason for the court to proceed to trial in the case of *Victims of Sucumbios Contamination v. Steator Energies.*

Epilogue

The Following Spring; Bodega Bay, California

There was a long, narrow strand of sand that jutted from the high cliffs on the east side of Bodega Head that was Jack's favorite birding area in the world. It was his home field. Anytime he felt down, he'd set up his spotting scope at the end of Doran Beach Road across the narrow tidal inlet from the strand and wait for low tide. He'd watch for hours as the tide ebbed and flowed, first exposing and then inundating the vast expanse of mud flats. At first, there would be diving birds—ducks, grebes, and cormorants—searching for algae, invertebrates, and fish under the surface. They were replaced by the long-legged, long-billed shorebirds—marbled godwits, whimbrels, and willets—that would probe, knee-deep, the shallow waters for the critters buried deep in the mud. Finally, as the water fully receded, came the new group—plovers, sandpipers, and sanderlings—which would exploit the exposed mud.

In a moment, five thousand birds on the flats would take to the air in a seemingly endless wave as the shadow of a peregrine falcon made a lethal ninety-mile-an-hour dive into the flock. One small dunlin would be sacrificed to satisfy the predator, and as fast as the flock departed, it would return to feed until the falcon's next stoop or the inevitable return of the sea.

It was Tom's idea. He knew of Jack's connection to this spot from their few talks about favorite birding areas. The response from the others was immediate, for all had felt a similar longing.

They met at the sand spit: Marsha, a recovering Ben, Vincent, Tom, Carlos, and Gary. To all of them, it seemed inexplicable that their ordeal had occurred because of something none of them had really seen, or if they had, never had any concern about. But because of fear and greed, they had lost a friend. Gary often thought Reynolds's plan probably would have succeeded. The only thing that had brought it down was the kidnapping that Reynolds thought would save it.

"Look!" Carlos shouted. "An osprey." Dressed in a bulky down jacket and woolen hat and gloves, he was still trying to adapt to the fog-heavy chill of the northern Pacific. While he enjoyed the company of his friends, he was looking forward to a trip to Colombia in the next few weeks. "Perhaps it is the one from the lodge," he said with a laugh.

The bird soared to a height of a thousand feet before he leveled off. Silhouetted by the golden morning sun, his feathers glistened in the soft rays of light. He hovered momentarily, appearing almost motionless, and then flared his tail feathers and extended his legs. Barely visible at that height, a foot-long twig from a Douglas fir dangled from his sharp talons. In an instant, he tucked his wings, lowered his head, and dove straight down several hundred feet. At seemingly the last instant before crashing to earth, he pulled out of the violent dive and gracefully began his ascent for a repeat performance.

On a nearby cell-phone tower, a female osprey sat on what remained of last year's nest. She appreciated her mate's sky dance, as she had for the past six years. *But why*, she wondered, *must he prove year after year that he's worthy to sire my young?* Really, what she needed most was the twig to repair their weather-beaten nest.

Jack would have loved it.

Acknowledgments

When I wrote the first paragraphs of *Sky Dance* three years ago, I really never imagined I'd get as far as an actual story, let alone a complete book. And I certainly could not have gotten this far without the friendship, assistance, and encouragement of many friends and family. They all made *Sky Dance* a much better story, and any shortcomings are totally mine.

I want to thank my sister-in-law, Victoria Henley, and my neighbor, Judy Maben, for graciously and without complaint slogging through the first drafts. I can only imagine how they had wished I had taken fewer science courses and more English classes.

Gary Wilson, my best friend since grade school, provided helpful input on cellular and satellite communication systems. Dr. Sid England and Kevin Guse, my birding and baseball buddies, provided invaluable advice on all things ornithological. However, they share no responsibility for the species I contrived for the story—a little birding license.

My sons, Casey and Andrew, provided help with questions I had about guns and ammo. Thanks, boys.

Linda Gonzalez helped with formatting and editing suggestions on later drafts, and Sage Smith created the map.

Angela and Lora at CreateSpace provided editing and plot suggestions that were invaluable. What great mentors!

Thanks to Bella, my GSD, for the walks, swims, and dog-park forays occasionally missed over the past years when my concentration was diverted. I owe ya one, girl.

Finally, thanks to you, Carol, for forgiving my absences and the chores unattended. I could not have done it without your support and inspiration.

I thank you all sincerely, and if I missed anyone, I apologize.

38831225R00196

Made in the USA
Charleston, SC
18 February 2015